Penguin Books
Edens Lost

Sumner Locke Elliott was born in Sydney,
Australia, in 1917, the son of the well known
authoress Sumner Locke. He was educated
in Australia, served in the army, and later
became an actor with the Independent
Theatre in Sydney, where his first stage plays
were produced. He went to America in 1948
to become one of the first dramatic writers
for CBS and NBC and in nine years he
wrote over fifty plays. He became an
American citizen in 1955 and now lives in
New York. His first novel *Careful, He Might
Hear You* (1963) won the Miles Franklyn
Book Award, it was followed by *Some Doves
and Pythons* (1966) and *Edens Lost* (1969).

Sumner Locke Elliott

Edens Lost

Penguin Books

Penguin Books Ltd, Harmondsworth,
Middlesex, England
Penguin Books Australia Ltd, Ringwood,
Victoria, Australia

First published by Michael Joseph Ltd 1970
Published in Penguin Books 1974

Copyright © Sumner Locke Elliott, 1970

Made and printed in Great Britain by
C. Nicholls & Company Ltd
Set in Linotype Granjon

For Marie

Where the apple reddens
  Never pry —
Lest we lose our Edens,
  Eve and I.

—BROWNING, 'A Woman's Last Word'

1. Angus

Suddenly he became again the boy in the gardens of the crematorium sixteen years ago and again Eve said, 'Come to *us* if you like.' When she crossed back over that barrier she saw herself in the red dress at the funeral, handing him her card and him standing, blinking in the sun in the earnest navy-blue suit; his shoes seemed too big for him and he was altogether so painfully trusting that what she was doing had seemed like daylight kidnapping. She had got back into her waiting taxi and she was all fleshed out with success (she had been thin and starving for some time) because she knew for certain he would come; the event seemed extraordinary to her and fatalistic . . .

At the funeral there was only, apart from himself and Miss Quinn and old Mr Dart, this stranger in red.

No, he whispered.

No, he didn't know who it was. He would not turn around and peer at the woman. He sat very rigidly, staring at the fake-walnut lectern with his eyes dry and reflectionless.

'But *red*,' Miss Quinn whispered, nudging him, 'isn't very reverent.' Was it so very reverent of Miss Quinn to have in her handbag a half-eaten Violet Crumble chocolate bar which she had surreptitiously, pretending to reach for a Kleenex, taken a large bite from? But he knew what Miss Quinn was implying. The woman in red could be his aunt transmuted. It was widely believed in this escoteric circle that the dead were curious (and rightly so) about the undertaking of their own funerals.

'You ought to just nod,' Miss Quinn whispered. 'It might be a friend or –'

He shook his head and by an attitude of his body declared that he had no part of the proceedings about to take place. He wanted to say fiercely that Aunt May had only become embroiled in the Society because she'd had nothing to do on Thursday evenings, *any* evening, and that she had been so desperate for distraction she would have gone to a hanging.

Well, now they were hanging Aunt May. Or they might just as well be and it might have had more dignity than the suffocating charlatanism of this reverent-but-nevertheless-cheerful ceremony abetted by the dazzling weather and the sun blazing through the marmalade-glass windows of the chapel, which were ornamented in coloured bottled-glass scenes of bibulous-looking saints who appeared to be picnicking and engaging in spiritual orgies.

The hired organist was playing the closing bars of 'There Is a Bright Land' and at the same time meaningfully indicating his watch. Mr Dart rose, all six foot four and massive white mane, huge hands arranging Bible and books on the lectern, clearing his throat and saying loudly in the emptiness of the chapel that, friends, as it appears no one else is coming, we might as well begin.

Mr Dart read from the book of Revelation and from the works of Sir Oliver Lodge and Arthur Conan Doyle. He asked those present to rejoice that the spirit of Irene May Collins had been joyously released from the endurance test of this [cheerful smile] troublesome stage of the journey. It sounded as though Aunt May had been delayed by traffic.

They stood. A bronze door slid up and the organist played 'Softly, as in a Morning Sunrise.' The unadorned casket rolled away.

He went down the aisle with Mr Dart, looking straight ahead and insulted.

Outside in the glaze of sun and deafening cry of locusts the hired limousine was waiting and he went directly towards it and heard from behind his name called.

'Angus?'

Coming up fast in dazzling red and under the large hat an angled face, little delicate pointed ears with hoops of gold in them, thin and proud of it. She spoke in a dawdling voice as though she were very slightly drunk.

'I'm Eve St James.' Something then about buying china in Beard Watson's store, where she had read about it in the paper. This was extraordinary, she was saying, rarely seeing death notices. 'I knew May years ago but I knew your mother better. Victoria and I went to school together. I now live in the mountains.'

At least she did not pretend grief for him, press his hand and say that it was for the best perhaps. Instead, she flicked open her bag and scrambled in it for something: A card.

'Here. If you want to, come to *us*.'

Mr Dart and Miss Quinn were approaching, readying smiles and hands of friendship.

'*Come* to us,' Mrs St James said and by the alteration of inflection and the way she narrowed her eyes implied that she knew everything about him. She understood.

Then, ignoring Mr Dart and Miss Quinn, she walked quickly away to where a taxi waited.

'A friend of my mother's,' Angus said and put the card in his pocket. Mrs St James waved a white glove and the taxi flew off.

'Fancy a taxi all the way from town,' Miss Quinn said as they got into the limousine. 'That'd cost over a pound, I'd think. That *was* kind, dear, wasn't it?'

Then, as if Angus might have been overcompensated, she added, 'Mind you, dear, that chapel would have been more than half full if all those who were so fond of your dear Auntie May – if all of *them* could have afforded to take a taxi all the way out here. You do realise that dear, don't you?'

She paused and Mr Dart took up the flail.

'Now, Angus, you're not to feel sad, dear boy. Your dear aunt isn't sad.'

Miss Quinn laughed at the idea.

'Oh, far from it, dear.'

'She's as happy as a sandboy.'

'She's rejoicing.'

'She's merry as a grig now, dear.'

'She's dead,' Angus said, in order to restore an inner balance and prevent the feeling that he was tipping over into their terrible unreality. She is dead, he kept repeating to himself.

She is dead, that's all.

But he didn't turn around to look (as they did) when the car circled around the last curve in the road leading away from the crematorium.

In case, floating above the tops of the eucalyptus trees, there might have been a thin blue vapour.

'So your auntie kicked the bucket, Angus,' Miss Hammer said without looking up from her work. She had a long tongue, which flicked in and out as she bent over her painting. Come to think of it, she was not unlike an anteater with her hooked, extended nose and her tongue flicking in and out. 'How old?'

'Fifty-one,' Angus said and sat down at the table next to Miss Hammer. The room where they worked for Lipton Advertising Slides was narrow as a shoe box and necessitated their sitting very close together. There was a smell of stale tea leaves.

'Fifty-*one*. That's too young to go, isn't it? Heart, was it?'

'Heart failure.'

'That's right. I wasn't surprised when Mr. Lipton said she was gone and you wouldn't be in yesterday. In this heat they're dropping like flies. Cremated, was she?'

'Yes.'

'Yes. It's better that way. Especially in this heat. Provided you don't have any religious problem.'

Only two days ago just before lunchtime sitting here as usual with Miss Hammer, painting the slides, and Mr Lipton had come in from his office, breathing harder than usual, and had said, Angus, your landlady Miss Quinn was on the phone and your aunt's been taken ill and you'd better leave off now and go home, here's two bob for a taxi. Nothing had changed here. Nothing had happened to the ugly green vase of dried shivery grass on the window ledge. But in that time a slit had opened in the earth to show the fires below and closed again.

Never mind, Miss Hammer was saying, we all have to go and it's better to go quick like that. Like her own mum had gone, sitting at the dining table of a Sunday evening just as they were serving the tea. 'I said, "Mum, you're not eating your lovely veal . . ."'

Angus held a glass slide up to the light and read with difficulty, mistily, that the next attraction at the Plaza would be Errol Flynn in *The Dawn Patrol*.

The glass slides that he and Miss Hammer painted so carefully were flashed on and off the screen in the intermissions while the Mighty Wurlitzer played. Sometimes the theatre managers gave out passes and he took Aunt May or Audrey Bundock, who lived two doors down from them in Victory Street.

Somebody who knew Mr Lipton had told Aunt May there was this marvellous opportunity to start in the advertising business and what with Angus being artistic and all and two pound ten a week . . .

'Well, love, you could look on it as a stopgap until something better turns up,' Aunt May had said when he came back from the interview and told about the dirty, dark little warehouse studio and the thing growing out of Mr Lipton's face which was difficult to look at.

'But *love*, two pound *ten* . . .' He was reminded of the enormity of the sum and of how he could save enough to go to art school at night.

And, 'Different if your mother and father had *left* something.'

Two almost forgotten faces looked at him regretfully.

'All right.'

That had been nearly two years ago, an infinity. Now he was seventeen and still climbing the three flights of greasy stairs every day past Finkelstein and Son Fabrics, Tillock and Co. Imported Lace and Peebles Dental Surgical Equipment; every single morning to hear Miss Hammer say, 'Hot enough for you?' or 'Cold enough for you?' or 'No seat on the tram; my poor feet,' and always after taking off her jacket and putting on her old paint-spattered smock, 'Oh, well, no rest for the wicked.' In winter a small electric radiator smelled up the room without sending out the slightest heat and in summer an equally small electric fan merely disturbed the languid, stifling air. But at seventeen you were told you had your whole life before you, you lucky boy. Years and years. Wait until you're as old as I am and you'll be sorry you ever bitched about being seventeen.

Oho, what I wouldn't give to be seventeen again, everyone said. Being seventeen didn't make that clock move any faster towards five-thirty. At seventeen you could feel as much in a rut as someone who was thirty. There was a difference only in that you had more of the same to look forward to.

Angus thought again of Mrs St James.

'Have you ever been up to the Blue Mountains, Miss Hammer?'

'Oh, yes. I went for my holidays once to Katoomba. Oh, it's terribly picturesque. Mountains and waterfalls as far as you can see and we stayed at a very select guest house with nice verandas all around it and three meals. But my rotten headaches started coming on like billy-o. It was the elevation, you see. I can't stand heights so we had to come home after only three days and of course they charged us for the full week because it was the season and so there I was, poor me, no holiday and out of pocket . . .'

She was off now on a tale of woe. No matter what you brought up. If you dared to hope something might turn out well, she said she'd believe it when she saw it. Or that *that* would be the day. Things, Miss Hammer said, would be worse

And not just her. Everyone. Everyone he knew and had ever

before they were better.

known was at pains to persuade him there was no hope. They thrived like mushrooms in a dark world, scoffing at the light and putting aside a little something for the rainy day that was sure to come because 'You never know what's just around the corner' and it was bound to be bad. They bought State Lottery Tickets every week, laughing at their own foolishness because, as everyone knew, only the already rich won the big prizes. Cheerily, they reminded each other they would be a long time dead. However, it was no use complaining because if it's not one thing it's another and you can say *that* again.

There was another country Angus saw in dreams. Not geographical but an idea, a scheme. Something to do with imagination and viewpoint and not necessarily the sole property of the well-to-do. He could recognize the people who knew about it. It was on their faces and in their overheard conversation and because of a difference in their laughter and even the way they walked. They were capable of being amused in some different way. They might even enjoy themselves without worrying inordinately over the prospects of the flu season and the electric light bill and having to get their teeth fixed and . . .

Their colour was not grey but bright red. Like Mrs St James.

Come to *us* if you like.

Lightly, the implication of saving him in her dawdling voice and the suggestion that she knew, understood absolutely everything about his perplexities and dampened hopes and the fraud of being seventeen with all your life before you.

Then, changing the inflection:

Come to us.

I dare you to.

'It rained,' Miss Hammer was saying, 'every day my friend was there and when the rain stopped, up came this mountain mist. You couldn't see your hand in front of your face and so they were cooped up in the hotel and never saw the view, not once. "Trust my luck," she said and I said —'

'It never rains but it pours,' Angus said.

'That's funny. That's what I *did* say. It's true.'

'You can say *that* again,' Angus said, getting in first.

'Did you enjoy it?' he asked Audrey. They'd been to the Regent to see Irene Dunne.

'I didn't mind it.' It was the extent of her praise for anything.

They were waiting in line for a table at the California Coffee Shop in the din of the Saturday-night crowd.

'Funny, didn't you think? That bit with the dog and the bowler hat when Cary Grant gets the wrong hat.'

'Oh, yes. I couldn't help laughing at that.'

What *was* funny, Angus thought, was them standing here not enjoying themselves. All dressed up in their Saturday-night clothes and Audrey wearing her new orange-coloured ankle-strap shoes, her hanky, not to be used under any circumstances, tucked in her imitation-gold bangle, and going to have a Cheese Dream at the California and not enjoying themselves.

'We'll get a table in a minute,' he said.

'I wouldn't want to *bet* on it,' she said.

'We've been waiting twenty minutes,' a woman ahead of them said.

'Sydney gets worse and worse of a Saturday night-time,' Audrey said.

'You can say that again.'

'Four and a two,' the hostess screamed at them and they went forward through the tables, Audrey mincing a little in her new shoes and wearing the expression of disdain she used for restaurants lest anyone think she was new to them.

All the way upstairs and then over near the kitchen, where the waitresses, dressed as Swiss peasants, flew in and out of the swing doors. The worst table in the California.

'Trust our luck,' Audrey said and let her knee stay against Angus. There was a slut inside Audrey densely guarded by beautifully ironed underwear and overlayers of prudery.

'Going to have a Cheese Dream?'

'Oh, I think I might be reckless tonight.'

They said the same thing every Saturday night. A peasant whipped by, took the order sulkily.

'Cigarette while we wait?'

'Ta.'

Audrey took a cigarette occasionally to show she was sophisticated. She held it at arm's length as though it might explode and took genteel little puffs, being careful not to inhale in case she got the habit. It was all right Angus having the habit, because now he was seventeen it wouldn't stunt his growth. Now he had grown to a lanky six foot he could do the drawback. Audrey was seven months his senior and something about this fact gave him a feeling of security with her, an older-sister feeling he did not have with other girls his age.

Audrey, apart from the slut in her occasionally showing like her petticoat, remained indifferent. Her incurious grey eyes looked back at him steadily. He'd drawn a sketch of her one time and she had said, 'Well, you'd know it's me.' Occasionally he kissed her on her buttoned mouth and the result would have been the same if he had kissed her handbag.

'One of the girls at the office ...' Audrey was saying and Angus debated whether or not to tell her about the note which had come at last and which said in violent handwriting: Yes, of *course* I meant it, dear imbecile. Come *any* time for as *long* as you want. Eve St James.'

In violet ink.

The printed letterhead showed a view of mountains and read: 'Hotel Ritz, Medlow Bath, Blue Mountains. Sole ownership and management: Heath St James.'

Weeks ago, in a blue, despondent mood, he had written to Mrs St James, using as an excuse his thanks to her for coming to the funeral, and, after much consideration asked in a post-script if she had meant the invitation. Then, when no reply had come, he had felt by turns relief and disappointment. Yesterday morning Miss Quinn had said, 'There's a letter for you on the hall table,' and stood by, holding her cat in her arms, while he read it through twice, realising he had brought himself to the edge of a chasm.

'Good news, dear?'

He didn't know. Was it or wasn't it? 'Just a note,' he said. Should he or shouldn't he? It seemed the smallest decision but he was aware of the significance of it. As long as he could remember he'd been indoctrinated with the dread of change. Change to Aunt May meant Usually For The Worse. No, watching Audrey daintily scoop up her Cheese Dream, little finger extended to show she was genteel. Better not to confide in Audrey. Not until his mind was made up anyway.

And, Audrey was saying about this girl Una in the office who thought she was so smart ha-ha and yet couldn't read her own shorthand notes and . . .

On the other hand, he thought, to get another opinion — any opinion. Just to *tell* someone.

'Aud.'

'Yes?' Audrey stopped in the middle of what had happened about Una.

'I think I might go up to the mountains.'

'You don't get your holidays till June.'

'Not holidays.'

'How do you mean then?'

He told her about Mrs St James. Let her read the note.

'Funny *writing,* isn't it? Funny ink and all. What's she calling you an imbecile for?'

'It's meant humorously.'

'I wouldn't want her making fun of *me* like that.'

'Well, I might go.'

'How would you get the time off?'

'Just leave.'

'*Leave?*' Nobody they knew ever just *left*.

'I might.'

'Give up your *job* and all?'

'I'm not going on painting advertising slides all my life.'

'Nothing wrong with it for the time being.'

'How long's *that* ?'

'What would you do when you *got* there?'

'I don't know.'

'*She* doesn't mention anything about a job.'

'I know.'

'How do you know *what* she wants? '

'I don't.'

'Well, if I was you I'd find out. '

'No.'

'Why not? '

'Because if I found out first I mightn't *want* to go.'

'Are you *feeling* all right?'

'Perfectly, thanks.'

'You don't know *what* you might be getting yourself into.'

'That's the *point*, Aud.'

'Pardon me?'

'That's why.'

'How do you mean ?'

'Just for once take a risk.'

'Why?'

'Because. And because we might be going to have a war.'

'Oh, there isn't going to be a war.'

'How do *you* know?'

'Hitler has TB. My dad heard.'

'Yeah?'

'Yes. That's why his voice is so hoarse all the time. He's dying of TB, my dad says.'

'Anyway, war or no war, I can't stick it much longer.'

'Stick what?'

He extended his arms to take in the enormous radius of his terribly small world.

'The lot. The whole bloody lot.'

'Nice boys don't swear in front of girls.'

'What have I got to *lose*?' he asked, afraid of what he would hear. And heard it. Same old song and dance about birds in the hand and looking before you leap and never knowing what you might be getting into and something fishy about people you don't know asking you to stay with them.

Well, if you wanted *her* opinion, Audrey said primly, she wouldn't trust this Mrs St James as far as she could spit.

'Besides, it's safer not to get to know *strangers*.'

'You *said* it,' he said.

Thanks for making up his mind.

At a place called Valley Heights, the mountains having begun, an additional steam engine was put on and the train shuddered and stayed panting, taking on water, preparing for the climb ahead. The air had grown cooler. You could (and he did) take a deep breath and be instantly aware of the change of texture. But would he mind, the elderly woman opposite asked, if they had the window shut? The soot was fearful, all over the seats and their faces and hands already grimy, their eyes quaintly lined around in black.

Thank you very much, she said. She was getting off at Katoomba and she wondered if then he would be so nice as to help her to get her suitcase down from the brass rack. Really, the trains, she said. It was a disgrace to the state government, these ramshackle old boxcars even for second class. She smiled and offered him a piece of chocolate, which he accepted gratefully. He'd had nothing but a cup of tasteless tea and a dry scone at Sydney Central Railway Station.

'And where are *you* off to?' the woman asked him.

'Medlow Bath.'

'Oh, it's pretty there. Whereabouts are you staying?'

'At the Ritz.'

'Oh.'

She appeared to be looking him up and down. Wondering how a young chap like him in second class with a Woolworth suitcase and his shoes shined up with a banana skin could be going to stay at the Ritz. The Ritz had about it the feeling of mirrors and footmen.

But she merely said kindly that he would see sights that had to be seen to be believed (and she had once been to Bavaria in now cut-off Austria). He would see the Megalong Valley, Govett's Leap, the National Pass and the Valley of Waters; and the Three Sisters, which was a mountain that indeed looked like three giant figures and for years had been expected to collapse into the Kangaroo Valley thousands of feet below. What a sight it would be, all that roaring stone giving way at once. In fact, once when a new crack had suddenly appeared, they had run special trains up and hundreds of people had come to watch the terrifying sight and had camped out at Echo Point for days. But nothing had happened after all. The Three Sisters had stood for a thousand years and most likely would stand for another thousand. It gave you a sense of being unimportant, now didn't it?

Not something Angus needed at the moment.

The train curving slowly higher through steeply rising cliffs of dripping stone and overhanging trees cutting off light, and around deep ravines at the bottom of which water glinted, was reaching a plateau of colder, darker air. With every stop at little flower-tubbed stations, the fact of the air and of the crisp, unusual light brought a sense of nearing Mrs St James. A coil of nervousness had begun to wrap itself around his stomach.

So he asked, 'Do you know Mrs St James?'

'Oh, you could hardly live around our part of the mountains without knowing Mrs St James.'

'It's them I'm staying with,' Angus said.

'Oh, yes?'

Possibly a look of something crossed her face or else a darting shadow of a rock flicked a second's darkness in and out of the carriage.

'Well,' the woman said, 'I shouldn't say "know". Met. But I often see the girls doing their shopping in Katoomba.'

His look of innocence spurred her on.

There were two St James girls and one boy. The older girl, Stevie, was quite a beauty and they were all bright, bright as buttons, although –

Angus blinked at their brightness, bewildered by the unexpected entrance of all these St Jameses into his dream.

'– not to be wondered at when you consider *him*. But nobody sees much of him. He keeps out of sight most of the time.'

'Mr St James?'

'The Judge.'

'Oh, yes,' he said, leaning back in his seat, not wanting all these facts so soon and dismayed at the idea of a Judge. Saw the Judge, tall and glacial and having caustic things to say about the impulsiveness of the invitation. Could this have had anything to do with the long delay in Mrs St James's replying?

And then when he had finally got through on the weak telephone line and she had not been there, somebody sounding both busy and official and at the same time vague had said, oh, yes, that he was expected. 'I believe you're expected,' a man's voice had said through crackling static, and that someone always met the trains.

He had retired from the bench quite young. Young for a judge.

'Had a breakdown, I understand, and so they came up here looking for –'

A whistle screamed, drowning her words as they were sucked without warning into the darkness and smoke of a tunnel; could no longer see each other and for minutes, it seemed, while the train roared through smoky blackness, Angus imagined she was talking to him through the noise about the St Jameses; pictured her mouth moving, spilling out dire facts about what lay ahead for him and too late now to turn back, heed warnings, because the tunnel had become the dividing line between past and present and on emerging he would have already entered, crossed into the strange country.

But when they burst suddenly into daylight again, coughing from the acrid fumes into quiet late afternoon, the old lady was saying only that it was her opinion that 'they never would have made a go of it if it hadn't been for the experienced hotel manager they'd enticed away from the Carrington in Katoomba.' Just the merest suggestion that she could say a great deal more about the St Jameses if she'd a mind to but let it drop, folding her hands and looking out the window.

And later, 'Have a good time and thank you. Well, cheerio,' when he helped her out with her bag.

Medlow Bath was the next stop, she reminded him, and waved as the train moved, rushed on impatient to discharge him and be done with it.

He tried to take his mind off his disquiet by putting the pieces of Mrs St James together in his mind, trying to reconstruct her face, but none of the faintly remembered angles fitted; refusing to reproduce anything that looked like her, so that, with the wheels slowing down, grinding horribly as they began curving into the long, thin Medlow Bath station, he put down the window and leaned out, hoping her face would materialize from one of the little apostrophes growing larger and larger and turning disappointedly into station guards and into placid, country-looking folk who began seeing, waving and running to someone else as the train stopped and he got off with shaky old-man legs, inhaling the queer sharp air with pine in it and thought then that he saw her, wasn't that her, thin and walking quickly, raising arms in a warm, welcoming gesture, and taking off sun-glasses to become a hag greeting someone behind him.

Was he for the Hydro? The what? An angry little man wearing an old-fashioned duster coat marked HYDRO-MAJESTIC was planted in his path and waving a pencil threateningly as if to grab clients away from the Ritz. Only about a dozen people had got off the train and the majority seemed to have been personally met. A skinny young man was calling out that there was a bus waiting that went to all boarding houses. The train screeched and puffed out and the platform was emptying, ready to close for the day, when a man with a Punch face and wearing a green linen coat with RITZ stitched on it in bright red appeared around an advertising sign for Old Dutch Cleanser and asked Angus, was he Mr Weekes? Took him in tow.

On the road an old dark-blue six-seater car with its canvas top down waited. On the side was painted: SCENIC TOURS: MEGALONG VALLEY, NARROW NECK, GOVETTS LEAP, JENOLAN CAVES. An elderly couple sat in the back seat, wrapped around in car blankets, and two young girls sat primly on the jump seats, wearing Audrey-like looks of protective disinterest. They darted Angus a glance of hope, took in his age and then stared ahead at the dusty road.

'You hop in the front with me,' said the driver, whose name was Charley. Ask for Charley at the desk, he said, starting up the car, which choked and trembled. Cars and charabancs went to all the sights every day, full or half-day trips, whatever you wanted, and night trips too to see the Three Sisters and the Bridal Veil Falls floodlit. They roared off on a gravel road. The cold air tore at their faces.

Great gum trees sped past. Glimpses of dark-blue peaks showed between them. Occasional wooden houses with verandas stood back from the road and had signs advertising GUESTS as though the guests were on display or for sale.

Then, racing towards them, a sign HOTEL RITZ, TURN LEFT, and in a moment gables showed over a clump of tall pines and they turned off into a private road and through a large crumbling stone gate topped by an iron-filigree arch bearing the words HOTEL RITZ in peeling gold paint and down a driveway of white pebbles as the great Victorian brick structure built itself over them, adding cupolas and towers and steeply dipping roofs of slate, erecting itself through the pines into storeys and a wing to the right, hugely rising to meet them, dormer windows and balconies, gigantic stone lions couchant on either side of the front entrance and then, astonishingly, ending, deteriorating suddenly without warning, into blackened ruins, one whole wing falling away into pitiful rows of silent, gaping windows showing through them only sky and collapsed walls behind which bore on them the spectral drawings of staircases and upper rooms where weeds were growing now and birds nested, where mountain lichen grew wild, bright rock flowers sprouted and in the distance where tennis courts had been built in the burned-out area of wind and space.

'The fire,' Charley said as they stared up at the ruined walls. The great bush fire in the terrible dry summer of '28, ten years ago, that had engulfed the hotel as suddenly as death and in the night (he enjoyed the story) the whole west wing had gone up in flames that had been seen as far away as Blackheath and in the holocaust had gone the great picture gallery with its price-less works of art and the original dining-room with its chan-delier that had been sent all the way from Italy. All but three wing falling away into pitiful rows of silent, gaping windows seeing the three screaming figures silhouetted against the blaz-ing, falling rooms. Wind blew through the apertures. They shuddered pleasantly, being alive.

The hotel hung poised on the edge of a precipice, and they could see through ruined arches the mountains just beyond. From the valley miles below, Charley was saying, you could look up from anywhere and see the Ritz. From down there, he said, it looked like a doll's house, as they would see for them-selves when they did the Megalong half-day trip (handing out grubby cards), which included a delicious Devonshire tea, the speciality in this part of the mountains, nowhere else. And now if they'd just follow him and leave the suitcases for the boy; young Stan would get the suitcases.

They went up broad stone steps between the lions, sheepishly, like people on a conducted tour of a palace. On one side a veranda extended the full length of the east wing. A few people sitting in canvas deck-chairs looked up from books and knitting.

The carpeted lobby was only half a lobby. On one side tall tarnished mirrors rose into convolutions of gold cupids and masses of tormented gold plaster moulding, into riots of twisting curlicues, into great apples and sheaves of wheat from which, at points, Venuses held out terrible burdens of weighty glass lamps tinted red. On the other side a plain cement wall, unadorned, cut through the lobby like a snub. The ornate, richly carved reception desk had run into the cement wall and stopped dead in its tracks so that it was now out of proportion, truncated horribly at its midsection. At the Victorian side of the desk, a massive oak staircase rose to a landing and went on up into late-afternoon shadow.

A good-looking man with greying hair, wearing a double-breasted fawn suit with the nonchalance of a dandy, said he was Mr Marcus and touched a bell lightly, welcoming them all to the Ritz and dispatching bags, handing out keys with quiet efficiency.

'And you are Angus,' Mr Marcus said, coming over and smiling and taking Angus by surprise (gazing up at the peeling painted ceiling of cherubs blowing trumpets and writhing on pink clouds) so that Angus involuntarily shot out his hand before realizing that Mr Marcus was not to be shaken hands with.

'You're to go over to the bungalow, Angus. So if you'll sit down and rest your aged bones, I'll find someone to take you over.' Mr Marcus had little tired lines around the eyes and his smile was weary from years of overuse . . .

Like the brocaded chair Angus sat down in, admiring Mr Marcus's impeccable clothes and his elegant peacock-like walk and the slow, graceful way he seemed to do ten things at once, writing something, speaking softly into the desk phone, handing out mail ('I believe there's a letter for you, Mrs Humphrey') and the evening paper, and when a carload of chirping ladies came twittering in, all in similar floral-print dresses and some carrying wildflowers, greeting them individually by name, raising his eyebrows in astonishment at the fact that they'd seen a darling baby kangaroo.

Soothingly, Mr Marcus assured two excitable old magpies that they were on his list for the movie bus. 'Oh, I wouldn't forget *you*, Mrs Wadhams. You are engraved, like Calais, on my heart.'

There was a velvet fuzz in his voice and an arch to his shoulders which gave rise to doubts, yet was not effeminate, not like the wispy boys Angus was used to seeing in coffee shops. There was the softness about him of a pear turning brown.

'Hello,' Mr Marcus was saying softly into the phone (but now, with the chattering birdlike ladies dispersed, Angus could hear plainly). 'How are *you*? What's doing? Oh. With whom? Oh. Lackaday, then. Is *she* there? Know where she is? Her guest's here. Send Liesl over, will you?'

Then, listening for a long moment and smiling, he seemed infinitely pleased, stretched like a cat being stroked, ran a long thin hand through his hair, looked less weary.

'Rescue is on the way,' he said to Angus.

Mountains, Liesl said, meant nothing to her. She was from Innsbruck. She shrugged at the mountains. People coming up here and gazing all starry-eyed at *this*. After what *she'd* seen. Thinking *this* was something.

'Crazy,' Liesl said. She was far from home, her voice implied. Unspeakable things had happened. No one here in this lazy warm safe country could understand.

'But they are kind,' Liesl said, in the tone of one compelled to accept their kindness.

A refugee. One of the 'reffos,' as they were called, although no one meant it to be a slight. Hundreds poured in every month now. Everyone was kind to them and said, behind their backs, 'They'll take the jobs away from us, just you watch.'

'And the climate here, it's beautiful,' Liesl said, bitterly, as she clumped ahead of him through the strange air. She had a square, thick body on stocky legs, and close-cropped black hair around a plain, unpainted face. She would be getting on towards thirty, Angus guessed.

At the end of a shrub-lined pathway, a two-storey wooden house sat in a grove of thick pines, secluded. A board sign read: STRICTLY OUT OF BOUNDS TO HOTEL GUESTS. Arum lily plants grew untidily below the edges of the verandas. There were tennis shoes lying all around the front door, which was open.

Liesl led him around the side of the house to the kitchen door. The house was cold inside and had an aromatic smell of pine and cedar. They went up an uncarpeted stairway and in the breaking silence a dog barked distantly and a voice said, 'Now, now, Mr Foster.' Liesl opened a door into a small white room, overlooking the kitchen garden. There was a narrow iron bed covered with a chilly-looking white quilt.

'And the bathroom, it's across the hall,' Liesl said. 'Do you know how it is to work the gas bath heater?'

He didn't, he said, feeling as alien as Liesl, suddenly.

'Then I show you when you want to make a bath,' Liesl said. 'It is *very* dangerous.'

'Liesl?' a girl's voice called.

'Ja.'

'Can you come here a minute?'

'Ja ja. Wait. Where is your mother, do you know?'

'No.'

Liesl said, 'You soon find out here nobody knows where is anybody.'

A telephone jangled weakly. 'And now is the telephone. Crazy.'

She lunged heavily away.

He sat down on the bed and stared at the faded grass mat on the clean, bare floor. In the quiet, there was a feeling in the aloneness of not being alone, of other people in other rooms who were waiting, as he was, for a signal or perhaps to see what he would do first (he was lighting a cigarette shakily), for him to emerge first.

He remembered, suddenly, a game, years ago at a children's party. Sardines. He was *it,* the one to hide in the dark and be found under the stairs or in a closet, preferably some confined place so that each of the others, finding you, crept in with you with much breathing, squeezing, giggling, and the last poor dope, blundering in the dark from room to room was the loser. He had gone upstairs in the blackness of an unfamiliar house while they counted aloud to four hundred by twos, and had climbed onto the top of a tallboy in a silent room and waited and waited, pleased at first that no one could find him and then, unbelievable time passing and a nasty suspicion growing, had climbed down all dusty and come downstairs into light, to find they'd decided to play another game and he had not even been missed.

The light was gold now and he smoked another cigarette and then another, putting them out on the window ledge as there was no ashtray. Reality was so much stranger than imagination, which remained pleasantly rigid in any shape you chose (while reality changed from moment to moment, built itself into cold white walls and grass mats and people). All of this being unfamiliar on the mind's map where long ago he had carefully placed Mrs St James in a lighted doorway, her arms extended to him. Well, this was stupid, sitting here, waiting to be found, skulking in a bedroom. He was the dope, on top of the tallboy, waiting for everyone to come to him.

He got up and walked into the hall saw a line of doors to the left, some open and some closed. He walked down the hall, past bedrooms towards the front stairs, expecting, with the creaking boards, one of the closed doors to open and someone to look out (perhaps an irritable Judge, and what is the correct address – your honour? your worship?) and realizing, half-way down the stairs, that he was already tiptoeing.

A large, untidy living-room, choking with the smell of old log fires and saturated with magazines and books; awash with old leather chairs showing, in depressions and bulges, the outlines of people; a long black horsehair sofa, lamps with green glass shades, and large oil paintings, mostly of landscapes torn by wind; of lonely winter beaches threatened by immense surf. He sat on a wide window seat and picked up the *Illustrated London News,* not seeing a thing on the pages, and heard a distant train. Very likely going the other way, back to Sydney. It would be there, he calculated, somewhere about nine or ten that night, conscious of a surprising, ridiculous homesickness.

And, after all, if they are all nutty here or impossibly high-falutin and cold unfriendly, busy or whatever, so what? You can always get on a train and go home.

To where?

Home, such as it was, had gone up in smoke with poor, kind, dumb Aunt May. As one of his last acts of gratitude to her, he had told her how dumb she was. You are *so* dumb it's incredible, he told her in a frenzy of anger and frustration at the continuing sameness of everything, at dull food, slow trams, the bad news all coming together, and needing to escape somehow and being let off by some pinheaded remark of hers and then her getting up from the tea table and without saying a word, very dignified, going into her bedroom and shutting the door.

For the first time since her funeral he felt grief and, seeing her now, with her watery blue eyes and gentle rabbit-like expression, wanted to make amends, terribly to make amends, and felt the hot tears welling up and his throat constricting and, turning away to the window, saw or fancied he saw Aunt May coming through the trees, through his waters of remorse spilling down his cheeks, coming in a dawdling, unhurried walk, swinging a basket and wearing, unexpectedly, blue pants.

He was on his feet and streaking across the room to the stairs wiping his eyes and burning with the embarrassment of being found weeping, stumbling up the blurred stairs and then stopping because it was already too late and more disgraceful to be caught escaping, and turned slowly around, knowing she had spotted him.

She was standing on the steps of the veranda, one hand up to her eyes, looking at him, trying to make out who he was there in the shadows.

'Who is that?' she called.

Blinking, he went out onto the veranda. Behind dark glasses, Mrs St James's look was severe, the mouth forbidding.

Then, taking off her glasses, light flowed into her face like air filling a sail; warmth suffused her, transforming her as she came up the steps; smiling and making the outline of a caress without touching him.

'Oh, it's *you*.'

Years fell off her, peeled away from the faulty, badly remembered image he had been carrying around all those weeks of a painted and dyed woman. The angles were softer, the lines drawn lightly around the mouth and eyes and, hatless, the short bobbed hair was gold and grey. From being tall and spindly in his picture of her, she shrank into a boy wearing sailor-blue pants and a pink shirt open at the neck. She sat, curling herself lazily into a big wicker chair, crossing her neat legs, presenting small hands, small feet and such smooth whiteness of skin, it suggested in this insecure light that she might be in her twenties.

'How good, Angus,' she said. 'I had a presentiment that you might change your mind at the last minute. Your note was so *tentative*.'

He sat down opposite her, feeling stronger and remembering now her coaxing, dawdling voice as she said, 'I wasn't *there*. I was lost in something, coming down the path, and then I saw this man – boy – run across the room and I was startled. Did someone come for you? Did Liesl show you your room? Are any of the children around?'

She didn't appear to think any of these questions worth an answer.

'Beginnings are troublesome. There ought to be a way of avoiding them. I like to come in on things that have already begun. I'd like to have been born aged thirty. How old are you, Angus?'

'Seventeen.'

'Ah, yes. Well' – she might have been prompted – 'the only solution to being seventeen is to get it over with.'

She talked with folded hands, looking directly at him. With her, it seemed that the function of speech was in itself and not to be muddied by movement, not accompanied by the constant touching of oneself, the fidgeting, patting, fingering of furniture and all the other usually unnecessary things people do when they talk. Mrs St James simply sat and spoke.

'And this might be a good place to get it over with – a plateau. It seemed to me, when we met – what a dreadful *happy* funeral, almost *jolly* – that you were looking about uncertainly and needed a pause to think.'

'I'm very grateful,' Angus said hoarsely.

'That you can't tell yet,' she said abruptly. 'How old were you when your mother was killed?'

'Nine.'

'And May took you?'

'Yes, Aunt May.'

'Aunt *May*.' Better the river took him, her look said. 'Do you remember much about your mother? Your father?'

'I remember we lived in a lot of places, we were always moving,' he said, uncomfortable as always in their presence, unable to place them in any emotional reference.

'Ah, yes, she was always restless,' Mrs St James said. 'I adored Victoria. It's a pity you didn't know her *not* as a parent. One doesn't get to know parents. Oh, there was something so cogent and primitive about her. I don't think she ever had an unoriginal thought and of course then – back then when we were girls – she was so beautiful. Those great eyes and all that mass of shining black hair falling everywhere, and she had a kind of marvellous contempt . . .'

She stopped and looked away, as though listening for something. 'She and I . . . 'she said and stared towards the distant, darkening, fire-blackened walls of the hotel.

'Did you see our ruins?'

'Yes,' he said. 'We drove in that way.'

'I love them. I love to walk there alone, especially at night. and think I'm in Rome. People are always at us to rebuild the wing or at least put up cabins there. It seems to bother them. People come with very convincing arguments and want to tear down the old walls but . . . I think they'll stay.'

Hidden in the casualness of her tone was a pistol.

'The Judge dislikes changes,' she said, turning back to him, 'and we all respect that. Actually, we weren't alike, your mother and I. I was very subdued then and didn't have a thought in my head. You weren't supposed to then. You were sent off to boarding-school to learn how to be thoroughly useless. You were taught to be a young lady. So that having been cloistered with your own sex all your pubescent life, you were ready, virgo intacto, to be flung into marriage. That is our good old Anglo-Saxon way and it wouldn't have occurred to me there *was* any other way until Victoria came – erupted, you might say – into school, and oh, I was marvellously shaken by her. She pushed me out of the hothouse and made me breathe for the first time. Oh, to think, to be pulled apart by an idea was a unique experience for me, getting ready to be gracious under a hat piled with roses. Facts. She liked to get the stone out of the peach. She'd get *at* you. "Partridge," she used to say to me (it was my – disagreeable term – *maiden* name), "Partridge in a pear tree, Partridge you can't fool *me*." She *sensed* what people were. I remember we were reading about Dr Crippen's trial and I said how could he do it? How could this dreary little man with the walrus moustache be *capable* of cutting up his wife into tiny little particles and all the time be having tea and whatever upstairs with Ethel Le Neve, and Victoria said, "Eve, *everyone* is capable of murder." '

A gong boomed and Angus jumped.

'The dressing bell,' Mrs St James said. 'The dear ladies like to dress for dinner.'

She was silent for a moment, walking with his mother somewhere, and then she said quietly, 'I have found out she was right.'

She stood up.

'Come. I want to show you something before it's dark.'

He went with her along a sandy path of pine needles. The light was growing bluer, the shadows of moving branches on their feet, and going down narrow rock steps she took his arm lightly, talking all the while in her confiding voice (about his mother being caught with Oscar Wilde's *Salome* – outrageous then) and creating a sense of his having known her already and because she so disliked beginnings had moved their relationship forward like the hands of a clock. She stopped from time to time to point out a wild plant. 'Mountain heath, for which my husband is named, though I like to think it's the other way around,' she said and went on without waiting for him to comment. He was drawn along the pathway and into the texture of her strange, coddling voice, for she wove rather than talked.

About Victoria and her being punished unjustly for some minor infringement of the 'upper-class syndrome'; made to wear signs around their necks reading, 'I am ashamed of myself,' and of the delicious revenge (she drew out the word, lovingly). In front of the whole school, the headmistress lunching with the trustees, Victoria marching to the headmistress' table and saying in clarion tones, 'I wish to protest that the milk is *watered*.'

'Oh, she was like Electra, standing there with all that black hair and her eyes blazing.'

He saw it as an enormous canvas in a museum. Susanna before the Elders. Balancing it, at the same time, against his own fading memories of her, of a quiet woman, often lying down in shaded rooms and saying, not now, Angus, I have a headache.

Then Mrs St James said, as though seeing this too, 'The last time I saw here, some years before the accident I thought something had withered in her. I thought perhaps marriage had settled on her like frost. *Look*.'

She pointed to a prickly tree. A face peered at them from it, a face from the Inferno, misshapen head covered by bristling, disgusting hair, mongoloid face gazing at them with blind, blank wickedness, and he saw, as she pulled down a branch, the deceit of it, made of twigs, a nut face with pods for eyes, nose mouth ; it was an obscene cone.

'A Bad Banksia Man,' she said. 'Isn't he a fright ? The banksia trees only grow here on the mountains.' He saw there were dozens of heads on the tree, in different shapes and sizes but all with the wicked mongoloid faces. Bobbing in the wind, they looked like little traitors' heads on pikes.

Not to be confused with the mountain devil, which was also endemic to the Blue Mountains. A little nut (she was looking around, trying to see one) with devil's horns and a peaked face. 'We collect them for a friend who makes them into dolls – an old friend who is resting with us for a time. There are curious things here, Angus, as you can see.'

'It happened,' she said, 'in such a strange way. At a tennis match?'

The accident, of course. He was still not used to the way she had of jumping on and off a subject.

'Cricket.'

'Cricket.' She sounded affronted. 'In all the years I knew her, she never had the slightest interest in cricket. In fact, she hated it.'

'I think she did but my father –'

'Ahh.' It seemed to corroborate what she had felt about his father, her eyebrows rising in twin arcs of disapproval and of blame for the swift and peculiar end of her friend, capriciously killed when a grandstand had collapsed without warning.

'It seems mortifying to be killed watching something you don't give a hoot about.'

He hadn't ever thought about it that way but now he remembered a burned-out resigned look she sometimes had while listening to one of his father's long perorations and of her once saying, shutting her eyes against the endless words, 'Bert, you have made a well-known point there.'

'I think,' Angus said, surprised, 'they must have been very different.'

'Yes,' Mrs St James said, turning away from the subject and raising her arm to show the mountains.

They had come out of the pathway onto a rocky scarp and onto a concrete lookout built over air, over space that fell three thousand feet down sheer rock face to the valley, over a drop so dizzying that Angus, hanging onto the iron fence, felt the platform rock, felt as though he were being projected; the sense of falling into the gigantic chasm (the platform giving way, the grandstand cracking, hurtling down), and he drew back with a gasp.

'Don't look down,' Mrs St James said. 'Look level.'

The extraordinary thing was the colour. An eerie blueness lay on the mountains. It was not the colour of evening but a more intense blue, the blueness of seeing through tinted glass. Through it, the hard, clear-air daylight shot white glare onto cliff faces, creating giant shadows of deeper blue and, in the deepest crevices, blackness. From their crests in sunset and cloud, the mountain walls dropped in huge descending plateaux into a greyer light and then into darkness where at the lowest depths of the valley it was already night and where what appeared to be parsley was forest. Over the whole empty airiness of space hung an intense silence.

'There,' said Mrs St James.

As though she were presenting a gift.

Angus, hanging onto the rail, felt his stomach curdling.

'Do heights upset you?'

'Just a little,' he said, not wanting to admit that he could not look out of a third-story window without this nauseous feeling of dropping to his death in a falling elevator.

'The trick is to fasten your eyes to a level and look at one thing at a time.'

In the changing light of the sun going down and cloud banks moving, the landscape seemed to be in motion. Across from them a range of monolithic tablelands, which had been in shadow, caught alight and she pointed. 'The ruined castle. See it?'

He saw on a crest the outlines of abutments and fallen towers where a great castle had been built, incredibly, in the loneliness.

'Just rocks,' she said.

It was the peculiar light that caused things to take on other shapes, she said. Over there a face and there a camel. She caught at his arm. 'Quickly now, before the sun goes, see if you can find the emu.'

He felt the sickness subsiding in the distraction of this game. It was like those childhood puzzles in old-fashioned picture books where you hunted for the cat hidden in the tree.

'A giant bird, an emu,' she said. 'Away across the valley on a cliff face.'

No, he could not see it.

'More to the right. You can only see it just as the sun is going.'

It was difficult, but she seemed to imply, to implore him to find the emu, and directing him this way and that, up a little higher, now down. Quickly now before the light went. His eyes burned with the effort of looking and still he saw nothing emushaped.

Then suddenly, at the very last ray of sunlight fading, the

giant bird revealed itself hazily, rearing up a mountainside, its long neck and arching egg-shaped body sketched on a distant cliff.

'I see it,' Angus cried. 'I see it.'

Just as darkness swept across the cliff, erasing it.

Mrs St James breathed in deeply as though this pleased her, his having passed this small but important test.

'Some people *never* see it. So if you find it the very first time, it's considered rather remarkable.'

In this peculiar place where nothing was what it seemed to be, his finding the emu had given him status.

'So come and meet the others now,' she said, pleased with him, and put her arm through his as they went back up the dimming path.

'And now is sherry,' Liesl announced, bringing in the tray with two carafes and glasses, and with a glued-on smile.

'Sweet or dry?' asked Mrs St James.

Angus, not knowing either, chose sweet while the spectre of Aunt May raised its arms in horror.

Mrs St James said, 'Bea, will you take this to Angus.'

Lamps were lit in the living-room. Old lamps, Mrs St James explained, gave contrast. The house was fully electrified from the hotel generator but the Judge preferred lamplight.

Angus agreed it was much nicer, noted that he was the only one drinking sweet sherry.

Theodore, Bea and Stevie.

All of them in the yellow light looking so much like their mother. All of them stamped with her face in varying moulds. They had drifted in separately so he had been able to study each in turn. Theodore, the eldest, was Mrs St James turned into an athletic boy of twenty with outsize hands and feet (yet his hand-shake was disappointing, his brown eyes just missed you by a fraction), who moved with a great sense of physical power; the muscles showed through his white tennis sweater.

Beatrice was the youngest, a year younger than Angus, and she was choosing not to be a copy of her mother; in a year or she was choosing not to be a copy of her mother; in a year or coarsening from their thin inheritance (her mother's bones were mackerel thin), and something in her spirit was at work getting rid of the maternal vestiges in her face, the nose was lengthening (had gone too far already) and the St James chin lowering itself, preparing to make an oval sad face only fourth cousin to Mrs St James. She wore her heavy dull-blonde hair in a long thick pigtail and her glance told you she would be polite but nothing more; expect nothing more from her in the world, ever.

But Stephanie, coming in last, coming with the identical lazy walk and already in the middle of a sentence, the situation already begun, was closest to the original. It was extraordinary to see the two of them close together in the lamplight, the sharp angles and definitions of the faces so similar that one moved as in a mirror and, 'Here is Angus at last,' Mrs St James said and Stevie said, 'Hope you can bear us, Angus,' in the same dawdling don't-care tone so that the same voice might have spoken.

But, Angus thought, something is alike in all of them, a way each of them took a glass from Liesl's tray without looking at her, turned back to the fulcrum of the room, which was their mother, nodding at what she said, intent on her, not with filial politeness but curiously, as if they like him, were meeting her for the first time, found her equally fascinating.

What had she done all day?

Well, she told them, to be truthful, nothing. She had driven to Wentworth Falls to look at an advertised washstand but it was fake Victorian. 'Now, Liesl,' said Mrs St James, 'have sherry.'

'Oh no, no,' Liesl raised her arms, warding off Mrs St James's kindness. 'Too much to do but you are *kind*.' Flew off.

Mrs St James said, 'It's difficult to think of Liesl in actual physical danger and only barely escaping with her life.' Her parents, her brother and sister gone, all gone in the Anschluss, and only she remaining, at this great distance from everything and everyone she had ever known, all this way from Innsbruck, further than a star and yet . . .

'Yet I've heard her singing in the kitchen,' said Mrs St James, looking at the amber of her sherry. 'The survival of the human spirit never ceases to amaze me.'

'Penalty, Mother,' Bea said suddenly.

'I was expressing my personal opinion, Bea.'

'It sounded like a Dull Generality, didn't it, Tip?' Bea asked her brother.

'A Trite Conclusion, I'd say,' Tip said.

'Stevie?'

Stephanie, painting her nails, said, 'I didn't hear what Mother said.'

'I said that the survival of the human spirit never ceased to amaze *me*.'

'I don't know,' Stevie said. 'Banal Observation perhaps.'

'We have a game, Angus,' said Mrs St James, 'that the Judge invented to keep us from getting verbally sloppy. Daddy likes to keep us on our toes, you see, so we catch each other at things we call "Poorly Observed," "Dull Generality" and so on and we have to pay a penalty. Bea has by far the lowest penalty score. But honestly, Bea, I don't think what I said was Trite Conclusion. I am honestly concerned with the human spirit. Now if I'd said, "Just think what some people go through . . ." '

'But you didn't.'

They were in an argument; it was oddly important to them (with the exception of Stevie, who went on painting her nails and singing a little French song), and Angus, sipping his sherry, feeling the first delightful fire of it and his shyness slipping away, wanted to say something but could think of nothing (and how humiliating to begin, to open with a Banal Observation before you had even unpacked).

Then it was G. W., they decided. 'What's that? I've forgotten,' said Mrs St James. 'Grandiose Wording. Half a demerit.'

'All right, I'll accept that,' she said. 'I'll help Liesl with the washing-up as it was *her* human spirit I was being Grandiose about.'

The subject subsided. Mrs St James picked up intricate crochet.

> *Nous n'irons plus au Bois,*
> *Les lauriers sont coupés,*

sang Stevie in a faraway voice.

Which reminded Mrs St James that she had read in the paper that the Budapest String Quartet was coming to Sydney for two concerts and they might all go, she said, go down to one.

'We'll see what mood Daddy is in,' she cautioned.

Had anyone, by the way, seen Daddy today?

No one. Tip and Bea were absorbed in a gigantic jigsaw; Stevie looked out the window towards the lights of the hotel as though waiting for someone, someone to come and lift her from this giant lethargy.

The Judge's moods were tidal, Mrs St James said. They went in and out and when the tide was at dead low, they knew to leave him well alone. She said it casually but the importance of the Judge filled the room.

'You might say it's the only rule of the house,' she said. 'But the low-tide moods are very infrequent.' The Judge was working on a long and important book and sometimes didn't even come down for meals.

Her look was consoling but the Judge's shadow grew larger on the walls and over the lamplit group. (Had a breakdown, the woman on the train had said.) Was he given to rambling and sudden wild outbursts which would be embarrassing? There was just enough precaution in Mrs St James's voice to suggest that you had to be careful.

And the sign: STRICTLY OUT OF BOUNDS TO HOTEL GUESTS.

But the St Jameses were unconcerned or possibly insulated

against odd behaviour and completely incurious. Either that or they had the most perfect manners Angus had seen in anyone; no one having asked the tiresome questions as to his coming, and by what train and why? It was *she* who radiated this feeling (he could imagine her saying in her laconic way, 'Angus Weekes is coming to stay' and them scarcely reacting to it any more than if she had said, 'We are having lamb stew'). She had put him down in the group and they had simply moved over a little to give him room and gone on with what they were doing.

She was the centre of them, sitting now with her crochet and smiling and listening to two conversations (they were given to overlapping talk) and agreeing with Tip that yes, the music on the Katoomba radio station, where he worked as a junior announcer, was abominable and with Bea that someone named Nancy had an equine face. But then Nancy's mother had always looked like a horse, especially when she was a bride, Mrs St James said. They giggled a little at this, Tip's eyes flitting on and off his mother and sometimes to Angus, but never long enough to let Angus smile back.

They talked of Bach and horses and no one ever said, 'You can say that again' or 'Trust my luck.' They talked for the enjoyment of it, not caring if anyone listened particularly.

Then Mrs St James put down her crochet and turned her head towards the stairway and Angus saw, confidence deserting him, someone or some*thing* arriving. For either the Judge dressed peculiarly or . . .

But it was a ravaged-looking lady and, 'Here's Lady Cissie,' Mrs St James said, welcomingly.

A cloud of perfume preceded Lady Cissie, who sashayed a little. A fat brindle-haired terrier waddled ahead of her.

'Oh, I just lay and lay and lay in my bath. I had no ertia,' Lady Cissie said in a cooing, babyish voice.

All made up to hide the nooks and crannies that had split her face into sections, and wearing a mauve evening dress that was a decade or more out of date. Her hair was dyed an amateurish copper, cut in the shape of what had once been called the shingle. Small pieces of fake metal and glass flickered on her long blue-veined hands. Something curious was caught in the lace yoke of her dress.

'This is Angus,' Mrs St James said.

'Hello, hello,' Lady Cissie said, giving him a dry hand.

Slightly dazed, she might just have been an accident.

'And this is Mr Foster my companion in life,' she said, picking up the ancient terrier, who looked at her with mournful eyes. 'Oh, isn't this pleasant?' she asked uncertainly and Mrs St James said, 'Cissie, what's that in your dress?'

'Where? Oh' She gave a little scream. 'It's a bag of mothballs.' Lady Cissie rippled with laughter. 'Oh, I'm always getting myself caught in *some*thing.'

'That is true,' said Mrs St James, extricating the bag.

'Oh, thank you, my love,' Lady Cissie said, sitting down and putting the terrier on the sofa beside her. 'I get more nitwitted by the day and the air is abetting me, the delicious air here. Is that sherry?'

'Yes. Angus, would you pour Lady Cissie —'

'I'd rather have gin in something, my love, may I?'

'You may have anything you wish, Cissie. Bea, ask Liesl to bring the gin and some lemon squash.'

'Angus . . . the god of love in the Celtic language,' Lady Cissie said, taking a tarnished silver cigarette case from her bag. 'Are you here to estivate?'

Mrs St James, rescuing Angus, said, 'Cissie, you must remember Victoria Collins.'

'Oh dearest.' Lady Cissie lit her cigarette with shaking hands. 'I should, I should. Oh, my mind's a sieve.'

'At school we were inseparable; twins you might say.'

'At *school*. Oh, *that* Victoria.'

'Angus' mother.'

'Oh, a darling girl. Great dark eyes.'

'Yes.'

'Such a deep, serious girl.'

'Would you have said?'

'Oh, yes. Wouldn't you?'

'Hardly.'

'Oh, well, of course, my darling, you should know. She was *your* friend.'

'Well she was certainly that, whatever else she was.' Mrs St James crocheted rapidly and saw something painful in the stitches. Then if they'd been to school together, something dreadful, cataclysmic, had happened to Lady Cissie, because you would have guessed her to be perhaps nearly ten years Mrs St James's senior, Angus thought, watching her clutching the gin bottle Liesl had brought, clucking her thanks, spilling gin and ash into a glass, saying wasn't this pleasant Mr Foster? And what a sunset this evening. Had Liesl seen the sunset?

'Ach,' Liesl said, stamping out. 'Who has time for sunsets?'

'It *was* a beautiful sunset,' Mrs St James said, consoling her school friend and telling her that Angus had seen the emu right off.

'Oh, it's good *luck,* Angus,' Lady Cissie said and raised a trembling glass to Angus. 'I haven't found it *yet.* I've looked and looked.'

'You look at the wrong moment, Cissie.'

'Yes, my love. Oh, I've had a liftime of looking for things at the wrong moment.'

'At least you found *us.* '

'Ah, my dearest, no. You found *me,*' Lady Cissie said and, leaning towards her friend, clinked glasses with her so savagely that most of Mrs St James's sherry slopped onto the floor. 'Plucked me from the boat just as it was about to go over the rapids,' Cissie said, dabbing at the carpet with her handkerchief.

'Leave it, Cissie.'

'Oh, you never saw such a wreck in all your life, Angus.'

'*Leave* it, Cissie.'

'Oh, am I being a bore, pet?'

'Some*what*.'

'Was I being carried away?'

'Yes.'

'Oh, it's the *air*. It makes me so continuously elated and dramatic, Angus. But you'll get used to me. Oh, what a day I've had, Evie dearest. I made six little dolls and took them over to beloved Mr Marcus to sell to the daffy ladies and then that sweet Liesl lit up Vesuvius for me and I took a long delicious bath —'

'You said.'

'Oh am I repeating myself? Well, cheers. Welcome, Angus, welcome. Oh, isn't this pleasant?'

Lady Cissie lay back against cushions breathlessly and caressed her dog, spilled gin on herself, laughed and said, oh, that a big strange-looking blue bird had lit on her windowsill and looked at her very boldly while she was dressing. An omen. She was sure of it. Her eyes sparkled and her hands flew around. Something extraordinary was going to happen. Marvellous, she said, and at any moment.

'Do you believe in the next moment, Angus?'

'Mrs Saint, if you please,' Liesl said in the doorway.

'Dinner is what is going to happen,' Mrs St James said.

Under red and green lamps, buzzed by night insects, all of them could be clearly seen reflected in the dark glass walls of the enclosed veranda, their heads lifting and dipping over extremely strange soup: six here (one chair at the head of the table still empty) and six in the glass, all of them matched by their own flickering candle-lit reflections. The effect was delightful, quite poetic; the candles moving behind the coloured glass made some faces red, others green. Or could it be the wine, this delicious wine, Angus wondered, which Liesl had poured while his head was turned towards Bea on his left trying to figure out what the hell she was talking about (listening had become a little difficult, which must have something to do with the altitude or else they all talked too fast; either that or he was slowing down, delightfully, into a state of rapture so that smiles kept bursting over his face for no reason, smile after smile burst from him like hiccups), and so, 'Have your soup before it gets warm' Mrs St James said in her drawling way (such an odd soup, served cold and something floating on it) and, 'Oh, yes,' Angus said, happily. Oh yes to everything.

They were all truly delightful exotic creatures. He looked from one back to the other, up and down the table. To beautiful Stephanie in her peach dress, holding her spoon in an elegant disinterested manner, to Theodore, who sat erect and handsome, to Lady Cissie, who ate in a hurry splattering the tablecloth with soup droplets (for a titled lady her table manners were more like those of the old tarts who sat up at the counter in the Hippo Hamburger in Kings Cross), to Mrs St James on his right, who ate serenely, holding the spoon level with her mouth and looking at it lazily, taking a sip and looking at it again (he began to copy her but found it difficult to keep the spoon steady), and once she looked at him and he thought the look meant liking him, might mean a distillation of love.

So he was forced into frowning a great deal to disguise this intense happiness (which he knew was not entirely related to being unused to alcohol and altitude), to quieten the effervescence bubbling up which at any moment might break into laughter at nothing or cause him to brag dangerously ('I draw a bit'). He longed to say something witty but he was no match for these bright birds' swiftness in making and demolishing a point and could only nod and frown, nod and frown like an idiot, seeming to take it all in, and only once took courage enough to say aloud and pompously, 'I agree,' then retreated, pulled in his head like a turtle when Bea asked him 'Why?'

Then Liesl brought the roast and placed it ritualistically at the head of the table and behind it the Judge followed, and a respectful silence fell.

He was small. Except for the pure white hair and clipped

white moustache, he could have been a young boy with his un-lined face and alert blue eyes.

'*Here* you are,' Mrs St James said as if welcoming him home from a long and dangerous journey.

'Here I am,' he said and from the white-haired little boy came a voice to deal with, a deeply rich bass-viol voice which, even without intonation, could adjourn the case; instruct the jury; sentence you to be taken from thence to a place of execution.

'Good evening, Cissie, Theodore, Stephanie, Beatrice,' the Judge said.

And may God have mercy on your soul.

'This is Angus Weekes my dearest,' Mrs St James said.

'Good evening, Angus,' the Judge said and reached out a small hand which Angus managed to grasp, murmuring, 'Good evening, your-er-' and managed to regain his chair without falling.

The Judge took up a carving knife and carved beef thinly and with beautiful precision while Liesl held dishes for him. They waited in silence for meat and a pronouncement. In the sudden quiet Lady Cissie's terrier whined under the table and, 'Silly thing,' she said, 'it's your Uncle Heath.'

'Oh, Uncle Heath,' Cissie cooed, 'did you see the sunset?' She was the only one at the table smoking, spilling ash.

'Not while he's carving,' Mrs St James said and put a finger to her lips.

One by one, dishes were placed in front of them and silently Liesl went around with the vegetables.

At last the Judge picked up knife and fork and with that they began eating in the hush.

Nothing but polite knives and forks on china, wind outside glass, until the Judge said in his brass-gong voice, 'Supposing' – everyone stopping eating, everyone alert, all eyes on him – 'you have been the victim of a maritime disaster in mid-ocean. You have swum to a life raft, which you share with two others

47

for four days before being rescued. Name the two living persons of note you would choose to share your raft and give the reason for each.'

'Must they be living?' Lady Cissie said. 'Dead people are so much more interesting. Give *me* the dead, any day.'

'Living,' said the Judge and looked to his wife. 'My dear?'

Mrs St James thought, took a sip of wine. The attention of the table was riveting. Mrs St James stared at the Judge.

'Lord Louis Mountbatten,' Mrs St James said, 'and Bernard Shaw. The first because of his being an experienced sailor and the second for witty conversation.'

'*Jolly* good, *jolly* good,' the Judge said approvingly. 'Damnably good, my darling,' the Judge said. Angus was still trying to fit it all together in case he was asked. Something about a raft? They talked so fast. Little boiled onions, so difficult to get onto a fork with the table tipping about.

'Queen Mother Mary,' Lady Cissie shouted, her mouth full, 'and Mrs Wallis Simpson and me.'

'But, Cissie –'

'And my Mr Foster. Being a dog, he wouldn't count as an extra person. I'm not getting on any raft without Mr Foster. We would go down on the ship together rather than –'

'Your reasons Cissie. Heath has to have your reasons, dear.'

'Oh. Rapprochement, pet. I would seek forgiveness.'

'Then wouldn't it be more to the point to have Edward and Queen Mum?'

'No, no, no. It's the *woman* who must be forgiven.' Lady Cissie threw consoling arms around her own bony shoulders; her eyes were brimming with tears in a second. 'Oh, darling, do I have to tell *you* why? It's the woman who's always blamed, always, always, and it's the woman who has to be for once forgiven, darling. Oh, Christ, darling we've got to have some forgiveness between the *women* in this hateful world.'

She hugged herself bit her lip, smiled at them all.

'I hardly think,' Mrs St James said in a curdling voice, 'that the Queen Mother and Mrs Simpson would be likely to travel on the same ship in the *first* place, Cissie.'

'I would allow it,' the Judge said.

'You would, dear?' Mrs St James nodded. Apparently the Judge was the final arbiter and Mrs St James continued calmly with her roast beef, relieved that the matter was in his superior hands. His beautiful hands. Her eyes rested on them gratefully.

'Under the circumstances I would allow it,' the Judge said, 'the situation being apocryphal. Is there something interesting going on over there at the hotel, Stephanie?'

'No, Daddy.'

'Then what did I just say?'

'That the situation is apocryphal, Daddy.'

'Then whom do you choose for your apocryphal raft mates?'

'I would pick without hesitation Laurence Olivier and Tyrone Power.'

'Are they living people?'

'*Dad*dy.'

'Well?'

'*Dad*dy, *Dad*dy, you are so over the hills and far away, you are –'

'Stevie,' her mother said without looking up but like a little crack of glass breaking. 'That will do.'

'Who are these people?' The Judge as always turned to his wife for information. 'They are film stars, Heath,' she told him lovingly.

'Ah. I take it then they are both handsome fellows and possibly under seventy years of age?'

Stevie giggled.

'Yes, Daddy. My reason for the first is –'

'One rather grasps your reasons, Stephanie. But has it occurred to you that being alone with both of them at the same time might tend to neutralize your possibilities?'

'No, no. There would be this enormous big sail down the middle of the raft and –'

'You are ingenious, Stephanie. Also greedy, and I would hope both of the gentlemen would recognize the fact and ignore you, which would serve you right.'

But the Judge was looking at Stevie admiringly.

And I know who I'll choose, Angus thought blurrily, getting the hang of it, while Bea was saying she would take on her raft Unity Mitford and A. A. Milne.

'Bea, that dippy English girl who was in love with Hitler?' Mrs St James speared a roast potato. 'And why A. A. Milne, of all people?'

'They are both fantasists.'

'Interesting,' the Judge said. 'Putting Winnie the Pooh against the Third Reich.'

'Not *too* unlike pitting Chamberlain against it,' his wife said.

'*Very* good, my darling,' the Judge said admiringly and Tip without being asked said he would pick Emperor Hirohito and Joseph Stalin.

'Wouldn't you have a language barrier?' the Judge asked. '*They* couldn't speak to each other and you couldn't speak to *them*. No one would be able to speak to anyone, Theodore.'

'Then I would feel entirely at home, wouldn't I?'

There was a quick silence. In the long look between them, the table quivered and the Judge, saying nothing, looking icy, picked up his knife and fork again.

'You are not playing the game,' Mrs St James said to Theodore.

'Yes I am.'

'I rather think you're not, darling, but there's no need to be contentious about it.'

Lady Cissie broke in gaily. 'Let's do it again, only with *dead* people. Oh, let's have done with the living bores.'

'But Angus hasn't had a turn. Angus hasn't chosen anyone,' Bea said and faces turned politely to him.

Angus took a long sip of wine, gathering himself up in sections, found himself more or less on his feet, and, gazing down at them from a great height and filled with a new-found charm he said, 'I choose *you*.'

Looking down at her, spinning around a little down there.

'But I'm not a person of note, Angus.'

'Yes,' Angus said. His voice sounded uncontrollably loud. 'You are the person of note.' He had to get the words out separately like peas out of a tight pod. 'And I would rescue you because you have rescued *me*.

'Because . . .'

And they were being nice about it, a hand reaching out to his elbow to steady him and saying it was a game, see, just a little table game. No, you had to pick two celebrities and . . . why not sit down. A glass of water. Mrs St James rang a little bell. No. He had stood up to make a little speech, the first in his life, and a minute ago he'd had it all pat.

'Because you see . . .'

Now it was gone. Something about nothing. All the time of living with nothing and Aunt May and Audrey and Miss Hammer and now this person of *note* had rescued him and . . .

'And you see . . .'

Someone took his arm. His fork dropped on the floor and the terrier was barking and they were all talking to each other to save his embarrassment and, 'Altitude,' someone said, and, 'Eve, I shouldn't think . . .' About lying down a few minutes and he would be all right. Liesl had appeared out of the fog and he was now talking confidently to her. But the steps were difficult and he must have stepped in some glue and feeling worse every minute but Liesl was very strong, almost lifted him up the stairs, and guiding him, putting on the light in the bathroom and just in time.

'Oh,' Angus moaned, finding himself sitting on the bed and Liesl saying, 'All right now?' A nice cold cloth on his head and she was putting pillows behind him but he didn't want to lie down just yet, he said, for the room hadn't quite settled. She was kneeling. She was untying his terrible ugly shoes shined with banana peel that morning long ago back in Kings Cross.

'Oh, God,' Angus said, blaspheming for the first time.

'Crazy,' Liesl said. 'Everyone here is crazy, Ongus, but you'll get used.' She wrenched off one shoe then the other, was peeling off his sports jacket. 'I take this away to clean.' She asked could he undress himself? Oh, yes, thank you, Liesl. 'Crazy,' she said. 'But they are *kind,*' she said in a warning way, all the time in a strange low voice as if passing secret information to a foreign agent. 'Kind, kind people but they don't think. Sit and talk and all of the time play games. Ach, games. Day and night it's *games* they think about.'

She brought a faded eiderdown quilt and folded it on the bed. 'Here in the mountains comes cold in the night. You are better?'

'Yes, thanks.'

'Is here the switch for the light, this string over the bed.'

'O.K. Thanks.'

Liesl went to the door.

'Never mind,' she said. 'Soon comes the war and *then* they will think.'

Instant sleep. Falling over the edge of that lookout into the black gulf, dropping between the great chasms to land on soft pillows, turning over only into greater sleep.

Which would last, almost without breathing, the long night. Only once, stirring, he surfaced long enough to hear himself whisper, 'Liesl,' and, opening his eyes in the blackness heard that he himself had not said it; a real voice had said it.

'Liesl! Liesl,' the voice said urgently, under his window in the night. 'Liesl. Liesl.'

It became part of the wind.

'Hello, Angus.'

'You're doing a good job, Angus.'

'Thank you.'

'Lovely day. Haven't we been lucky with the weather?'

The similar lady guests waved to him and he waved back and pushed again. The trick was to get the heavy iron roller going, then it rolled itself across the tennis court and took you with it. The mountain sun burned but his naked shoulders were browning every day. You look like Gauguin, Mrs St James had said, admiring him.

'If I could only *draw* like him.'

He started back down the other side of the court. In the distance, through ruined arches, he could see Stevie in a hammock, one bare leg dangling, the other being caressed by Bill Seward, who was assumed to be Stevie's lover or fiancé and probably both, for Stevie was canny and the Sewards were rich, were Seward's Tea. ('Stevie will sustain, she's cactus-like,' Mrs St James told Angus. 'It's Bea who's in my bonnet.') One afternoon the silent house suddenly shook with music and Angus was amazed to find Stevie at the piano, ridding herself, it seemed, of something devilish or abolishing Liszt forever. 'My, you're good,' Angus said and Stevie (as she usually did) ignored him. 'My, she's good,' he told Mrs St James, who said, yes, she was. 'But she'll amount to nothing,' Mrs St James said, snapping cards (she was teaching him écarté). 'It's Beatrice who'll show us *all* up one day.' Bea was steadier. Stevie was incalculable; she played fast and accurate tennis, usually beating Bill Seward or other young men who came eagerly to her in bunches, but she was untrustworthy and was likely to throw down her racket in the middle of a set and walk off the court saying, sorry, but she'd had enough. She would lie on the veranda as still as death for days on end, then, rising suddenly out of inertia, would ride horseback in the same violent way she played the piano.

And it was a mistake to let her find out you could be shocked. She had taken Angus to Echo Point. 'Call out something,' she said and Angus, hanging on for dear life over the cloud-rimmed abyss, called, 'Helloooo,' and *'Loooooo'* the cliffs answered in unison and Stevie, cupping hands to that tapestry-shepherdess face, called out long and lovingly the ultimate word. It splintered on the mountains and returned in triple cadences as if the scenery were cursing them. A knot of sightseers drinking tea at a kiosk refused to believe their ears. Angus in a reflex of upbringing said, 'Hey, take it easy.' 'I believe you're a prude,' she said, her eyes shining with the delight of finding someone who is ticklish, and from then on she found little ways to outrage him. He was too awe-stricken by her to hit back and he realized it was futile to challenge her as did Bill Seward, lumbering around after her with his nice-looking, empty Australian face, who was now patiently rocking her in the hammock.

Angus, pushing the heavy roller, contemplated the guilt of his puritanism. 'I wish, dear, you didn't have such a puritanical guilt about not working,' Mrs St James had said. He had waited three weeks in bafflement and finally had had to ask what was expected of him, what was he to do here?

'Do?' She looked puzzled. 'You're not expected to *do* anything.'

'But I must do *some*thing.'

'No, no, you're our *guest.*'

'I can't just *stay* here.'

'Why not?'

Well, surely . . . He raised his arms. It was obvious. She sat very still. Not to her it wasn't. She seemed annoyed, disappointed in him.

'People might wonder –'

'What?'

'What I'm doing here.'

And that was what he wanted to know. They both knew he wasn't talking only about earning his keep. Rhyme and reason was what he wanted and Mrs St James, the great giver, refused rhyme and reason.

'Why must there be a reason?'

But, she said, she supposed there would be something he

54

could do to ease his conscience, if he felt it his bounden duty ('What a hateful word'). Made it clear it distressed her, his plebeian effort to settle up. 'Go and ask Marcus,' she said and as he was going she said enigmatically, 'If you're looking for a reason for being here, I daresay you'll find one.'

When he approached the hotel manager, Mr Marcus, smoothing a cream lapel, said, 'Oh, Mrs Saint wouldn't hear of it.'

Angus said he had had it out with Mrs Saint and was willing to do *any*thing.

'*Any*thing?' Mr Marcus gleamed faintly and smiled his weary little smile. 'Well I certainly can find a use for you when there are turned backs.'

Angus rolled courts, took down nets at evening, conveyed messages to rooms, helped sort mail and sometimes in a borrowed dark jacket called the numbers on bingo night.

Always, out of the corner of the eye, watching out for her, hoping for her approbation in his gluttonous desire to please her. To show her that he was happy, functioning, belonging, flushing with pleasure when, in her presence, walking through the cut-off lobby, the hotel guests greeted him warmly.

'You *do* get along with the old birds,' she said drawlingly, almost scathing about it.

It was true that he got along easily where nothing was required beyond a good memory for names and a sustained interest in family snapshots. It was in sharp contrast to the sudden discomfort falling on him when he approached the veranda of the bird house (Marcus called the St James bungalow the bird house. 'Going over to lunch with the birds?'), stepping into a pool of silence and calling out, 'Hello,' not realizing they were deep in one of their games and so someone saying, shhh, they were trying to puzzle out who Daddy was: a writer of note beginning with B. Are you Ambrose Bierce, Daddy? Their games were constant and curious. You might have to go a day without using prepositions. You might be the last fool to guess why on a journey you could take a cat but not a kitten, a blanket but not a sheet (Bea had finally rescued him from two days of misery by whispering fiercely, all her patience gone, that didn't he see he couldn't take anything that was spelled with a double letter; had been penalized for telling him). Worst of all, you could confuse the games with reality, like the time he'd come out on the side veranda and found the Judge and Mrs St James (and Bea watching from a distance) staring deeply into each other's eyes in silence, one or the other pondering an answer. He sat down at the table with them, smiling from one to the other in the combined silence which had gone on and on, no one moving until Mrs St James said, 'I absolutely will *not*, Heath. I absolutely will not, even for you. She's my oldest and dearest friend.' Then she had got up and left them in the situation, which remained horribly deadlocked until the Judge smiled gently and said, 'Good evening, Angus.' 'Good evening, sir.' 'Do you know how we play Last Chance? Beatrice, come and give us aid instead of sitting half on and half off the railing, which is indecisive.'

Whatever the quarrel between the Judge and Mrs St James, it surely was they under the dark tree late that night when he passed by. Surely it was her drawling voice saying, 'Let me have my way about this, will you? Ah, please. Will you? Will you?' And all the time her ghostly arms reaching around the Judge and kissing him between the words.

And Bea, sitting on the veranda steps with her knees at her chin, sitting in the half moonlight – half lamplight from the house, waiting.

'Hello, Angus.'

'Oh, hello, Bea.'

'Have you seen my mother and father?'

'No.' Lying because of the privacy of the scene under the tree, and Bea staring towards it as though she could see in the dark. So he had leaned against the veranda post and was about to say that the dew was very heavy tonight, my gosh.

'My gosh, the –'

'What do you think of us, Angus?'

'Why, I think you're all' – laughing – 'well, you ought to know.'

'What?'

'Marvellous.'

'Why?'

'Oh, I don't know. You're all so clever.'

'What about?'

'Everything.'

'Nobody's clever about *everything*.'

'No, but you're different from any people I've ever known.'

'God.'

'Well, you are. I never knew anybody interesting like you and your talk, interesting talk all the time and you all *do something*.'

'Oh, piffle. We're do-*nothings*.'

But talented, Angus said, and could if they wanted to. Stevie with her music and Tip with his political know-how (well, he made more sense than the *papers* did about Munich) and Bea with her writing (and stopping, remembering Mrs St James had said Bea didn't like to discuss her writing but that she was good, brilliant perhaps, and would show them *all* up one day).

'No spunk,' Bea said, glaring towards the trees. '*You* might have, though.'

'No talent.'

'I saw the sketch you did of Mother,' Bea said quietly.

'How?' Alarmed because it had been done surreptitiously at distances.

'I was helping Liesl change sheets. It was on your table.'

'Oh. Well . . .'

'If you had your choice, which one of us would you pick to save if the house caught fire?'

'I'd want to save you *all*.'

'No time. Which one?'

'I don't know, Bea.'

'*I* know.'

She was up and gone with that and whether from amusement or scorn he couldn't tell. None of them gave a clue about anything; they touched you on an inner soft spot and ran off yelling, 'Last one in's a rotten egg.'

Did it show so much? He thought he'd been able to conceal any outward sign of the elation that gushed through him whenever she paid him special attention or the feeling of divine faintness when she touched him lazily, saying, Angus, come with me and we'll buy figs for Daddy, and even when she reproved him, mowing the lawn, with, 'If you *must* be so active, don't do it around the house, Angus. Activity around him makes the Judge uneasy.'

The Judge. Daddy. It was always the Judge.

We'll wait and see what kind of a mood Daddy's in. That clock's four minutes slow; Liesl and the Judge cannot *bear* a clock not to be absolutely correct.

Moments of joy suddenly curtailed because of the Judge, that damned demanding child of hers. When they were going to drive down to the valley, take a whole day and picnic lunch because Angus hadn't yet seen it, just he and Mrs St James because the others had all seen it dozens of times and couldn't care less, and then at the last moment, 'We'll have to put it off today, Angus. Daddy's in a low and wants me with him.'

What a bugger. All week long looking forward to it. Bugger the bloody Judge and his childish moods. Everyone be quiet when *he* wanted to play games or read aloud to them for hours at a time while they sat, not allowed to fidget or move. Her listening as if it were to Virgil trying out the *Aeneid* on her.

Then, 'Thank you, Daddy. That was transporting, dearest.'

'What's really the matter with your father?' Angus asked Stevie, knowing Bea would never unbutton.

'Oh, he had a permanent sort of breakdown,' Stevie said casually but giving Angus a definite snub. Don't ask again, she hinted. But how and when and why?

And Lady Cissie, who surely knew, upset her tea. 'Oh, An-

gostura, I don't think Eve likes us to talk about it and I *barely* know the facts, I was away at the time, and oh, God, look what I've done on her green baize tablecloth. Run and ask Liesl for a towel, Angostura.'

He supposed you might live for years with the St Jameses and never know about the Judge.

Meanwhile you rolled the courts, as he was doing now, keeping an eye out in case she came quickly around a corner of the ruins with one of her excuses to stop him working. Now there was a call from the distant bungalow.

'Ongus.' It was Liesl standing on the steps waving.

'What?'

She beckoned.

'Who wants me?'

He picked up his shirt and went slowly towards the house. It would be one of Mrs St James's diversions; Liesl often came running from the house waving for him to come, come at once, and often he feared the worst, went running, fearing the war had broken out, running with a little icy fear only to find her puttering around in a garden hat with a trowel and wanting to show him a find: 'Look, a bottle brush tree.'

Apparently it wasn't trivial today. Liesl's face was patchy with red and white, clearly a sign of stress.

'Put on your shirt, Ongus,' she said. 'They want you. Crazy is what is going on.'

Cissie was edging downstairs carrying Mr Foster. 'He's having a *crise* so we're getting lost.'

He followed Liesl upstairs and to the back of the house, where the Judge's study was located, sacrosanct, almost always kept locked, and where now Mrs St James sat in a white linen dress, fanning herself, and Stevie, Tip and Bea stood or sat around a leather wing chair in which Daddy was installed in a judicial attitude missing only the grey wig. Mrs St James glanced up without smiling and said. 'Here's Angus now, Daddy.'

Angus had never before been in the room. He was taken

59

aback by the size and austere splendour of it. Things had been brought from elsewhere to set up this room with its Indian carpet, deep leather chairs, large mahogany desk with polished brass lamps. The bookshelves were lined from floor to ceiling with the leather and suede bindings of the books of law, to reach the highest of which you mounted a short polished ladder. On the desk near the Judge's chair ticked a little glass clock in the shape of a turtle.

'Stay, Liesl, please,' the Judge said and then, after a moment or two of silence, said, 'Angus you might be able to help us to clear up an uncertainty.'

His eyes were bright and strange. This wasn't a game then this must be one of the times when Daddy was a fraction off the beam.

'Have you been working outside?'

'Yes, Mr St James. On the tennis courts.'

'Have you seen or spoken to anyone from this household during the last fifteen minutes?'

'Well, Stevie was in the hammock with Bill Seward.'

'Did you see Beatrice?'

'Er . . . yes. I think I saw Bea once.'

'You only *think* you saw her?'

'No, I did see her.'

'What time did you see her?'

'Oh, about twenty minutes, half an hour ago – was it, Bea?'

'Don't ask her to confirm or deny it; I want *your opinion* as to the time and as accurately as you can remember.'

'I suppose about twenty minutes ago, Mr St James.'

'Did you hear the gong for eleven-o'clock morning tea at the hotel?'

'I suppose I did, sir.'

'What d'you mean, you *suppose* you heard it?' the Judge snapped.

'I mean, I suppose if it's after eleven, the gong must have rung.'

'It is after eleven.'

'Then I suppose I heard it, sir.'

The Judge sighed. 'I wouldn't want to be on trial for murder and have you as my defence witness, boy.'

'No, sir,' Angus said and laughed in a thunderous pause while Mrs St James motioned him with her eyes to be serious. This was a matter of grave responsibility. What terrible thing had happened?

The Judge held Angus in pinpoint gaze of glittery blue eyes that threatened extreme danger. Be careful then, entirely alert and –

'Was Beatrice coming from or going to the house?'

'Neither, sir.'

'Neither is not possible.'

'She was just sort of standing.'

'*Sort* of standing.' The Judge whipped the words. 'Explain how anyone can be *sort* of standing. Was the standing on one leg?' He looked around his little courtroom for an appreciative titter but all the faces were like agate.

'Standing, sir,' Angus said.

'Standing. Where?'

'Over near the ruins, sir.'

'And this would have been fifteen or twenty minutes ago, Angus? Eh?'

'Yes, sir.' Hoping to God it was, because the Judge made a note with a gold pencil. Mrs St James fanned, fanned.

'In that case it would have been before the tea gong went.'

'I suppose so, sir.'

'There's no supposing about it, boy, no possible supposing, my boy. Because the eleven-o'clock tea gong was sounded at one minute past eleven.' The Judge picked up the little grass turtle clock. 'I believe in this clock, Angus, because, unlike witnesses, it never supposes, it is always precisely accurate. I wish you to be as accurate about the time you saw Beatrice.'

'I wish I could be but . . . I didn't have my watch on.'

'Whom else did you see while you were working on the courts?'

'No one I remember, sir. No, nothing.'

'Nothing? Mind a total blank? Noticed nobody, nothing, the entire time you were outside? Your work requires that much concentration?'

There was a sandpaper of sarcasm in the throaty voice and, looking at the small man behind the desk, Angus saw that it was an illusion to think of him as small. Do try for God's sake to remember *some* item for him, said Mrs St James's quick leading look. Angus looked down at his dirty tennis shoes on the rich Indian rug and dug into the morning despairingly.

'Oh. A couple of ladies came over and told me I was doing a good job.'

'When did these ladies speak to you? Before or after you saw Beatrice?'

'I'd say . . . more or less about the same time.'

'*More or less about.* You have a passion for the indefinite.'

'Within minutes,' Angus said, swallowing his nervous saliva.

'Minutes are what we want.' The Judge now took out a fob watch and placed it neatly beside the turtle clock. 'What were the ladies doing precisely?'

'They were just walking by with their tea.'

'Carrying their tea?'

'Yes, your hon – Yes, sir.'

'Does that suggest a possible connection with the tea gong?'

'I guess so, sir.'

'You do?' The Judge began going a peculiar mauve colour. 'Does it suggest to you that the tea gong had already rung? '

'Yes, sir.'

The Judge was violet now.

'So that even if these ladies had sprinted, it had to be *after* eleven-o-one, which was the exact time the tea gong rang.'

'Must have, sir.'

'Therefore it was within minutes of eleven-o-one that you also noticed Beatrice.'

'I – I – it would have had to be, yes.'

'You said it was about the same time.' The Judge was purple now.

'Yes, sir.'

'So even allowing for a radius of error it had to be within minutes of eleven-o-one. Not supposing, nor more or less, nor about, but *within minutes.*' The Judge was apoplectic.

'Yes, sir.'

Something had been achieved, Angus didn't know what. Mrs St James fanned, fanned.

The Judge now returned through purple to mauve to taupe to his natural colouring, became reduced to his common denominator, shrinking into a little boy again, mild as sweet butter, smiled and say, 'Thank you Angus,' in the gentlest tone.

'And now Beatrice,' the Judge said, and the tone altered again, dropped into an exhausted cadence, carried in it roulades of the *Stabat Mater,* tragic flutes, deep organ notes of betrayal; all combined in an orchestration of sadness. 'And now, Beatrice, I will, having put the facts together, tell you what I think of your story.' Here the Judge leaned forward until he was only an inch from Bea's face and then spat the words at her: 'Cock and bull.' The Judge drew back. 'You ask me to believe that from a time just before or just after eleven-o-one until the time I came back into this room at precisely eleven-o-*four,* you came from some distance outside the house, climbed upstairs to this room, looked up a word you have already forgotten in my synonyms and antonyms, then rummaged in my desk drawer, disturbing my private manuscript and leaving evidence of this by replacing the brass-dragon paperweight so that it now points north instead of south, purloined two of my Turkish cigarettes from the tin where they are kept – there were six and now there are only four – and you did all this in the space of two minutes, by which time you were back in your own room at the far end of the house?'

'Yes, Daddy.'

'Cock and bull, my dear.'

But this can't be *all* it's about, Angus thought, looking around at the deadly serious faces. It had to be, by their looks, a more serious crime: something stolen or something valuable defaced. Angus glanced to see if, behind him, the filthiest word imaginable had been painted in tar on the wall.

'Now what I suggest you're doing, Beatrice,' the Judge was saying in Wurlitzer tones, weary beyond relief from years of hangings, 'is that from some misguided motive you are smoke-screening someone else. I think it is time for the real culprit to speak out.' He gazed from one to another of his family in a long ticking silence as a minute went by, then another and another. Then Tip stood up and, lounging to the desk, took from his pocket two crumpled eggshell-coloured oval cigarettes with gold tips, laid first one and then the other in front of the Judge. 'I with my arrow,' said Tip.

'*Gott,*' Liesl said under her breath.

'You took these yourself, Theodore – they were not quickly handed to you since we have been at this examination?'

'No, Father.'

'And you knew he had been in here, Beatrice?'

'I saw him coming out, Daddy.'

The Judge was highly pleased. He leaned back in his chair, he adjusted invisible robes.

'Now I put it to you. Which is the worse misdemeanour? The theft of the Turkish cigarettes or the attempt to cover this up? I ask you which does me the greater disservice? Now if I had accepted your story without fully investigating it, I would have judged the wrong party guilty. A minimum of two people in this house would have been aware that I judged a lie to be the truth. No doubt you thought you were being heroic – I take into account your youth and impressionable nature, your love of tales, a possible identification because of our mountain scenery with Flora Macdonald –'

A little laugh from the court, instantly quashed by the Judge's strong fist on the desk. '*But* consider . . .'

Consider, consider. The summing-up went on; weighing honour and justice in the scales with dishonour and perjury, citing precedents in liquid Latin, glissandos of rolling oratorical court language remembered from his days of glory (all the time Mrs St James's eyes rested on him continuously as they must have done so many times from visitors' galleries), and finally, warming to the point and rising to his full five-foot-six and pointing a finger at Bea: 'Think, think. It isn't the Judge who sentences you to life imprisonment, it is the lie. It's our lies that imprison us all.'

He sat down.

The verdict: 'No hard feelings.'

'Oh, these little judicial siroccos do him good. They breathe air into him,' Mrs St James was saying, pacifying Liesl, who was half-way into a tantrum.

Angus said, 'Bea, I hope you're not annoyed with me for spoiling your story.'

She was either puzzled or too furious to speak.

'I didn't know you were covering up for Tip.'

She went unexpectedly into peals of laughter.

'Oh, Angus, you are truly such an *innocent*. Didn't you get that it was all cooked up?'

'No.'

'Oh, Angus. We do it all the time.'

'Like a game?'

'Only he doesn't know that and you mustn't ever let on.'

'But why should you want to take the blame?'

'*That's* the game. Someone breaks a rule and we make up a tale about it. We always make it a bit wrong so that Daddy will be able to find the loopholes.'

'Does your mother know?'

'Certainly. You really are a dear naïve boy.'

He wanted suddenly to pull Bea's thick pigtail hard and jerk her head back painfully. He watched her walk away. It was this feeling of being always a step behind. They were like Chinese boxes, truth within truth within truth, opening one to find another.

'I won't *always* be,' he shouted to Bea, but she didn't turn her head to see who (a superior urbane sexually experienced sceptic highly regarded painter impossible to hoodwink) had shouted at her.

Well, I'm rolling the tennis court, Angus said to himself. I'm rolling the tennis court and that's *all* I'm doing and that's the only truth *I* know.

Suddenly Mrs St James said, 'I want to tell you about Daddy,' out of the blue, driving very fast up from Katoomba from an afternoon's shopping. 'A man was wrongly convicted of rape.' It was in answer to Angus' feeling her out about his future. It had to be, coming so soon after his talk with her that morning. She had looked at him in her mirror, standing behind her, and even her face back to front looked clearly startled. Moving?

On, he said. One of these days, soon. It was nearly February, the summer more than half gone, and anyway, 'All good things must come to an end.' She had winced at the truism. 'Are you unhappy? Bored?' Impossible to explain that happiness was part of his fear; that there were lately moments when he broke out of the lassitude of blue air into a cold sweat. Some mornings he woke up in alarm. A noise from the faraway outside world could come crackling over the kitchen radio, which Liesl kept on continuously (but turned low because the Judge wished not to know about the bad news from Bohemia and Moravia), and he would be shaken out of the dream long enough to feel the absoluteness of war coming, a moment enough to think that he must part today with this long mountain-drugging, bird-singing, no-time-passing holiday; what are you going to do with the little bit of time left before it happens? You must do something. Before the last of the little puny inheritance runs out, you must go.

Or a touch, a hint of danger in Lady Cissie's odd little remark to him in passing: 'The mountains'll get you if you don't watch out. You come here and you simply can't escape. Isn't it *divine* here? Oh, my God, I don't know *when* I'll ever get away.' Perhaps she was a little drunk. The voice was a mixture of elation and terror as she went mincing away in a tattered skirt leaving the cold fact. So . . .

'I feel I must get a move on,' he had said.

'Yes, I see.'

And now: I want to tell you about Daddy.

'One of those cases the evening papers like so much because everyone's so respectable. He was a young high-school teacher and the girl was in his class and in Burwood and if you know Burwood you'll understand that the details were even *more* shocking against that suburbia. I think the facts stood for themselves. I mean, if I'd been on the jury . . . but you can't, no, you can't presume to the legal mind. Mr Justice St James. It wasn't a title, Angus, it was his name. Oh, he lived by that name. The impartiality of him . . . frightening at times, really frightening, and I never dared in all the years have an opinion about one of his cases. Oh, the total impartiality – the hunt, hunt, hunt for accuracy. And he said later, you see – and this was so sad for him; this is what haunted him later on; *still* haunts him – he said that in his summing up to the jury he allowed partiality. Oh, I said to him, you are wrong, wrong. I have read it and it is absolutely and totally an equating of the testimony as it was given and he said . . .'

'Said what? I didn't hear you.'

'He said . . .' Angus had to bend near the wheel to hear her. 'Said, "It was in my voice." '

They drove for a minute or two in silence and she seemed to be unable to continue.

'You know his voice, Angus. But you can't imagine, nobody can imagine unless you were in a courtroom, what he could do with the shades of that voice. And he thought the man was guilty. He wanted a conviction and I know why, I know what he was thinking. He was thinking of his own two daughters. He said that he advised the jury of this not with words but with his voice. And of course they returned a conviction. Nobody but him would have thought a thing about it. The law – even the *law* is not infallible. Nobody else would have sentenced himself later on. Not another judge in the *state* would have retired from the bench at the top of his career – young and at the apex – because a mistake had been made. Of course the *papers* . . . Oh, the papers, when the other man was found and the similarity, you see, and then the girl – *married* by this time and respectable and mealy-mouthed as a bishop – admitting then that she could have made a mistake. Well, the rampaging in the papers and the sickening self-righteousness and moralizing they indulged in and Members of Parliament being called on to comment in the House. No *direct* blame was laid on anyone, least of all on *him*, but the inference was there . . . the inference was there as it had been, he said, in his own *voice*.'

She drove rapidly off the road, swinging into a pine grove and almost off a cliff, stopping a foot or two from it, so abruptly that Angus pitched forward, and then they sat in silence while she dispelled something in her from that time, glaring at the crests paling into evening.

'Look,' she said, 'there's a deeper blue today. That means we'll be getting the evening mists soon. They come boiling up and fill the valley and it's as though we were all on a ship sailing between islands on a great sea of milk and often it rises above the mountaintops and covers everything and everything disappears and *we* disappear too, which is sometimes comforting to me.'

And, possibly, she needs me. Angus was confirming, moment by moment, the startling possibility that this was the reason she was re-examining painful things, still so painful that she'd had to make a detour in the story.

'Well, he came to me about making the decision – about leaving the bench. He said he wanted a few days by himself. How could I refuse? He was the law. I wanted to say, you can't be alone in this dilemma, but I knew he didn't want me to touch him – I'm not impartial and I'm not as honorable as he is. I might have dissuaded him with a look. I had to be still. So I stayed still for five days and got ready for *any*thing because I knew he'd need me. I knew he'd have a tremendous *need* of me–'.

She had become quite aroused for her, sparks ran along the edge of her voice.

'– but those five days were costly to me. I didn't think anything could undermine his proportion – his geometric logic. And he wasn't prone to melodramatics. Thank God, I said to myself, he'll never do anything melodramatic ... but just the same, we'd known a most *reasonable* man who for no reason anyone will ever know had just recently gone out for a Sunday-afternoon stroll and thrown himself off Watson's Bay Gap into the ocean. Five days. "It's all right," he said when he came back to me with the decision. "All right with you?" he asked me. "All right," I said. He was the law. No questions were needed and no wounds showed but, in the effort of being still, I ... shortly after, I lost my last child. I lost a son and shortly after that – it was all very close together – he came up to me late one afternoon and I was in the garden. We had a very big house in Bellevue Hill and I remember him coming very slowly towards me, very slowly and not looking at me, looking away and looking, I thought, just tired, and then he said in this curious voice, "Did we have lunch today?"'

Angus caught sight of his face in the rear-view mirror and saw that it looked stupid; it had a fatuous look, the expression on cats when their bellies are being rubbed. He wanted to put his arm around her. She had slumped back in an exhausted way from the effort of telling and was running her hand through her hair.

'So now we play games,' she said.

What do you think about that? He felt she was presenting him with these facts in the same way she sent for him to come running to see a strange plant – so that he would come to her side.

She had said once that if he wanted to find a reason for being here, no doubt he would.

'Sometimes I feel as though I'm a displaced person.'

She was explaining far more than she was saying and he couldn't fathom it beyond the fact that she was telling him in her cool way she had some need of him and to ask her to spell it out would be gluttonous; it was enough just to know it. It was terrible and sweet to think of and he was swept with the importance of it. It made him mute with joy and he sat like a lump, feeling some word was expected of him and knowing whatever he said would be asinine, dull-witted, and she would be let down by his uncomprehending, thickheaded ... 'Oh, Mrs St James,' he said sadly and leaned over awkwardly and kissed her violently. She gave no sign that it had happened, just stared at the glove compartment.

'What's the time?' she asked.

'Quarter to five.'

'Oh. We have to meet a train.'

She backed out of the pine grove and, on the highway, speeded, blasting slow drivers with her horn and being blasted back, sworn at as they tore along the road to Medlow Bath.

'This is Tip's girl,' she said as they neared the railway station and saw that the train was already in, and her voice had recovered its old safeguarded cool self. But as they got out of the car she said, 'I don't want you to feel invaded by what I've just told you.'

And knowing that he was about to make some gesture, she got out of the car rather impatiently, leaving Angus with the wet words of fidelity drying on his lips like soap.

'*There* you are, Lesley Ann,' she said in her most high-handed way, almost undiscernible from, 'What a *bore*, you are, Lesley Ann.'

'Oh Mrs Saint. Oh, look, how jolly nice of you to come and meet me. Oh look, I could have got the bus, it wouldn't have been any trouble at all.'

She was pretty in a brown-haired, brown-eyed and everything-matching way and she was coming up to them, nearly falling out of her matching shoes in the eagerness of not putting anybody to any trouble by having to walk a step farther than they might. She had been caught off guard, probably expecting the son, not the mother and a strange boy. The way her eyes flew from one to the other showed her unpreparedness, and her quick handshake when Mrs St James said, 'Angus Weekes, who's also staying with us,' slipping in and out of Angus' hand as quickly as possible, sent the message that she was frightened.

'What a shame you had to come. I'd have been perfectly all right. Oh, no, look, I can carry it, it's not a bit heavy, really. Oh, well thanks so much. Oh yes not bad at all Mrs Saint. I had a window seat and it didn't seem any time at all. '

A nice girl. She couldn't hoodwink a snail. Like him.

But what a distance I have come he thought. What a long time since *I* got off that train. Looking at Lesley Ann's nervousness, taking Mrs St James's elbow (which she should never do) and saying it was so marvellous to be here, so marvellous of them to have her, and keeping carefully in step with Mrs St James while she also put her foot in everything.

'And is *Mr* St James any better?'

'Daddy is splendid.'

'Oh, isn't that marvellous. Oh, is that begonia? Isn't it nice, the way they grow little gardens on the platforms. Jolly nice of them.'

But he also knew that he was changed; his walk had changed, his height had increased so he could see at least beyond Lesley Ann and could feel fatherly to her, lead the way to the car and say 'You get in the back, Lesley Ann.'

'Oh, thanks very much. I *am* a nuisance making you come to the station.'

'You didn't make us come, Lesley Ann. Angus and I were out on errands.'

'Oh, that makes me feel better. Oh, isn't this a new car since I was here?'

'Yes, it's my little run-around Hillman Minx.'

'Honestly? I *like* a Hillman Minx.'

'I *am* glad,' Mrs St James said in sceptical voice, and in the ensuing silence and seeing Lesley Ann's desperate eyes and because he knew this girl's language, Angus said, 'You brought the good weather with you.'

'Oh, *thank* you. You've been up here for a while, have you?'

'Quite a while.'

'But he's getting twitchy,' Mrs St James said. 'Angus is getting the city twitch. We shall have to think of something to intrigue and divert him, Lesley Ann. We shall have to use our womanly wiles on him.'

'I didn't mean right *away*,' Angus said. 'I didn't mean as soon as all that.'

He would stay as long as she needed him now. Or as long as he could manage to love her or until she said she could no longer tolerate him or at least until, if there was going to be a war, he was dragged into it. And he would remain very still, very quiet, in the role she had chosen for him. The near and distant love which is there out of the corner of the eye and is the emu on the yellow rock at the moment before darkness to comfort her in the way she had said the mists did, coming to blot her out. And there would be, he said, nobody else, no girls, no affairs (taking a Trappist vow), no interference with the purity of it and nothing ever spoken. Because even to speak would put it on a baser level. It was the kind of love you only spoke of at death. At death you might say, 'I've loved you.'

'– and the bread was stale,' Lesley Ann was telling them. But jolly nice ham with mustard on it and he was such a nice little man, you know, you 'felt you couldn't refuse, so actually I'm not a bit hungry. Do they still have those lovely Devonshire teas down in Megalong Valley? Last time I made a real pig of my-self, I remember.'

'Oh, yes,' Mrs St James said, drawing out the word and turn-ing to look at him. So she might have been answering him. Yes, she said, that would be the way *she* would want it. Now did he see, as clear as the air whizzing past, the reason for his coming?

'Yes,' Angus said.

'But you haven't pulled down the ruins,' Lesley Ann said, eager to be alienated. 'I felt you'd have pulled down the old fire damage by now.'

'No, we haven't,' Mrs St James said, a Greek being asked why the Parthenon hadn't yet been disposed of.

'You could put up some jolly little cottages there,' Lesley Ann said.

We must seem strange to her. We must all seem a bit off the hook to the poor kid. Angus seeing them through Lesley Ann and this being a new and interesting experiment. Her standing there on the porch and saying, no, it was perfectly all right, look, not to bother with her at all, and the running about and shout-ing because almost at the moment of arrival (in the old days someone would have instantly said, 'trust *her* luck') the bath heater had almost blown up with a terrifying roar and Lady Cissie had darted out in a bathrobe and was still now hanging over the stairs, holding Mr Foster to her and soothing him while Liesl and Mrs St James had run up to investigate.

She hadn't wanted to bother Liesl, Cissie was saying aloud to anyone who would listen; saying she must have put the match to the wrong gas jet. 'A convulsion happened, Angostura,' she said as he came upstairs with Lesley Ann's suitcase. Then Cissie leaned towards him and said in a conspiratorial way:

'This is the little girl whose mother drinks, isn't it?'

'This is Tip's friend.'

'Yes, but she's the girl whose mother drinks, I think.'

'I don't know.'

'Yes, I think so. What's her name?'

'Lesley Ann.'

'Yes. Tip's little girl. I *think* it's booze, dear. Not absolutely sure. Has to be *something*.'

'Something?'

'You know what I mean, love,' Lady Cissie winked at him, prodding him to admit it with her. 'They only bring the wounded *here*.'

Himself? Cissie? Liesl?

Liesl looked up darkly as he came into the kitchen. She was cutting deeply into an onion and she gestured towards the ceiling with her knife. She was a study in rage. She was almost beautiful with rage; her squatness and square features under her cap of black hair dissolved in prisms of flashing lights.

'I don't say anything, Ongus, understand? *Gott*. It is *very* dangerous. Don't I tell you that? But they play games. Crazy. I'm not having a day off in three weeks. I say nothing. I ask for in here a shelf. I ask sixteen times maybe. No shelf. I say nothing. Well, they are kind. All day today up and down stairs because of the Judge in a bad mood. Terrible. All day long goes the bell. Liesl, I want tea. I want lemon squash. I wonder is there a piece of cake. He wants *her* and all afternoon she is out. Where? I don't know. Where? he wants to know. What time is she coming back? Comes the man to fix the Frigidaire, which is buggered. He makes dirty everything, look, and no time even for mopping. Then *boom* upstairs, we are nearly blown up. I say nothing. But *now* comes this *girl*.'

Liesl lifted both hands to her forehead, pressing the knife to her brow, breathing deeply in and out, in the throes of pain, in agony while freshets of tears ran down her face and no sound of crying escaped from her.

'No, Liesl. She is scared to death of being a nuisance.'

'She is already a nuisance.'

Liesl threw the knife on the table.

Well, she could leave, of course. She shrugged helplessly. She was a 'reffo'. Everyone wanted to help the 'reffos'. Everyone was so kind to the poor bloody refugees. 'It's a free country,' Liesl said, demonstrating with her arms that she was free as the wind outside. She sat down heavily and cut an onion without hope.

'Oh, well,' she said. 'Say nothing, Ongus.'

'No, Liesl,'

Oh, poor, squat Liesl. Voices under the window in the night and he'd thought it was one of the boys from the hotel. One of the waiters, very likely the Czech who worked in the bar.

And Lesley Ann without a clue. Not a clue. Tip in Liesl's bed every other night and not a clue.

Here she came now, exactly at the wrong moment, changed into a pale-blue dress with a pleated skirt, smiling her shy smile and saying, hello, Liesl, how are you, and goodness don't you look well? Jolly nice to see you again.

She had brought Liesl a little gift. Oh, it was nothing. Just something she'd seen in a shop window. Liesl unwrapped it silently and found an angel. A little carved wooden angel.

'From Austria,' Lesley Ann said.

'Ja.'

'You know them?'

'Ja. Of course. We had them at Christmas.'

'Oh, I'm *so* glad. Well, I thought it might be a little reminder of home for you.'

'Ja.'

Liesl put the angel as far away on the kitchen dresser as was possible. She smoothed and folded the wrapping paper as tenderly as if it were the last piece left in a free world; then dropped it in the garbage tin. Hothouse flowers would have burst in the heat that was in the air.

'Sherry on the veranda, I would *think*,' Mrs St James said, passing the kitchen. She had changed into a white dress and was wearing a string of lapis lazuli.

No one had sent word but alone in their Chinese boxes each had decided to be gala. Stevie was in a silver dress.

'I love your dress, Steff,' Lesley Ann said.

'Do you?' Stevie, who disliked being called anything else, instantly withdrew into one of her favourite disguises, massive indifference. Bea hid in a book. Mrs St James crocheted.

Yes, it's a lousy beginning and we must seem a bit off the hook to this poor little blighter, Angus thought. It had been a long time since he had caught a glimpse of the St Jameses through the conventional telescope. He had become immured. He was one of them now. Decidedly now, today.

But something of his old constitutional self rose to the occasion to help the uneasy guest and so, because they *never* did, he made small talk.

Where in God's name was Tip, was what Lesley Ann was begging to know, although she was asking about the golf course. She had gone to some trouble to be pretty. She smoothed her pleats. One would have thought he might have phoned or made some gesture, she implied, asking was it a more difficult course at Katoomba. But anyway, she was a 'duffer' at golf, although she'd be pleased to play with anyone who wouldn't mind putting up with her.

You'll have to be smarter than this to survive, Angus told her silently, answering her questions; your face value is rock bottom here where self-effacement is considered rightly to be a conceit and where every second thing you say could be given a demerit as a Dull Observation. You haven't a Chinaman's chance of surviving this Chinese group unless you learn the ropes as I have.

Imagine if she got caught in one of the 'trials'.

'There's a beastly sand trap I got stuck in there,' Lesley Ann was saying, looking towards the hotel in despair.

'I'm not much good but I'll go around with you,' said Angus.

'Oh, will you? Good egg, Angus. I warn you I'm just rotten though.'

What was her attraction? What could Tip possibly want from

her? Maybe (Angus undressed her for a moment and she was a peach all right) she was somebody entirely different with Tip. Maybe she was passionate and uninhibited, this gentle doe, when roused. Madness might overtake her in the dark.

'I've been taking lessons but –'

At last Tip was coming, although in no hurry, no eager rush, no bounding up the steps to greet her but dawdling along, untidy in floppy old grey flannels and turning his good looks towards them, faintly disinterested as Lesley Ann pretended suddenly that a night insect had landed on her; was brushing away a spectral gnat to cover up her joy.

'Hel*lo*,' Tip said.

'Hel*lo*,' Lesley Ann said.

'So you got here, eh?'

'Got here, yes. Got here safe and sound.'

They shook hands solemnly. Most *certainly* wild things had taken place between them. A bat could see that.

'Well, *you're* looking pretty fit,' Tip said.

'So are you.'

'Sorry I couldn't get here sooner.'

'Oh, look, don't apologize. I've been having a marvellous time. We've been having great fun, haven't we, Mrs Saint?'

'What's going on in the big city?'

'Oh, the usual. How about you?'

'I'm still at 2KE. I'm a junior announcer now.'

'*Are* you? Good for *you*.'

'Oh, it just means I announce the time and weather if someone's away.'

'Just the *same*.'

'How's your mo– your family?'

'Oh, she's – they're fairly all right on the whole, thanks, Tip. Oh, look, I remembered you said you couldn't get a decent pipe up here and so I got one for you. Here. I hope it's what you like.'

'Oh, thanks, Lesley Ann. Oh, *yes*.'

'Oh, good. I was hoping it would be what you liked.'

'Oh, yes. You shouldn't have.'

'Oh, it's *nothing*.'

Liesl was handing round the sherry and little hot cocktail sausages and, coming to Tip, she looked steadily to the right and he to the left.

'Oh, *Liesl*.' Lesley Ann gave the prescribed social squeal. 'Goody *gum*drops. I say. Mmmmmm. German sausage. May I dip? Aren't we lucky having *you* around?'

The dish might just have tipped a centimetre, might just have tipped scalding sausages into her lap, but Liesl kept it level and in the quick triangular look that for a second joined Liesl to Tip and Tip to his mother and she to Liesl and in the soft way Mrs St James said to Liesl to please have some sherry, yes, please, I want you to, it was clear that Mrs St James knew.

'You are kind,' Liesl said bitterly.

And Tip was being fatuously polite to Lesley Ann (without a clue but with a scalded mouth, open, full of sausage, trying to get her breath, shaking her head helplessly, apologizing by waving her hands in the air). Tip was being the attentive lover to a degree that he had slipped into a parody of her. 'Got it down? I say. They *are* jolly hot, aren't they? Have another? Righty-ho. And what else have you been *doing*? Still going to Berlitz? How's your French coming along? Oh, good for *you*.'

'Oh, *merde*,' Stevie said. And Tip said, witheringly, '*A toi, aussi*,' and smiled and Angus saw a hammer fly through the air. The smile, the politeness, the kindness was what made you uneasy with Tip. The arm around your shoulder and the intent look of deep interest. Are you all right, old cock?

The sun had been directly in his eyes. Angus, mooching through silver shivery grass towards the house, preoccupied with certain recent things *she* had said, things he carried with him because with a slight change of emphasis you *could* translate them into love, and one he'd misplaced, something said at supper the night before; so wrapped up in trying to recreate the actual wording he could have walked off the edge of the world and right into that blazing sun, and, *'Look out –'*

And the thing, whatever, flew past his ear, the wind from it sang and something thudded to the ground behind. He turned round stupidly and saw the hammer lying on the grass.

'Are you all right? '

With his hand to his eyes, he saw the figure against the sun on the roof, waving violently to him. It seemed to be on fire against the light. It scrambled down a ladder.

'Are you all right, old cock?' Tip asked.

'I'm O.K., yes.'

The arm around him.

'It just flew out of my hand, honestly. I was fixing some loose shingles on the roof and it flew out of my hand.'

Tip had picked up the hammer and swung it.

See? See how easily it could go? It flew away.

'It's got a murderous head on it. If that thing had hit you . . .'

They walked towards the house and Angus resented very much not his possible murder but the way Tip was holding him, with each step giving him a little squeeze, hauling Angus along with an arm around him tightly, and with each little hug there was a suggestion of being taken into custody by an extremely affectionate cop.

'I wouldn't want you getting killed while you're up here. Not *you*, old cock.'

Hug. Hug.

All the time Tip's eyes were blazing with what seemed to be delight or venom or perhaps just the sun. Something phony, something wrong about the whole incident, and Angus, being too young, had yet to learn that most reasons for things are obvious.

'Oh, one thing, if you can remember,' Tip was saying to Lesley Ann. 'Don't call them *German* sausages in front of Liesl.'

Years later, in strange places, under khaki tents, billeted in lonely unfamiliar towns, when he conjured up these days, counting them in later, dark times as being halcyon having carefully forgotten their perplexities, Angus thought of this particular day – when she'd confided in him – as the beginning of an end, the moment of finding the dry brown leaf on the stem. The constancy of the mountain light was deepening and defining everything more starkly. The blueness now was thick and changed and they (looking around them on the veranda) were changing with it and with the colder air currents, like birds sensing winter, they flustered, fidgeted. A touchiness ran through them.

Not then noticed but in later times he would have said, 'then' and 'about that time' that they were, gala in their clothes that night, gathering themselves inside. Preparing for some inevitable change. Whatever the feeling (perhaps the war could not again be staved off by an umbrella; perhaps nobody would be here next summer and the hotel vacant, the bungalow left to the possums), they all felt it secretly and were getting ready. So, seeing an old bureau that had stood for countless years in the same place without comment, someone would be likely to say it must go, today, out with it – look, it is eaten all the way through with borers – and then, having heaved it out, be touched with sadness for it lying, legs up, on the dump. One might feel one's own deterioration. The borers in oneself.

They had fiddled, fussed through an excruciating dinner. The Judge was in a thunderous mood. He was wearing an aged dinner jacket; the satin revers were ravelled. The lamb was underdone and the potatoes woody. He carved in disgust.

'The six-fifteen is to be discontinued,' he complained. Although he had not been on a train for nearly twelve years he followed the timetables assiduously and changes of any sort upset him.

And Bea said, unwisely, 'Hardly anyone takes that train.'

'That is not the point.'

'It might be to them.'

'Who is "they"?'

'The railways.'

'Are you agreeing with them?'

'I'm not supporting them, Father. I'm only saying I *suppose* they know what they're doing.'

'Which is the same thing.'

'Which is *not* the same thing. All *I'm* saying is that they run the trains.'

'*And* they know what they're doing.'

'Yes, I suppose so.'

'Which means you are taking the attitude that they are within their rights.'

'I mean they *have* the right, yes.'

'Therefore they are right and I am wrong.'

'I didn't say you were *wrong*, Father.'

'Oh, yes you did. Oh, indeed you did.'

'I didn't. I did *not* say you were wrong.'

'You said *they* were right.'

'I said they *had* the right.'

'Which is as good as saying *I* am wrong.'

'Which is not saying that at *all*. I'm not saying you are wrong or right. For*get* you for the moment –'

'*No*. My personal opinion is being questioned.'

'It has nothing to *do* with your personal opinion.'

'Oh, indeed it has. If I'm being told that I can't say it's wrong but *they* can say it's right.'

'Do. They can *do*.'

'I see. They can say what they like and I must be quiet, is that it?'

'I didn't say "say." Of course you can *say* whatever you like – Don't *hush me*, Mother. I've got a perfect right to deny the fact that I am saying Father is wrong. I am only saying –'

'– quite enough, Beatrice.'

'– if I might *just* be allowed to make my point on the same

81

terms as Father – that the railways have the right to be *wrong* and Father doesn't.'

The Judge threw down his napkin.

'I do not have the *right* to be wrong at my own table?'

Lady Cissie laid a shaking hand on the Judge's arm. 'Now, Uncle Heath darling – No, listen, listen, sweetie pie. You see, you are *both* right in a way. What Bea meant – Sweetheart, listen to Cissie a moment, love. Listen, all right? Now, what Bea really means when it all boils down is that the *right* people – now let me get it right – the *right* people have put off the train at the time *they* think is right but which to you is wrong.'

'That is *exactly* what I've been *saying*,' said the Judge. He got up and left the table in a second. He was almost tall, ashen with hauteur, going inside the house and leaving behind a vibrating silence.

'Oh, this roast lamb is super*duper*,' said Lesley Ann.

Why not go dancing tonight, Mrs St James suggested in a lazy indifferent voice, but she looked pinched, sitting under the red lamp, and when people hesitated she grew tense and said, yes, please to go over to the hotel and dance and get out of the way while Daddy was in this mood. Yes, you too, Angus, she said, seeing his reluctant face. Go and take Bea with you, she said (as Bea had no one to take her, it must be his chore). Bea was still solidified with rage.

They made quite a stir coming into the sparsely filled ballroom with its old-gold ceiling and overdone murals of Blue Mountain scenery, the big orange-yellow lamp hanging in the middle and casting a curious satanic light on the pathetic dancers, an awful parody of a ball: the middle-aged couples walking, rather than dancing, holding each other with reluctance and with set faces enduring it, circling the floor joylessly. The unattached women dancing with each other, the taller one usually being the man; oddly Sapphic and out of keeping with the spirit of respectability that hung as a pall over everything.

The tin-pot little band bea away on a dais without ever looking at the figures on the acres and acres of bare yellow ballroom floor (which made the heart sink to look at it, Angus felt, the terrifying huge expanse he had to manoeuvre Bea around; she was already bunched resentfully in his grip, she danced mechanically without any grace). 'A-tisket a-tasket' went the tinny music, the foot drum banging the time unmercifully, and around they went, taking minutes to make one circuit of the enormous floor and passing these sinking hulks on the way, little flashes of gleaming false teeth; the withered velvet flowers in the hideously permed hair all crimped and set in water, the skittish ladies in emerald-green lace and electric-blue voile dancing with each other for lack of men; the ghastliness of it all set Angus' teeth on edge and, turning to Bea to shut some of it out, he started to say something but she cut him brusquely with, 'Oh, you don't have to make conversation, Angus. I'm sorry to be the cause of all this.'

But the St Jameses had made things look up a bit, the band had perked up the tempo at the sight of Stevie in silver and lofty handsome Tip with pretty Lesley Ann and Bill Seward romantic in a dinner jacket. The only turnips in the group were Angus and Bea and, 'You'll have to dance with *me*, I'm afraid,' Bea had said and he had felt wordlessly sorry for her.

But relieved when the band leader called out, as to cattle, that next would be the new rage from London, 'The Lambeth Walk'. A progressive dance, changing partners (the ladies stuck with each other gave a little cheer and, 'Whoopee, Muriel,' one of them said) as the circle began spinning, and Angus was relieved of Bea and embracing a clutch of dumpy matrons before Stevie swam into him. Dancing with Stevie was unlike anything else that had ever happened: dancing with Stevie was pure sex, not intended on her part to be provocative but naturally so. It was the nearest thing to being allowed to hold Mrs St James. The replica. 'Oh, Stevie,' he said. 'What?' she asked in her mother's voice, casually surprised to find she was being held by him but turning away immediately to swim on to Mr Marcus, impeccable in navy-blue suit and a polka-dot bow tie, who was gallantly joining in to help alleviate the acute shortage of males. As each lady of uncertain age was passed along to him, Mr Marcus gave an elegant little bow, a slight twitch of the lips (there was no doubt about him, Angus was thinking), and leaned towards them with some obviously daring remark at which they squealed, ricocheting around in his arms, begging him to stop, stop, he was killing them. But Angus noticed that when Stevie circled gracefully from him to Mr Marcus, Mr Marcus took Stevie very seriously because he said nothing, only accepting Stevie in embrace, and she accepting him, letting her hand curl around his neck, and they being perfect for each other ('a real Astaire and Rogers,' said Mrs Wally Petersham to Angus, coming enthusiastically for Angus in brown lace and with a flash of china teeth), and Angus began to relinquish Stevie reluctantly for Mrs Wally Petersham and Mrs Wally Petersham ('see you next time round, chum') even more reluctantly for stiff-as-a-board Bea as around they circled in this interminable dance, accelerating now and singing the words 'Any time down Lambeth Way,' screaming 'Oy' to each new revolving partner ('Oh, not a *bit*, you're jolly *good*, Angus, *I'm* the duffer,' said Lesley Ann for the fifteenth time), and Angus turning whirling seeing the wheeling parade of orange-coloured faces, felt a migraine-like depression coming on, the beginning of one of his hunches that there might be, well, bad news about something.

It was nothing. It was just this sombre, decayed old ballroom and the terrible festivity of the old dears who would all be dead soon. It was just everybody being so touchy tonight and Bea's outburst and Mrs St James's cold white look and knowing about Tip's deception. Stevie in a calculating mood and honestly making an idiot of herself on the floor with that middle-aged fairy, Mr Marcus. A sense of disintegration, the group breaking up. His group. The only one he'd ever belonged to and it mustn't happen (he was singing loudly to drown it out, but couldn't stop the thoughts), he must keep them all together somehow.

Signifying the fact that they were soon getting the hell out of this mausoleum, the band played 'Good Night, Sweetheart,' and looking around he saw that everyone was paired off right: Stevie giving herself luxuriously to Bill Seward rather than to the music and Tip holding Lesley Ann like an investment. Angus was so busy keeping them in sight that Bea said, 'Are you looking for a cab?'

The band raced through the National Anthem and Mr Marcus called out that there was cocoa and sandwiches in the main lounge, dears.

But crowding out of the doors, the others had gone. He couldn't see them.

'Where are the others?'

'I don't know,' Bea said.

'Don't they want cocoa and sandwiches?'

'You'd better ask *them*.'

'Well then, what about *you*?'

She was looking at him in her pent-up way.

'No, thank you, Angus. I'm going to bed.'

Bill Seward was in the billiard room with some men. 'Stevie went to bed,' he said, chalking a cue.

It was the end of the evening then. They'd dispersed, gone their separate ways. But Angus was left with this spooky feeling of disintegration.

He walked through the fire ruins, across the dark tennis courts, looking over towards the bungalow through the pines, which showed one light fitfully. It wasn't the night to go in hoping she would be crocheting in the drawing-room or playing solitaire, looking up over her glasses at him to say, 'There you are. Sit down by me and bring me luck.'

Towards the parapet which ran along the side of the tennis courts and looked down over shaded walks with benches overlooking the valley, now wrapped in darkness and night wind, he went, collar up. A figure, embracing itself against the cold, leaned over the parapet wall.

'Hello there. You getting a breath of air too?' she asked.

'Thought I would.'

'Yes. A*ha*.'

'Where's . . . Tip?'

'Oh, you see, he has to get up most frightfully early in the morning so . . .'

Only the minutest quiver in the voice signified that it was tough to be abandoned at eleven o'clock on your first night here. Lesley Ann hugged herself.

'They are –' A law unto themselves, he was going to say, but she cut him off quickly.

'Marvellous people. So hospitable really when you get to know them. They've been most awf'ly kind to me.'

'Me too.'

'I'll bet. Golly.'

' "*Any eve*ning – *any* day," ' he sang.

'You're a friend of Bea, are you?'

Poor little simp. She was wrong about everything, wasn't she?

'No. It's *Mrs* St James who's *my* friend.'

'Oh, look, I absolutely adore her. Isn't she wonderful? Oh, golly, I think she's . . . and she's so pretty, isn't she? Don't you think she's pretty?'

'Yes.'

'Oh, for her age she's – oh, she's . . . scrumptious. I could just sit and look at her for hours.'

He just wouldn't reply to such bilge as that, even to make the poor bitch feel a bit more cheered up.

'Would you like some cocoa if I go and see if it's still on?'

'No, thanks, no, really, thanks. But don't let me keep *you*. I'm fine, just fine. Oh, I could just stay out here for hours and hours. This night air just makes you feel . . . oh goodness, I don't know. Look, you run along.'

'No, I'm happy,' he said.

'Mmmmmmmm. So am *I*,' she said, hugging herself.

Laughter or what sounded like it came from below the parapet and they both leaned over to see. Down the path that led to the lookout something moved in the paleness of the light from the stone lamp; something silver moved and two cigarettes burned close together, moving down the path away from the hotel, and again there was laughter from where the silver dress moved under the dark eucalyptus branches; it could just as easily have been weeping, it had such an excessive sound, the repudiating ring of someone being told a monstrous thing they will not believe. It was naked and embarrassing to overhear. They froze into themselves at the sound of it dying away down the walk and Angus knew that the situation was as brilliantly lit for Lesley Ann as it was for him. By turning their heads an inch, they could plainly see Bill Seward (having taken off his dinner jacket) chalking a cue in the lighted window of the billiard room.

So Angus and Lesley were joined as witnesses.

'Oh ho ho ho *ho*,' came Stevie's unbelieving laugh, as distressing as retching. 'Oh ho ho ho ho *hoho*.' She was being told about murder perhaps and she was hanging on desperately to the person who was telling, holding on to whoever it was and sick with laughter.

'Trees are weird-looking at night, aren't they?' Lesley Ann said, meaning it was none of their business but . . .

And if there were the remotest sense to things, Angus thought, then long ago Lesley Ann and Bill Seward should have discovered each other's potential for a lasting illusion of happiness, finding they were equally matched in the virtues of being well-mannered, pleasant, predictable, pedantic and easily duped. They were the salt of the earth, poor boobs.

'Do you see that glow over there? Way over to the left?'

Yes. Lesley Ann said she saw it. (For want of anything else.)

'That's the Three Sisters floodlit.'

'Oh, *is* it?'

And because they were both for different reasons feeling bereft and afraid, he kissed her.

At night the mists came and by day people began leaving and baggage stood every morning in the driveway while at the bungalow they played games of Has Anyone Seen? and What's The Matter With?

What's the matter with Liesl today? Has anyone seen Bea?

Lesley Ann changed dresses frequently and stood on the veranda a great deal of the time wearing a tight smile and not asking where Tip might be and Stevie played the piano a lot and for the first time became aware of Angus. Although she still kept a distance between them, she added a dimension and drew him subtly towards her in little bursts of confidence.

'If you were only older, I might throw myself at you.'

Very likely she'd spotted him at the window that early blue morning when, by accident, awakened by cold to grope for the fallen blanket, he'd looked out and seen her walking through the long shivery grass in her silver dress and carrying her shoes, coming back from her skylarkings on the dark cliffs with secrets that made her look towards the house in a dazed way, lifting her hand to ward off the coming day, which would be too painful to face. She must have seen him dart back. Next day she started referring to him as Angus darling. She borrowed him from her mother and tacked him onto her driving excursions and together they raced around in her little beetle of a car. After a few days it began to be remarked on and Bill Seward, making a heavy joke, reaching for her with a mammoth arm, said in his dumb pleasant way, 'Is this your new bloke? Are you giving me the old heave ho, eh?' and Bea said in an extremely quiet and penetrating voice, 'Everybody likes you, Angus. Why is that?'

With Stevie's new interest in him he was flattered and wary.

'Angus darling, I *want* you.'

She was looking very serious and beautiful in a dark-blue

plaid skirt and a sweater and had come around the door into Marcus' office, where Angus was typing the dinner menus.

'Be with you in a minute.'

'No, now.'

'I have to finish this.'

'Let him do it.'

Like her mother she had the knack of getting you to drop whatever you were doing. You left your nets and followed *her*. Because she was such an erratic driver, always veering suddenly off this road and onto that, Angus thought nothing of it when she turned onto a dirt track which became grittier with shale and grey dust, the trees becoming sparser, and said, 'Oh, I believe this is the track to the old shale mine; let's see if it is.' He hadn't caught the fakery in her tone or become aware they were doing anything but taking a drive because, as she had said, she was feeling so bloody bored she *must* drive somewhere, so come with her, please, please, Angus darling.

Not until they were standing in a hideous, plundered, denuded clearing at the top of the open mine shaft surrounded by hills of blue shale on which weeds sprouted. It was a grey and desolate spot on the sunless side of the mountain and the continuous wind blew eddies of dust into their faces.

An empty gondola perched on the tracks, which ran rusted down an open cut in the mountain at what seemed to be a ninety-degree angle and disappeared over a cliff.

Even standing at the top you felt the earth pull at you from wherever the bottom might be and, shrinking away from the sense of pulling gravity, Angus saw Stevie was carrying on a conversation with two greasy men who were leaning out of the window of a tin shack which housed the machinery.

She came dancing back.

'I gave him a pound and he says we can go on it.'

'Not me.'

'Don't be a sissy.'

'Not *me*.'

'Oh, come on, it's thrilling, Angus. I've been down lots of times.'

'Then *you* go.'

'No. They won't allow me to go down alone. You have to have a man with you.'

She was already clambering into the iron gondola. Angus hung back.

She held out her hand to him. 'Come on.'

'No, Stevie.'

'Scared?'

It was horribly like being back at school. Playing dares.

'They're *watching* you,' she said. Angus saw the men watching him hesitate. Saw two greasy taunting smiles.

'It's perfectly safe. Look at the thickness of the cable, idiot. They take ten men down in it all the time so don't be a little fool.' Don't dare make a fool of *her*, she warned, and her eyes were as flinty as the hills of shale.

'Get in, mate,' one of the men called out. Angus climbed in, scraping his knee on the sharp iron edge.

There was a thin wail, a squeaking, clanking of groaning wheels and the gondola shuddered and started down the narrow track, dipping as it went until they were seemingly perpendicular, slipping slowly but inevitably towards the edge of the cliff ahead. As they tipped over, they were released into space, which opened up around and beneath them, the air sang up to them, dank and smelling of moss and tree fern; they swung out over nothing, the thin rails shook under them grinding on brittle shale and they fell constantly in harmony with the falling of the gondola, arching their necks and shoulders rigid against the pitching-forward feeling of being vertical.

It was the crack in the nightmare, the spasm in sleep when, dreaming of falling, sprawling, the leg kicks in bed.

All the time Stevie was yelling. With her hair ballooning up in the wind and her face contorted into terror and delight, she looked demented.

Then he saw that the crazy girl was standing up, that she meant to throw herself or be thrown out of the rocking, careening vehicle, the giant tree ferns overhead just missing her by inches, holding onto the handrail and screaming with exultancy or fright. He caught hold of her skirt and held on with one hand, gripping the handrail with the other while she resisted, beating at his arm and face until she lurched over, fell back onto him, and they collapsed together on the floor of the gondola and lay in a bruised embrace in the dust and stones, his arms tightly wound around her, not allowing her to struggle, master-ing her until the rattling, bumping, swaying descent was over and they felt the gondola straighten out at the bottom of the valley and run tamely like a child's train onto a small siding and into a tunnel which smelled of dark mould.

During the ascent, he continued to hold her to him, ready to sock her, to knock her unconscious if necessary, until he heard, at last, the moaning of the winches and felt the car straighten out on the approach to the top level.

Once they were out of earshot of the two men, 'You damned stupid bloody idiot,' he yelled at her, feeling the reaction in his shaking, collapsing legs and his pounding heart. 'I'm not jok-ing, Stevie – irresponsible – I *mean* it – maniac, that's what you are. I mean, what the hell, Stevie?'

'What the hell what?'

'What the hell *what*? Good God *almighty* – standing up in that thing. I mean, there's a sign as big as your — You've been in the thing before. What kind of lunatic are you anyway?'

'Oh, we *are* angry, aren't we?'

'I think you're mad. That's what I think.'

'Well, there's a little madness in the family.'

'And don't treat this as a joke.'

'No, sir. No, my lord.'

'When you deliberately endanger –'

'I was hanging onto the rail.'

'I'm not talking about you, I'm talking about *me*. To hell

with *you*. You damn nearly pulled me out with you. I could have got *my* neck broken and you treat it all as if it were – oh – just nothing, just a little lark, ha-ha.'

'Look, you couldn't fall out of that thing if you tried.'

'Oh, really? Oh, well, I didn't know that, Oh, I see. I suppose that's why they have a sign saying: DANGER. KEEP SEATED AT ALL TIMES UNTIL TRUCK STOPS. Oh, thanks for telling me.'

'I mean, unless you de*liber*ately –'

'And of course you weren't deliberately standing up, no. Well, next time you decide you want to kill yourself, you do it by yourself. Don't involve *me* in it.'

'Did you really think –'

'Next time if you want an audience –'

'Oh, now, listen. I'm sorry. I truly am, Angus. I'm sorry I did it. I forgot you have a thing about heights and – I truly truly wasn't trying – swear on the Bible – What's the matter? Feel faint?'

'Excuse me. I think I'm –'

He was very sick, holding onto a tree.

'Poor Angus darling. I am an awful bitch, aren't I? I agree with every word you say. Better now?'

'Mmmm. I'll just sit a minute.'

Later, in the car, she said, 'Funny you'd think I'd go to all that elaborate trouble to –'

'I don't want to talk about it any more if you don't mind.'

'Funny,' she said. 'Funnier than *you* think.'

'Come in here, dear,' Lady Cissie said. 'I've got a little bicarb that will settle you. Eve's out and anyway, dear, probably better not to bring it up – if you'll pardon me – with her. I mean – *you* know, dear – let it slide, if you know what I mean, Angostura.'

She brought a glass of water, mixed bicarbonate of soda and

put a cushion behind his head. 'Why didn't you just say no to Stevie?'

'Who says no to *any* of them?' Angus burst out.

'Oh, you've *spot*ted it, Angostura, you *hit* it, my dear.' Cissie patted him lightly with her many-ringed hand because he had accidentally said something profound. 'Oh, it's true. The St Jameses have a talent for making "no" impossible. They stare *through* it ... Stare *through* it,' she repeated louder to her dog, who looked up at her with rheumy, loving eyes and coughed. 'He has a wee bit of a cold,' she said. 'The thing is, you can say no but you'll find yourself doing it anyway.'

She put a brass candlestick against the open door in case. '... in case anyone comes upstairs, dear, and might think we were talking about them, which we are. But somehow talking about them behind a closed door is worse, don't you think? Conspiratorial.' She winked. She was full of secrets.

Her cracked, chipped hands flew about, bending pipe cleaners into the shapes of elves, gnomes, satyrs and gaudy little people with heads made out of mountain devils, the little pods with horned faces which she went around constantly gathering from bushes. She clothed them artfully in scraps of shining velvet, brocade and spangles and they sold for two shillings each at the gift kiosk. Now none of the usual clumsiness, none of the butter-fingery slipping, lurching, slopping, but rather the coordinated hands bent, fastened, glued (a mountain devil becoming a circus queen) while her tongue flicked in and out and the tired, ravaged face shone under the fiery false copper of her dated shingle. In her patched old spinach-green bathrobe, tasselled and frogged, she was a magnificent wreck, she was exiled royalty.

Up here at work in her crowded little room, she shone. One could suppose she was all right, that she could even pick up and go on, pick up and go back into the world again.

She *would* go, she said. Pretty soon now she would pack up

her duds and go. She would get a job as a paid companion to some old bird, she said. The idea of Cissie looking after anyone was so ludicrous you could only nod.

'But every time I've got the suitcase packed, Eve puts out a dainty foot to trip me. Well, you know how she gets me, Angostura. By my weakness, darling, by my besetting sin, dearie. Vanity.'

'Vanity? How?' Angus asked.

'Knowing that Eve St James *wants* me here.'

'Oh, yes, I know what you mean.'

'I'll tell you a secret, love, which you might not suspect, looking at the two of us. I'm the stronger one.' She winked. 'But it's the weak who always get their own way. Have you noticed?' She put a grubby finger to her lips. 'Say no more.'

She imparted this truth as one prisoner slipping a note to another. 'Well, you might as well fight flypaper as tussle with *her*. I've always been the loser with her right back to the very beginning at school and partly because I've always looked up to her, dear, can't help it. I'm sunk in admiration of her. Lots of reasons. Some of it's envy. Wish I had some of that divine coolness and built-in chic and dignity which I've craved all my life. I, who spill and slop my way through life. That com*plete*ness of hers, so *achieved*, and then – Was that someone on the stairs? J'ear anything? But to come a time in my life when apparently for some reason I'm a comfort to *her* ... well, say no more, Angus. It's too much for my vanity as I'm sure it is for yours. We're putty, you and me, except that you don't owe her anything whereas *we* – Mr Foster over there in the basket and me – well, you see, we were pulled out of the boat just before it went over the rapids. On the brink as 't were. All I need tell you is we were down to raw hamburgers and gin and we'd decided we might as well fold the show, as they say. No light, no gas, no phone. Oh, it was a comic situation, dear, for reasons too hilarious to go into in full detail. So I said to Mr Foster "I think we might as well call it a day, don't you?" We'd really given the game away a long time before that; given up the living people outside and they'd given *us* up and so to hell with them, we said, Mr Foster and me. Let *them* do the living if that's what they want – let them do the fussing and coping and putting on a brave face. So, Angus dear, what we did – him and me – was we just lay down together in the dark and waited for the end to come . . .'

'And *she* came?'

'She came.'

A little pulse throbbed in her temple. She sewed with steady hands. She was lost in contemplation of past things moving before her eyes. Her cigarette had rolled out of the ashtray and lay among the scraps of velvet. Angus reached over and picked it up just before it set fire to a piece of spangled net. Cissie laid down the doll and smiled with a semblance of long-ago coquetry.

'Did you know I was the "Rexona Girl"?'

She got up and pulled open a drawer and, scrambling through multitudes of scraps, unearthed a yellowing thick concertina of paper which unfolded into a cracked poster, unfolded into a beautiful girl with thick auburn hair, swathed in a gauzy cloud of tulle which allowed her lavish nude body to be seen hazily through it. She was perched on a rock in a wooded glade and was projecting one toe into a mountain spring. One hand was raised provocatively, a finger extended towards the dimpled chin, while the other hand held out a glistening white cake of soap from which coloured bubbles blew into the air. The girl was gazing down at her own reflection in the water. The smiling full mouth, turning up at the corners to laugh at itself in the rippling waters, the vivid blue eyes and something about the proudness of the head were faintly reminiscent of the woman holding the poster and looking back now at the young girl who was staring into the trembling future and who, had she seen in the waters the face now looking back at her, would have dropped the soap and run from the pool in terror and disbelief.

'Me. Can you *believe* it? Isn't it a camp?'

The dated lettering said, 'Be a good Rexona Soap Girl like me.'

'I was *every*where,' Cissie said. 'Dearie, you couldn't get *away* from me night or day. I was all over the country. You could drive hundreds of miles back of the beyond out into Woop-Woop or Buggeryville and there I was. You'd be driving through the bush and coming to some little tin-pot town. There I'd be saying, "Welcome to Warnambool, a good Rexona town," and, going away, there I'd be again saying, "You are now leaving Warnambool, a good Rexona town." I met everybody, dear. I was on floats in all the parades wearing just this bit of wisp and handing out soap, and I got photographed with all the visiting stars and boxers and what have you. Oh, I was putting it on like mad, love. In fact, that's how I came to meet my Honourable. The Honourable Clive Heaton Lovejoy, who was an aide to the Governor and who asked me to trip up to the altar with him. That was when they all started calling me Lady Cissie. "Look at *her* putting it on, will you," they all said. "It'll be a quid to even speak to *her* soon." But it wasn't being grand or the money that made me drop the soap. It was his shyness. That's what got my *vanity*. It was wine to me, you see, that this adorable, really adorable sweet shy creature wanted to depend on *me*. Oh, I felt so *bold* that I let my eyebrows grow. Dearie, my heart still goes out to Mrs Simpson and King Edward because I went through a bit of what they did – the papers being bitchy, rather nas-ty about him marrying the Rexona Girl, with such mean little unfunny jokes about how I must have "soft-soaped" him and especially because unfortunately he had an estate near Bath. Imagine. Say no more. Oh, I didn't care. I didn't give a fig, love. I was gay as a grig because he was ...'

Cissie drew him in the air. There he was.

'He was – well, anyway at first – one of those you want to – oh, you know – constantly love, guard, say, "It's turned cold, you'll need your coat," and he'd give you that grateful look as if you'd given him the word of the Oracle and a bag of gold as well. That's what did in Miss Rexona.'

Cissie folded up her former self and tossed it back into the drawer.

She took a ripe peach from a saucer on the bureau and began stripping the skin feverishly. Her eyes were very bright; some of the glitter ('six bridesmaids *and* St Andrews Cathedral *and* the Bishop') was still on her, she sashayed, she twirled a little, boasting of it all.

'Annblullbull,' she said with a mouthful of peach.

'What?'

'Annulment. Say no more.'

Sucked her fingers, put the peach stone on the windowsill, sat down and sewed rapidly on a doll. The lines around her mouth were very deep.

'*Again* there she was. *Her*. With outstretched arms. *Oh,* Christ, the goodness of her at that time to me. Help! There was Eve. No questions asked, just there. Her only criticism was that I didn't fight it in court. You see, I never told the details to anyone. Couldn't. Still can't. Lavatory walls, dear. But after a while, after quite a while, I told *her* just little bits, skirting round the edges, and she said I was mad not to have dared them, the Lovejoys – *suitable* name, ducks – not to have come right out in the open and dared them to bring it into open court because they would've settled for a fortune *not* to have it heard in court. But as I told Eve, where do you get a good lawyer in Ceylon? That's where I was, you see. I had got off the ship in Ceylon. Ran, dear. In the middle of the night. What they did – his mother was with us by then – what they did, after some considerable debate, was agree to an annulment and my fare home if I signed this and that, swearing away all claim to anything of his – to even a waistcoat button – and the *way* they did it . . .'

She closed her eyes for a second, then shook her head violently; got the record started again.

'Well, love, I *think* – I'm not absolutely sure but I *think* – I was not quite altogether right in the head by that time and I think they knew it and they also knew I would have signed on with the *Bounty*, I'd have signed on with Captain What's-his-name, Charles Laughton – *Bligh* – because he was a per-ince compared to the Honourable. I said, give me the pen. So, my dear, I got nowt, nowt. Except that I got home; I was lucky to have been only badly wounded. Oh, no, I'm wrong, there *was* something. A little gold pin he gave me which I kept for a while. It was rather sweet.'

Now she arranged the false copper curls around her forehead, with sudden expectation of important things ahead. She preened for a moment, then darted for a box of raisins.

'I'm so hungry all of a sudden, aren't you?'

She began to eat raisins ferociously, all the time keeping an eye on the door and all the time continuing the now wound-up recording of her life and in increasing haste as though, glad of the unexpected opportunity, grateful beyond belief to have someone to tell, Angus must hear as much as possible before anyone came and then must escape to the outside world to get help. Therefore she skipped; jumped about in time, darted backward and forward so that he often lost the track.

One moment she was almost married again, this time to a Dutch physics expert who turned out to be not an expert – well, not of physics anyway – and not even Dutch, and then she had overslept and missed the boat, literally, to New Zealand and so lost her chance to tour the islands with a rich and childless old ex-barmaid who might have willed her the whole swag if only her alarm clock had worked. She flitted, shifting ages like a quick-change artist in vaudeville; she was twenty, forty, six-teen; she was robbed of her sealskin coat before she told of meet-ing the young man who stole it . . .

Yet she didn't want Angus to get the wrong idea. She'd had a great time of it, she'd met Chaliapin, she'd had good friends like Eve, and after all there had been *the* man.

'Peace and quiet, dear,' said Lady Cissie, a raisin sticking to her chin. 'Almost heaven. Nearly seven years of almost heaven. He was the man who gave me Mr Foster as a puppy. Mr Foster is named for him.' She and the dog exchanged a definitely understanding look.

'Now, this is funny because of what we were talking about earlier, about Eve coming to rescue me, about taking in the wounded? I tell you there is a danger to taking in the wounded because they may take *you*. Not even meaning to. They may break something, understand? Dearie, that's why I try not to break anything in Eve's house – oh, cups, saucers, bath heaters, just leave it to *me* – but not to break anything of hers even if it's a misconception she happens to like. Oh watch out you don't do that; you can do it so easily in a second and not even know it.'

Cigarette smoke curled around her head; she prodded the air with a chapped finger to make sure Angus was being properly warned. 'Not even know it, like a dear pal of mine, a dear darling feller, who very quietly, without meaning any harm to me, very neatly put the pot on my seven years of peace and plenty, and it wasn't even his fault. Oh, he came to me in distress, in a bloody great big perplexity, and what was I to do? I was stashed away then, see. Mr Foster – the *man*, not the dog – liked me stashed away and *I* liked it and I had this tiny little house on Lake Pittwater with *him* whenever he could come. He was married, what else? Say no more. I hadn't seen a soul for years. Didn't need to; had what I needed, darling. Had *him*. Then along comes the old pal to the front door and with a bloody dilemma, so what do you say? You say, "Come in," you listen to his troubles, you put him up on the sofa for a few nights when he asks you because if you *don't* you might be liable for him going over the Gap, which a mutual friend of ours had just recently done – taken the dive at Watson's Bay Gap, dear – the bloody last dive, baby. So naturally I took my friend in. Now, *he* didn't mean to break anything of mine. He just wanted ... comfort. But what I didn't count on was Mr Foster – the man, not the dog – was Mr Foster having a prudish streak.

Mr Foster turned up while the pal was there and ... oh, I wasn't accused, no scenes, just ... something was broken that we could never put back. The End.'

Angus was seeing a man go off a cliff, saw the body, clothes torn off with the force of the wind and water, and hearing someone say he was a most reasonable man who had gone for a Sunday-afternoon stroll and 'just recently,' someone said, telling surely about the same thing, and 'thank God he'll never do anything melodramatic,' Mrs St James had said, 'but just the same we'd known a most reasonable man who had just recently thrown himself off Watson's Bay Gap.'

So that's who it was.

The two voices blended together, both expressing the identical fear for someone who had been in such trouble, such a dilemma, that suicide was not to be ruled out.

'Just the same ...' said the two voices.

Angus looked away so that Lady Cissie would not be aware it was written all over his face that he knew without any doubt who had been her visitor, coming with such unfortunately bad timing to her little idyllic cottage on the lake. The wounded man asking to be taken in had been the Judge and, of course, this must be one of the links between Cissie and Mrs St James, the debt being paid back and now Cissie being rescued (whether she wanted it or not) by her good friend Eve. One of the many curious paradoxes about Mrs St James became suddenly clear: remembering the coldness of her, face to face with the Judge when Angus was thinking they were playing Botticelli, and she had said, no, not even for you, Heath, she is my dearest friend. A request not granted. In those five days, both women had suffered a loss – a child, a lover – and so (Mrs St James had meant) Cissie would stay as long as she wanted. It was something between *them* only, between Cissie and her that no male protest would ever budge. Not even the Judge, who had gone off the deep end in spite of both their efforts and as effectively as if he had jumped over the Gap.

Drawn perhaps by sensory powers, by some antenna of her own perception that Angus and Cissie were rummaging through old drawers and coming across things of hers that she didn't want seen, Mrs St James walked suddenly into the room carrying a white jug filled with bright-orange Bottle-brush. 'Gathered for you,' she said to Cissie in her smoothest voice, her brows arched in surprise at finding Angus here. She might be just a shade annoyed and Angus got up quickly to offer his chair to her but she passed him by and settled the jug on the washstand.

'Reminiscing,' said Lady Cissie, who had become, in the moment of Eve's entrance, clumsy, scattering pins, 'about when I was the Rexona Girl in 1875.'

'Seventy-*six*' said Mrs St James softly, and the two looked at each other, smiling old knowing smiles, understanding each other perfectly, and now Angus knew why.

'But your little old boy is sick,' Mrs St James said. She bent over Mr Foster's basket and he stared at her uncomprehendingly.

'It's only a cold,' said Cissie. 'He always manages a little cold at the change of season.'

'Do you think the vet should take a look?'

'No, dearest. We don't like vets. Vets tend to worry us with their probing and fussing, don't they?'

'Just the same –'

'No vets. No vets.' Cissie was adamant. While Mrs St James was turned away, bending over the basket again to pat Mr Foster, Cissie quickly poked one of the little mountain devil nuts into her unruly hair. The gesture was so rapid, so sleight-of-hand, that Angus wondered if it could have been accidental.

Now the real blow was that they were losing Marcus, Mrs St James announced. He was leaving at the end of the month and he would be impossible to replace because he was in every way the perfect manager.

'But I won't plead,' she said, 'I won't plead with *any*one to stay.' Her eyes swept over Angus and Cissie, including them in this in case this might have been what they were discussing in private. She was conscious, like Angus, of a subtle undercurrent, a breaking apart of the fabric, first this, then that – ugly little rips in the pattern.

'You have something in your hair, Cissie.'

'Do I, love? Get it out for me, will you?'

'Sit still, I don't want to hurt you. Oh, it's a mountain devil. Now how could you get a mountain devil in your *hair*?'

'I can get anything, dearest, given half a chance.'

'There. It's out now.'

'Thanks, love. Oh, if I didn't have you to comb me out every now and then I'd be as twiggy as Ophelia. Oh, what *next*?'

Cissie gurgled, was all fingers and thumbs again, and Mrs St James seemed pacified and calmed by finding the mountain devil. So it was a little secret game they played. Rescue Me. Cissie played it the better of the two.

'Such a mist is coming up,' Mrs St James said, leaning out of the window and smelling the mossy late-afternoon smell. 'Come and help me roll down the canvas blinds, will you, Angus.'

Going downstairs, he took her elbow to reassure her that things were not going to fall apart: he would help her hold everything together.

He said, 'I'd like to help with the day-tour bookings when Marcus goes.'

'You were good to listen to Cissie, Angus.'

'Oh, nothing of the kind.'

'She doesn't get much chance to unwrap the Rexona Girl.'

'Gee, she was a simply gorgeous-looking girl.'

'Not gorgeous.' The word distressed her. 'Much subtler beauty with just enough wrong with it to make her tantalizing.'

She led the way along the cold veranda, where they wrestled with ropes stiff from being tied all summer to lower the heavy green-and-white canvas blinds.

'I believe it's cold enough for a fire. Did she tell you about the husband?'

'Yes.'

'Mind you, she's always been one to leap into the volcano just because it happens to *be there*.'

'This last time when you came to the rescue, was she . . . absolutely –'

She put her finger warningly to her lips and he saw that Cissie had come around the side of the house and was going towards the hotel carrying a paper bag of her mountain devils to sell and walking skittishly, a pretty walk that knew she was being watched and that likely there were photographers lurking behind hedges with flashbulbs.

Beyond her, the thick mist was clotting. The peaks floating in it appeared and vanished; appeared again and in the cold air as sharp as cheddar they could hear that Cissie was singing as she went.

'What I found when I got to her, got in, got the neighbours, got the ambulance was . . .'

Must have been horror. The dirty room, the wreck on the bed with the dog in its arms and refusing aid desperately. 'No, we've closed the show, closed the show.'

'She was all gobbledygook, Angus. She'd been so long alone in that filthy little flat she'd given up bothering to use a knife and fork and ate with her fingers, feeding the dog at the table and eating with her fingers at the same time. I just said to everyone, "Don't watch, don't stare," and we didn't. And the day she picked up the knife and fork was the first step.'

'Well, you've done marvels having –' He stopped before nearly saying, 'having *two* dotty people around.'

'I didn't do anything.'

'You took in the wounded.'

'Ugh.'

'Well, you did.'

'No, I mean, what a horrid *ornate* way of –'

'It's how *she* described it.'

She laughed. 'Oh, I *thought* it sounded like a quote.'

Their hands touching on the ropes, he said, 'May I just say—'

'No, you may not. I can tell by the look on your face that you're leading up to one of your compliments. I don't want medals and flattery or gratitude. I detest gratitude. All I try to do is create a *possibility* here for people and let them alone, let them *be* and not be asked to take up cudgels for them. You've often seen me not take up the cudgels, often.'

Yes. The things she knew about and never stirred, watching them all with her cold generosity.

'That's for people who want to start wars, of which the world is chockablock. People who can't leave well enough alone and can't let each other alone. I lived in constant war as a child. People barging in and out of other people's rooms and lives and screaming. Not here. I've kept that out and *them* out. I told my brood when they had something to scream about to go and scream it out at Echo Point and hear their own silly angry voices coming back at them. Go and scream it long and loud but not here. Here is—'

She lifted her arms, taking in sky, whiteness, crumbling ruins, cedar and eucalyptus in a parabola. Here was her, keeping the forces at bay; here was pulling down the blinds against winter, turning on warm lamps and turning off radios with bulletins. '– is liberty.'

And what she'd done, if anything, if there was any secret to it at all, was defend the constancy of that liberty, that ease. So she went on down the long veranda surveying her citadel built on a rocky peak, safe from everything, safe both for and from her own kith and kin forever.

Then Angus said (it only took a second or two to say it), 'I don't think it could've been easy taking Cissie in. Any more than it was an easy thing for *her* to take in the Judge when *he* was in trouble.'

When there was no reply, glancing around from untying the

blind ropes he realized she had gone around the corner of the veranda. So probably she had not heard him.

Unwinding the stiff and tangled cords, he had started to hum, picking up the tune Lady Cissie had been singing and coming to the end of it before recognizing it was 'Bye Bye Blackbird,' which his mother had occasionally sung to him in his bathtub.

'Do you want me to cover up the wicker chairs?'

But she must have gone down the steps out of hearing.

So when he turned the corner he was surprised to find her, almost fell over her.

She was holding onto a blind rope and being very still in a curious attitude, crouched slightly in the position of someone who has been gripped suddenly by a violent gastric pain and who must stay very still until it passes. She had turned very white and her eyes had narrowed snakelike into a piercing stare in the direction of the far, disappearing heights where, looking, he saw that Liesl had started a huge bonfire of leaves and fallen branches and apple boxes and in the glare of the fire surrounded by thickening mist, in orange and white, Liesl swore and cursed and poked at her blaze, the flames leaping up at her so that momentarily she was a Valkyrie and Valhalla burning.

Mrs St James didn't move or take her eyes from the fire, beyond which the hotel shivered and wavered through the heat as it must have done on that night when it was half consumed and people stared up at the figures trapped in the windows. She neither moved nor breathed, never taking her hands off the ropes, not blinking for as long as a minute, two or three, and then she turned and stared at Angus glassily.

'. . . did you hear that?' she asked and it could have been the conclusion of a long unspoken sentence or a simple inquiry, her ear keener than his to a faint noise in the house. Then she drew herself up and, with strength returning, she went very quickly past him and into the house; so quickly that when he followed, startled, to the doorway, asking, 'Did I hear *what*?'

she was already through the room, almost to the stairs, gone in a streak with no reply and some instinct told him not to follow.

Not until after he had taken out the gummy old tarpaulins and covered all the wicker chairs and sofas did the sickening thought begin.

Or had she said '*Where* did you hear that?'

No, it was merely that the Judge had called and she had heard him as she did at all times, in the depths of the night and from any distance away, by a sixth sense.

The impossible thought persisted, though he brushed it away as continuously as a wasp, returning louder each time and, like all unlikelihood, gathering feasibility.

He went upstairs and shut himself in his room in order to let it occur. If, supposing . . .

Not possible but . . .

Allowing it to be possible for a moment.

Suppose she hadn't known.

Now it was out and he felt better seeing the absurdity of it and was able to say, 'Ridiculous,' out loud and force a laugh and take hold of his shoes to polish and at the same moment the doubt returned so forcefully that he sat down on the bed holding the shoes and felt the ice-cold conviction that it was true because of its very unbelievability and he saw, very clearly, Cissie posturing, winking, sticking nuts in her hair; Cissie with the door open in case someone should come . . . might think . . . finger on the lips, don't tell, and being so careful not to break anything in the house even if it was a misconception. Cissie wholly dithering, twittering, fumbling, playing the bird with the faked broken wing that leads the nest hunters in the wrong direction, and the strict avoidance of any least familiarity between her and the Judge – the always almost calculated formality of them together. 'Good evening, Cecilia. Good evening, Uncle Heath,' and never looking right in the eyes, covering themselves with the gauzes of the most superficial remarks,

106

grateful that they had their mutual oddities to cover them if there were the slightest slip . . .

This was it.

This was the game that Cissie and the Judge had played, called Protecting Eve.

Their method of screaming at Echo Point so that this episode which might be misconstrued, misunderstood, would not be brought into her warm, safe house, where she moved softly, asking not to be told, to leave alone.

Well – he tried a laugh – that was it and now it was out and could be looked at and declared unconvincing and untrue and, because of the unusual nature of the person involved, horribly possible.

Here was the proof coming now. Alarmed to hear her quick footsteps coming down the hall and waiting for his door to open and see her blazing face there asking how dare he, how dare he have made this mischief, this crack in her world? He waited, fascinated with the thought of her fury . . .

No, funnily the footsteps went past and downstairs and a moment later the coughing, choking of a car having difficulty starting in the cold and, pushing open the window, he caught a glimpse of her backing, turning and driving off very fast.

Was there a connection in the fact that she would suddenly have had to drive somewhere in the coming, possibly danger-ously heavy mist? It was precipitous, the way she drove off, headlights pricking on irritably, gears wrenching, it was unlike her (the car tore off) to be making all these jerky, abrupt, slam-bang . . .

This was all guilty imagination. Nothing had happened. She was not angry. She had remembered a necessary errand . . .

But the house was creaking with the ominous echo of those quick angry footsteps. He lay on the bed and tried to think calmly about what to say. He went through it in his mind, he reasoned with her calmly, assuring her that it had only been assumption on his part because (truthfully) Cissie had never actually said *who* had come to her cottage asking for help and even if it was true, surely this minor, minor deception years and years ago needn't . . .

So, exercised beyond his strength in trying to find tinny arguments and excuses for letting a dead cat out of a bag, he felt exhausted, closed his eyes, and, in trying to balance his amazement at her vulnerability with his desire to nevertheless put right, put right, put back, back everything where it had been ten minutes before decided to move all this weight off his chest for a minute or two, dozed . . .

Woke hearing this strange bird cry perhaps ten minutes later, perhaps half an hour?

Ossssser. Ossser, cried the bird, a long way off, the thin note rising at the end in a shriek. A crow.

Asleep nearly an hour, looking at his watch, getting off the bed to reach for his jacket. Walls of white wool outside now blotted out the trees but glancing down as he passed the window he saw that wherever she had been, she was back. Saw with relief that the car was there.

He went quickly downstairs to face it, whatever it might be, with assurance and a sense of balance restored by sleep.

'*Fooooooooster*,' called the bird, nearer now.

He paused a moment and then went on out to the veranda into the opaque white night.

Cissie had just met Mrs St James at the steps, coming at a run to her, and they reached out and clutched at each other in apparent joy. Mrs St James telling Cissie something that was apparently transporting her with joy and amusement, surely must be amusement the way she held onto her friend, putting her head down on Mrs St James's shoulder, rocked back and forth with her and then, as Angus came forward questioningly, lifted her head and, holding Mrs St James slightly away from her, quacked, squawked at the joke between them and, giving Mrs St James a little push away from her, turned around in a circle and then sat down on the bottom step, bent over and holding herself in the pain of too much laughter, her head moving back and forth opposing Mrs St James's telling her any more.

Mrs St James came and knelt by her.

'Quickly is better, he said. The vet *said*, Cissie.'

Cissie raised a ghastly head that shook slowly from side to side. She said in a quiet voice, 'No you didn't.'

'A mandatory *kind*ness . . .'

'No you didn't,' Cissie said.

'A kindness.'

'No you didn't,' Cissie repeated again and again. 'No you didn't, you didn't.' Her hands would not stay still. 'Did you?' Angus knew now and felt the crack under his feet that he had made, felt it widen, and in the next few seconds saw things fragmented. Saw Cissie start to get up, sit down, pick up a pebble and drop it and sometimes nod to Mrs St James, who was trying to reach for and control Cissie's hands, which, every time she caught, Cissie yanked away from her, nodded in agreement and yanked away her hands from the figure bending over her and talking about kindness, kindness.

'Oh, Christ,' Cissie said at last in agony.

And because some deity of ill-timing could not resist this perfect crowning moment, a figure loomed out of the mist calling out, 'Hello, hello,' jovially, and, 'I say this is a humdinger' said Lesley Ann.

'I almost couldn't find the path' she told them eagerly. 'I could hardly see my hand in front of my face.'

Then they remained like statues until after a while Cissie said quietly to Mrs St James, kneeling by her, 'I want to get up. Would you let me get *up*, please.'

She got up then and slowly went up the steps in the dignity and majesty of someone very drunk, refusing aid, and there was nothing unusual to note about her, nothing to cause a glance until she suddenly put her hand to a veranda post and then, embracing the post, she called out, 'Oh, God,' to someone a long way off.

'What we have to realize is that when a dog is seventeen . . .'
Mrs St James began and Angus turned to look at her in disbelief
and saw a total stranger, half-smiling, self-pitying woman with
a mottled face and wild eyes who was speaking in a wheedling
voice, in the most supplicating tones, about murder, and she
was unfamiliar to him; she could have been a demented beggar
who had wandered off the mountain road out of the mist.
Minute by minute Mrs St James was altering, peeling away from
her former shape until the cringing, half-apologetic victimized
self was showing through. Wait, hear me, she was pleading to
him and to Lesley Ann, who was seeing the horror of it too,
seeing all dignity gone in the desperate, persuasive little jerks
and movements of fingers through her hair turned to string in
the dampness.

'. . . the only humane thing,' she said. Her voice was hoarse
and urgent. She was transformed now into a beseeching dark
figure against clouds of white. '. . . is a whiff of chloroform, the
RSPCA man said.' She was ugly. She might have been a bush
or a tree or one of the Bad Banksia Man faces. 'You must accept
the *fact*,' she was crazy all right. 'Help me explain that to her,
darling,' she said and the little tin word coming from *her* did it.

'Freak.' He spat the word on her.

He started to walk quickly.

'Angus,' she said. At first only chidingly in her hurt, then like
a bullet in the back. 'Angus!'

He walked faster into the density and heard her call out his
name once more in a long-drawn-out cry for help that frightened
him into running, cutting through sharp bushes and through
the vague outlines of ruined walls and arches in the fear that if
he heard her cry out again it might touch him with pity, imagining she might be following him through clouds and arches,
through the maze of the burned-out hidden walls and, not understanding that he had successfully pulled down all her precious, guarded ruins, reach out for him and stop him with pity.
So he ran on through what had been a dining-room, half of a

vast lobby, out of all this until he felt himself on gravel, and the drive, opening under his feet, swept down in gradual descents, pulled him with it, running fast now until he came to a stop under where the big RITZ sign was hidden in mist over the arched gate. He waited listening for the *scrunch* of footsteps with the terrible expectation of seeing her once more, to catch a glimpse of her following him, hurrying out of the impenetrable curtains that surrounded him.

There was only an intense, brooding silence. Everything was gone now; the only thing remaining in sight was the gate where he was standing. The hotel was gone; might never have existed. The bungalow was gone, melted away, and everything and everybody in it vapourized, and now there was only himself and the sound and sight of his own breathing that remained in this place.

He was already so far away that he was another person on another planet.

Yet when he turned and groped his way to the road towards the railway station, the gate being instantly swallowed up, the RITZ vanished, swallowed up behind him, and everything gone now, he was possessed by the sense of being followed. Once he stopped to listen but there was nothing, nobody, and hurrying on he realized that what was pursuing him, gaining on him (and the thought of it, like the last glimpse of her, was colder than any mountains), was the beginning of a long memory.

2. Bea

By the sixth year of the war it had long ago become an obsolete and extravagant gesture to offer cigarettes to anyone excepting high-ranking officers, persons of great note or age, and known non-smokers, and yet a certain atavistic politeness survived, an apologetic turning aside to grope for and light the one cigarette from the half-concealed package. A deftness was required to produce just one cigarette from inside the jacket pocket or from out of the purse or, as in the case of a flamboyant actress, from the breast (although it had been suggested she hadn't got hold of a real party trick until she could produce it lit). The offering of cigarettes, like many other useless peace-time civilities, had vanished along with gasoline and genuine Scotch whisky. So when eager little Miss Ring from the *Radio Times* held out a luscious fat pack of Lucky Strikes and said, 'Go on, *do*. Really, I've got a whole carton,' Bea took one partly because Miss Ring obviously must have an American in tow and so could always get more (though even the Americans were getting scarce) but also to put on a semblance of a better face than she had been showing since the beginning of this interview, which she had not wanted to do, had known would be asinine, had been proved right.

Because right off Miss Ring had said the wrong thing. Right off Miss Ring had seemed taken in. Miss Ring still seemed sceptical. 'Oh, but I expected a *man*,' Miss Ring had said, coming in. 'D. K. Durfee sounds like a *man*.'

'I'm a wartime substitute,' Bea had said, 'like powdered eggs.' She suspected Miss Ring was one of those 'we' writers who would begin her piece, 'We were as surprised as you would be to discover that D. K. Durfee is a girl. The young authoress of those countless radio serials greeted us wearing a dress she had made herself out of pre-war used lampshades . . .' It would be that kind of piece Miss Ring would write. Very succulent girls-together-modestly-eschewing-notions-of-grandeur kind of thing, and her hair would be described as blonde and luxuriantly braided.

'I'm going to be wicked, dear, and ask you how old you are,'

'Twenty-five,' Bea said.

She usually lied about her age. Something about her being only twenty-two caused people to burst into an angry hilarity at being caught taking her seriously. It was bad enough to have to admit to being enthralled by one or two or three of the D. K. Durfee serials but to discover you had been hooked by a twenty-two-year-old girl, a big, ovine, placid, cool-eyed girl with plaited blonde hair, was too much. So they sought to pull her down, laughing at her and trying not to believe it. Are you really D. K. Durfee? But then you don't do it all yourself, you *can't*. Isn't there a team of you? No, she told them solemnly, ashamed of being ashamed of her freakishness, she did it all herself, every single word of it herself, plots and outlines and characters and everything. 'But how do you manage it?' Miss Ring was asking (naturally), and writing with a very blunt pencil, possibly to make sure that most of it would be inaccurate.

'Four very fast shorthand typists.'

'But the *strain* . . . five continuous separate stories, all going at once? I mean, I'd think you might easily get one confused with another?'

Already Bea was feeling a dangerous jocularity bubbling up in her. It often got too much of a strain trying to defend and explain D. K. Durfee so she escaped into absurdia.

'I find,' she told Miss Ring solemnly, 'that if I eat a raw-onion sandwich, it helps to keep my concentration going.'

'*Really?* That's *very* interesting.'

Because she couldn't explain her odd powers. The stuff flowed out of her. Often she went so fast dictating that the girls would cry out that they were way behind. Often they couldn't read their own hieroglyphics and came tapping on her door, interrupting the next episode spilling out of her, to ask if she could tell them what some character had said here just before Myra smelled fire and always she would have to make something up because she could never remember what she had said, it was gone from her in the instant of being created. All she did was come in every morning and they would bring her huge cups of scalding tea and she would look at the recording schedule that Mrs Helena Ambrose left on her desk (sometimes with a note: 'We are dangerously close to air date on "Jezebel's Daughter." Can you manage six?'). Then she would buzz and Maisie or Nancy or Pat or June would come in with her notebook and she would ask where she had left off and one of them would read back to her the last few exciting cliff-hanging moments of the previous episode, which was often a surprise even to her.

And Maisie, who had humour, would say, 'Now let's see you try to get out of *that* one, D. K.'

Then she would close her eyes and begin. Slowly at first and the words as stiff and dry as sticks until she felt it starting to take hold of her like drink and then faster and faster until she was drawn back completely into the timeless and brightly lit countries of her mind through which she journeyed disguised as many fabulous people passing from one extraordinary event to another and, with the intense lustre of fake jewellery, these creatures outshone the real world around her, everything real darkened and dimmed, aware of nothing else until Maisie, who was now on her fourth pencil, would call out, 'You're on page seven,' and she would bring about a climax.

Gulp tea. Next.

Next girl. More tea. Where were we?

Yet she was as removed from it as a medium in a trance and as unaffected as a prostitute. She was astonished, coming out of it, at her own doodles. Great Rorschach-test things, bats and curious machines of death and ugly misshapen bursting stars that had been heavily pencilled on her blotter by a lunatic.

All day long her voice droned on, growing gradually hoarser, being men and women engaged in passions and emotions that she had not experienced, in foreign countries she had never seen, and in the freedom of her innocence she was able to stop at nothing; knew also that if she ever gave a thought to the absurdity of it (she never, never listened to her own stuff on the radio) she might see the paper and chicken wire it was made of and her power might dry up in her.

So in order to protect it from her own devaluation and sense of humour, she attributed it all to D. K. Durfee.

Well, pick a name then, they'd said to her when she had stoutly refused to use her own and (ashamed of being ashamed of her work) gave her parents as her excuse.

So Durfee after Durfee's Milk of Magnesia, which was sitting on Mrs Ambrose' desk, and the initials because she was always having to say she didn't know how she did it. D for *don't* K for *know*.

Just as it was impossible to control D. K. Durfee's wild fecundity, so was it to ignore the spread of Durfee jokes and jibes. It had become eponymous in some circles to say, 'Don't do a Durfee on me,' meaning 'Don't keep me in suspense,' and recently a *Sydney Morning Herald* editorial had commented that the curious attitude of the Minister for Defence over the camouflage netting contract scandal was as dark a mystery as would delight D.K. Durfee.

'We're getting famous,' Mrs Ambrose said, accepting the credit, which she did when it was considered a good plug for the shows, and Bea, to show her utter disregard of the Defence Ministry and D.K. to boot, emptied her ashtray onto the newspaper.

One thing she treasured. Someone had sent her the *Army News* which circulated only to troops stationed in the remote Darwin area of the Northern Territory and which featured a cartoon strip called 'The Nuts,' in which two unkempt Bad Banksia Men dressed in grubby tropical uniform each week bemoaned their fate of being part of a forgotten army in this desolate outback. The caption of this one read: When do we bloody well get to the *war*?' 'Maybe D. K. Durfee knows.'

It was signed, 'Cpl Angus Weekes, 8 AOD, Darwin.'

She had it framed and hung over the desk and then, quaking, she wrote sixteen letters to Angus, none of which got beyond the second line, and which were so stickily coy or rigidly formal that eventually she gave up trying altogether. When it came to writing a simple letter to a soldier, D. K. Durfee left Beatrice St James to her own devices.

But it titillated her to think that Angus had heard D. K. Durfee all the way up there in Darwin where there were no radio stations that would carry the Ambroses' blood and thunder, and also she was curious to know if Angus had any idea of the identity of D. K. Durfee and even more to know what, if any, his reaction would be to it, and sometimes she looked at the Bad Banksia Men nuts and thought about the night on a train about three years ago when, stalled in a siding, a troop train had drawn alongside and, looking up, there was Angus staring at her from about two feet away – their faces were exactly framed in the two train windows and she had gasped at the sight of him, gaunt, much too thin with his stringy neck sticking out of the khaki collar which was too big for it. She waved but he remained slumped by the window, leaning his head against the dirty glass. She tapped on her window; she tried to open it but it was glued shut with years of soot. She stood up and gesticulated wildly to attract his attention but either the feeble brownout lights in her train were too dim or else *Angus* was only seeing the reflection of his own weary face in the dark glass, and then his train jerked and moved on, carrying him away, leaving her with the suspicion that he *had* seen her doing fandangos and cold-bloodedly ignored her, and she sat down gulping her disappointment and the hurt of being publicly snubbed so that when one of the amused people in her compartment said, 'Didn't your boy-friend see you?' she gritted her teeth and said, 'My *stupid* cousin.'

Miss Ring said, 'Hobbies?'

Bea bit her tongue to stop saying, 'I collect lint.'

'No time,' she said.

'Well, what do you do for recreation?'

I stand nude in the Archibald fountain in Hyde Park. 'I'm not *in*teresting,' she said. Miss Ring's voice was so saturated with condescension that she could hardly bear another moment of it. These people could never believe that her outer life was so commonplace. She came and went in overcrowded trams. She went to bed and got up. She occasionally took herself to a Town Hall concert. People didn't want to hear these things; the truth embarrassed them. They didn't want to hear about her, they wanted to hear about D. K., and (she bent to move the little electric radiator away from the legs of the imitation-bamboo sofa which in damp weather was as sticky as toffee and gave off a smell of nail varnish) any moment now if Miss Ring persisted in trying to worm the tame, flat, dull truth out of her, she would get a dose of D. K. she hadn't bargained for. D. K. was struggling inside her like a dybbuk to get out.

'Any ro*mant*ic little situation I can hint at? You don't have to say who it is . . .'

'Oh, I don't mind telling you who it is . . .' There. D. K. was out in the open and dangerous. 'But you must give me your word you won't print it for security reasons.'

'Heavens. Really?'

'I mean, I wouldn't want to get you in trouble with the War Office and I'm sure somebody in Security reads your *Radio Times* if only to see what time the news is on.'

'You *are* a dark horse, Miss Durfee.'

'There are reasons.'

'Can you give me a clue? Top Brass?'

'Very. Mind if I tell you obliquely?'

'Oh, no, whatever way you like.'

'Who went to the cupboard?'

'I've no idea.'

'Who went to the cupboard to get her poor dog a bone?'

'Mother – You're engaged to one of the *Hubbards*?'

'Shhh. Mustn't use the name.'

'Oh, I give you my word. But which one? David? Bunny?'

'No.'

'I thought I knew all the Hubbards.'

'Give you another hint. First name the same as the American band leader Heidt.'

'Horace?'

'Right.'

'Horace *Hubbard*?'

'That one.'

'You do mean the Hubbards?'

'Not the feed-and-grain Hubbards, *the* . . .'

'Well, isn't that funny, because before the war I used to go up to Cobbity a lot to see the Hubbard boys play polo and I don't remember a Horace.'

'Oh, he wasn't one of the polo-playing boys because of his eye.'

'His eye?'

'You see, he has one eye lower than the other.'

'Oh, I'm –'

'Oh, it isn't *very* much lower but he's sensitive about it.'

'Well, of course one wouldn't be *un*sensitive about ... but I'm wondering where he comes in the family. Older or younger than Bunny?'

'Oh, he isn't a brother, he's an uncle.'

'An –'

'Uncle. And don't confuse him with Curtis, who is Army.

Horace is Navy. Commander and attached to the Ministry on top-secret work so that's why you can't say . . .'

'Well, he's . . .'

'What were you going to say?'

'. . . a bit older then.'

'Oh, I don't think fifty-eight is old. Not these days. What do *you* think?'

'Mmmmm. You know what I think? I think you're pulling my leg.'

'Oh, now why would I want to do *that*?'

'Gosh, is that the *time*?'

Miss Ring gathered up her notebook, black gloves and Lucky Strikes.

'Well, Miss Durfee, you've given me a very interesting half hour and now I'll do my best to make up something about you that they'll believe.'

'I'm sorry but, you see, I hate interviews.'

'So do *I*,' said Miss Ring bitterly and went.

She looked a bit dusty as she went and not so young come to think of it and perhaps she didn't have an American after all; perhaps all she had was a black-marketeer.

'Now *why* did I have to do that?' she asked Maisie, her head stenographer. She was feeling remorseful now and Maisie the Impassive was a cushion: imponderable, unemotional, superbly mundane.

'You asking me?'

'Yes. Why do I have to play games?'

'I suppose because she got your goat.'

'She was so *sincerely* commonplace I couldn't help it.'

There was something about Miss Ring, a pathetic thing that had sparked her merriment right from the start. She was asking Maisie to understand and give her a lead and Maisie did.

'Well, I'll tell you what *I* think: it's ten minutes to five and you've got more than half an episode to finish.'

'Just the same, she'll probably be venomous now.'

'Oh, who cares? Nichevo. It's goin' to be a long war, you know.'

'Yes, yes, that's right. Well now, back to work. Where did I leave off?'

'Varonski says, "Is that Josette I see across the lake?"'

'I think I'll send her some flowers.'

'Is this you or him talking?'

'Me. Will you get Stewart's to do it? See if they've got snapdragons and take a note: "Dear Miss Ring. Will you please try to overlook my bad manners this afternoon?"'

Absolved, she was able now to close her eyes and erase Miss Ring entirely in the further adventures of Ignace Varonski in the Crimea, so when Maisie brought the typed note to sign she looked at it blankly. 'To go with the flowers,' Maisie reminded her and she signed it in D. K. Durfee's big bold handwriting.

There, joy of joys, across the street was a taxi and she ran to it, but two young American lieutenants reached it at the same moment.

'No, you saw it first,' she said, backing away as they held open the door politely.

'We're going up to the Cross,' one of them said. 'Any use to you?' Kings Cross was exactly where she was going. 'No use, thanks just the same,' she said and, walking away, felt that they were saying something both amusing and ugly about her. Taxi sharing was mandatory and it was a rare luxury to ride alone. Everyone had amusing stories about exasperating fellow passengers: about riding with men who made passes at you, drunks, mad old ladies, vulgar servicemen. But it seemed to her these stories were greatly exaggerated. It was blood-curdling, what had not happened to her.

She waited for the Kings Cross tram in the brownout winter twilight. Cars went by sluggishly with their muffled headlights and overhead the filtered street lamps gave out a weak gingery light, and when the tram came grinding up King Street, it too was lit with the same weak, muddy light by which people strained their eyes to read the thin evening newspaper. Like everyone else, she was inured now to the colourlessness of everything – brown lights, khaki, yellowish newspapers, books printed on cheap paper which turned brown and then quickly to fine dust. The dreariness of brown was everywhere. She could not remember Sydney before the war and, like children who were now beginning to grow up never having seen neon signs, she could not imagine the city starting to glow and twinkle at dusk. She could not visualize what the General Post Office had looked like before they had taken down the clock tower and stored it away somewhere against the possibility of Japanese bombers. She was accustomed to the big stores with unlit show windows and wire where there had been plate glass and all these precautions which, like the air-raid sirens, regularly practising their dismal warnings, had been made for invasion, death, parachutists, in the terrifying days of 1942 when these things had seemed possible, when they had drawn the secret, invisible line across the huge continent to the north and said we will defend from below here, before the Americans came and the threat had gradually rolled back to New Guinea, the Philippines, the Marianas, and had left behind it the drab colour of war and a feeling of anticlimax.

And what is a more ridiculous-looking thing than a camouflaged double-decked bus? Could anyone conceive of the 6.22 bus to Roseville being set on fire by a dive-bomber?

There was something unreal about it all. It might have been a huge hoax on the population, mesmerized into believing a mighty war was being fought. Even when the *Queen Mary* appeared overnight in the harbour like a giant grey squid, one had to deny it was the *Queen Mary* in case the Enemy Was Listening. So Bea felt (climbing into the packed tram, the smell of damp khaki, damp newspapers, such a grubby wet little woman conductor shrieking to 'let them on ... let them on or we'll sit 'ere all night, you bludgers' – everyone was a bloody little satrap these days) the war had nothing to do with reality and certainly nothing to do with her even though Tip St James was lost, caught with the Army in the fall of Singapore three years ago and presumed to be in Changi prison camp. If alive. If alive, you said, and it meant nothing any more, no more than the daily casualty lists. Everything brown and colourless like the war itself. Nothing surprising in this grey life everyone lived; it had become matter-of-fact. There was no longer anything unusual in the fact that the US corporal (his stripe still seemed upside down to her) strap-hanging next to her, his hand occasionally nudging hers when the tram jerked forward, and reading the *Evening Sun* through thin steel Army Issue spectacles, was, let's say, from Racine, Wisconsin, where he had worked in a bank and was now attached to Base Headquarters in the Grace Building so now went back and forth on the Kings Cross tram. War had simply transplanted him some thousands of miles into a new rut.

And most people glumly agreed it might be years yet before the last Jap was routed out of the last foxhole on the last unheard-of little island.

'That'd be O.K. with me,' Maisie had said. She had a chubby major in Base Headquarters who fed her on T-bone steaks and exotic confections like banana splits at the American Officers Club. She had a seemingly unending supply of Kleenex. But Bea shied away from the Americans and their largesse. They made her uneasy. They were a queer lot altogether, so open. Anyway, she didn't need distraction, living as she did a lot of the time in the Crimea.

However, the idea of the young corporal in his new rut pleased her as if she had designed some truth about the war all by herself, and so . . .

'Excuse me,' D. K. Durfee asked politely. 'Do you happen to know where I should get off for Darlinghurst Road?'

'Yes, you get off at the Kings Cross intersection and it's right there,' the corporal said.

'Oh, thank you,' she said. 'I'm a stranger here.'

'You're welcome.'

He seemed pleased. It had made him feel good being able to direct her, him being a resident. She read his paper over his shoulder until he said, 'Next stop you get off.' 'Oh, thank you,' she said. 'You wouldn't be from Wisconsin by any chance?'

'No, ma'am, I'm from Buffalo, New York.'

On the corner of Darlinghurst Road an audience was watching an altercation taking place between a young GI and a girl. She was one of the little unprofessional tarts who wandered up and down and in and out of the crowded coffeehouses, all pompadoured and tricked out in sad little gay dresses and paste jewellery, and she was weeping uncontrollably. As Bea went past she began swinging at the American boy with her bag. 'No, no, no,' she screamed, 'don't you bloody dare, you fat-arse don't you bloody tell *me* what I am.' 'Now, Gwen, Gwen . . . c'*mon*,' the boy said gently and the girl struck him again with her bag and the buckle cut his face; there was blood. The faces watching were expressionless. 'Don't tell *me* how to behave.' She was hysterical. 'I take domestic science and dressmaking; you ask *any*one.' The boy was trying to grab her arm but she wheeled away, screaming, 'Don't you touch me, you fart. You Yanks think you own the country.'

Two American provosts were hurrying up.

Six o'clock was a bad time, pig-swill time. The bars closed at six o'clock. It meant that the boys had pushed down six to seven big schooners of heavy dark lager in perhaps ten minutes to beat the clock and then hit the cool air of the brown, cheerless street frustrated; nothing to do until the cinemas opened at seven-thirty, nowhere to go except the coffeehouses of the barren, spiritless Y M C A's and Red Cross Entertainment Centres. Just after six o'clock the streets were crowded with fiercely thirsty adventurers, brawlers and the lonely.

Sometimes in the blur of faces in the six-o'clock stampede Bea thought she saw Angus; once she had been so certain he had passed her by that she'd run and caught hold of a beery soldier who had then pursued her for several streets, drunkenly shouting, 'Yes, you'll do, you'll do.'

Six o'clock and nowhere to go but home, where Adina, who shared the flat with her, would have some disaster to relate (the flat was always reeking with the smell of her cooking) and it was Friday night; there ought to be some kind of jollification on Friday night. Instead of turning off at her corner she continued on towards Bayswater Road, pretending for a moment or two that she might buy a lemon meringue pie at the home bakery and, having bought or not bought it, could then say that, after all, she was only a step from where Marcus lived in the old Ersildoone Towers, so . . .

He never minded her dropping in. They would talk for hours on end, sipping his sherry, and Bea with her shoes off stretched out on his sofa and Marcus in the wing chair and the firelight on everything, flickering on the high, baroquely festooned ceiling, and there was absolutely no strain with Marcus. 'I was passing,' she would say, coming up the wide circular staircase and, 'Like Pippa,' he would remark and kiss her on the forehead. He dusted her off, shined her up and very soon she was sparkling, exhilarated as always with him. Later, much later, they would have dinner at the Elizabethan Inn or sometimes he would dish up scrambled eggs or kidneys and bacon in a chafing dish in front of the fire. Marcus was Marcus in war and peace. Marcus was as ingenious at promoting comfort as when he had been manager at the old Medlow Bath Ritz.

She was entirely comfortable with him. There were books and records and additional luxuries not provided in the ration books and, above all, talk. She was so comfortable with him that she never once mentioned that there was a thorn in her side.

'Come up on winged feet,' he said when she called up on the house telephone, and she climbed the circular stairs, smelling the cedarwood smell of the once elegant house now cut up into flats.

He was standing in the door. He was the only impeccable

thing left in these dingy days. Behind him was firelight, flowers, damask draperies reflected in the big gilt mirror.

'Saint Beatrice James,' said Marcus.

'I've come,' she said, 'in answer to your advertisement for a Last Ditch Conservative.' They made up want ads for the personal column. 'Born Mischief-maker would like to share flat with Longwinded Storyteller.'

He kissed her on the forehead and took her coat.

'Inveterate Gossip welcomes you,' he said.

'Oh, your *roses*,' she said. She swam into the serene room, light as air, and was instantly turned to lead.

Two feet in little red slippers projected from the end of the sofa.

'Come and meet Muff,' Marcus said and led her around the sofa on which she usually flung down. A woman lay looking into the fire and didn't move for a moment, then started and turned her face. White hair cut short around a sharp-boned face. Bea was reminded of her mother.

'Oh, *hello*.'

'Muffet Beatty . . . Bea St James.'

'Oh, *hello*.' Muffet raised herself slightly, waved a hand in Bea's direction. 'Are you *the* Bea?'

'She is the Bea.'

'The Bea? The Bea that writes all those madly divine –'

'Which you've never heard, Muff.'

'Which I've never heard because you, you monster, never remember to tell me when the wretched things are on, you *abso*lute beast.'

They must have been drinking all afternoon; Muffet's voice was thick and glutinous. Words hovered on her mouth and fell out lopsidedly. Perhaps if she was good and soused she wouldn't stay very long.

'Oh, look, you must tell me when you're on. The station and things. I abs'lutely go wildly mad for thrillers and things. Divinely clevah of you. How'd you do it?'

'Don't know,' Bea said. She sat down heavily on a leather ottoman, sunk in the blank disappointment of her spoiled evening.

'Sit here ... lots' room.' Muffet drew a place on the sofa. Her head was not steady.

'No, no. I *always* sit here.'

She took her sherry from Marcus, who bent and again lightly kissed her on the forehead. Probably they'd been drinking since lunch.

'Cheers,' she said without warmth. She was the interrupter, the skeleton at the feast.

Muffet said, 'Dreff'ly wuffish out, ist?'

'I beg your pardon?'

'Ist – *is it* dreadf'ly wuffish? Rain 'n' things? Haven't b'n out all day.'

The woman was definitely drunk. Not tight, drunk. She moved all the time in twitches and jerks. 'And now, my Muff,' Marcus was saying, 'can I get you a gin? Is it time?'

'Oh, I think's time *now*, my darling.'

For her twenty-seventh gin probably.

'Only allowed wunnaday. *One a day*,' Muffet said. There was a hint of Eve St James in the voice and it ruffled Bea; it was someone doing a poor imitation of her mother, insulting. Her mother was dry and witty and scornful and not absurdly affected like this woman. The accent was Put On British, frightf'ly Mayfair, so obviously she was one of the expatriates who rushed at the beginning of the war, fled London while the going was good, while you could still get a ship out, fled to the Antipodes on the excuse of caring for a second cousin to whom they had not even sent a Christmas card for twenty years and who, once safely here, ran down everything; everything was too ghastly, too provincial for words, too abominable. Bea took her sherry in almost one gulp. She felt it spread and warm through her hostility and hoped that she had not really heard Marcus say that, 'Muffie has taken Don's flat.'

'Don?'

'Don Dawson in the flat next door's been moved to Melbourne and had to get out of his lease overnight . . .'

'Wasn't it fantas'ic, Bea?'

'And here was my Muff practically on the streets.'

'Onnastreese, lit'rally slip'nna park.'

Bea felt she had swallowed a huge piece of pastry and it had stuck where her heart ought to be. This caricature, nodding and bobbing over her gin, was here to stay then? This was what they were both chortling about? My Muffie was here to stay?

Never again the long delightful evenings playing his records (shall we put on Mahler and talk or Marlene and listen?) or reading aloud from *archy and mehitabel* or *Cold Comfort Farm* or Benchley. And what hurt like hell was that he had never even mentioned the flat to her, knowing how she would love to be in Ersildoone and close to him. Knowing she'd been on the lookout for a flat to herself for two years. But that his preference was for this mass of tics, this tippling old boozer.

'Wuffish, slip'nna park and got all my furn'chure in stor', dear.'

'Oh, you're madly lucky to get in *here*,' Bea said and gave Muffet the most terrible smile she could muster. The realization had begun to spread through her with the sherry and she was sunk, right down to her boots.

Well, Muffet and he were of an age, for one thing, they laughed at the same time, and also my Muff played gin rummy like a barracuda, Marcus said.

Bea, who could keep five stories going simultaneously in her head without ever getting their characters or events confused, had difficulty in distinguishing clubs from spades. 'I can't understand *why*,' Marcus said in exasperation, 'when you're so clever.'

So they tried chess but it was disastrous; she had no grasp of outmanoeuvring.

'You have no cunning,' he complained. 'Anyone could take you. The Flopsy Bunnies could beat you.'

'I know,' she said with a fierce contrary pride that she was no good. She clung to her inadequacy in the same way that she persisted in her old-fashioned braided hairdo. Adina, picking up hairpins in their flat, would say, oh, Bea, if you'd just try a long soft bob with perhaps a little chignon to put on at night? No, she said, thanks, but you have to have a certain kind of face to sustain a long soft bob.

But Marcus had said 'Aren't you clever not to run willy-nilly with fad?'

That had pleased her. So when it had been carefully brought back to her that someone had said Bea St James dresses as if she were going to sing in a lesbian madrigal group, she naturally brought it to Marcus, who merely looked bored and said:

'Are you lesbian?'

'Of *course* not.'

'Then forget it. You're never going to get on if you flinch at every little sling and arrow. You're a success and that's not easy to forgive and you're daring, which is worse. I think it's very smart of you, Pippa, to aim at being a big girl.'

'I *am* a big girl.'

'I've always admired the way you don't try to deny it, you come right out with it, big bold stripes and big wide lapels and pockets and oversize purses. Top marks to you, dear one.' So here she was, big and bold and daring, striped and braided and wide-lapelled in a broad-striped daring green-and-white suit (about which Maisie had said, well, you'll never get run down by a bus in the brownout in *that*, D. K.) and wondering why she was so small. 'Can I have some more sherry?' she asked and Marcus took her glass and said, 'Are you O.K.? You look somewhat solemn.'

'Oh, yes,' she said.

Never again, after tonight, after perhaps she finished the next glass of sherry. Never again the nice things. Like the time after listening to the ecstacy of the finale of *Rosenkavalier*, he'd been silent for a long time and then reached out for her hand and said, 'Generally, people are extraneous, don't you think?'

Except for her, he had meant.

Muffet, twisting her neck in a spasm of effort to appear sober, said, 'And d'you get mally passhona' finletters and things?'

'Do I get what?'

'Do you get madly passionate fan letters,' Marcus said very softly.

'Oh, sometimes.'

Everyone that you let yourself get fond of leaves you.

'But how madly clevah of you to kippit – *keep it* all in your head.'

Angus had walked off into the mist without even saying good-bye.

'Mus' havva make masses 'n' masses of notes t'yourself. . .'

Angus had walked off leaving his only suit hanging in the wardrobe and his best shoes and overcoat. Not that he had an inkling about her secret and sexual longings. But then, all she could be was a big lumpy girl who sat around saying prickly things. She tried. 'You may be talented,' she told him but somehow it came out like a curse. Then they were dancing and he was sorry for her because she was in a small disgrace and he had kept looking at her steadily and waiting for her to speak and she was so congealed with love and desire she was speechless and could only clump around in his arms in silence trying to think of something to say that might give him a clue to her, but just as she had prepared the little verbal clixir he'd twisted his head away to look for Stevie and so the spiteful ventriloquist in her had said, scathingly. 'Looking for a cab?' Well, so Angus walked away into the mist and never came back and when it was clear that he'd gone for good (she would open the wardrobe and hug his suit, fool that she was), only then was something released in her and she had made her first honest connection with another person, she had wept to Marcus.

'Just *went*,' she cried out, about the unreasonableness of it, about the end of her chances, 'without *even* his overcoat.'

'The only original thing he's ever done,' Marcus said and suggested she'd have her first 'spot'. Haig & Haig and sympathy had freed a log-jammed river of confessions, of admissions of love and despair and panic, all of which strangely enough was news to her.

She had rolled back to the bungalow, important and exhilarated.

'I'm tight,' she told her mother.

'Good for you,' her mother said in the way she had of absolving and so punishing you.

But the connection had been made too late. Three days after she had successfully transplanted her untenanted emotions from Angus to Marcus, Marcus had left.

And now was going again.

She sat woodenly, her big legs drawn up and uncomfortable on the low ottoman, and smiled grimly at Muffet, who was leaning towards her and seemed to be having trouble keeping her head from falling right off onto the floor. Whenever she jerked it back just in time, she gave a peculiar little snort, showing tiny rabbit teeth discoloured from smoking. The way she smoked was a sideways grab for the cigarette, a swoop up in the air, a hesitation and then a hit-or-miss to the lips and a jerky downward swipe, a jab at the ashtray and up again.

Difficult to understand what she was saying, slurring, slurping, and Marcus interjecting a word of encouragement to her whenever she got stalled.

'Williamorm made massanmassa notes.'

'Willy Maugham made masses of notes,' Marcus translated.

'Massonates. Like you, Bea.'

'Muffie stayed at Cap Ferrat,' Marcus interjected.

'Yes. Stay with Willamorm in Cap F'rat, darling, and made him a wildly mad-camp little rug frisnees.'

'For his knees.'

'F'ris poor ole knees.'

'Muffie used to hook the most exquisite mohair lap rugs.'

'Eckwiz*ite*, darling.'

'Eckwiz*ite*. I'd forgotten that. Who was it used to say eck-wiz*ite*?'

'Mermaid.'

'Mer ... oh, your maid.'

'Mer-maid, darling. Mad Marg'ret. Mad'shatter she was, Bea. Too wild. 'dored her. She wazza one use to wash all my money, Marcus. Wouldn't let me touch a penny till she'd washed it in hot water and lye and all kindsa mad mad things, my dear. Frightenna germs. Oh, she's awfully wuffish about dirty money and I saidda Willamorm, you've got to put Mad Marg'ret in a book – Willamorm had met her in my house, see – but Willamorm said it was too late, and give her t' Noel.'

'Give her to Noel. I never. Muffie and Noel were also chums.'

'Oh. Know Noel wellz I know *you*.'

Perhaps Marcus was more at home with ancient, tedious, out-of-date talk like this, about tired celebrities on the Riviera before the war. He lived in a bubble of beautiful glass and fire-light and gin and probably Muffet belonged in it too. Bea knew it had been a mirage. She was too far behind in years and she had come to Marcus like Mad Margaret to Mr Maugham, too late. She would accept her defeat, she would drink her gall and go. She had better go in a minute because she had begun to feel that she might like to break something violently.

'Tell Muffie your dreadfully dumb actor story.'

'Oh, no, Marcus,' Bea pleaded. She was not going to be put on display for Muffet, at least not now, now at the end.

'Oh, do, do. 'dore dreff'ly dumactor stories. Never knew an actor who wazzn't dreff'ly dum' 'cept Larry maybe.'

'Tell, Pippa,' Marcus ordered.

'No, it isn't germane.'

'Doesn't matter. Muff will love it.'

'Will 'dore it, tell, tell.'

'I had a very unnerving experience coming home on the tram,' Bea said suddenly, feeling D. K. Durfee take over strongly and hearing at the same time a tiny crack in the glass bubble that housed Marcus. 'An American soldier asked me where to get off for Darlinghurst Road and so I said, without thinking, that I got off there. He seemed O.K., they all do at first. He was from Wisconsin.'

'Oh. The *Lunts* live in Wiscozzin.'

'Yes, my Muff, but let Bea tell.'

'Well,' Bea said, 'he practically told me his life story. You don't want to be unkind to them, lonely boys in a strange country, so I listened politely and then when I got off at the Cross, of course he got off too and then it dawned on me I'd been picked up. The whole thing was a ploy. He knew his way around as well as I do. He just wanted to pick me up. So then I couldn't shake him off. He walked all the way down to Macleay Street with me and so I said, "Well, I go this way, good night," and he said, "I'll walk with you," and I said "Oh please don't I'm in a hurry and really ... good-bye," but he kept on with me until finally I said, "Look, will you kindly stop following me," at which he got nasty and started to catch hold of my arm. So I said, "Get away from me." I said, "You Yanks think you own the country." '

'You should have called a cop ...'

'Oh, have you ever *seen* one? All the time he was pulling at my arm and saying, oh, come on, come on. I don't know what he was saying really, I was so mad ...'

'Dirty things?'

'Oh, no, not dirty, oh, not obscene, nothing like that. Quite polite really and glasses and smaller than me – so the whole thing was awful so awful what I did. Specially as he was smaller than me ...'

'What did you do?'

'I hit him with my bag.'

'And ran?'

'Yes, but first I hit him with my bag in the ear. I hit him *twice* and cut his face open.'

Now something very definitely was broken. They were looking at her, subdued, the firelight flickering on their faces. Marcus looked concerned and sorry and Muffet was twitching in the changing spikes of light, and finally Marcus said, 'Oh, well, they *are* inclined to be a hazard.'

'Who, the Yanks?'

'I'm ready to go on record,' Bea said, 'that I have *had* the Yanks up to *here*.'

'Got to remember they sav' arnex.'

'What, Muff?'

Muffet caught her head and tossed it back on her shoulders, snorted and said, *'Saved our necks.'*

'Ah, yes,' Marcus said.

Muffet tapped Bea on the knee. 'Trouble is that one has to admit they sav' arnex, Yankssav.'

So she wasn't to criticize the Yanks. Put in her place. Well, she shouldn't have borrowed the story, stolen it for effect, for revenge; it was too D. K.'ish for words. But all the same, she didn't see why she should be admonished by this relic of the Riviera, who, safe in her bubble with Marcus, assumed that she was some little Nell from the Mountains who knew nothing. She got up to stretch her uncomfortable legs and caught a glimpse of her feverish face in the mirror.

'Oh, well, I should hope nobody will ever forget *that,'* she said. 'Were you here when the Japanese submarines came?'

'I . . . waddn't tin Sydney then.'

'Well, they snuck in, you know, under the Manly ferry while the submarine net was open and they got up as far as the Cocka-too navy dock. We weren't told till after that they almost got a big American flattop. But when the depth charges went off . . .' She drew the picture. The black night, the city shaken by explosions. Everyone terrified but obediently refraining from using the telephone, filling their bathtubs; crouching in their hallways for the all-clear which never came; so shocked, everyone imagining their last moments had come . . .

Marcus and Muffet seemed to be spellbound at the graphic story. She was very effective; she had her audience by the ears all right until Marcus said quietly, 'Of course, you weren't here yourself then, D. K.'

The D. K. was so very quietly interjected that a second passed before she got it.

'Well, no' – damn him – 'but I know people who were – for instance Adina, the girl I share the flat with. It practically looks down over the navy dock and she told me *not knowing* was the worst part of it. She sat hunched up in the hall all night with her clothes on.'

Marcus looked at his nails, Muffet at the floor. After a while Muffet said, 'Yes, well, sort thing would make one feel mildly wuff – wuffish.'

A singing, silent sadness came down over the whole room. No one said anything until suddenly Muffet reached out her arms to Marcus.

'Think'll go fra nappy-poo 'fore dinner.'

'Nappy-poo time,' Marcus said and took Muffet's hands and helped the swaying woman to stand. Holding her to him with one arm and reaching behind the sofa for something and the thing was a cane.

'Got your keys? Got your bag?'

'Gommy keys. Gommy bag.'

You couldn't tell until she stood up about the leg, one leg distinctly shorter than the other and the foot twisted away almost backward and dangling in a little-girl flat shoe.

'Bye-bye f'now,' Muffet said.

And hanging onto Marcus, up and down she went, lurching through the room, and the journey to the door was over giant sand dunes.

'Made it,' Marcus said, opening the front door.

'Maaaaaaaade it,' Muffet said.

When Marcus came back, Bea looked up despairingly but he crossed the room without a glance at her and, taking the poker to kill her, poked at the fire, put on coal and poked away.

'Bomb victim,' he said.

'Oh, God.'

'She had to – um – learn how to speak again.'

'Yes? Oh, God.'

'Among other more ... personal things so ...' He put back the poker and looked at her with no expression.

'Oh, God,' she said and covered her eyes and waited for him to start in on her but there was no sound except the crackling of the fire and when she uncovered her eyes and looked up he was leaning on the mantel and fingering his moustache thoughtfully.

'Well ...' she said, stretching out her hands towards the end: let it come now.

'You want a sherry?'

'No, thanks.'

'Cup of tea?'

'No, nothing. I've got to go in a minute.'

'You don't have to go.'

'Oh, yes, yes, I must.' She lay back on the sofa and groaned. 'Oh, I don't know what to say.'

'About what?'

'About *what*? About my piddling on about the midget subs and she was in the Blitz.'

'Oh, Muffie wouldn't mind. She doesn't think of herself as a heroine.'

'She left.'

'She was tired.'

'Really? I think she was offended.'

'She liked you.'

'Oh, *now* ...'

'She just said so.'

'Well, she's just being polite. The English are always polite.'

'She isn't English and she isn't polite.'

'Well, kind then.'

'Nor kind. Although she is one of the kindest people I know.'

'You could have given me a hint.'

'What? "This lady's disabled" or something?'

'Well, to let me go on . . .'

'Who was I supposed to be saving?'

'Oh, well, if *she* didn't mind . . .'

'Pippa, you should worry less about your loss of face and more about your lack of intuition.'

'I couldn't have known about her leg. I couldn't have *divined* –'

'Her leg hasn't anything to do with it, my love. Her leg doesn't suddenly make her interesting or gay or even especially brave. She's always been brave and campy and fun. She isn't here because she's a *casualty*.'

'No,' Bea said, reminded of someone else.

'If she thought that it'd *really* kill her. That would *really* do the poor love in.'

'Yes, and I'm sure she's grateful . . .'

'Well' – he laughed – 'let us *hope* not.'

But she will have to be, Bea thought, knowing when he said 'poor love' exactly what Muffet's role would be. Say what he liked about her lack of intuition, she certainly knew more than he about the nasty little duties of gratitude and the rewards of taking in the wounded, as Lady Cissie used to call it, and her mother being too vain to understand. Just as Marcus was too vain. The fact of Marcus' vanity was as sudden and surprising as if she had noticed for the first time that he had one brown eye and one blue.

'You were about to say?' he asked.

'Nothing.'

'Something about you suggests disquiet.'

'I was thinking about Muffet,' she said.

'You thought she was a silly, affected woman.'

'Something about me suggested that?'

'Every pore.'

'Did it? I'm sorry.'

'And now you think she's a spunky martyr. Neither is true. I wish you would get to know *people*.'

'So do I.'

'This is your Dutch uncle speaking.'

'Ja, ja.'

'Oh, you're running for cover, I can see.'

'No, no I'm not, Marcus.'

'Don't just *write* people, Pippa.'

'The right people?'

'Write – as with a pen – people.'

'Oh. Make them what I think, do you mean?'

'Yeah. You don't give anyone time. Snap snap. Angel or devil. Snap snap. Someone passes you the olives. Snap. Lifelong friend. Someone says you look a bit dykey in that dress. Snap. Lifelong enemy.'

'Yes.'

'It's instant canonization or . . . you know, like the American – whack with the handbag.'

'What Amer – oh, *that* American.'

'That was pretty snap snap.'

'Yes, well . . .'

'Your reflexes are too agile, my dear love. I warned you when you were sixteen you were going to be an unhappy extremist when I tried to explain to you that that boy Andrew was not worth a trip to Calvary.'

'Who's Andrew? Do you mean Angus?'

'Angus. A weevil, a favour-currying little inveigler who caused the trouble between your mother and Cissie.'

'Angus was a victim.'

'How so?'

'He was used.'

'How?'

'My mother needs adulation.'

'Well, he was a born ingratiator. I never once saw him when he wasn't smiling at someone.'

'*I* did.'

'I think you've decided that after the fact.'

'After what fact?'

'After the fact of his sudden going, which you decided to accept as a loss, when you decided to adopt him as a lost love and you were having a most gratifying time being Niobe-all-tears...'

'Oh, bosh, Marcus – balls, in fact.'

'That was all right when you were sixteen – all pubescent girls have lovely little ethereal affairs and unrequited love is marvellously fulfilling – but, my darling, you are now twenty-two and past the age when you should believe your own romances. It's a matter, if you don't mind my saying, of a lack of self-value, my Pippa. Your trouble is...'

Her trouble, she knew, looking at her big knees, was facing a growing and terrible conviction that as well as being vain he was commonplace under this drag he wore of being a witty savant. He'd rather be thought queer than square and God knows (she felt the thorn in her side) he was anything but queer. But now all of a sudden he was being unoriginal, was saying the same things everyone said, things she knew backwards, and worse, he had begun to sound, as people invariably did when they gave advice, gratuitous and smug (for your own good if you don't mind my saying and only because of my fondness for you), which always led to the inevitable truism that she was a fantasist who must stop hiding and get out, break loose and have a Real Experience with pain and joy and so become the Real Person she was and because of the terrible pleasure it gave them to rain down these truisms, they peppered their feeble denunciations with endearments. What I mean, my darling, is that you are a horse's ass, pet.

'See what I mean, pusscat?'

'Oh, yes, yes.'

She was miserable at the news of him. She would get up and run before he got to his coming clincher that she was letting D. K. Durfee imagine her life for her.

'I think you are funking out.'

'P'raps I am.'

'I want to see you open up like a great big *clam,* silly. Open up to everyone, even people you dislike. Nobody's all good or all bad, Pippa.'

'*Really?*'

'Nobody's *all* black, loveboat.'

'I suspect my brother might not entirely agree with you about Jap prison guards but then –'

'There you go, see. Darting into *extremes*. Running behind the joke. The dramatic situation. I'm rather afraid that what you're doing is –'

His eyebrows were drawn together in two arcs of concern, he was having intense pleasure but either God or herself must stop him from saying it.

'I've got to go, Marcus.'

'Just a second – wait just a second. Sit down and let me finish. I'm afraid what you're doing is living a secret life away from all of us on the Bosporus. '

'On the . . .'

'Bosporus. The last time I tuned you in someone was planning an outrageous coup in Odessa.'

'Odessa is on the Black Sea.'

'Stop wriggling out of it, stop getting red in the face, now. I'm not making fun of your plays, cupcake, I think they're bloody good escapist fun and entertaining nonsense and I'm just as gripped by them when I *do* happen to tune in as your great unwashed public from coast to coast. But . . . darling, stop, do stop using *them* as a substitute for living.'

She closed her eyes and felt him sit beside her and he put his arm around her. So in the very last moments it was going to be flatulent and fatherly.

'Now, now,' Marcus said. 'Isn't it better to have the truth?'

Now she'd had her bitter medicine she supposed she was to be given a chocolate.

'It's not so *terrible,* is it? Now it's out, shall we have a smile? Shall we have a big kiss of forgiveness?'

It was the first time he'd ever kissed her on the mouth. She felt the surprising bristles of his moustache and his very warm mouth and then she opened her eyes and finding him so very close to her was jolting. She could pick out every single clean white hair and his mouth a little spitty and his pupils dilated in the intense pleasure of his goodness to her.

'After all, I do love you, you know,' he offered her. 'I love you.'

So she took the thorn out of her side and said, 'You are confusing me with my *sister,*' and got up, stepping not by plan but heavily on his velvet foot, and she went across the large room with considerable calm and took her coat and bag from the brocaded hall chair and opened the front door and went out and down the curved staircase with immense dignity and thought she heard him call out something – pig or frig it sounded like – and she knew she had photographed for her lifelong keeping his face at that moment when she said it and would use it to insulate herself against any pain she might have in the future about him and then when she reached the lobby he had come out onto his landing and he called down, 'Beatrice,' like an imprecation and, looking up, she saw him leaning over the balustrade and even from such a distance she knew the wound had been deep and would bleed a long time.

'Beatrice, *Be*atrice.'

'Good-bye, Marcus,' she said because it was the only true thing.

Adina had left a note on the hall table that she had gone to the movies. 'Off to the flicks,' said Adina's skimpy, stingy writing, and, 'Phone your sister when you come in.'

But Bea, without taking off her coat, sat down and asked a girl with adenoids what would be the delay to telephone Medlow Bath. The trunk lines were busy to the Blue Mountains but she placed the call. She went into the small living-room, which was wallpapered in hexagons and cubes of a thirties style and furnished like a dentist's waiting-room; the residence of two girls who left notes for each other, rarely met and even then only exchanged brief pleasantries and reminders of bills due. Adina was stingy. There were forty-watt bulbs in the lamps and so the dingy brownout persisted even here. This was not home, this was exigency.

Bea was thinking of home and seeing the long dark veranda and the rose lights of the bungalow and the big darkened hotel, which was closed for the duration. She felt she was six and wanted her mother, needed her mother, and of the things she would say on the phone, completely undramatically, sincere ...

Mother, could I come up for a few days or will you come to town, because I need to talk to you. I need ...

Like Marcus, her mother never credited her with any intuition, only that she was clever. Bea is clever, the clever one. But what her mother put away from her was the fact of their twin identities, their exact alikeness, so much craving for mutual admiration that they had had to conceal it under repudiation of each other, vying with each other to see who would deny it first, and so year after year they had circled each other in silent admiration and fear and spoke only in wit and scorn and sometimes, out of shame, in deep sarcasm about the possible truth of themselves and so drew blood. And oh, it is just *nothing*, her mother had said, but for your birthday she had said, giving her a darling little fur hat, and in her delight, in wanting then and there to fling her arms around this thin, beautiful cold creature and cry out all kinds of sugary cooings, she had welled up with tears at the desire and burst with the shock of it and so had pulled on the fur hat hard down over her ears to make herself look as hideous as possible and said that she would most certainly look like a great big *otter* in this, she'd better not go out in the woods in this lest she be shot dead by a hunter, and her mother had said, well, Bea, you are never much without a gun of some kind yourself, and turned and gone out of the room with the tall and don't-give-a-damn dignity that Bea had inherited and just now used on Marcus and . . .

But now she must steel herself, screw up her courage and also screw being a big horse's ass and afraid.

And Eve would listen, D. K. Durfee said, and now she saw them together, not in a sentimental blur but really together for the first time and talking all night on the veranda with the mountain mists coming up towards morning and one day, soon, not too long, her father would be dead and her mother would come to live with her. Now she was coming into their nice big flat with the best of the mountain furniture brought down and they had Mrs Dutton to look after them and oh, good, you thought of a fire, darling. I brought some of those nice little Norwegian sardines you like . . .

It spread, it coloured and took on life, expanding like one of her serials. Marcus arrested as a black-marketeer and they got his apartment and her chess had improved. Her gin rummy was brilliant.

She had reached the point where she had discovered for Eve a charming and well-to-do widower when the telephone rang.

'I have your call for you.'

'Hello.'

'Hello.' The line was bad. 'Mrs Dutton ? This is Bea.'

'Hello.'

'This is Bea.'

'Who is it?'

'Beatrice. Is Mother there?'

'Sorry, would you speak up, please?'

'Bea. Bea.'

'Oh, is it Bea? Oh, how are you? It's a bad line, isn't it? You keeping fine?'

'Yes, yes, thanks. Is my mother there?'

'You keeping up the good work, dear?'

'Yes, yes.'

'Oh, you're lucky to be where it's a bit warmer. We had a bit of real snow today.'

'Yes? It must be pretty.'

'Do you want to speak to Mrs St James, Bea?'

'Yes, please.'

'Yes. Hold the line, will you? She's at dinner but I'll go and call her. Hold the line.' After a long pause: 'Are you holding the line?'

'Yes, I'm holding the *line*.'

'I'll just go and get her if you'll hold the line, dear. Just hold on.'

She gripped the phone; this would be the time she would not fail herself, she would grab her mother's attention; things must now be said out loud.

She shook from nervousness waiting, following Mrs Dutton down the dark hall to the dining-room, where they would be sitting under the Tiffany lamp, and Mother would be in a heavy cardigan because of the cold and her hair very pale in the lamplight and now getting up and laying down her napkin, wearing the look of sardonic long-suffering she put on for interruptions and, 'Bea,' she would say to Daddy, who might or might not tonight be hiding in his delusion of lunacy.

Whatever the evasions, she would insist they must meet.

'Hello.'

Even with the bad connection the voice was the voice, drawling and unsurprised. Mother was never, surprised, never shaken.

'Hello,' Bea said.

'How are you?'

'All right, all right. You?'

'All right. Freezing here.'

144

'Hear you've got snow. '

'Yes. Pretty much want to come to town.'

'*Do* you? When?'

'What?'

'*When?*'

'When what?'

'When . . . I didn't understand. What did you say?'

'I said it was pretty watching it come down.'

'Oh . . . oh, yes.'

The lines crackled between her and the mountains and beneath the static she could tell her mother was curious, waiting for the reason.

'Daddy all right?'

'. . . want those long knee socks you left last time you were here? I was going to post them to you.'

'No. I don't need them; it's not cold here.'

'. . . yes, freezing. Well, I'll put them in the mail and there was a piece about you in the Katoomba *Times*. I'll enclose it . . . a laugh. We roared . . .'

Something about D. K. Durfee. This is what always happened by accident or on purpose when she phoned – an evasion.

And the three minutes ticking away.

She grabbed a pencil and dug into the table, then said very loudly, 'Are you coming down soon?'

'Down?' Mrs St James disappeared into the static and was gone for a while, then reappeared loudly. '. . . cope with the damn blackout and having to stay overnight at an hotel unless I really have to, Bea. They've discontinued the six-fifteen, did you know?'

'No, I didn't.'

'Daddy's *very* put out. But it means virtually impossible to get back unless . . . '

'Yes, well . . .' She broke the pencil and gasped, 'I had a fight tonight and I feel rather lousy. In fact, I'd like to talk to you.'

'. . . I s'pose at the Y M C A. I mean the Y W C A, but so cheerless.'

'Three minutes, madam. Do you wish to extend?'

'No, I guess . . . yes. Yes, hold it, will you? Hello? '

'Yes, well, that's the three minutes, Bea. I better hang up now.'

'No I extended.'

'Oh, did you? Well . . . '

'I was saying I had a fight tonight.'

Either her mother again hadn't heard or wouldn't hear. Go and shout it to the mountains, she told them, not to me; don't bring your troubles into this house. Turning away so as not to hear even when you stood right next to her and said what you hoped was comforting on the veranda that morning when Mother had lost her toy, when Lady Cissie, who no longer had to be a toy, no longer had to pretend to be helpless, took all the twigs out of her hair and packed her straw suitcase and came down and said that the hotel car was taking her to the train and, being all cried out and able to speak without emotion or anger, said, 'Fancy *you* being jealous of *me*,' and kissed Eve on the cheek and went off, shaking her head and laughing at the wonder of it and Eve just stood there under the hanging ferns scrutinizing the mountains as if she had been told to find the emu on them or die and after a long time you said, 'Never mind,' at which she had turned her head at last with a look of beautifully contrived curiosity and said in a tone as flat as reading a timetable, 'Never mind about *what*?'

And now it was just as painful having to raise the voice to say, 'I had a fight.' To have to raise the voice to say I am depressed, I am in pieces tonight. Do you care that I am? To have to shout these things on a telephone was to humiliate the heart.

'A fight,' her mother said distantly. 'Do you mean business?'

'No, a friend,' Bea yelled, informing the relay operators all the way to the mountains and back.

Characteristically the line cleared at that moment; the operators wanted to hear.

'Oh, that's better,' Eve said. 'I can hear you now.'

'Me too.'

'Go on. What were you saying?'

'I said I had a fight with an old friend tonight.'

'I see.'

'And . . .' And what? The lines hummed. 'Well . . .'

'Is it serious?'

'Yes.'

'I mean, is this a man? Is this a serious thing?'

'Well . . . yes and no.'

'I see.'

'I suppose it was more serious with *me*.'

'Yes?' They both waited, miles apart, to see who would speak next and eventually they spoke together. 'An affair?' Mrs St James asked and at the same moment Bea told her mother that she would like to talk to her. 'I thought I might come up,' Bea said.

'. . . the wrong chap perhaps?'

'What?'

'I said, do you think you picked the wrong chap perhaps?'

'No, I said it wasn't an *affair*.'

'Oh.'

Some crickle-crackling then occurred but through it the message came very clearly from the mountains that perhaps this call was irrelevant.

'Not an affair in that sense of the word, hard to explain . . .' Hard to explain why I'm calling at all. 'But someone I'm madly fond of and so I feel rotten about it. I'd like to talk to you.'

'Yes, glad you did. Well, is it repairable?'

'No, never. I absolutely did it in forever.'

'Well, if it isn't repairable I'd say — Just a minute, Bea, hold on a minute, will you? Mrs Dutton, take the Judge his dessert, serve the Judge his dessert, don't wait for me. Well, Bea, if it isn't something you can patch up, the best thing is to forget it. No use regretting . . .'

'Quite so. Awfully wuffish, regret.'

'I didn't hear you.'

'I said I agree. No use.'

'No use, you see, if you can't mend your fences.'

'No, I can't.'

'Best advice I can give you.'

'Yes, yes, thanks.'

'What?'

'I said, yes, I know.'

'I'd say come up for a few days but Daddy's having a gloom . . .'

'No, no, I can't – couldn't.'

They hung on now, waiting only to be rescued.

The lines hummed, crackled a little.

'Six minutes, madam.'

'Have to go now, Mother.'

'That's the six minutes so –'

'Talk to you soon.'

'– try not to be depressed about the thing.'

'No. No. No, I'm not depressed, not depressed. Give –'

'Drop a line.'

'– my love to Daddy.'

'I'll tell Daddy. Good night, Bea.'

'Good night.'

She hung up the receiver.

Go to hell, she said.

The telephone rang immediately. She snatched it up.

'Yes?' Go to hell, whoever it was.

'Welllll,' said her mother. 'You are in a stinky, bite-the-head-off mood, aren't you?' said her mother's voice drawlingly.

'Who's this?'

'Who's *this*?'

'Oh, it's you.'

'*C'est moi*,' Stevie said. She sounded martini-ish. 'You have been gaggling on that phone for hours.'

'I've been talking to Mother.'

'What's the matter with her?'

'Nothing. Just something she wanted to discuss with me.'

There was a crash of ice falling into the phone and Stevie said, 'Can you come over for a snort?'

What, *now*?'

'Yes. *S O S*.' Stevie reduced her voice to a husky croak of intrigue. She was constantly intriguing these days; she turned her head frequently to see if she were being overheard.

'I'm in the bedroom,' she informed Bea. 'I can only talk a minute. Can you come?'

'No.'

'Do you have a date?'

'Yes.'

'Come en route, come just for half an hour.' There was another deafening crash of ice. 'Gabriel's here. '

Gabriel was Stevie's American Colonel. Bea had decided not to make him an issue although Stevie was intent on doing so; she glittered with inference and made large gestures of pretending Gabriel was nothing to her in order to publicize her affair.

'I have to keep my voice down, Bea. Gabriel's here and the maid is off and Bill's mother's just arrived.'

'I see.'

'Old Mum Seward has walked in, see? She's in the nursery with Miranda now but you grasp the situation.'

'Yes and no.'

'Which?'

'Yes, I understand the situation, and no, I can't come.'

'Please.' Stevie sounded desperate. 'I don't want her writing to Bill that I entertained a man here alone.' Someone had come into the bedroom because she pealed with laughter and said. 'Oh, Bea, how funny, oh, you *are* a funny chicklet. But get here, will you, you're late as it is.'

'No,' Bea said to the dial tone.

Snap snap. I do not run – snap – when everyone calls. Is that what Marcus said among other things?

She went into the kitchen and took down a frying pan. Adina's weak kitchen light only cast muddy shadows on the sickly blue linoleum and the walls painted stale turnip. The colour of the kitchen alone was enough to depress a manic. The refrigerator always smell of the odds and ends Adina saved, wrapped in wax paper. Bea unwrapped something that might be a baby's hand. She found bacon but only one egg. The bacon rashers were stuck together and tore.

'Oh, I don't know,' she said.

She could not avoid hearing the tap dripping into the sink or the unpleasant tooting of ferries outside in the brown night. She sat down at the kitchen table and rested her chin in her hand and felt the cold, silent room contain her and her alone and remind her of it with its little noises, drips, creaks. She could see her shadow on the wall. She was gigantic.

'Oh, well,' she said.

She thought now about the gas: about how long it would take before someone smelled it and whether at first it would be very horrible, whether she would vomit violently and twist and turn on the floor, trying to escape it, and turn it off. Someone had said that what saved Lesley Ann when she did it was that halfway through she must have changed her mind and that she had crawled towards the door and clawed away the blanket she'd put down and when they found her, almost gone, she was breathing through the crack.

It would be like Lesley Ann to do the thing wrong, change her mind, be an anticlimax.

She went to the stove now and opened the oven and looked at the jets and knew that she would put her head right in there and get it done before anyone found her. Also she would leave no note. Let them wonder for the rest of their lives which one of them had been guilty.

The kitchen clock ticked away loudly. Well?

Oh, hell, she said, I'll go to Stevie's.

When Hilda, Stevie's housekeeper, opened the door, Bea said, 'Oh I thought you were –' Off for the night she had almost said, realizing immediately that, of course, she had been tricked.

'They're in the study,' Hilda said and then clapped her hands angrily. 'Bed. Bed,' she called out and Bea looked up to see Miranda's face peering through the banisters with the look of supreme indifference she had inherited from Stevie. Bea waved but Miranda continued to stare. She was able to withstand all exhibitions of human affection with the same equanimity with which she withstood hurt. She had been handed down from her grandmother. 'And here's Bea,' Stevie said, unsurprised, knowing without a doubt Bea would come. The two Americans stood up in their beautifully pressed beige uniforms.

'My sister, Bea St James. Captain Alcott.'

'Orcutt.'

'Orcutt. Corey Orcutt? Oh, American *names*. And you know Gabriel.' The Colonel, the older man, said, 'Hello there, Bea. What will be your poison?'

'Scotch,' Bea said, seeing there was plenty of it. Stevie's house was stocked with genuine Scotch, American cigarettes, Juicy Fruit, Kleenex, Coca-Cola, the GI editions of new novels. She handed out lipsticks and said 'God-awful' a lot. The American voices so constantly around her were infectious and little burrs and flattened vowels had penetrated into her speech.

'Good to see you, lover,' she said.

She was stretched out on the red leather sofa. In her black velvet pants and white silk shirt tied at the waist with a wide scarlet sash, she looked like a young *vivandière*. She seemed slightly above everything; she was swimming in her success. If she said there would be fish for dinner the Colonel seemed to find it entrancing; so discovered to be dazzling and adorable, she glowed. She had never been so extraordinarily a beauty as she was now and she had acquired a whole new set of mannerisms to go with it. She had always been a sometimes haughty and often scathing girl but she had now softened and was full of little winning ways. The Colonel called her 'baby' and patted her affectionately.

'Go on with the story,' Stevie said. 'He was telling us a story about what's-her-name.'

'I was telling them,' the Colonel said, putting Bea's drink by her, 'about Evalyn Walsh McLean.'

Stevie said, 'But tell, go back a minute and tell how it happened. Tell Bea the name of the man you were with.'

'H. Dean Longswiller.'

'H. Dean Longswiller,' Stevie said. 'Don't you love it?'

'Anyway –'

'If I didn't know you better, I'd say you made it up. H. Dean Longswiller, Bea. Are you ready?'

'Anyway' – the Colonel patted Stevie gently to cede the floor – 'I was with H. Dean at this purrticularly large party in this purrticularly large house in Washington. Washington, DC, that is, and H. Dean had to go to the john – '

'The loo,' Stevie translated.

'The john. Had to go to the john and he was gone a helluva long time. Well, finally he came back downstairs and ... you see, this is a tremendous big house in Washington –'

'D.C.' Stevie said.

'Let me tell it, baby. So eventually, after a helluva long time, H. Dean came back and this is what he said to me, this is no paraphrase. This is exactly what H. Dean said to me.'

Here the Colonel paused for attention and spread out his large pink hands as he probably had done a thousand times telling the story.

'H. Dean said to me, "Gabe, I opened one of the bedroom doors by mistake, and here's what I saw. Upstairs in one of the bedrooms Evalyn Walsh McLean is lying asleep in her evening dress. There is a crack in the ceiling. On the floor are her shoes and in the toe of one of her shoes is the Hope diamond." '

Whoever this Evalyn Walsh McLean was and what the Hope diamond was and why it should cause even a smile, let alone a cacophony of laughter, was beyond Bea but the Colonel had let it be known that it should by throwing back his head and roaring. His laughter was artillery fire, mowed them all down, mowed Stevie down first and she fell towards him in agony and then back again with her peculiar laugh that started low and went up the scale to a point and down again.

'Oh ho ho ho ho *ho*,' Stevie went and then down: '*Ho* ho ho ho ho.' Concealed under this fusillade, Captain Orcutt leaned towards Bea and said, 'The Hope diamond once belonged to Marie Antoinette and is supposed to bring its owner bad luck, which may or may not have some connection with the crack in the ceiling.'

'Thank you,' Bea said.

'Now that is the God's truth,' the Colonel assured them.

'Oh' – Stevie was gasping convincingly – 'it's the crack in the ceiling I like best.'

'And in the toe of one shoe ...' The Colonel began again and Captain Orcutt sighed and looked deeply into the shine on his shoes. Containing, he implied, no diamond, no hope either. The Colonel, having expelled all his laughter, lay back in his chair and looked rather joyless, looked seriously to Stevie for whatever trick she would like him to perform next. It was a look of patient canine faithfulness and adoration. It was the identical look that had frequently been on Bill Seward's face; Bill Seward's kind, honest, dull face, as open as a blank cheque onto which Stevie could write thousands if she chose; good old sweet Bill Seward of the tea Sewards, searching for an expression to put on that empty face, but until he was given the hint, the clue to what was expected next, drifted, peered around doors to find her, an empty face painted on the balloon was Bill looking around a door (someone outside holding the string might let go and the face would go smiling up to bump against the ceiling), then, oh, here you are, he would say, did you call me? No, darling. I thought I heard you call me. No precious. Are you O.K.? Yes, angel. What are you doing? I am reading, my love. Any good? Not bad. Had you thought of wanting to go to the tennis match? I am too pregnant. In a deck chair? In any chair. Do you feel queer, old thing? No darling, I don't feel queer if you mean in the physical sense. Want anything? No. Want an orange, if I get you one? What about some grapes? Like some grapes? Nnnnnnoooo, thank you, sweetheart. What would you like? I think I'd just like to go on reading.

The balloon floated away.

Nice Bill, for some years now existing only in a silver frame on the bookshelf, looking out, resolute, determined that We Will Win, unquestioning about war and not afraid of flak or candour, and so wrote across his RAAF chest in unimaginative handwriting, 'To my Beloved Wife . . .' wrote down to below his navel about this photograph watching over her until (few read on past his navel out of acute embarrassment) he returned. Your own Bill. Dear Bill had been on the shelf for some years now. It had been with the same obtuse candour that he rose to his feet to reply to the wedding toast by reciting in a deadly honest and painful monotone, 'She walks in beauty like the night,' while holding stiffly at arm's length a champagne glass extended towards his radiant Stevie, who had closed her eyes, surely, everyone guessed, because she was so dazed with happiness, but Bea crumbling bread nearby, could see that Stevie's hands were clenched so tightly that her new ring was sunk dead white into the flesh and that when she did open her eyes and look at him, her smile was clever. Then when everyone drank and the unwary turned to each other in renewed conversation he had held up a hand for silence and then begun a careful inventory of the merits of the St James family, beginning with his honour and being sweetly grateful to each of them in turn, ticking them off on his prepared notes as 'my gracious and lovely mother-in-law, Mrs St James, my brother-in-law and soon to be brother-at-arms ... last but by no means least my little sister Bea' – which had *had* to cause some mirth, Bea being the biggest bridesmaid you ever saw, sitting there in her tent of pink tulle and her pink satin shoes the size of canoes. But she frowned at the laughter not because of herself, but because there was not a chromosome of wit or malice in dear Bill. He thanked the Reverend Mr Thomas, he thanked the organist, he thanked the choir and lastly, leaving them modestly to the end, his parents. Then he asked everyone to rise and join him in the most serious toast of the day, to the success of the allied fighting forces everywhere. He might be the last of the heroes, Bea thought. He might be the very last of the dying believers in the golden future, the dream, a just and lasting peace with honour; the spirit of Anzac, the flag, the Empire. The eye of God in the sky.

And 'I'm bloody lucky,' Stevie kept saying. She had hiccups. She sat on the bed in her slip and avoided all efforts to get her into her going-away suit, staring out at the sad blueness of the mountains, getting up to light another cigarette and then sitting down again not looking at anyone and saying resentfully, 'I *said* it, didn't I? I'm bloody lucky.' Then when he came upstairs looking for her for the first time (in what was going to be a marriage of looking for her) and bringing with him a deadly dull and witless telegram someone had sent them urging them to 'get started with Shell,' Stevie had dutifully laughed and worked hard at it to please him because it was from a chum of his and he actually thought it was funny. She had worked herself up into her Oh ho ho *ho*'s but all the time she pushed at him with her hands, pushing him a step back at each ho ho an then she had not been able to stop and had lain on the bed in such a fit of laughter that she kicked and rolled in it and every time they came to her with the dress, with the shoes, she went off into new paroxysms. When Bill, baffled, said he didn't think it was all *that* funny, she rolled off the bed onto the floor and said, '*You* are the funny one,' and acted out her hysterics until the girls in their tulle rushed for water and cold cloths but it was her husband who took command, who pulled her up onto her feet and shook her like a rag doll and barked air-force orders at her to stop it, who then held her and rocked her and said certain quiet and private things to her that seemed to calm her. She put her arms very tightly around him and said, 'I'll be good now. I'll be very very good,' and when she finally came downstairs she looked subdued and dutiful on his arm as if by a certain pressure of inner force she had turned adult.

When she kissed Bea good-bye, delaying with Bea longer than the others, she gave her a secret look that implied, 'You know,' and Bea replied as secretly, 'Yes.'

But not for years did they ever speak about it. Not until long after Bea had begun the sequential relationship with Marcus did Stevie bring it up.

It was before her Americans started coming, it was while Stevie was being the war wife and home-front mother. She was ostentatiously knitting khaki socks for Bill; the needles clicked and darted as if the outcome of the war depended on her alone and Bea was in the middle of an opinion which happened to be one of Marcus', so much Marcus' opinion in ideas and in words that she was caught stealing it red-handed. Stevie suddenly said, 'Are you and Marcus having an affair?' And Bea, startled at finding herself partially exposed, alarmed at finding Stevie so close to the wish, drew herself up into an enormous denial. 'He's *fifty*,' she said. As if that had anything to do with it.

Stevie stopped knitting and was suddenly very still for a long time and then said:

'If it's true that it only happens to you once in your lifetime, I've *had* it.'

All over, kaput, she said. She talked in her own voice for once, without modulations. She told Bea about Marcus from the beginning to the painful end. From the time she first sensed him. She had scarcely taken off her school hat for the last time and

156

was lowering hems when he had first looked right at her, pushed her off dizzy heights in herself she didn't know previously existed. From then on they careened towards each other on a collision course and whatever was to happen was preordained, as it was in their natures and their cards that whenever it came to an end, it would be violently and with a mutual feeling of disgrace. Stevie talked of herself in the past tense. She talked of herself as a survivor might tell of a dead victim and Bea, tracing the days and nights of that time, saw the plaster fruit on the ceilings of the bedrooms of the Ritz Hotel in the yellow waning afternoons when sometimes, Stevie said, they had nearly been caught by a maid or the housekeeper. All the long sad days of Stevie and Marcus, leaving bedrooms separately, wearing looks of innocence. All that long time, Stevie said, when she came to life in the late afternoons, all the series of codes and signals they left for each other and the times when she waited in 107 or 16 or 12 and sometimes he didn't come. 'But just being alive . . .' Stevie said and left it unfinished; talking of herself during the time of her life. Now dead, she implied.

'But the *end* . . .'

Well, she had really put the screws on him, because she knew that it was useless anyway and so why not put on a display of fireworks and go out with a big explosion of stars. They had been standing at the lookout in the dark with only the faint reflected glow that came from distant floodlighting, and then without giving him any warning she had climbed over the fence and hung on.

'You know where there's only about a foot or so of gravel beyond the fence and then it drops away two thousand feet?'

Bea saw her plainly in the dark. She had on a silver dress, she said, and Bea said noncommittally she remembered the dress, go on. Stevie had cajoled Marcus and threatened at the same time to let go of the fence if he took a step near her. She had kept him in the sweat of it for nearly twenty minutes while she appealed to him in the language of screenplays not to desert her, to take her with him wherever he was going. There she was in the faint light in the silver dress and just a hand's length away was space over air currents and darkness that went down two thousand feet and all the time she held Marcus at bay and spoke to him in a vibrant but hysterical voice saying things like, 'What do I have to live for?' 'I'd go to the ends of the earth for you.' 'Tell me that you love me,' she said in the language of films she had seen. 'I can't live without your love.' All the time she hung a second from death.

'Oh, poor Marcus,' Stevie said and picked up her knitting again and went hell for leather at it for dear nice Bill.

'Oh ho ho ho *ho*. *Ho* ho ho ho oh,' Stevie went and, leaning towards Bea, gave her a gentle push with every ho ho. Her eyes were as dark and sad, as empty of reflection, as the great darkness of the abyss in the mountains over which she had swung years ago.

'Oh ho ho ho ho,' went Stevie, knitting in time to it and seeming to be as sad and empty as all the deserted hotel bedrooms in the old Ritz Hotel were now, the wind blowing against their locked doors.

'Now,' the Colonel said, alerting them, synchronizing watches was in order. 'Now dear, are we going to Romano's? Do you want to dance tonight, dear?'

'Up to you, lover,' Stevie said.

'Well now, the only reason I'm asking, baby, is that if we are going to go to Romano's, then I should call up now and get a reservation and also you should start to think about getting dressed.'

'Fix me one drink and then I'll go get dressed,' Stevie said and the Colonel put a large pink hand on her, taking her glass, and said, 'You know what occurs to me, baby?'

'What, lover?'

'That I let Corey here take my car – I have my staff car here, Corey – and send it back for us.'

Oh, no, Gabe.'

'You'll never get a cab way out here ... Now, he can run you in to town and then by the time he gets back here, we'd be ready. Don't you think that's a better idea, baby? You'd have time to change then, baby.'

'Fine, lover, divine.'

'See, he can run you in to wherever you're going right now and then by the time he gets back, Stevie will be dressed. I insist, Corey, no trouble, man. Now finish your drink, no rush. Did you have a coat?'

'Well, it's been fun – er – Stevie ...'

'Oh, look ... come again.'

'Say, Corey. Here's something just occurred to me. Look, maybe you could drop Bea wherever she's –'

'Oh, no, no. I'm no distance –'

'You have to go by the Cross, right?'

'Yes, but –'

'Fine, that'll be fine, see. That way we get to get Bea where she's going and get to take you and so on and everyone's in luck that way, see?'

'Swell. Well, I guess –'

'Glad I thought of it. Not at all – don't say another word. This your coat? Look here now, you give me a call while you're here – you make sure you give me a call if there's anything at all I can do.'

'I certainly appreciate –'

'Think we're all kind of tied up tomorrow, aren't we, baby? Still, give a call ... mighty glad ... and you too, Bea.'

'I think we have been processed,' Captain Orcutt said in the car a few seconds later while the Colonel gave the driver his orders. The Colonel loomed very large in the doorway of Bill Seward's house; the Colonel – Stevie had let it drop like a pin – was in civilian life a Wall Street broker and, as a matter of no interest, a widower with two married daughters.

'Off you go,' the Colonel called out and saluted them off.

'Anywhere near Macleay Street for me,' Bea told the driver.

'Is that in town?' the Captain asked.

'No, that's Kings Cross, a suburb.'

'I guess I'm in town, in Sydney, or whatever you would call it.'

'That's town.'

'Town. Well, they've put me in a place called the Royal Park Hotel.'

'Oh, yes, I know it. It's by Hyde Park. It's a private hotel.'

'As opposed to being a public hotel?'

'I think it means they have no bar.'

'It has no bar. It has no dining-room. It has a kind of creeping inertia about it and I must say I was surprised when the lady at the desk said I was lucky because it's so modern.'

'Yes, it is modern.'

'It is?'

'I mean, they only built it just before the war.'

'Oh.'

Well, she was grateful he didn't make that crack they all did about 'Which war?' He wasn't one of those grab-bag Americans who tried to latch onto you in the first second of meeting with a hello there, little lady, you and I seem to be the only ones here not screwing, Hank's the name.

'I could've gone to one of the officers' clubs, but this is the first time I've been in an honest-to-God city for ten months –'

'Oh, really?'

'– so I felt I'd like to sit my fanny down in a huge marble tub.'

'Ah, yes.'

'Not knowing anything about Sydney – never been able to get down to Australia up to now – I had pictured something like the old Monteleone in New Orleans – something old-fashioned with tall ceilings and the gilt wearing off of everything, kind of Victorian with ferns around, which I like. But I got modern. You're very lucky, the lady told me, to get into a modern.'

His voice in the dark was strong and very American and not self-pitying in any way but his face, flashing on and off next to her each time they passed under a brown street light, looked thin and bewildered and a bit angry at being put in the modern sterility of the Royal Park.

'Maybe you can get them to move you,' she said.

'Oh, I only have till Monday,' he said. He gazed away from her and they drove through Rushcutter's Bay towards Kings Cross. Something caught his interest. 'Is that a castle?' She looked too, sorry to have to disappoint him. 'It's the tram sheds,' she said. 'Oh, yeah?' He sat back, he sighed. It might be just as well if his leave were over, the way things were going.

Yet his voice was not sorry nothing was happening; she liked his voice, very strong and very American.

Lonely as hell.

She was tempted to ask if he was having a bloody awful time but that could lead to perhaps having to offer to do something about it, take him to the zoo, the Botanic Gardens.

But he had sat back, had disappeared into the darkness and was no longer visible except for a flash now and then of his perfectly tailored pinks and his officer's shoes. He may have gone to sleep, they went for so long in silence, and anyway what did it matter because they were climbing the hill now to the Cross and in a moment or two she would never see him again.

'Anywhere near here,' she told the driver.

'Where is this we are at?' the Captain asked, not showing his face.

'This is the Cross,' Bea said. 'Good-bye.'

'Good-bye,' he said, shaking hands and, as the driver opened the door, alighted with her. 'I guess I'll get out here, Sergeant. It doesn't look any worse than Sydney.' He returned the sergeant's salute and then they were walking down the browned-out crowded Friday-night street.

He walked beside her, his hands in his pockets, saying nothing, crossing when she crossed, turning corners when she turned. He seemed to be neither enjoying himself nor bored.

He appeared to have utterly forgotten she was there, looming up beside him. She was so conscious of not being with him that it wouldn't have surprised her at all if she had swung away from him and seen him stride on ahead without even noticing. Very faintly he was singing something under his breath that sounded like 'Abide with Me'.

Then, passing a small park where there were benches of couples embracing, he said, 'Anyplace around here we could get a drink if you would like?' He had an odd way of not parsing sentences. Nowhere after six, she told him. 'You're in blue-nose Sydney, not New Orleans. But you could go to one of your own clubs.'

'I don't feel like drinking with a lot of lonely guys,' he said.

She thought for an uncertain second of inviting him up – 'Well, I only live a step' – but it might look like a feeble solicitation (not on a small girl, but on a giantess invitations up could sound like a last bleat of hope) and she wasn't sure there was any booze in the house and Adina would be certain to come in and ask did she really need the light on in the hall.

So they stood looking in opposite directions while she grew hot with shyness and then he said he figured he would walk back to his modern hotel.

'Well . . .'

'So . . .'

Right. O.K. Hope you have . . .

He was gone and instantly she was cooled off but with the niggling thought that it was true she always funked out. She saw him walk away. He looked unfamiliar among the familiar things. He was out of place. He didn't know whether to turn this way or that at the corner. He was miles and miles from the heart of anything. He stared at the strange public telephone box as if by a miracle it would ring and be for him. At that moment one of the pompadoured little sluts approached.

'Look,' Bea said, amazed at herself, having run, 'I was just thinking . . . I haven't had dinner yet, have you?'

Tried to be as casual as possible because the effort had made her heart rock and again she was blushing strenuously.

'You seemed to be in a hurry,' he said.

'But we'll go Scotch,' Bea said and then had to explain that it had nothing to do with drinks. Pay their own. 'Oh . . . Dutch,' he said and laughed for the first time. He had a very deep cleft in his chin and, with his black eyes under their big brows, his face was formidable until he smiled. He must be tall because she could look up to him just a fraction.

When they pushed through the blackout velvet strips at the door of the California it was packed and it would be twenty minutes, 'at *least,*' the hostess told them sourly, with pleasure. At the Tulips a gaunt ham bone of a woman in Dutch costume said, 'The kitchen goes off at nine o'clock.' 'With a bang probably,' Bea said. The Elizabethan Inn was shutting for the night after their ten-minute walk there. When they finally got seated at the Oriana in the garden annexe (and this is nice, she said, because if you lean very far to your left you can see the moon) the waitress brought what she said was 'the supper maynu'. No, dinner was off. They ought to know better, her look said and went up and down Captain Orcutt as though he were standing in the shower and then cast a scornful look at Bea. How did *you* come to cop a nice one like him? 'Butterfly cakes and cream *tarts* and a nice cup of tea,' Bea said witheringly. 'What we'd like is a *steak*.' 'Arf-past nine,' the waitress said. 'There's a war on, you know.' 'I don't know how to explain our way of life to you,' Bea said as once more they hit the street, 'but this is a good sample.'

'War is hell,' the Captain said. He might possibly have come through some nightmare of a beach landing and be making a crack at her life of little inconveniences as Muffet had done earlier, so she bit her lip. He stood by, waiting for orders.

There was nothing for it now but the last resort. 'Come on,' she said, hating to do it, but they had to go somewhere now she'd got them into it.

She led him up the stairs where a sign said THE SALZBURG and a large painted pink hand pointed imperiously up. There were people waiting on the landing and she pushed past them to the door and looked around the crowded room under the red lamps cloudy with cigarette smoke; the smell of deeply frying food was everywhere.

She caught hold of a busy waiter and said, 'Could you get Mrs St James for me.' He looked around and pointed and Bea waved and held up two fingers dramatically.

Under a stag's head, Liesl stood and ignored them, ignored Bea's uplifted arm (paying her back for never coming and then wanting special favours); looked deliberately away and spoke to waiters, ordered a table cleared, beckoned to four people to come and seated them, presented them with menus and spoke to each one in turn, recommending her specialities. Liesl had taken to dressing with calculated disregard for the limitations of her figure. She was boxed into fuchsia silk, from which burst, at curious points, paper-napkin-like stiff lace. Two huge hoops of silver, each big enough for a canary to swing in, hung from her ears. In the atmosphere she'd created of an Austrian shooting lodge she looked ready to burst into song, accompanied by the waiters.

Bea said, 'My sister-in-law owns this ersatz *schloss*.'

'Think we'll make it?'

'If she ever looks this way . . .'

'Bea. Come.' Liesl swung towards them in a blaze of fuchsia, her stout feet planted into fuchsia shoes. She led them, one arm raised in what seemed to be a threatening gesture, to the little closed-in balcony room, where she squeezed them into a narrow corner table, forcing them into a tremendous intimacy of knees and thighs touching, Bea's great legs fighting with the Captain's, their feet mingling, stepping on each other as Liesl trapped them against the wall with the table.

'You are lucky because I keep this one for someone who doesn't come.'

'Thank you, Liesl. Liesl, I'd like you to meet Captain Orcutt.'

'Gut evening.'

'Happy to know you, Liesl.'

'You see, come at six when nobody is here.'

'Yes, but we couldn't come at six, Liesl.'

'Come at six, everyone is standing around, no one here. Then at nine o'clock comes everybody. Crazy. You want a good schnitzel? We have one tonight. This means here chicken livers but I think is off now. Here is, if you want fish for Friday, a bream in butter. Maybe you like the pork, Bea. You are stationed here?' Liesl looked at the Captain severely.

'No.'

'Captain Orcutt's on a few days' leave.'

'No I'm not.'

'Oh, I thought . . .'

'No. I'm on special-service duty. Requisitions.'

'Oh. Could you . . . would you mind moving a minute. You're sitting on my hand.'

'I'm *sorry*. Hurt you?'

'No.'

'Sure?'

Bea wagged her hand. Liesl was staring hard at them. Probably thought she'd picked him up. Liesl hung over them, her hoops swinging, and advised the pork in the threatening manner she used nowadays to family members. She was Mrs Tip, don't forget it. You like this with sauerkraut? Otherwise – she shrugged – it might be a matter for the *polizei*. But *do* come in the room, Liesl, the Judge doesn't feel comfortable with you half in and half out of the door, Eve said, and Liesl came in, looking at the floor, and Tip in his badly cut stiff new uniform explained rapidly in too many words about the shortness of time and leave and so it would be just the registry office and only the family *if* they wanted to come and all the time Liesl studied the floor with big red blotches on her neck as if she had been caught stealing and of course, her mother had said, no question about arrangements because it's entirely yours and Liesl's business, not ours. The Judge listened and made imaginary notes to counsel. Well, *any*way, Tip said to the silence they were all making, it's all fixed, his voice breaking in the brittle coldness of the room, the reception as bitter as the mountain air outside; he put his arm protectively around Liesl, who stood hunched up, ashamed and accepted; the court approving, the Judge was nodding listlessly to an inner thought and then (Bea thought with grace and ingenuity) Eve said, now does Liesl have a dress? I don't think you have anything to wear, do you, Liesl? Well then, as I don't think Daddy will terribly want to go down for the wedding – will you, Daddy? – well then, I was thinking that you and I, Liesl, would go down a day earlier on the morning train Wednesday and together we can shop for a really lovely dress, and Liesl, who had never taken her eyes off her shoes, at last raised her head and looked directly at Eve with an extraordinary ferocity but with a totally new and chilling dignity and smiled at Eve and said, '*I* get the dress.' Very well. Liesl. 'No, *I* get the dress.'

The dress was orange shantung with a hideous yoke and an orange velvet hat, orange bag and shoes. She looked hot to the touch even on this cold, rainy day; gusts of rain blowing against the dirty windows of the registry office, bare floors and the smell of government about it, smell of carbolic soap and the clerk in a greasy, shiny navy-blue jacket, wearing a dingy brown pullover under it and asking the required questions in a low voice, never once looking at them and mumbling, more like night court and them arraigned on a charge of having indecently persuaded for a lewd purpose a minor on said train station ... but they agreed solemnly, glumly, to take each other as husband and wife; it seemed more like a sentence, watching them from the back, Liesl bursting in orange finery, Tip in new khaki as stiff as undercarpet. Her hands, taking off her gloves, had swollen in fear and anxiety, fingers thick as parsnips so that they had trouble getting the ring on – ouch, she cried, *Gott* – and her wide face twisted in pain at the wrench. At the very moment of marriage he had hurt her, Oh, *Gott,* she cried, and then they turned and kissed in a jerky movement, banging their mouths together, and then held each other desperately and with such need (and disregard of anyone watching knowing about their need now) that Bea and Eve looked away.

Then a really dreadful lunch, chicken croquettes, Pimm's Cups first, at the Carlton in the Pink Room, which had been designed for gaiety in the twenties and let go; all gaiety gone now, it was a vast anachronism of pink and grey enamelled lattices and mirrors and made more depressing by a little *thé dansant* orchestra playing Lehár and dated pieces from old musical comedies, more like the sound of continuous weeping, and hanging around in the mauve air, under the chandeliers, was the sense of everything being over and done with; the war had ended everything. Your chicken all right? they asked each other; can I pass you the bread? Such was the wedding-feast conversation until Mrs William Seward, coming late, coming by some demonic perception in watermelon pink that managed to clash violently with the bride in orange, managed by her assumed gaiety and the glassy tinkle of her laughter to be insultingly gratuitous and rattled democratically on ('Do you realize, Liesl, I've never known what your other name was'), managing to convey subtly that they were sitting with the servant girl in public, and Bea saw that Tip had looked at Stevie with hatred and had drawn Liesl into the circle of his arm, where she rested uncomfortably propped against him, balanced on one buttock, while Tip murmured caressingly to her, saying, did you go upstairs and take a look at the room? Ja. Did you think it was all right? Oh, ja. They said we could've had a room in front but I said I thought we'd rather look out towards the park. Oh, is fine ja. So you're happy with the room, are you? Sure, sure. Because we can easily change it, Tip said, and drew Liesl closer

to him, almost off her chair, a halter around her neck, percept-
ibly examining her as wife and saying in a voice clotted with
possession that they had very good lemon ice-cream here; would
you like some lemon ice-cream to finish off with now, eh?
Would you?

All the time the little band playing 'Tea for Two' and 'One
Alone To Be My Own'. They talked of nothing over the melancholy violins; impossible to feel anything except Tip's tower-
ing resentment of them all. At last, the ordeal over, Stevie fled
on a flimsy excuse, they stood in the lobby and managed the
good-byes. Well, good-bye, Ma, he said, and thanks, you know
thanks for coming and kissed his mother said so long, Bea
thanks. Eve half bent to kiss Liesl who drew back, looking
astonished, and so Eve pretended she was removing a hair from
her and said, now, Liesl, you know you are to come to us any
time, *any* time you please once Tip's gone. Yes? Liesl said as
a question, yes? Then, opening her bag, Liesl took a clean
handkerchief and wiped her husband's mouth free of his mother's lipstick. Well, good-bye, Eve said and walked very fast
out of the Carlton lobby, the transfer having been made, and
Bea, scurrying along behind, managed to get the umbrella over
her mother, Eve was going so fast along the wet streets to get
away; surprised Bea by saying (because it was three in the afternoon), I want a drink, do you mind? They went into the Wintergarden and sat in the almost empty forest of black glass
tables and honey-coloured mirrors that showed them to be very
isolated and Eve drank two brandies one after the other, looking pale, looking old, and waited for Bea to make the comment,
for Bea to do something to restore her prestige to her, her priv-
ileges and opinions, for all these things had been turned upside
down and emptied like a wastebasket by Liesl. Well, something should be said. Had there ever been a sadder mating?
Had there ever been such a mismatch; even Liesl seemed
secretly to know it because what was the boy hoping to prove?
Bea was ready to reassure her mother on these points, that it

was poor Liesl who should be pitied, poor Liesl in her bright array, poor sow's ear, being drawn into Tip's fantasy and his need to make a sign of independence and what would become of poor Liesl when he at last understood what he had done and would then perhaps despise her? Bea leaned forward with these restorative thoughts, leaned towards her mother and said, 'Ugh, brandy. I hate even the smell of it. Oh, how can you *bear* to drink that stuff' and then, cramming on her gloves in her misery, looked around the handsome room with disgust. Well, Eve said at length, we've got three hours before our train. What do you suggest we do, Bea? Is there a good film at the Prince Edward?

'*Not* schnitzel,' she told Liesl, who was leaning on the table, her hoops swinging. How dare you insult my mother, how dare you that day when you wiped her away with your handkerchief. 'Nor do I feel like the sausages with sauerkraut.' Bea studied the menu, which stated rather pompously that the sole proprie-*tor* and directo*ress* was Liesel St James. There was something hermaphroditic about the idea which would be wasted on Liesl. Liesl was immune to ideas and safe from irony; she also saw nothing of other people's struggles not to offend her.

Come look, now here is her new home. An immense apart-ment in the old converted Wentworth mansion, a whole floor through, which held the harbour in a circle of gracious regency windows, blue water wherever you looked. 'Sun comes in day and night,' Liesl said straight-faced and, 'Look for the ceilings, Bea,' which indeed one might for they were lost in height. The bathroom was marble and the tub immense. This when God Almighty could not find a flat, when Bea had endured the shar-ing of Adina's depressing low wattage for nearly two years without hope of finding anything where she might live at least alone if not in comfort. But how did you *get* it, Liesl? Oh, I get. And look, and look, here is the carved wardrobe she bought for a bargain. Do you like, Bea? In the bedroom an acreage of double bed waiting for Tip if he ever came back. For Tip and the directo*ress*.

Oh, Liesl, how beautiful, how superb. Oh, yes. Liesl took it all in stride. The difficulty in being kind to Liesl because she had suffered so much was in her not noticing.

'And after that I have for you a torte, with honey,' Liesl said, appraising Captain Orcutt up and down. They had decided on stuffed cabbage. There appeared to be the possibility that dinner might actually happen. But, 'Are you still working on the radio, Bea?' Liesl asked.

'Yes,'

'I'm hearing something last Sunday night. This is the dark fate of somebody. Is this you writing this?'

'Oh, "Dark Destiny."'

'This is you?'

'Yes, Liesl.'

'But they say this is by Dokey . . . Donkey . . .?'

'Durfee.'

'Ah, Dofey. This is you?'

'Yes.'

'Oh, because I said to my friend Hedi, this is perhaps from my sister. Now I find this very hard to understand, you know? I find it very hard to make head and tail out of this.'

'Well, if you only tune in now and then –'

'This I know. What I'm saying is this is not real. This is not real people, you know?'

'Well, but this is what they *want*.'

'Yes? I think not. I think what is good is when you say, "Ah, this I know. This happens to me too." '

'I'm not paid to write works of art, you see.'

'But I'm not talking about works of art. I'm talking about what is real. What is real is good, yes? But this . . . All the time is some woman crying, crying she has found out her boyfriend has put time bomb in the Eiffel Tower. Is not possible.'

'I see you have that delicious Passionola fruit cup. Let's have some of that, shall we?'

'Sure, I get. How does he get it up there, this bomb? This is not likely, I think. And why does this woman not call up right away the police?'

'She will in a week or so.'

'But she is crying, crying all the time nobody believes her. Why she is not going right away to police?'

'It's what we call the love-duty conflict, Liesl.'

'This is to me ridiculous, you see, Bea, why you don't write something everybody will say, "Ah, this is true, this every day is happening to somebody"?'

'Because if I did two million people would stop listening to "Dark Destiny." That's why.'

It was like being on trial, with Daddy making a point, and Bea could feel herself growing hotter. It was like Daddy in front of Angus and she felt Captain Orcutt watching her.

'They *like* this?'

'Apparently, Liesl.'

'No, this I find hard to believe.'

'Well, *you* may, Liesl, but the general public and the makers of Oxo, the delicious consommé that heats in seconds, *adore* it.'

'Oxo. Is terrible. I wouldn't serve it. *They* like it?'

Count to five. 'Well, I think they like it, because we get over seven hundred letters a week.'

'This is not making it good.'

'I didn't say it was *good*, Liesl.'

'Then why you write this? I don't understand.'

'So my mother can stop having to work in the glue factory. ... Do you have a cigarette on you, Captain? No, Liesl, let's not bore Captain Orcutt with any more of –'

Liesl turned her attention to the American.

'You're listening to this "Dark Fate"?'

'No, but we have the same thing in America.'

'This is being heard too in America? Of *Bea*?'

'We have the same *type* thing – serials, soap opera. Oh, sure, it's very popular.'

'Ah, but *this* you don't have in America. Not Bea. No, because I know you *don't*.'

'He didn't say ...' Oh, God, why must you pick tonight for this?

Liesl leaned on the table, her hoops swinging.

'You want to know why for me this is ridiculous? I tell you why.' Liesl's face was scalding. 'I go through too much that is *real*. I see it happen all around me.'

Liesl lined up the salt and pepper shakers so they stood at attention; she breathed in deeply as she used once to breathe in the mountain air. She was expelled of something, relieved. She was grateful for it and now could be generous.

'She is good, you know? Bea. She is clever.' Liesl beamed on Bea, her sister-in-law. 'She is too good for this screaming, crying. Otherwise I wouldn't say, you know?'

'Right,' he said.

'You say only this to people you care? I am right?'

'Right.'

'She is baby now but *I* am experiencing these things. When she is experiencing something, she writes then something we will all say this is real because making *us* cry, I am right?'

'Right,' he said.

'Yes. *You* know. You tell her this.'

And Liesl, smiling at Bea, patted her on her braids with a nod of congratulation and left them jammed together there in bed.

After a while the Captain said, 'I think you ought to know my secret mission is to blow up the Sydney Harbour Bridge and it might make you feel better to know nobody will believe me.'

'I apologize about all that, Captain.'

'Oh, don't.'

'It's usually water off a duck's – but somehow she always – it's not what she says, it's a *way* –'

'Well, you know about the girl they used to say, well, she don't say much but what she says is awful pithy.'

'Ha.'

'But tell me more about what you do.'

'I tell you what, Captain. *I* promise not to tell you about that if you'll promise not to tell *me* about Evalyn Morse McLean.'

'Walsh McLean.'

'Whoever she is when she's home.'

'O.K., but I wish you wouldn't keep calling me Captain.'

'Major, then?'

She made bread balls urgently, wishing he wouldn't make sly attempts to put this on a pseudo-intimate level; Americans seemed to her to be always pushing their friendliness at you. Something to do with their fondness for public image.

He got the rebuff. He said with stiff mock etiquette, could he offer her another cigarette, Miss St James?

Leaning towards his polite lighter, she said, 'Didn't mean to be – thank you – to be curt, but nothing to do with Liesl or you. I've just had a Götterdämmerung of an evening.'

'Have you? I'm sorry.'

'Not your fault.'

'No, but I was beginning to think mine was taking a turn for the better.'

The sly American compliments, the way they had of slipping the pass in under the camouflage. Expecting you to be flattered.

'Jolly nice of you to – er – could you just reach the ashtray? Oh, isn't that ugly, isn't that the ugliest ashtray you ever laid eyes on.'

Angrily she excoriated the ashtray, creating, she hoped, a dampener on any more felicitous little prods on his part; they were just unlucky partners for dinner in this hideous little café. 'And all those stags' heads,' she said, deploring them.

'One of them just heard you.'

Well, he made the effort of a little joke and one must smile, at least. Looked at sideways he had a strong and handsome profile, but full face he widened and the planes of the face flattened into a disappointment. He had the features (he was thirty-four, she decided) that just miss; were he in the movies he would always be the co-pilot who at the end loses the girl to the pilot. 'However,' she said, 'it's a damned shame they had to pick July to send you so that you would miss the surfing.'

'Everyone tells me that. In fact, it was the very first thing the lady at my modern hotel said. You've missed the *surfing* ... ah ah. Well, I've been a little way behind everything in this war. From getting into it to always missing Bob Hope wherever I have been.'

'What's your assignment here?'

'Restricted.'

'Oh, forgive me.'

'Very very hush hush.' He held up a finger and looked at her darkly for asking.

'Sorry, Captain.'

He continued to hold up his finger, then after looking left and right said, 'Ping-Pong balls.'

'What?'

'I am here to requisition, among other things, five hundred Ping-Pong balls. Mine not to reason why but bats are not included on the requisition.'

'Are you a ... what would they call you?'

'Captain for Special Services. You've heard, I guess, of them getting the serum through but you are talking to the man who in the Second World War got the Ping-Pong balls through.'

'Oh, here's our Passionola.'

'This is a fruit drink?'

'It's made with the juice of passion fruit.'

'Passion?'

'Fruit, which is absolutely delicious and – what's the word – invidious to this country?'

'Indigenous?'

'That's it. But this is the bottled; not as good as the real thing but unfortunately the real thing is out of season this time of the year.'

He said, 'That wouldn't be surprising; my just missing it.'

'Taste and see,' she said and saw that he was holding the glass, waiting for her. Well, he had good manners.

'Cheers,' they said and he smiled at her. 'Terrific,' he said, sipping the Passionola.

'Mmmm. Not bad,' she said. '*Ping*-Pong balls? Really?'

A cold rain had begun at the ferry and then hardened into a stubborn downpour on the tin roof and therefore there was no point in getting on the boat, no pleasure tramping around the zoo in the rain just to see some miserable wet lions. Too bad, she said, that he wouldn't be able to see the zoo, one of the finest in the world. They had stood in the draughty wharf, him in his officer's raincoat, wondering what to do now. Too late for the matinees, too early for a drink, they had had their separate lunches so. . . . He said, 'It's up to you.' Well, Bea said, she didn't have an idea now that the zoo was out and the Botanic Gardens too. Well, there was the National Art Gallery or perhaps the mammal and reptile museum or . . .

But he had frowned, looking away, looking bored as he had done since they had met at three o'clock. A flop. She had no bright suggestions and (the thought struck her coldly like the falling rain) no Marcus now to call up and say, look, can I bring this American for tea? Adina used up Saturdays to clean the flat so . . . They had stood on trapped together in her indecision until he said, why didn't they go back to his hotel, where at least they'd be warm, order tea and maybe look in the paper and see if there was a show they could . . . Well, but . . . She was caught in her own folly of having made the date in the first place and while she was looking at her watch for help he called, 'Taxi.'

'The lounge doesn't open till five,' said the lady at the desk at the modern Royal Park Hotel; the lady was spiderish and unloved and wearing a verdigris velvet dress and vicious-looking steel beads. 'Ice?' she said. 'Well, I don't know, I'll *see* . . .'

She gave Bea the hard look of a searchlight. 'Not giving you very good weather, are we?' she said, handing him the key.

Very glad (going up in the little slow automatic lift to the third and top floor) that she had chosen to wear a beige wool dress with long sleeves that ended in hard white cuffs and had a turned-down white collar that gave her a subdued, secretarial look besides, hopefully, making her seem reduced in size.

She stood at the window now, looking down at Hyde Park, at the ugly hulk of the memorial to the war before this one, and she pulled the cuffs down over her wrists, feeling and looking secretarial and neuter being this mole colour, ready when he got off the phone to take a letter to the Adjutant Commander Ordnance Division about the order requesting file number et cetera; subject: Ping-Pong balls.

The phone had been ringing as they came into the room and for twenty minutes he'd been perched on the bed with papers spread around him and talking to someone about a missing voucher. Twice he had looked over and formed the word 'sorry' and twice she had pantomimed that she was happy as Larry, perfectly at ease, which she was not.

Coming in, she had been filled with a sense of recognition, had almost drawn back at the door expecting to see something she could not immediately remember, a sudden strong sense of the past not connected with the green walls or the unfriendly furniture. It was instantaneous, It was the subtle masculine smell, sweet and mysterious, which could be of shoe polish and hair oil and shaving lotion and clean after-bath man smell that had made her giddy with a nostalgia that was both sorrowful and exciting. It made him more defined now in his own place, sitting on his bed in the smallness of the room (even standing at the window she could have reached and touched him) in the pink glare of plastic lamp shades and with his old brown kid slippers under the dressing table; he was newly defined to her in great detail so that even with her back turned she could see every furrow on his face and tell the expression he was wearing by his voice. She stood at the sluicing window so touched by the immediacy of her feelings of having crossed into strangely familiar territory (another room, another time) that it was difficult to retain her secretarial stance and, in order to forget the other room, she turned and forced herself into the present moment and felt relieved at finding herself wrong; he had not been staring at her, was cradling the phone against his shoulder while he wrote left-handed. He was asking for a number to be repeated and he spoke loudly and with authority in his deep American voice and told somebody they had better shape up at their end and that he'd damn well report to H Q on their lousy duplicate index system. She wondered if this might all be to impress her (he was roaring away and some browbeaten sergeant was really getting it). Then when he winked at her in the thick of his tirade she was sure of it and the idea of it stretched in her and touched a hidden core of conceit in her, pleasantly. When he made gestures that he needed a cigarette, she took his pack and lit one and put it into his fingers.

Apart from his physical presence on the bed, running one hand through his thick, dark hair, there was no clue to him that she could see. If he was married, there was no picture of wife and children on the dressing table (and she glanced in the mirror at her curious face, prying), no snapshot of Mother and Dad. But patting her neat braids, she looked down and saw among the clutter of things that his breakfast coffee cup had been put down on top of an airmail letter and that the first line of the page read, '... bear to think you would consider me first. Dearest, I hate ...' The 'me' was underlined heavily three times and the handwriting was girlish; the *i*'s were dotted by little halos. He had spilled coffee onto this personal anguish.

'Now,' he said, standing beside her, and she turned guiltily from the inroads of a D. K. Durfee reverie about the girl so far away, writing tearfully in an empty room at night in a town in an American state – perhaps Kansas – and even in her loneliness and possibly some despair about him being careful to make her little halos over her *i*'s.

'Lucky we came back,' he said. 'They'd been trying to get me for two hours.'

'Oh. All straightened out?'

'Straightened *them* out, as you could hear. Nonpriority ... Oh, they love giving me that nonpriority bit but I won't take it, no, sir.' He exulted and rubbed his hands in delight, expanded. Energy flowed back in him and the gloom of the afternoon departed from him.

'Now,' he said, 'as a reward for your kind patience, what can I get for you that you would like?'

'Did they say no tea?'

'No tea. No ice in this splendid modern establishment. What do you think of it?'

'Well, it's more or less what I imagined; no taste but' – she sat down in the only armchair – 'at least it's clean.'

He was moving bottles around because, he said, the sun not having come out, we can presume it has gone down.

'Hey, can you bear bourbon and tap water?'

'I've never had it.'

'Tap water?'

'Bourbon. Is that how you say it? I always thought it was *Boor*bon, like the French kings.'

'Or there's rum.'

'You don't have any sherry?'

'No. What is this Sydney thing about sherry? I've noticed that.'

'It's mostly offered. It's – um – indigenous?'

'Invidious?'

'Intransigent? It's has – oh, listen to me: "*It's* has," and I haven't even had a drink – it has a kind of decorum about it. Very proper old ladies can get quietly potted. And clergymen. Won't you have a drink, Reverend? Oh, just a spot of sherry for me if you're all ... I mean, my mother, for instance. When we

were quite young we all had a glass of sherry before dinner because it's supposed to spark the appetite and be quite harmless
and. . . . Sorry, I'm going on and on. What?'

'I said, which. Rum or –'

'Oh, I'll try just a little bourbon then with a lot of water,
thanks.' She stared at the poor reproduction on the walls while
he went to get water from the bathroom.

'Oh, what a wretched, wretched day,' she said.

'Doesn't matter, does it?'

'Oh, no.'

'Doesn't matter to me,' he said.

'Except the zoo's –'

'– can put up with my lodgings.'

'–crowded on Sundays if you wanted; I mean, being your
last day.'

'– from Kentucky,' he said, coming back from the bathroom.

'You are?'

'The bourbon. I want you to know you're drinking real Kentucky bourbon. That enough water?'

'Touch more. Fine.'

'There we go, mate. That what you say?'

'Mate. Yes. Cobber. Good on you, cobber.'

'What do you say for Cheers?'

'Cheers.'

'Cheers.'

They pointed glasses at each other and they sat down on the
bed and drank deeply, with satisfaction. She took a gulp and it
was like bitter burned honey. She made a face.

'Don't like?'

'Not quite sure yet.'

'Take slowly.'

'Oh, I will, don't worry. Oho, don't worry. Mmmmm,
nice. Yes, really nice. Kentucky. Isn't that where they have the
Darby?'

'The Derby.'

'The *Der*by. The Derby. Burbon. I'm learning. I do like the sound of your American states.'

'I'm glad, mate,'

'I mean the names. Some of the names are quite pretty, I think. Montana, Wyoming, Ar*k*ansas.'

'Arkan*saw*.'

'Oh, is it? I thought it was like someone sighing. "Ah, *Kan*sas." '

'There's also Nooo Jersey and Nooo York. "N'Yooork." That's how *they* say it. Ugliest accent. "I'm from N'Yooooork." '

'What state are you –'

'Sit still.'

'What?'

He leaned forward, right into her face as she drew quickly back.

'Stay still a minute.'

His hand went gently towards her, up to her cheek and then away.

'Something caught in your eyelash, bit of fluff,' was all it was.

'Oh.'

But imagining for a second ... thinking he (the world upside down for a fraction of a second) was what? Her heart snatched up in amazement at seeing what she had done: she had reached out her hand to grasp his.

Hopefully, he had not ... or just thought she was warding him off.

'Maryland,' he said. 'I'm from Maryland.'

'Maryland,' she said, looking on the map for it; the invisible map was spread out on their knees between them to cover her embarrassment over the reflex of her hand let loose from her discipline, reaching without her knowledge to – 'Is that east, north, south ...' her voice said and she stared at the fabric of her skirt to find Maryland and she could not for the life of her remember his name. If the police burst in at this moment, she could not to save herself from arrest tell them his name.

Corey. But what? Oakley? Uffland?

It was the ambrosia in the room, sweet thought of heavy lilies and a blanked-out feeling of amnesia and now, with the shock at herself subsiding, she fought for his identity to bring her back to normal and so, looking up from her map, she looked him full in the face (he was hunched forward on the bed with his elbows resting on his knees, glass in one hand, and he seemed to be asking her with tremendous sincerity to try to remember his name) and while he was, in point of fact, exactly pin-spotting his home for her, she sought for it.

'Exactly – you could measure it if you wanted – between Philadelphia and Washington.'

'Ahh,' she said (but what is your name?).

'Afton.'

'Afton?'

'As in flow gently sweet.'

'Ah, yes.' She was wandering through the alphabet in desperation. Afton was his town, where he was co-owner of the Mingoes-Ennerva Electric Tool Company, a manufacturing town but pretty. 'I wish I had a postcard or could draw it for you.' He seemed to think she wanted to know all about it. He was assuring her in his funny, serious, authoritative way that it lay between two low banks of hills and that the downtown area had scarcely changed in fifty years because they had a strict town ordinance about store fronts and signs. 'We don't allow any gooping up, no neon signs, no tacky modernization that isn't in keeping with the mixture of American Colonial and Victorian . . .'

The rules of the game were these. She must remember his name before he finished this drink in his hand (the amber line was already half-way down the glass). If she could not remember his name before he finished his drink she would be cursed and doomed and something wretched would happen to her before midnight. If she could remember his name before he took the last sip, then something unexpected and delightful was going to happen to her before midnight. Starting now A? B? C? D?

His mother was on the town council, his mother was a conservative, from an old Maryland family, she was a Scopes, he explained, and she was as a ramrod against change.

'You can be sure of one thing. As long as Mama is alive there will be no drive-in movie in Afton.'

There was a curious linguistic dissonance in the way he said Mama – the word seemed to rob him of some of his height. He grinned as he talked about her, rubbing the back of his neck and bragging in the way children do about the severity of their teachers that *his* mother was the biggest dragon in the county, what would you want to bet him?

J? K? L?

Mrs what? But Bea could see her, the guardian of the red-brick fronts and Colonial façades of Afton, a small grey-haired woman who drove, he said, a 1934 Packard and a hard bargain with the same will power that got her out of bed at six every morning of her life except for the time when she had double pneumonia and even then she struggled with the nurses, and who, being opposed and beaten by the A & P and by the fools who had plumped for a supermarket on Fort McHenry Street, now drove to a general store six miles away.

'Because when Mama chooses to do away with something it just ceases to exist for her.

'I know that kind of disregard,' Bea said.

Bits of his mother were being put rapidly together. She had been a fine horsewoman and had ridden to hounds right into her forties. She adhered to the notion that the newspapers printed nothing but lies. She wrote frequent scathing letters to the editor. Most of all she was the sworn foe of a radio couple named Fibber McGee and Molly and consequently never missed their programme in order to excoriate them with her remarks of 'rubbish' and 'how can people *lis*ten to this hogwash?' It had been said, but not sworn to, that she had outstared an angry bull in a field and won.

182

He was on the sled of memory, winging down that slope where it is impossible to stop, the past hurtling up to meet him; his mother had just now pushed him on the sled, his curious, cold mother who could outstare a bull and who now turned her slug-grey eyes on Bea and looked her up and down and didn't too much approve of this antipodean large girl alone with her son in a small room; didn't too much approve of any girl for that matter and so had quietly – Bea felt sure this was so – tightened her hold on him without it being apparent to anyone save the girl in question and later to him, surely to him because he was not naïve and from under his beetle brows so black that the hair had blue in it he sent scattered messages in between the casual dialogues about his mother. Something else, something secret was being imparted underneath and in code and if she could decode it . . .

His hand went up and down, the glass grew paler and suddenly the game had become important and not merely diversion. She felt that her game was connected with what he was trying to tell her. He was explaining something about himself disguised as anecdote; he was being rueful and funny about the time his mother opposed his going to Europe one summer with a bunch of college friends and yet when he finally capitulated to her she had sent him a goose to Princeton.

'A live goose all crated up and with it a note in Mama's characteristic way saying, "Corey, you'll never get anywhere, even in Europe, if you don't learn how to say boo to this."'

Because in a perverse way she wanted to be opposed; it was no fun if she got her own way without a battle.

Bea laughed along with him and prayed for him not to lift the glass for the last time because the game provided for no cheating, no extension of the time set; just as in childhood she had set herself such ultimatums as for instance she must see a wasp before she reached the hotel gate or become a nun.

'Enough of that,' Corey said. 'How's your drink?'

'Oh, fine, fine. Don't move. Oh, I think that's fun though –

your mother sending the goose so you'd fight her. She sounds tough but fun like Edna May Oliver. What we would call a "corker" – which has nothing to do with drinking by the way – just a very strong individualistic, characteristic, strong . . . person like – mmmm – you describe Mrs *Orcutt* and . . . oh, thank God, thank *God* – for *them* I mean – in the world and everything, Corey . . . Oh, I like the sound of her, I really do. Oh I really like the sound of Mrs Orcutt.'

The bolt unlocking, the stone falling away, light pierced her and flowed through her and having won, watching him drain his dregs, she was able to observe him and to notice by certain nervous movements, the jerk of his glass upward and the way he turned his head towards the now dark window and studied it industriously, that he didn't know where to go next.

'Well, well, well, well, well,' he said and drummed his fingers on his glass.

He was nervous; now that he was out from behind the camouflage of big, amusing Mama, no more to tell, he was only himself and possibly that was not enough, was it? This is what he had been hinting at, peeking at her around his mother.

'Is it still pouring?'

'Cats and dogs.'

She was as certain of this as she was certain there'd never been a piece of fluff in her eye.

He was afraid.

The fact was that everyone said she knew nothing about real people and that this was what so phenomenally unhampered D. K. Durfee but she knew her intuition about Corey Orcutt was the truth, was as tangible as the chair and bed and the sound of the silence and their breathing in this indecisive lull; was the undeniable and astonishing truth. She was filled with tenderness at the new pleasure of it.

'Now if I may,' she said and held out her glass and, when he reached for it, instead she gave him her hand.

'But nothing disturbs the serenity of my mother.'

They played dominoes with sugar cubes. She put one down and a little later Corey put one down. All the time they looked severely down at the table. Sometimes their hands touched and, for a moment, brushed, wanting to touch again, joining sugar cubes under a candle, their heads close, both of them moved by the story of Bea's life. A lot of it was sadder than she'd imagined, not because she was making anything up; she held strictly to the outlines of truth (her father was insane, her mother cared nothing for her) but along the way she discovered glens and arbours haunted by ghosts and spirits, who, being disturbed, emerged and touched her with icy fingers. Exhilarated sadness. Because behind it lay the last few hours and pieces kept coming between her and the narrative, like the way Corey kissed her. The discovery that she had been kissed apathetically, parentally, sexually, offhandedly and for the purposes of home movies but never in her life that she could think of, lovingly. The way, after kissing and drawing apart, no reference was made to it and they spoke in breathless voices of mundane things, breaking off in the midst of a sentence to kiss again, but never spoke any obvious word of love, knowing this would spoil it because there was a transcendental feeling of naturalness and of belonging. And he said, this is Timmie, taking out his wallet. Somehow his showing her this was a personal thing, judging by his serious eyes, and she sat up, pushing back her fallen braids, and took the snapshot and, surprise, it was a wire-haired terrier, prick-eared and eager and a girl with a disappointed face in a white dress sitting on a summer lawn with her arm around the dog.

Who was Alice he said, who was looking after Timmie while he was gone to save Mama. He skipped over Alice lightly and with a slight shrug, indicating a suspension, indicating there was a problem here.

'Is this your house?'

'No, no, that's Alice's house.'

So she knew by his emphasis all about Alice's house and that it was in Alice's house that letters were written in the long lonely evenings and that very likely Alice was suspended indefinitely and knew it, her arm around the dog; both she and the dog had the same cocked expression, looking up expectantly into his camera and waiting on the good word from him. Only Alice looked less optimistic than Timmie.

Once the telephone had rung and he had spoken to a superior officer, saying, right, sir, check, sir, and that he would be at HQ in the morning but holding onto her all the time. Then, hanging up, took the cigarette from her and stubbed it out and clasped her as if they had been separated for three weeks.

Their conversation had become physical then, conveying by motion, hands, mouth that he — no, she — no, he — was the more tender, more surprised, and eventually, hours passing, it seemed, the repetition of their increasing tenderness exhausted them and they knew it, coming to the end of their repertoires in this prologue and so it began to be urgent and decisive and frightened her and, feeling she had not seen his face for these hours, she had struggled away from him, turned on the bed lamp and, as he twitched in the painful light, she had whispered as though both their mothers were in the room, that because of the idiocy of restaurants closing hadn't they better. . . . Fled into the bathroom, where she looked at her flushed wanton face in the mirror and thought about having respect (hoped it wasn't respectability, that deadly suburban thing that sometimes she feared was in her), cooling her boiling feelings in cold running water, looking at his shaving brush and smelling the clean man smell that had so affected her when first coming into the room because it had reminded her of the only two other men (well, one and a half really) and of how she felt compelled to explain to them her passion, and so had never seen either man again. So, wondering what to do, how to prevent this happening with Corey, she washed her hands for a long time and then took ages with hair-pins, braiding, until she had been able to bolster herself with some shaky reasons, using poor Alice for one and for the other that there was only tomorrow left and the improbability that he would ever come back here so...

She would be like her mother, who, when the facts of love were presented to her, pointed out a tree. So if he were to say something about them, make a comment, refer to love, she would ask, what about? About *what*? She rehearsed. She would take a leaf out of her mother's book on the economics of passion.

Returning from this intermission, she was once more beige and very secretarial and he was looking correct in his cap and holding her coat ready and they went down in the lift with their secret safe from each other. Well, it's stopped raining, they told each other. Then gradually, over dinner, their cleverness began to desert them and as time went on they began silently to admit their disappointment to each other that they were in this restaurant and not alone still and now the chance gone by (certainly for tonight) because of an implacable card in his hotel lobby that said: NO VISITORS AFTER II P.M.

So they played sugar dominoes and Bea's story went on and on past Angus, past Marcus, past D. K. Durfee, on and on, and whenever she flagged and sighed Corey said go on, go on, until they had used up all the sugar cubes and most of her life and the waiter was troubling them by almost sitting on the table, for the check. They wandered then, arm in arm, through late-Saturday-night crowds and, having no aim except not to part, they walked relentlessly, they trudged, crossed streets purposelessly, dawdled down quieter alleys by darkened houses all the long way down to the harbour, where they sat down on a cold concrete bench directly under the gritty brownout street light and looked out on the water, which seemed oily, dimly refracting stars and street lamps and slurping thickly at the little moored boats tippling at the pier. There was an unpleasant smell of rotting seaweed which carried to them on the night breeze as they sat close together, collars turned up against the sharp wind, and she wanted to say and fought against saying that she didn't see how it would be possible to let him go away on Monday morning and never see him again, she didn't think that she could do it, and clearing her throat of these mistakes she said, 'Stars are out, see?' 'Hmm,' he said. 'So we could, if you like, probably make it to the zoo after all. If you'd like, tomorrow afternoon,' she said and he was so long in replying that she was sure he was ruminating as she had done earlier on the uselessness of their ever seeing each other again. 'I was just thinking,' he said at last, 'looking at that dark water. There are some birds they told me about in Hawaii, little water birds they called the shear-waters, because they sort of shear the water and land on it, and on nights like this after rain the reflections and lights on the wet streets confuse them because they mistake it for water and so they land on the wet pavements and injure themselves and are unable to take off again and so they die.'

One way of telling her.

'Too cold,' she said and stood up, stamping her feet and unhappy. So they walked again in silence until she told him these steps led up to her street and they climbed.

'Look, Bea,' he said at the top of the steps. 'About tomorrow. I don't think –'

'I was just going to say the zoo's so dammed crowded on Sundays anyway.'

'I don't think I want to bother with it, do you mind?'

'No, no. And I know you've got paper work and people to see.'

'Bea, what I would *like* is to plan nothing for tomorrow.'

'Naturally.'

'Provided we can be together.'

'Well . . . we can.'

'That's what I'd like very much.'

'Yes.'

'So what will we do? Will you come to *me* then?'

'Yes.'

'Then I'll wait for you at the hotel.'

After they kissed, he said, 'But you will come, won't you?'

'Of course.'

'Because it sounds as if I'm making use of that standard ploy – the soldier's last evening before returning to hell and assuming a lot more besides.'

'Not assuming anything. Not a thing.'

'Good.'

'Not a thing. Unless tonight was an optical illusion. Or is that what you mean when you were telling me about the birds?'

'Maybe.'

'Was it?'

'In some ways.'

'Corey, say what you mean.'

'Just that I'm one hell of a doubter.'

'Well, so am I. But let's not be. There isn't time for it and if I thought it was only a ploy, as you say, I wouldn't come.'

'Thank you, Bea.'

'So . . . don't doubt me, please.'

'All right, but I –'

'No more talk. No, just let's say good night now. No *more*, Corey.'

'I just want to say one thing so come here, come here, will you, just for a second –'

'What? No, not now, not here –'

'Just – '

'Just *what*? I didn't hear you.'

'I said just *be* there, will you? Will you?'

Only to people with time ahead of them is given the luxury of playing at being late and so, although no hour had been mentioned, she was dressed and ready by four, ready to go, with purse, gloves, topcoat laid out on the bed when the clock struck. Then she strictly admonished herself for this whorish indecent promptness and made herself sit down and slowly remake her

189

hairdo from scratch and then forced herself to drink two taste-less cups of tea while she turned the dial of her mind to very low and tried to rest for a few minutes from the terrible combination of happiness, fear and longing that had kept her awake almost all night and drawn blue shadows around her eyes. She had watched herself doing sly things, covering her insomnia with Max Factor and putting on a soft biscuit-coloured chiffon dress and her Tecla pearls, and had pretended there was nothing un-usual about this until Adina said, 'That's a summer dress, isn't it? You'll freeze your bloody arse off in *that*, ducky.' 'Oh, no, and we'll be inside most of the time,' she said and blushed fur-iously and lit a cigarette. 'You already have one going,' Adina said, pointing to the ashtray.

Yet he might already be wondering, doubting, (he showed up about every three minutes on a big moving-picture screen on the wall; he was looking at his watch, glancing impatiently out of the hotel window to see if he could spot her coming down the street). Even so, let her not get there before five o'clock, especially decked out as she was for a Command Performance, so she washed up the cup and saucer with slow deliberation un-til Corey appeared over the sink and said something like, hurry it up, will you, so that she dropped the saucer and broke it.

Then she sat down in the living-room and, assuming an atti-tude of extravagant annoyance, made out to Adina that she was suffering fools gladly to have to get all dressed up and go out on a Sunday to meet 'these people' when what she would give her eyeteeth to do would be have an egg and tuck cosily into bed and listen to the 'Lux Radio Theatre'; appeared to be deeply interested in when and where Adina was going to vaca-tion this year until Adina said, 'I take it you're remembering this clock's ten minutes slow,' at which she became a debutante and ran about in a panic, in and out of her bedroom, grabbing her things, and out of the flat and then all the way to the tram.

It wasn't until she turned the corner by Hyde Park and saw the hotel that she had been able to slow down to a walk just in case he was looking out of the window, which he wasn't. The hotel, which had not been burned down or bombed during the night, stood placidly in the deserted Sunday street and the only thing was that, turning the knob, the entrance door was locked.

She looked around and found a bell and rang, breathing deeply to arrange herself calmly before going up in the lift, and then rang again because whoever was on the desk must be away on a brief errand. The next time she rang, she kept her finger hard on the bell for quite a time because this person perhaps could be hard of hearing though, she said, one would think that even in wartime there must be *some* hotel employees available, even to a small private hotel such as the Royal Park, not necessarily aged or handicapped.

Giving herself time to laugh at it, she walked back and forth outside the entrance and made sure that her slip was not showing, her seams were straight, and after that she stared at the door until she saw through the crinkled glass that finally someone was moving inside across the lobby and then after a curious wait that this was the reflection of herself and her chiffon dress blowing in the wind. Now she pressed the bell in sharp jabs, one long burst after another. After a time, she knocked as well and rattled the door handle.

Well then, she would have to telephone. There was no public phone in sight and she was sure, hurrying around the corner, they would open the door while she was gone. A block away on a side street she found a phone booth, the number, and then that she didn't have the right change, then four blocks before she found a little newspaper shop open where she bought a packet of Life Savers and got change. Well, at least, she thought, waiting outside the now occupied phone booth and keeping the situation light and supple, I will have a valid excuse.

She decided she must not think that the way her heart was beating had anything to do with any sense of alarm, merely that she had hurried, but listening to the telephone ring and ring and, after she had hung up and again looked up the number, again listening to it ring and ring perhaps twenty times with the flat undeniable buzz that switchboards have, she could no longer resist the beginning of real fright and, wrenching open the booth door, she ran all the way back to the hotel.

She took off her glove in the hopeless assumption that fingers wrapped in leather may not make electrical contact and that now somewhere in a far-off pantry someone dozing was alerted at last.

'I'll tell you this,' she said to herself aloud, 'even D. K. couldn't have thought up *this* one.'

Within the next half hour she went back twice to the telephone booth, stubbornly believing that this time somebody would attend to the switchboard, but the long flat unanswered buzzes began to take on the sound of someone raspberrying her. The undeniable fact was that the Royal Park Hotel did not answer calls on Sundays. Well then, nothing could be done except to wait until someone came in or out. She had not brought her watch and so made herself believe that it was only probably five-thirty or a quarter to six at the very latest. She examined the brickwork around the door. Occasionally, but with no hope, she rang the bell.

'Although he mightn't even have expected me till six,' she told herself aloud but knew this was not so, not with the sweet urgency he had said, just be there, will you? Then why didn't *he* do something? Why was he so stupid as to just sit up there in his room? Because he didn't know. Hadn't he gone out all day? Hadn't he said he had to go to HQ in the morning? Then wouldn't he know there was no one on duty in the lobby? But maybe there *had* been someone in the lobby in the morning and maybe he'd been doing paper work all afternoon and had not even lifted the phone and being American he wouldn't have the faintest knowledge of the archaic Victorian behaviour of Australian residential hotels, who ignored emergencies on God's day.

When the street lights came on, she ran down the steps and

into the street. A few lights showed under drawn shades and she could not be sure which was his window but cupping her mouth she called, 'Corey'.

'Cor-ree,' she called to what she thought was his window on the top floor. Then, though she was attracting some attention by risking her life standing in the middle of the street, head up and not looking to see if cars were coming, she continued for some time, hopelessly calling his name, and her voice sounded to her thin and uncarrying. Trams came by and drowned her out, cars tooted angrily at her and she saw she had attracted the admiration of two Australian privates and when they began crossing towards her, grinning, she turned and ran into the brownout shadows along the rim of the park and didn't stop until she had reached Oxford Street. Then for luck, to change her luck, she walked in the opposite direction away from the hotel, hurried as if she had urgent business until she came to the dark windows of Mark Foy's, where she peered in, idiotically, through the chicken wire at sneering wax ladies wearing their wartime substitute outfits furred in rabbit. She deliberated on the ladies preening in the unlit show windows because if she delayed long enough, then on returning perhaps the night staff would have come on from their long afternoon naps and the hotel door would be open, blazing with light. When, quite nearby and startling, booming, she heard the clock in Town Hall strike seven, she ran all three long streets back to the hotel to find it continuing to sleep in darkness and desertion. It seemed at this point that she reached her height of desperation, so high that she considered the police; walked up and down thinking quite seriously of the police being the only way that she could get in. But the thought of questions and answers handicapped her; the thought of breaking locks and forcing entry with a cordon of police, paying for property damage, a curious crowd watching, in order to keep an appointment with a man she had not known until Friday evening held her back with its unlikelihood.

Then what else? Americans of course could do anything, get anything they wanted. Could she call Stevie and ask if the Colonel would mind trying to get in touch with HQ and – but no.

But after a while even desperation wore down into a kind of sulky acceptance. She sat on a park bench across from the hotel. The fact that she could not walk away interested her. The fact that she would keep up this cold vigil if necessary until midnight or until he came out in order to prove to him that she had not let him down interested her. It was a side of herself she didn't know existed. She had not until now been called on to prove such a thing to anybody in such physical terms. All she'd ever done was to proclaim in lofty prose her feelings of passion for the two other miserable and, now she came to think of it, puny affairs, which she had only disgraced by calling attention to beauty and depths they did not possess, and to embarrass the other participants, like praising out-of-tune-music. Now she was being called upon to perform a service of faith which was important, sacred to fulfil . . .

And she was so impressed by the thought, so carried away with this searching and not unpleasant discovery that she had strength, that she found she had failed to notice a man and woman coming out of the Royal Park and screamed, wait, screamed across to them and ran almost into the front of a taxi. 'Stupid f'kin' sheilas,' the driver yelled as she almost fell into the gutter. 'Don't shut the door,' she called but the man and woman had already come down the steps.

'Oh, I want to get *in*,' she panted. She must seem strange to them – enormous, blown-about, hysterical – the way they were staring at her in the half light.

'I've been trying to get in for *two hours*. There's no one on duty.'

'There's no one on on *Sun*days,' the woman admonished.

'Not after *lunch*,' the man said as if that was only proper, the only civilized thing.

'Are you expected?' the woman asked.

'Oh, yes, yes.'

'Then they'll come down and let you in if you're expected.'

'They – *he* doesn't know I'm *here*,' she almost screamed.

The man and woman looked dubious as if waiting for references.

'Captain Orcutt. He's on the third floor. He's *expecting* me,' she said, almost in tears. 'But he doesn't know I'm *down* here.'

So, knowing everything now and with looks of sorrow for call girls, the man wordlessly took out a key. 'Tch tch,' said the woman.

'Thank you.' She fell into the dim lobby, fell into the little lift. The lift ascended with the rapidity of treacle.

Corey's face was as unreceptive as the bell downstairs. He was pressed and polished, all pink and American-eagle-gold-buttoned, parade-ground beautiful he was. She clutched at him untidily. 'Dear *God*,' she began, fell, into the armchair and because of the relief, became suddenly brilliantly amusing about it, pouring out the saga. How she went back and forth to the phone booth, the Aussie soldiers, how she stood and called and called. But he was either so glad or so compassionate that he seemed not to find it amusing and finally cut her short quickly by saying in an exasperated way, 'You're not in the phone book. There are only four St Jameses and none of them are you.'

'No, it's under Glaspell. I never thought to tell you.'

'Because I wanted to call you.'

'I *knew* you'd be wondering what in hell –'

'No, this was this morning.'

'Oh?'

'Because I wanted to tell you what had happened.'

'What?'

'I'm leaving tonight, you see.'

'Oh.'

'There's air transport going tonight via Darwin and they put me on it.'

She shut her eyes for a moment; she'd noticed the bag on the bed.

He said, 'I wanted to get you to say could you come in for lunch or as soon after if you could . . .'

'Oh, I wasn't doing *any*thing . . . I was just mooching around filling in time. Oh, but *why*?'

'This is the Army, Mr Jones.'

'Oh, damn the Army to hell and damn this frigging hotel and –' Why, she wanted to say, in Christ's name couldn't you have had the sense to see if someone was downstairs or look out the window or . . . But he looked so serious and stern that she knew not to say any of these things.

'What time do you have to go?'

'Have to report by twenty hundred hours – eight o'clock, in other words – but by the time I check out and find a cab . . .'

'For one thing,' she said with a last-minute ridiculous hope, 'you won't be able to check out because there's no one downstairs.'

'I don't think that my colonel in Manila is going to regard that as sufficient excuse for my missing my transport.'

'No, I suppose not. Still, what will you do about the hotel?'

'Oh, I guess I'll leave them a note with the key. I imagine Major McMurtrie's staff is on to the quirks of the Royal Park Moderne.' He scribbled a note while she tried to stop a hammering feeling in her choked-down heart. Corey put his room key down on the note. Then she saw what he was doing was putting on his cap and picking up the valise and raincoat.

'Well?' he asked.

She hadn't thought he meant right now, this very second.

'Sure you have everything?'

'Think so.'

'Haven't left anything behind?'

She looked hopelessly in the empty wardrobe for him, peeped into the bathroom and then, as he was holding open the door with an air of impatience, she went with him obediently out of the room forever and he rang for the lift while she looked at a small hole in her glove. But going down in the lift she said, 'What is happening is unbelievable.' He made no move of comfort, no gesture of putting an arm around her; he looked angry and stern beyond words as they crossed the lobby and he opened the front door for her. She had been inside, she reckoned, close to four and a half minutes.

As she walked beside him, she pretended to be busy straightening her belt so she might give an air of being impassive. He said nothing and they crossed over towards Oxford Street and she finally said huskily, 'Where are you going?'

'To Transport HQ on Bathurst Street.'

'Oh, *yes*,' she said as though this were interesting.

They stood on the corner waiting for traffic to pass and he said nothing so she had to say it.

'Will you ever be back?'

'Oh, who knows? God knows. I have a hunch the next trip will be to the States.'

'Yes, I see.'

'Who knows? If the war drags on another five years they might – oh – hey, there's a cab. I better nab him. Taxi. *Taxi*.'

They ran a few steps.

'Yes, well . . .'

'Well . . .'

'Take care of yourself.'

'You too.'

Then he said grimly, 'As far as timing goes, I still hold the track record for perfect misses.'

'Oh, Corey.'

Then they kissed like relatives and shook hands at the same time. There were two American lieutenants in the cab. 'Going up to Bathurst Street?' Corey asked. 'Hop in,' one of the Americans said.

He got in.

'So long, Bea.'

'Good-bye,' she said but it was lost in the noise of the wheels.

She would manage to get home by resolutely not thinking about anything until she could reach the medicine cabinet, where, she prayed, there was one last sleeping tablet in an old bottle left over from a period of self-induced insomnia, and so in the tram grinding very slowly towards Kings Cross she leaned her forehead against the window and simply saw lights, dimmed headlights and the outline of her head and at some point the indefinite outlines of another head behind her, wearing a Women's Army hat, and then that the Army Hat was bending, lowering with sidelong dips, and then that an unrealistic musical-comedy-cheerful voice had said, 'Excuse me, but it *is* Bea, isn't it?'

Turning towards the Army Hat, bright brown eyes and hair and smile, she almost said no, said, oh, go away, it is just a little more than I can stand.

'I bet you don't remember me.'

'Yes. How are you?'

'Do you? It's been over six years I'd say. *Do* you? Lesley Ann.'

'Yes, yes, how are you?'

'Okeydoke. *You* look marvellous.'

'Oh, thanks.'

'And look, you've been absolutely *heap*ing glory on yourself, haven't you?'

'Have I?'

'Lord, yes, *have*n't you. Aren't you still writing all those little radio skits?'

'Yes.'

'Good Lord! I don't know how you keep it up. How do you?'

'*Don't* *K*now.'

'Good Lord! Good for you though. Good for you, Bea. Though it must be tons of fun.'

'Yes.'

'Good Lord! I'd say. More like play than work, I'd say. I see you've just come from a party.'

'Sort of.'

'And, Bea, how are the folks?'

Oh, the old folks at home? Fine, thanks. Yes, she's fine. Yes, he's about the same. Yes, she's fine. Yes, she did. A girl. Yes any moment now the Europe war's over. Com*mander* Seward now. Yes she's counting the days.

(What he meant to say was, 'Glad you came, glad of everything, you know, hope you know.')

'I was sorry to hear about . . . Theodore. Rotten.'

'Rotten.'

'No word, I suppose.'

'Don't know anything. Hope for the best.'

'Aha. Aha. Yes, rotten for *her*. Ingrid.'

'Liesl.'

'Liesl. I *meant* Liesl.'

And I wonder, Bea thought, if she knows that *I* know that she crawled across the floor and pulled the towel away from the door? And I wonder what she'd do if *I* tried it now in front of her. Leaped from this moving tram under the wheels of another one?

'And what about *you*, Bea?'

'*What* about me?'

'Haven't gone and got yourself married or engaged or anything?'

'No.'

'Well, you're a ce*leb*rity anyway. I have cousins who listen to you in Western Australia, three thousand miles away.'

'Oh?'

'Look, it's funny me running into you like this, because I was talking about you only the other day with someone.'

'Yes?'

'Yes, and it was someone you know too. I wonder if you can guess who it was?'

Whoever and Whatever Divine Affinity that I have Grievously Offended, she said to herself, you must soon get off my back because this is overdoing it for one evening.

'I wouldn't have the remotest idea.'

'Want to give a guess?'

'Excuse me, what street is this? I think I get off next stop.'

'Angus.'

'Angus?'

'Yes. Weekes. Angus Weekes. You don't remember him?'

'Remember him? He was one of the old folks at home.'

'Yes. Well, he's also at the Barracks now. I'm in Q and he's in Admin. so we've been seeing quite a lot of each other in fact. I'll tell him I saw you. Oh, look, he'll be tickled to death.'

Bea got up and tugged at the bell cord, thinking how all in a flash it couldn't matter less to her if Angus were in Tanganyika.

'Angus doesn't approve of the St James family in any way, shape or form.'

'Oh, no, Bea, no,' Lesley Ann said urgently. She couldn't be quite cured of her neuroses, judging by her leather gloves, strangled things which all the time she kept twisting and garroting.

'Oh, Angus is all over that long ago, I can assure you. I happen to know him rather well as it happens and I can tell you he doesn't hold any grudges against *any* of you.'

'Tell him how glad we are, will you? Tell him Bea said that's a real weight off our shoulders.'

'And now, Bea, I don't want any more Alibi-Ike-ing between you and I,' said Helena 'Hank' Ambrose, giving Bea ten minutes, twenty if she liked because of the crisis that had come upon them, and this in itself was the top mark of esteem in the whole network, for hadn't Hank herself conceived the idea and character of 'Fair-go Baxter,' now in its ninth year?

'Is it – and I repeat this is behind closed doors and absolutely between you and I – is it a matter for a doctor?'

'No.'

Hank moved her diamonds, which were as hard as her eyes and never off her day or night. Three on each hand.

'Because you could tell me in strictest confidence, absolutely – put my hand on the Bible – between we girls.'

Hank was looking at her with genuine concern. It was the way everyone in the office looked at her lately. If she had changed sex overnight it would have caused less curiosity and most certainly less alarm than the mysterious drying up of her fountain. At first the cynics said she was angling for a new and more lucrative contract but as daily, weekly, her invention petered out and the once prodigious flow became a dribble, the fear began that she was genuinely ill or (and this was scarcely spoken) written out and the girls sitting across the desk from her with their idle pencils, doodling while she gazed out the window, began replying to her silences with hostile coughs and wrigglings and tappings on the desk because of their own fears of what might, could, happen if D. K. was finished. That was the problem with freaks – everybody's job depended on their freakishness, and where could she be replaced? There was no one, never had been anyone, to approach her output.

They brought her tea and enticing little cakes, suggested aspirin, Dexedrine, that she try to dictate lying down, and in the outside office unfounded rumours grew that she had been found crying in the ladies' room, that she had begun to drink and had a bottle hidden in the filing cabinet, and, worst of all, that (somebody unreliable in the mimeographic room swore to it) her father was nutty as a fruitcake and locked up in some mountain fastness and that she was showing the first signs.

She was aware of all this and, like someone in a deep and serious illness who has fleeting moments of response and pushes at the sides of the oxygen tent, she would arouse herself, sit up straight and ask, 'What did I say last?' and the girls would patiently read back perhaps for the fifth time the line of dialogue she had left dangling in space. Words dripped very slowly from her like water and she bit into pencils while her eyes followed her mind to some other country. 'Oh, dear,' she said, 'Ummm,' and then, 'I'll finish it tomorrow.' When precedent broke, it broke across the backs of everyone in Ambrose Productions. This was on the dark day when the Oxo Soup people rejected one of her scripts with the incredible word *'Unexciting'*, causing one of the less highly paid staff writers to remark, not without relish, that they might as easily have written, 'Mene, mene.'

And now she had been summoned to the Presence and now Hank herself was doing her damnedest to ferret out the cause.

'Know what I think ? *I* think it's a man.'

'What makes you consider such extremes?' Bea asked.

'It's got to be something, hasn't it? Someone as talented as you doesn't just lose their talent overnight.'

'Don't they?'

She wanted to tell Hank that she cared, not so much about the fact that some states had only enough recorded Jezebels to last about two more weeks but that she longed to turn back into the countries of her invention, longed to throw herself into adventures on the Blue Train to Paris, but that she could no longer conjure up her fantasies. The fatal thing had happened. Whenever she closed her eyes she saw only one room and one person.

Now Hank was growing threatening. If she couldn't keep up the output, then they might have to consider ... well, perhaps four other writers would have to take over.

Hank said, 'I'll let you in on a little secret. *Wireless Weekly*'s putting your picture on the cover next month so whomever is worrying you, Bea, they aren't worth it. A girl your age with five *night*time shoes ? Oh, think about it. This is your *life*.'

Bea thought about it. Particularly the fact that everything that had happened (and wouldn't they be disappointed to know) could be shown on the newsreels.

The only person who could conceivably understand about the sadness of near misses and bad timing might be Stevie, whose own timing was immaculate. Not that Bea was jealous but she could not help envying Stevie's uninterrupted good luck that enabled her to say long and loving farewells to Gabriel, her Colonel, during an extended house party in Palm Beach and still be home two days before Bill Seward's squadron was welcomed back with a ceremony involving the Prime Minister in Canberra.

Of course Stevie had noticed no change in her, droop as she might, but then it might have had to be pointed out to Stevie that the oceans had dried up. So, hurting on the skin with the need to talk, to confide in someone, Bea put down her coffee cup, wet her lips.

'Lover, I have a problem,' Stevie said in her slightly American voice. 'How do you tell the returning hero that he is a bromide? Oh, I tell you and nobody else that I've had to bite hard on the bullet not to scream. Oh, honey, if there is a Dull Observation – Do you remember our old game? How many demerits did we give for them? But if there is an Obvious Statement to be made he will make it. I stand and wait for it to fall like the other boot, you know? How do you point this out to the beribboned boy?'

Stevie hurried on for fear Bea might answer or try to advise her. She had the strong look of Eve St James being vastly amused at finding her favourite vase smashed and warning that it was to be taken lightly and you were not to sympathize. Whatever her private misery, Stevie was disguising it as vaudeville, and when clear bubbles of water gathered in the corners of her eyes, she became doubled up with mirth and punched the sofa because Bill's remarks were truly hilarious (you should put him in a play, Bea) and his banalities were so comical, while upstairs his daughter, who better appreciated his humour, yelled with joy at him and from the walls his tea-planting ancestors gazed down at Stevie with miraculous tolerance. Repeated around the walls in their high collars and lace fichus, the Sewards bore no ill will, because they had handed down compassion together with their high foreheads and their money to the pilot upstairs, whose voice could be heard saying, 'Whazza moo cow?'

Help, Stevie said, but in reality said, 'Oh, I'd forgotten he actually says things like "Where are you, helpmeet?" and I may shortly go psycho with all the Air Force Roger Apple Baker Charley dialogue,' Stevie slumped, slid down on pillows, just about laughed out and her cheeks wet.

I am in love, Bea said, but there was no one to listen.

Whom had they ever turned to? They had been brought up to leave their troubles outside with the dirty tennis shoes and not to bring emotions into Mother's spotless house.

Now if they could talk about this, if they could console each other about having been abandoned as children, then perhaps they could be like sisters in real life who confided in and comforted each other and could then have a good cry followed by a nice cup of tea and cheer up and sit with their arms around each other glancing through a fashion magazine. There they were now in the old swing on the bungalow veranda whispering together. But the sentimental scene was instantly eclipsed by two giant figures of a constantly recurring nightmare and as in the horrifying dream she was only five years old yet able to think and rationalize at her present age, she saw that someone for a callous joke had cut off her hand, and she had screamed for bandages and aid and comfort and her mother had said so lovingly, there, there. There, there, her mother soothed, soothed and petted Daddy because he had seen the bloody stump and was rightly appalled at the sight and so led Daddy away from the nasty scene of the accident and, walking away slowly, arms around Daddy, Mother whispered and comforted and confided as they walked away. They always walked away, walked away, walked away on a treadmill so that they got no farther in order that you could scream but they would always be in earshot and always walking away.

This was the dream that she had told about sitting in the restaurant and moving Domino sugar cubes, only she had told it in terms of reality, which is why she had found it so sad and Corey had found it so sad.

This man, the American, understood me, she told Stevie and looked over there at the chair where he had been sitting the night she came in to rescue Stevie and the Colonel and found him sitting there looking at his shoes and all the talk about Evalyn Walsh McLean.

Stevie was saying something about apple pie. 'Me. He tells me I keep the bed – I mean the house – in apple-pie order, old girl. I have the Order of the Apple Pie. Me, who could untidy an empty room.'

But you see, Bea went on, and I say this as one who no longer writes exaggeration, if he were to materialize in that chair now, the scene would be that I would kneel at his beautiful feet and say thank you for knowing me and understanding me and for your sweet and understanding listening and for saying, 'Not the zoo, *you*,' which might be made into a song and so on about love, love, love you, may I cut off my hand if I'm –

But he may well be back in Afton, Maryland and he may well be saying to Alice that thank God the hotel door was locked and so I didn't have to listen to any more stories about her life according to the book of St James.

'Oh, well,' Bea said aloud, 'who knows? I mean, who knows? If someone were to walk in the door this minute –'

'No, better,' Stevie said 'if we were on the *Lusitania*, whom –'

'– would we save.'

'Oh, *better*. Whom would we leave on board?'

'Do you know,' Bill said, coming in with logs, 'this is the only warm room in the house?'

'Is it?'

'Just go into the hall and come in again; it's *degrees* warmer.'

'*Is* it? Could it be the fire, do you suppose?'

'There we are, troops,' Bill said, dumping the logs onto the funeral pyre of what they'd been thinking and dusting his big hands over the grate so, let the chips fall where they may, they didn't fall on the carpet of Stevie's apple-pie-order house.

'The Double Bay Deluxe has got Alice Faye,' he said.

'I'm too torpid for Alice Faye,' Stevie said.

'Check. Just thought you wanted to go to the flicks.'

'Too comfy to move,' Stevie said, full length. 'Anyway, with Alice Faye isn't the outcome predictable?'

'Roger,' Bill said and made a fist and punched at her cheek, the dear little assistant gunner. He sat down and looked at the crew, at a loss without orders. As if Bremerhaven or Cassino had been scrubbed tonight.

'Ohhhhhhhh,' Stevie yawned. 'Isn't this bliss?'

She had shut her eyes, leaving Bill alone with Bea.

So Bea said, 'Have you heard about the plight of the shear-waters?'

She told him about the birds landing on the wet pavements.

'Ah, yes,' Bill said. 'Now I'll tell you the reason for that, Bea. The reason for that, you see, is air currents.'

Now if I count very slowly to twenty, she said, and I see no-body I know in that time it means he is back in the States and I will never see him again.

She was sitting in the lobby of the Hotel Australia, where she came two or three nights a week at cocktail time with a variety of imaginative and sly excuses like (talking to herself aloud, which she did most of the time now, often being caught and having to turn it into a song) hopeless trying to get a cab now so I'll kill time by sitting in the Australia lobby and see if there's anyone I know. Because it was rumoured that should you sit long enough everyone in the world you knew would pass through and where it was true that every American in Sydney eventually came.

At five o'clock the big circular leather seat in the black-and-white-marble Palm Court flowered with pretty girls wearing open-toed shoes, Ann Sheridan hairdos and expressions of confidence. Some wore engagement rings and to them came the captains and the corporals to salute their patience and bear them chatteringly away. They sat in their spring dresses as fresh and graceful as delphiniums and among them oxlike sat Bea St James playing her game of accidental encounter, waiting and watching the street door revolve endlessly and sometimes spotting him, the exact curve of the jaw under the peaked cap. Often in the gauzy light someone the right height and wearing the right face came straight towards her, almost up to her, before changing into a stranger.

Her ritual never varied. She came into the lobby, glanced around casually, looked at her watch to find she was early, so bought an evening paper, sat down among the floral dresses and waited, watching them come and go from the Wintergarden bar until she was alone on the horseshoe seat and only bellboys and statues were left to observe her get up and go to a phone booth, where she apparently dialled and spoke to someone, after which she left the hotel briskly, sometimes at a run.

Once she had gone further, gone boldly into the Wintergarden and asked for a table, but an enormously sissy waiter had asked if she was alone and then had said in a loud voice that they didn't permit unescorted ladies at the tables. Then she heard someone say, 'Oh, there you are,' and caught a glimpse of an American uniform, saw a dimpled puce face, sprouts of dying nicotine-coloured hair, saw he was pulling out a chair and beckoning; the smile was desperate. 'Thought you'd *never* get here sweets,' the Major said and the sissy waiter's look was withering as she blundered around trying to get out of the door like a great whale. So that had been the end of playing this game for nearly two weeks until she began to get little metaphysical jabs again that he was trying to get in touch with her: was waiting in the lobby, giving it one last try, having forgotten entirely where she could be reached at work and so (running the length of Castlereagh Street) she returned to the waiting game and occasionally a little terror took hold of her at the thought that after all it was possible that he *could* walk in and see her sitting there waiting like that dismal dog Greyfriars Bobby on the master's grave.

Tonight the Palm Court was jammed and she had to wait for a while to get her seat on the horseshoe sofa. She sat and read in the *News* without interest or credulence that they had dropped the new bomb for the second time. Turned from that to something she could comprehend: a dramatic turn in the Gladesville trunk murder (fiancée identifies torso) until someone said, 'D. K. Durfee, isn't it! Once of Medlow Bath? Can you come and have a drink?' and she looked up into a face that had added a moustache and whose features had come to an agreement since she had last seen them. 'Come,' Angus said, taking her by the hand and propelling her to the Wintergarden while she muttered that she had ten years to kill. 'I mean ten *minutes*,' she said as he led her through a field of hats and hair to a window table where Lesley Ann was sitting.

'Look who I found,' Angus said.

'Just for a minute then,' Bea said over Lesley Ann's clutching arms. 'Oh, this is marvellous, Bea,' Lesley Ann said.

'This is marvellous,' Angus echoed and waved to a waiter. 'Gus, Gus.' Angus summoned with a pipe. He had become proprietary. He appropriated the waiter, appropriated their drinks. He leaned back smoothing his moustache and asked for a window to be closed. 'Bring some of those little baby sandwiches,' he said in his deepened voice from his increased weight, and ground embers from his pipe with a steel chisel and took out a tobacco pouch, showing his new cultivated lethargic gestures, and, looking at Bea, smiled with his eyes and this in the total reconstruction of chromosomes and genes was all that was left of the boy.

'You might say,' Angus said, 'this is a bit of fortune's handicraft that us three should be together on the last night of the war.'

'Is it the last night of the war?' Bea asked.

'Could be, I'm told. Pal of mine in Intelligence at Barracks.' It was now only a matter of the de-deification of the Emperor, he told them in his new voice of experience.

'It'll seem funny without the war,' Lesley Ann said.

'Bea, Bea,' Angus said and put a brown, golden-haired hand on her arm. He was immensely fatherly. 'You've grown a charisma with success, old bean.'

He'd become a faint imitation of someone. 'And you've been,' Bea asked him, 'where exactly?' He was so changed that she heard herself pose the question in tones she used for strangers on buses. 'Three years in an ordnance depot in the Never Never country, so called because you would never never believe it,' Angus said and obligingly drew a map on the tablecloth with his pipe stem and gave them, in his rich basso, a description of the far north, where there were cities of red anthills six feet high under vast cobalt skies where in rainy seasons next-door neighbours sixty miles apart never saw each other for four months in this gaunt, this ruthless country. All the time he spoke of such hardships, Angus took little nibbles from tiny chicken sandwiches, wiping his glossy moustache fastidiously and addressing Bea as 'dear girl.' So had she been to blame for harbouring a vision of him all these years so totally wrong? This large grown man, thick knee pressed up against the table in his staff sergeant's uniform, smoothing the moustache that looked attached with spirit gum and in his velour voice saying it was prebiblical, one might say preflood, unchanged except for the roads built by the bloody Yanks and that it was atavistic, nudging you with its eternity, and so he was going back, away – Angus intimated the marble and glass around them with scorn – 'away from all *this*,' Angus said with disgust, reaching for another tiny sandwich. Well, he was buying a tenth of a small tin mine in a spot so desolate it took two days by dirt road from the nearest settlement; there was no name for it on any map. 'And if she behaves herself I may take along this delightful dryad who is temporarily disguised as a lady captain.' He placed the other brown hand on Lesley Ann, who lavished doe looks on him and, to hide her exaltation, pretended to be angry at his presumption but, being a terrible actress and without humour, the effect was that of pique in a sheep. 'You're being very bossy,' she said and hit at him with her gloves; this girl who'd crawled away from the gas across the floor, happily slapping at Angus with her army gloves while he tried to grab her hand in a way that told Bea their sexual rompings had been extravagant. There was a fierce innocuousness about them as they bantered each other saying, 'Is that so?' 'That is so.' 'Oh, you think so?' 'Yes, I think so.' 'Do you know?'

Bea dreaded they might rub noses. Glancing away from them, she stared at the crowd and saw Corey sitting in a group not too far away, which was a usual mirage about this hour and at this temperature of her emotion, feeling deprived by the happiness of Angus and Lesley Ann and because of Angus ordering two rounds every time the waiter passed them because already the lights had winked the first last-drink warning. She felt a little dizzy. 'So far away, Bea,' Angus was saying, 'that should they ever drop the big A on civilization — and looking around this room, dear girl, can you honestly say it would be much loss? — so far away that we wouldn't even *know* about it.'

'I would *want* to know,' Bea said thickly, resenting being left in the holocaust while they lived out their idyll. She admired and hated his new full-grown confidence, his consoling fatherly arm around her, and telling her in the kindest way about primitive latrine conditions, and because this appalling dream they had might very well work out for them. 'If you're crazy for ants . . .' she said and hooded her eyes like her mother, not because of their predilection for ants but because of the structural change he'd brought about, this absorption of himself into a coarser frame. Perhaps he'd planned this absolute disappearance into a new body when he'd walked away into the mist that evening and vanished, leaving his blue suit and his squat Sunday shoes in the wardrobe. The mystery never satisfactorily explained; the stationmaster had seen him get on the train so they knew at least he wasn't in pieces at the foot of a cliff but nothing more (that it was not to be mentioned to Mother was palpably obvious); vanished leaving those ugly painful-looking shoes holding his shape and the drawing he'd been doing of Eve, which Bea studied intently for a clue of some kind and found that either by accident or by lack of craft he had made her mother look evil. There was a subtle malice around the mouth and eyes. It was as if he'd predicted a cruelty in her and left behind this evidence to prove he'd been right and it was in itself cruel of him to do so, Bea thought, even inadvertently. It occurred to her that he had the true cruelty of people who are oversensitive. She saw him on his first night with them, his first drink (watching him put them away now, it was funny to think he could have got plastered on a little light wine), and making, trying to make, an elegant little speech to Eve, poor boy falling over syllables with his reverence for her and all the jokes they made about his blind adoration of Mother. Yet he had predicted cruelty in her.

Now, pitching in the wake of the big talk from this big man beside her, Bea wanted the mystery cleared up.

'Angus, why did you run away?'

'I'm not running away, Bea. I *want* to live in the Never Never. Don't we, chicken?'

'Why *did* you, I said.'

'Did I what? Funny how people take the attitude that doing what you want to do is wrong unless it conforms to their ideas – but I don't expect that from *you*.'

'Why, Angus?'

'Because you are one of the few originals.'

'Why?' she persisted. 'Something to do with that fuss over the dog?'

Angus was looking at her now.

'The cat,' he said, 'out of the bag.'

'Oh, Bea,' Lesley Ann said, 'you never did cut your hair, did you and how jolly wise of you. How wise of you. It *suits* you.'

'How wise of you not to get involved,' Angus said. '*I* got involved. Didn't *she* tell you?'

'No and I never asked.'

'What did you think?'

'Just that it was original of you to just go – without your shoes.' Angus leaned back and gave a delighted laugh, too loud. 'That is my Bea,' he said. His gestures had become too ornate. Now, for God's sake, he was holding up her arm in the air and kissing her on the elbow for everyone to see.

'Tell why,' Bea said, 'in five words.'

Well then . . .

He had been such an innocent but then he'd had no life whatever and when he was inducted into *theirs* . . .

'You can't imagine the impact on me you all had. Well, it was like never having heard there was cold Senegalese, never having thought about *thinking,* of being educated to have values – you were all so educated.'

'I think,' Bea said, 'we were educated about unnecessary things – like knowing a great deal about swans.'

She wanted to put him off, lightly, but he was not going to be put off. He held up an admonitory finger to her. He would explain to her her family. Delightful creatures, entrancing, oddish . . .

'And I was just a nice little nothing,' Angus said and knotted her fingers tightly into his in case she had any idea of escaping. 'Such a *nice,* agreeable, obliging *rabbit*.'

He was furious with the idea. So apparently he had been at great pains to make up this new aggressive worldly man (the smile was crooked and wry). 'Well, *you* warned me about being such a bloody innocent.' Had she?

He was describing her to herself now and it was like hearing an opera based on your own life in a foreign language when only your name is recognizable occasionally through the mass of incoherency; all about how she was the only one who saw through the fakery; she had been the only one untouched by it.

'The only one of the bunch without a secret drag,' Angus said and Bea began to feel alarmed. 'I must go,' she said but Angus had her hand tightly and he may have waited a long time to impress her with his aggressiveness. He was determined to explain her curious family to her.

It seems they were a wild bunch underneath. 'Your loving brother once threw a hammer at me and missed my head by inches, but it wasn't *intended*,' Angus said, laughing. And then Stevie, knowing about his acrophobia, had trapped him into a wild nightmare ride over a mountain in a shale-mine trolley and had tried to throw herself out of it. Perhaps he had had a touch of the sun up in the Never Never. 'And much more that wasn't obvious to me then,' Angus said, his eyes sparkling. 'Oh, Bea doesn't want to hear all this,' Lesley Ann said. She'd begun to twist and throttle her gloves. 'Let's get the bill, can we? It's getting so hot in here.' 'I haven't finished my drink,' Angus said. He'd begun to sweat lightly and there was a hint, a gleam of purposeful malice in his good humour. He was one of those quiet drinkers who look and sound harmless until in a twinkling they've got you by the throat. '*You* know what I'm talking about,' he said. 'Haven't a clue,' Bea said, trying to unknot her fingers from his. 'What killed me was that *she* could be so corny and obvious. Like something out of a – forgive me – a radio serial, Bea. Her of all people.'

'What?'

'Why, *you* know. For her to have had the dog put away and then to pretend it was out of *kindness*. For her to be *paltry*.'

'Why did she then?'

'Well, *you* know: *mea culpa*, of course, because I let the cat out of the bag about your father and Cissie.'

The only way to forgive this was to realize he was either nuts or he'd made it up to compensate for some imagined hurt and in seven years had come to believe it. There was no way possible to confuse his meaning.

'You're the one who should be writing radio serials,' she said.

'Now, Bea, old *dear,* could I make up a thing like that?'

Only one meaning. Her father and Cissie.

'You are getting fat, do you know?' she said.

She stood up but Angus still had hold of her hand and, when she tried to wrestle it away, held on. He was strong.

'Facts, Bea. You can't escape from them. Only *you* did.'

'. . . have my hand, please?'

'Darling girl, I'm paying you a compliment and I want you to listen.'

'Will you kindly let go of my hand?'

'But then you knew about all the fakery going on.'

She got her hand free but the jerk unbalanced her and she fell against the table and then hugely onto it and bottles went over, beer all over Lesley Ann, glasses onto the floor. 'Drunks,' someone said loudly. Angus looked amazed and hurt. 'Don't *be* like this, Bea.' Her elbow was in the ashtray. 'Good-bye,' she said and managed to right herself but in doing so dropped her purse and Angus, blundering up to help her, knocked over his chair. Keystone Kops all in a flash. Heads turning, waiters coming at the double. 'Hurt yourself?' Angus asked as she grovelled on the floor. She was trying to get her purse but Angus was standing on the strap; she pushed at his foot, hit her head on the table getting up, dizzily. 'Closing time,' the waiter said severely. 'No, no, I'm leaving,' Bea said loudly to the room. There was beer all over her skirt. 'Not in *anger,*' Angus said angrily. 'I won't have it.' He was puce in the face in the blinking lights. He attempted to block her way and a man had stood up at the next table.

'All I said was you got away.' He wasn't so big after all. 'You got away from them like *I* did.'

'Not like you,' she said, 'because *I* belonged there in the first place.' She pushed past him and started through the aisles of tables and upturned amused faces. Several people had stood up to see where the fight was going on and then, disappointed it was over so soon, turned attention on her and her departure, intersecting her way through the knots of tables in her beer-dripping skirt, and so she enclosed herself in wraps of sedateness and made her way to the faraway door in time to the music from the band as though she had just been the recipient of a trophy and, looking neither to right nor to left, was conscious only of stares and shadows and so was too occupied trying to vanish to be surprised at the blur of three tall figures slightly to one side. A hand reached out and, Hello, one of them said, thought it was you. 'Hello,' she said and closed her eyes for a second and then opened them again and, 'Well,' he said, 'they told me if you sat in here long enough you'd get to see everyone in the world you know.' Apparently he had hold of her arm to save her from sinking into suds covering the floor.

'Major Lenahan and Captain Tunley, I'd like to have you meet Miss St James,' Corey said.

This isn't too bad a place. Medium rare for me. Maybe you can help us: should we go to the Minerva or the Tivoli? The Tivoli's acts and girls. Girls is for us. You go call Charley.

Someplace called Broadcast House. No, they're the noncommercial network and extremely parochial and they would not have heard of me on principle. Oh, well, Corey said (or this man who looked like Corey said), our lines of communication were never very good, remember?

But iced water, for God's sake. You'd think we were asking for mint juleps. American custom, Major (her head was full of splinters, the result of being made to take in too much at once). Ask if they have an aspro. It's sort of an aspirin.

You didn't think you'd ever get back (sideways he was very much like she remembered but full face, a total stranger). Fluke. No, this time they put me at the Roxbury, know it? It's just around the corner from where I live. No kidding!

Her head was clearing a little now except for one dark lump of unpleasant thought. I'm sorry about this, she said, the lobster's *usu*ally excellent here. Is yours like rubber too?

Is this the best they could do, Charley? Corey asked; they were in the very back row with the standees breathing down on them and dropping jelly beans on them. From time to time she glanced left at him in the light from the stage but try as she might, she could not take it in nor could she by any amount of effort get her heart to lift up one centimeter.

Who's this Bobsy Le Brunn? Home-grown comic. I doubt if he'd go in Des Moines. Now we have the Ten Little Trotters, performing pigs. I think the Major's nodded off. The girls are a bit on the mature side, wouldn't you say? Direct from the Folies Bergère! Via Tibet, would you say?

Perhaps she had spent it all in thinking, imagining it happening, to have any real spark of emotion left but her deflated mood continued through the massive all-Viennese finale which had a curly Johann Strauss and baby grand playing the 'Blue Danube' through a net cloud and produced genuine emotion in Captain Tunley, who was the youngest.

Raining when they came out. It always rains when I'm here, he said. He'd taken hold of her arm the way he used to and she was beginning to understand that it had happened, he was here. Now a nightclub. He insisted, it being their last night. 'Whee,' Bea said in the cab, making an effort, but he only said, 'What?' Not three guys and one gal, the Major said properly. He and Tunley would cut out. See you in the morning, crack of dawn.

How very very very pink it is in here, Corey said. What do you think about our bomb? I drink to you, he said, in this somewhat acidy champagne I suspect of being hock.

They held onto each other tightly on the crowded floor, unable to move more than an inch or so. Don't they ever get tired of 'White Christmas'? Corey asked and they went back to the table and had something called Fig Delight and Bea tried and tried but could not get her spirits up, they continued on down until she knew she was looking glum and that he knew it; he glanced sharply at her once or twice almost as a husband might, as her husband might say, Oh, for God's sake, can't you cheer up when I'm spending all this damn money and try not to be a bloody wet blanket on my last night. 'Funny, I thought you smoked Philip Morris,' she said gaily. Well, whichever way you look at it the bomb's a gigantic achievement for peace and makes us the front runners of the *world,* he said a bit severely as though she might treat the bomb with levity, her being British and it American. 'I can't take it in,' she said. 'I can't believe it may all be over in a minute.'

Come on up and have a nightcap, he said. Well . . . Oh, yes, come on up and anyway it's teeming now, you can't get home in this.

Oh, miles better, miles, miles better, she said, and you have a little kitchenette and a view too.

And what would *this* be? He'd tried to figure it out for days.

They gazed at it postponing possible outcomes; concentrated on this object.

Eventually, one of them having to break the silence, she said that it was either a little stepladder for extremely short people to climb into the rather high old bed or a shoe rack.

A shoe rack. He was so grateful to her because . . .

'Because . . .' trailing off and abruptly kissing her, 'oh, I've thought about this, Bea, many times.'

Now in the dark it was no longer possible to push back the lump of unpleasant thought that had been sticking in her mind all through the long long evening and made her feel like a dead weight, a mere physical contraption, manufactured and patented with all parts working correctly, arms and legs, automatic response, but not resulting in the furious joy guaranteed in the brochure. It was this dead-at-the-heart feeling which she tried to deny by assuring him with tenderness and abandonment to him but, full of love, she felt a failure. Felt absurdly in the closest moments as though she ought to be thinking about something else, as though she knew in the back of her mind she was already late for some urgent appointment and here she was roistering in bed. Typical of her, she thought, to be distracted at the time of this miraculously granted occasion, to not be there, only to know the deep dark sweetness and pain of it at its boundaries, before and after but not during; which was for those who only play it safe, for cowards, for the heartless and wary, and the thought of this drove her to deny it to him with excesses and a startling vocabulary of delight.

Then, over lapsing, diminishing, whispering, turning away and a stealthy apologetic setting of the alarm clock's phosphorine hand, lying there she became suddenly the thing she'd been warding off, a hurt child, an extremely lonely and high-principled child, and it was this child that had gone through all the motions of the expected and surprising, angry and gentle but with the sorrow of her hurt, and this was what had been wrong with it. No better way to flatten lust than to feel sadness and an enormous longing to be just hugged and kissed.

So although he was stretched out beside her, their toes touching, and he'd taken hold of her hand under the sheet, she was lying beside him fully clothed in her school uniform, a tartan skirt with a silver pin in it and a middy blouse, and she had on her black woollen stockings and strap shoes and her school hat with the badge in front. She could feel the elastic strap around her chin and also that she was on the verge of tears, wanting immensely to be comforted by hugs and kisses. Because, face it, if there ever had been at any time something between her father and her mother's (always presumed) oldest and closest friend, then . . .

If what Angus had blurted out so deliberately was true (and unhappily he was not deep enough for guile and not sour enough for malice), that would mean that the inviolable had been violable, that the immaculate love which had excluded her, excluded them all because it was so all-enveloping and self-containing (now she was on the veranda, hugging her knees and watching them, heads together as usual, walking close together

218

with their almost insufferable love), had after all contained a breach.

She put it to herself meticulously: all her excluded lonely girlhood she had been able to justify the exclusion by saying there was not room in this total love they had for anyone else. Period. That was how she played that game. The no-room-for-me game. But now if this had not been so – and there was Cissie's dog to prove it and her mother's mottled face when she'd said, 'Never mind,' and her mother had said, 'About *what*?' – then to what purpose? So then, if they'd all been kept at arm's length, told not to disturb, keep out for something that all the time had been flawed, not the great white pure-as-topaz . . .

'But tell me, what *is* it? Corey's voice sounded hoarse in the dark, concerned but also exasperated now at three in the morning while she wept and wept.

'I don't hear you,' he said as she wept and murmured into his chest.

'I want to tell you something.'

'What?'

'I love you.'

So, that out, felt relief; something had to be the truth, something had to be said and meant.

'I love you.' She found her damp handkerchief ball and blew into it. 'And I wasn't crying because of that but because it just occurred to me that in my whole life nobody around me has ever said exactly what they mean and *I've* never said exactly what *I* mean and there's got to be one time when you do, otherwise what's it all for? What are we all so afraid of? People ought to *tell* people they love them, why not? What's so terrible about it they're ashamed to? If they mean it, long as they mean it desperately with all their heart, why not tell?

'Well, anyway, I have to tell you that. Simply that I love you. Just simply that.'

'Well . . . that's – that's very sweet, Bea.'

'Very deeply and sincerely with all my heart, Corey.'

'Very dear.'

'That's all. Period. End. Oh, except for one thing – and I only tell you this so you don't think this is one of those things people say in the dark in bed – I'm not just saying this in an emotional state because I'm not – actually I'm very cool about it – have to be – what else? I mean, it wasn't entirely accidental.'

'Mmmmmm?'

'I mean tonight.'

'I don't quite follow you.'

'I mean us . . . meeting.'

'How's that?'

'Coincidental more. I mean, I've been going in there on and off for months . . .'

'*Months*?'

'I mean, it seems months – weeks anyway, since you've been gone. I also used to go by your old hotel – just in case – I said to myself I'd have practically mended roads if –'

'Oh, now –'

'No, it's true.'

'I know but you mustn't –'

'I know this isn't the sort of thing I ought to confess to but –'

'No.'

'But I want to tell you the truth, the whole truth, Corey, on our last time – do you see?'

'Yes, sure, sure . . .'

'Oh, God, if you can't admit it just once in your life . . .'

'Yes, no . . . It isn't that I mind your telling me. I just don't want to be . . . Could you move just one second, could you move over a little, there's something sticking into me. It's a hairpin, I believe . . .'

'But you *do* understand?'

'Sure.'

'You understand I have this great need . . . not to play games.'

'Yes, of course.'

'Because I love you.'

'Yes.'

'Because . . .'

Because there was nothing more to say that wouldn't be repetitious, she lapsed into silence and he gave a huge sigh and turned on his side away from her and they were back to back and, looking down from the ceiling, mightn't they look like bas-relief bookends, she imagined, but almost immediately she was in this canoe and it being very narrow she had to lie with her arms close to her side all night and be most careful turning around not to capsize it. Only once in thickest sleep she bumped into the warm fleshy side of it. 'Sorry,' she said and kept her arms to her sides for the rest of the journey, remembering she mustn't stray far or turn over but not fathoming the reason why anyone should have thought it amusing to put sharp barbed wire down one side of her bed leaving her only this narrow patch to lie in but they had at least taken pity on her and shortened the night considerably because only eleven minutes after she'd closed her eyes the light was coming up from the wrong side of the boat – bed – and morning was spreading through a slit in horrendous looped curtains patterned with scenes of executions, it looked like, half opening her eyes and hearing the little stealthy noises around her; from the bathroom very quiet brushing and then gargling, a tap turned on and off and then shaving sounds and more water running and then suddenly the old brass snap bathroom light switched off and creaking, tiptoeing around in the gaining light and she lay still supposing he must have beaten the alarm to it and peeping sometimes through her own disordered hair watched him snap on garters, later belt, looping tie, stooping a little to see if his parting with the comb was straight, jingling noises, things put away in knapsacks, creaking, zipping, closet door open and shut, wire hangers strumming, beginning to wonder when he would speak her name or touch her but nothing happened except continuous going back and forth, bags strapped and keys gently lifted from glass and finally in some trepidation now she opened her eyes fully and sure enough he was in his cap and raincoat perched on the armchair and writing something and, turning, saw her sitting up with the sheet around her.

'I was just leaving you a note.'

He crumpled it up. It was a much older face full of bumps and lines, crepeyness around the eyes in the early light. A note and bags ready by the door. Just as if she were a call girl. Wondered if he'd left twenty dollars under the ashtray.

'Will you be all right?'

He spoke with icy consideration. He came as far as the end of the bed and looked down at her, a complete stranger and seriously offended. 'If you call down after eight, they'll send up coffee,' he said. It was more than offended, the tone of parting forever from a friend discovered to be false. 'Everything is taken care of,' he said and he'd been cruelly hurt seemingly, 'but if you remember, just drop the keys off at the desk as someone else may be using it tonight.' She just sat hugely there with the sheets draped around her and hair hanging down and it was true, the bed was littered with hairpins and the thought that she'd brought her untidy emotions into it.

'Too bad,' he said.

'About *what* ?'

'That it had to be so short.'

But he was already breaking loose, frantic to be gone from the disappointment of coming ten thousand miles to go to bed with the same girl with the same problems as Alice who also loved him over and against the wishes of his fierce mother (he was twisting the brass ball on the bed rail as if he could see in it what he was going back to), so this was no fun, no fling to be caught by another emotional girl, sitting in the bed holding her sheets around her and big and mute with pain, possibly going to brim over into tears any moment . . .

Oh, Jesus, he seemed to say — and he twisted the brass ball,

spun the ball furiously – any time now I may just cut out altogether from the whole goddam female bit, me and the dog.

'Hope you find Timmie O.K.,' Bea said hoarsely.

He brightened just a little.

'Oh, yes, I'll be seeing Timmie soon.'

She got out of bed, draping the sheet around her; she was
massive and majestic going to the bathroom and she was going
to be munificent too, get him off the hook, saying thanks as
Mother would wish her to. 'Wonderful time, thanks. Can't
think of a nicer way to celebrate the Bomb.'

Went into the bathroom and locked the door and turned on
both taps into the basin and just listened to the rushing water
washing everything away, all presumptions and dreams down
the drainpipe, and she let the water run a long time before washing her face. Then she went back into the empty room and
dressed and did her hair. Then she opened the piece of crumpled paper and it read: 'Dear Bea: Have to be on the wing and
didn't want to wake you. Thanks (crossed out). You are the –'

Dearest? Worst?

She wondered what he had been going to write. Wondered
what she was.

The gracious lady at the desk told her. The lady had a beautifully carved face and blue hair. 'And don't you ever show your
face in here again,' the lady said.

'*Honi soit,*' Bea said.

'*And* kindly keep your gutter language to yourself.'

The End, she thought, seeing the two large technicolour words
and, crossing the street, everything suddenly agreed with her,
the morning exploding, ripping the air around her, hooters
whistles, klaxons taxis honking, ferries hooting as she put her
hands over her ears and it began to rain paper, insane people
ran out of houses and shouted to her, children ran to attack her
with squeakers, blattered at her face. She stood still in the fun-
nel of deafening noise not knowing where to go. A mad-
woman in curlers grabbed her. *All over,* the woman screamed

in her ear. You are dead right, she answered the woman, who was capering with a doorman. Now a soldier waving a bottle at her. All over. But nothing to *be* over with in the first place. She cupped her hands around her mouth and yelled *nothing* into the hurricane and was jostled along towards Bayswater Road into confetti storms. *Nothing,* she yelled into the wall of noise. *Nothing,* she yelled to the mountains and then, remembering that she had scores of friends and untold lovers waiting to be created, not even begun to be imagined, indefinitely, was infinitely better off than any of these nincompoops gesticulating in the blast of peace, she called out as she'd many times had cause to, alone at Echo Point, *So what*?

Because of the noise she couldn't hear the reassuring echo yet. It would be a while, after things calmed down again, before she got the answer to that.

3. Eve

Somewhere in the depths of the house a clock struck seven with
little hurried golden strokes and then, contradicting it, a deep
brass-gonged grandfather whirred and slowly struck six. All the
clocks in this house disagreed and their indiscriminate chiming
became constant unhappy music in and out of every room, in
the grand front hall and under the stairwell, sepulchral in the
shaded library (nobody could locate by day the little monster
that pinged-pinged in the night), solemn knells in the dining-
room. The clocks rang out their false times, clanging away in
empty rooms when it was not the hour and consequently were
not looked at, never put forward or back, ran riot among themselves in a secret conspiracy, some running fiercely ahead and
others dropping behind until there was no truth to time anywhere in this house. The owner, who had brought the clocks
together with selective love, was not present now and so they
were wound by a sulky servant. The assumptions of the clocks
added to the general unease of the house, which was unhealthily
silent, full of warpings, creakings and, the sea having remained
deadly calm, it gave rise in the dead of night to speculation
about hearing muffled oars and, in the daytime, the maids,
subdued by the malaise in the atmosphere, had taken to tiptoes
and, big girls as they were, they teetered upstairs and down,
whispered, winced at creaking boards as though perhaps someone lay desperately ill behind one of the ivory doors and sometimes someone would call out, is that you, Mabel, and would be
shushed and a door would close in the distance when all that
was being asked was had Gristede's delivered six melons yet

and then the silence grew intenser, hard to take a nap in the intensity of such a silence, startled by a dried pod dropping from a tree through the open window, such a silence that hearing nothing brought suspicions of sounds, starting up from bed, heart beating wildly to find no reason but a faint stirring of the pale dreamlike curtains wafting with breath into the room and back again and only chirrups of crickets towards evening.

And, Eve thought, what is needed, if only (she was sitting at a low wide dressing-table mirror repeating herself three times and she was putting cucumber cold cream on her arms very deliberately and very slowly and counting the wrong clocks) – if only someone would suddenly put a record of a Sousa band playing 'Stars and Stripes' at *full blast* and shake the house from top to bottom with shock and blare and fright and break the spell of this sick modulation which even at dinner caused such muted voices and the sad sounds of knife and fork so quiet that one evening she had distinctly heard Mabel swallow, standing behind her holding the white dish of escarole.

As if they wouldn't hear the phone when it rang (extensions all over the house). But constantly they said, was that the phone? I thought I heard the phone, did you? And when the phone rang they were stricken and, like paralysed people, could not move for a moment, took a sip of water before turning to the sound and then one of them rising from the table or the deck chair to go to it while the other waited and did useless things, scraping crumbs on the tablecloth or pulling a blade of grass, straining to hear what might be being said to and from New York.

The owner of the clocks had gone into the city. Gabriel had come across the lawn dressed unexpectedly for town on a Saturday evening at cocktail time and said without emotion, 'I'm leaving now,' and Stephanie had said, while all the time she carefully examined her small toe for any signs of age, 'Oh? How long will you be gone?' and Gabriel said, 'I'll let you know when *I* know that. I'll call you.'

That had been over two weeks ago and therefore the longest of all his absences without calling up to now. Meanwhile they played Stephanie's game of Gabriel Who? But guesswork like Gabriel's clocks ran riot and communicated itself to the staff so when the phone rang the house stiffened and stood stock still (the cook in the kitchen with saucepan lid poised in the air, the gardener having turned off the power mower) until Stephanie had asked Mabel or Linda who it was and been informed it was Saks of Southampton, so, everything resuming, the cook put on the saucepan lid, the gardener powered the motor.

And the silence got thicker. Leaning over their interminable games of Scrabble they murmured their scores to each other listening towards evening for the sound of the cars. But when a big car turned into their lane it invariably went past their gates and continued on towards the Lindquist house.

They became aware that it had been Gabriel who was the source of this house, the power and magnet that drew people to it (and why not, as this was his house, his neighbours, his friends and his way of doing things in this same house since 1925, when he was married on the lawn to Frances, whose portrait hung in the library and looked down at these interlopers with dead anguished eyes), and Gabriel had the flair and so his parties were much favoured. He collected people in the way other men collect deadly weapons; he showed them off, polished them with attention and affection very knowingly until they glistened or believed they glistened and then, trying to outshine each other for Gabriel, they caused a kind of éclat. Eve had watched it work for him. He caused such a current of importance to circulate among his friends that it made them feel lavish, which, they being rich, was a comparatively rare emotion for them. In return for being made to feel they were all delightful, it was understood that Gabriel must be allowed (if he wanted, which was mostly) to recite 'Casey at the Bat' with gestures.

Had Eve and Stephanie put out a sign warning of cholera they could not have become more alienated from the other big

227

houses, word having been brought by their staff to other staffs that Gabriel in the middle of August had gone into town on a weekend and not returned. Omitted was a better word, Eve thought, when on weekend nights the sounds of parties floated over to them across the salt lagoons and all evening the big cars rushed down the lane past their gates and on to the Lindquists or the Crowleys. Well, thank God, Stephanie said, because they were bores and could only talk about two things, money and more money. But she looked at her mother as if she expected to be corrected or told she was insular in the wrong way. So Eve said nothing but on occasions wished for guests, one guest, any guest to break the strain of being alone with Stevie in this sense of desertion that had spread through the house now that the impetus was gone from it.

'Just what *do* you want?'

Suddenly in the soup course. He had stood up and flung down his spoon. 'Just for God's sake tell me what you *want*, Stephanie.' They were incredulous, open-mouthed, spoons poised over their cold sorrel soup; it was incredible that this was Gabriel, heated and irate, breathing heavily, fiery-faced. It was as unexpected as an archbishop spitting and then, as if to back him up, all his clocks rang and bonged on cue. Then, with Stevie giving him that too-affronted-for-words look, Gabriel left the room. That had been on the Friday night before the Saturday evening when he had come across the lawn cool and estranged to say he was going into town. Eve couldn't remember exactly what had preceded the explosion. Dinner had been going along much as it always did, with her exactly balanced between Stevie and Gabriel, and something had been said about Nancy Ackerman buying a peacock, which Stevie began disparaging, making so very little of it in so big a way as to make it sound fatuous and typical, typical and linked to a social decay surrounding Gabriel, who said once and with a flicker, 'She *likes* you.' But Stevie could not care a rap for anyone who'd bother buying a peacock (her sceptical voice droned on in a way that at times made Eve feel herself being parodied), which only went to prove that everyone here, her so-called friends, were so punky, really punky. It was kooky how really many punky people lived around her . . .

Just what do you want? He yelled, this glad man (always glad to see you, glad to get you a drink, glad to put you onto the right person to get you a Flemish tapestry), and went out of the room and nothing had been said about him since. He might as well have gone to Tibet.

His caps and hats hung in the back hall, his carp swam in the Japanese pool, his Waterford crystal inkwells were ready on the desk, his squash rackets and golf clubs waited for him on the game-room closet and his English setter waited for him on the main drive with frantic eyes. His snow-white terry-cloth robe hung behind his bathroom door as he himself might have hung himself on the hook, sleeves hanging in a gesture of the uselessness of further trying.

'And I want to thank you for coming, but I mean greatly truly thank you, Eve, for being here, my dear,' he said to her a month after she arrived, leading her away presumably to see his new giant rhododendron bushes and putting a very muscular gold hand on her arm but speaking with gentleness and such sincerity that it rocked her for a moment. The terrible niceness of him shook her so that she had to pretend she had a piece of gravel in her shoe and stamped her foot and said with all the scorn she could muster '*If* you're happy to have a white elephant around . . .' 'Oh, now come on, why do you say that, Eve?' he asked; he was genuinely disturbed and worried that she possibly was not happy here. 'Oh, you know how much good you do for Steff.' 'Really?' She made the word curl. 'I can't imagine what.'

That much was true, though not in the wooden warped way she had spoken of it, but she still awakened in the night with this feeling of acute displacement, wondering where she was, in what strange bed thousands of miles from home (but yet where

229

was home anyway?) and what was she doing here for God's sake and for how much longer? Not that she was homesick. She had been a displaced person in her own mind and body for some years now and so it made little difference whether she was here in Long Island on this estate or living back with Bea (far more illusory than being here, far more mysterious) or in her own empty bungalow at Medlow Bath full of ghosts.

But Stevie had telephoned and spoken to her unhurriedly and in a pig's voice; exactly like a pig speaking to her from New York via Honolulu and Fiji all the way along the ocean's bottom to where she sat at three o'clock in the morning Sydney time in the hall in Bea's huge drafty duplex apartment. Stevie called and said in her pig voice to come; she and 'Daddy' wanted Eve to come and she put Gabriel on and a fortune was spent in his telling her not to bring this, not to bring that, nor her furs as they were midway to spring there and asking such things as did she like lobster, well then, the lobster would be waiting for her on the night she arrived ... But (she went back to bed hugging the strange thought) it was possible that one of her children wanted her.

'Oh, tip-*top*,' Bea said. 'Oh, you *must* go. You mustn't *think* of *me* for a second. Go and roll in Stevie's luxury. I've met him, you know. He's the kind who's always snapping open a great bloody gold cigarette lighter for you whether you want to or not and could get you *Life* magazine back issues in Lapland. Oh, well, you go.'

'I thought I *might*,' she said, making it sound onerous, 'get it over with.'

So she came.

All the way a spark kept lighting up in her. She put it out. It lit again. She doused it firmly. It came over her even in sleep, strapped in her seat in air pockets. She put it out because she coud not bear hope but she had not felt such a spark since she was very young and it would not be doused with all her cool dew she kept for any little weaknesses such as this. She stood in the hospital death light of the rest room on the plane, swaying, standing on air currents, and saw her own thrilled face in the mirror; her eyes were dilated by excitement and she was breaking out into a smile, all pretty crinkles and bridlings, and when by habit she raised her eyebrows in cool disdain at herself she merely looked asinine with a kind of bridal happiness. She was being transported rather than airborne and she let the smile happen before breaking it into the basin where it belonged. Because if . . .

So she sat down on the toilet seat and, taking out of her big duffel bag her new excellent-for-arrival crocodile shoes, she put them on with the expression of someone donning filthy muck boots and battened herself down against the feeling of appalling excitement and joy at being summoned, wanted, and against the perturbation of the heart at being roused from the dead, not sure after all this time it was a good idea to leave the tomb, come staggering out into the sunlight to see what they wanted of her. When one has been accustomed to nothing for a very long time, the something happening, the bell ringing in the night, is an alarm, waking the dead . . . Sometimes best not to answer it. But she had answered Stevie's call in the night.

She was trembling at the back of her knees at Idlewild Airport, walking slowly through a seeing-eye door after being whisked through customs by unseen pull and seeing Stevie hurrying towards her, Stevie breaking into a run and waving ecstatically, beckoning her to hurry as if seconds more of waiting were unbearable. Stevie's eyes were bright with excitement.

'Look, there's Averell Harriman,' Stevie said as they exchanged lipstick smears. They stood and looked at Averell Harriman until the chauffeur came with the bags so it seemed she had come seven thousand miles to get a glimpse of a diplomat and later, with no clue forthcoming, to sit and look at grass lawns. She sat and looked at grass. She sat and looked at water. Sat and looked at sky. She dressed herself carefully every day to sit and look. Sometimes she sat in other people's gardens and looked at their grass, water and sky. The spark in her died.

'And I want to thank you for coming. But I mean greatly truly thank you for being here, Eve my dear,' Gabriel said and she had sprung a leak with tears, damnation, stamped her foot on the gravel at finding herself vulnerable to this kind impervious man almost old enough to be her husband, an older version of Bill Seward (except that Stevie had exchanged dullness for the sameness of prodigality), and she touched Gabriel's arm and an old child in her cried out, you must tell me why I'm here, you must explain this rapidly deteriorating situation and moreover you must expand your kindness to let me explain myself in all my lifelong fearfulness so that I can speak to my daughter about it. Gabriel was waiting for some reply. In a moment they'd be lost in the rhododendrons; his hand was reaching out to touch a leaf. The words rushed to her. 'If you're –' Estranged from life, she began to say and instantly Heath St James appeared and bade her shut up. To explain herself she needed to explain him also and the vision of Heath St James dared her to. He was sitting in his chair with the knit rug over his knees just as he had been on the last afternoon and seemed to beckon to her and make an effort to speak. She tried to resist going all through it again but in memory he was just as strong as in life and again she bent over him, again she heard the two whispered words as she always heard them. She closed her eyes and lived through the horror again for perhaps the ninety-sixth time. It didn't decrease with repetition.

'If you're –' Something about being a white elephant, she said to Gabriel weakly, failing the chance of confession, and then that she couldn't fathom why Stephanie would want her here and Gabriel soothed her with airy platitudes because he was that kind of man, who constantly put things to rights on the surface and trusted them to take root; he was a mathematician who dealt strictly in black-and-white figures and emotions distressed him (and how well Eve understood this and how to brush them under beds) and he became clumsy, his big hands moving painfully around the situation to make the best of it with gifts, drinks, cheering up everybody. Nothing but the total collapse of Wall Street would have seemed to him worthy of such catharsis as she was going through: the act of suttee, of throwing herself alive on her husband's burning funeral pyre.

'Did you know,' she asked her son-in-law, 'you can change the colour of hydrangeas by putting nails under them?'

She had the feeling that she was vanishing away from want of cause. They'd find her empty chair on the lawn one day with the glass of everlasting iced tea beside it.

One morning she went into the library and began pulling books out of shelves and fingering them around. 'What are you doing?' Stevie asked. 'Thought I'd get this into some kind of order,' she said and began a systematic stacking in alphabetical order. 'But why do you feel you have to *do* something?' Stevie asked and then continuously hampered her by wandering in and out, picking up books and reading aloud to her. So she gave up and went back to sitting and looking.

Anyway the atmosphere worked against activity. The great warm soporification of salt, humidity, wine, food and the pastures of white bed.

Dear Bea, she wrote, I am being rested to death on the American Plan. How are you?

No matter how she tugged and stretched at events, she was never able to fill an air letter and the flaps remained unwritten on. Such parched little letters but what the hell, just a courtesy. I'm still alive. Bea had no time for her letters or for her. She could see Bea now standing up for breakfast because she had no time to sit and reading her uneventful notes impatiently, standing in her horsey tweeds and sipping her breakfast tea in a hurry. I hope, she wrote, you are over your cold. Affectionately, Mother.

As early as August she began thinking of going home. She telephoned BOAC and discussed going back the alternate route via Singapore and the BOAC girl was so charming, interested, enthusiastic that it had given her a momentary illusion of communication; someone was paying attention to her. So much so, that she felt she might lose all restraint and spew out everything to this sympathetic girl, Miss Quigley. Now, Miss Quigley wanted to know, would Mrs St James care to have a stopover in Jakarta, which could be so easily arranged, no trouble whatever. Eve wrote down the word 'Jakarta' on the pad and looked at it. It seemed so vital to Miss Quigley, her life might have depended on it. How do you *feel*, Miss Quigley asked. Well, rotten if you really want to know, Miss Quigley. Seeing you've been kind enough to ask I'll tell you: I feel curiously as if I am vanishing into nothing. You see, I'm estranged from life. Oh, not at all, not a *bit* of it – Miss Quigley laughed – not *you*, Mrs St James, you can be redeployed, rerouted, redestinationed without extra charge because I'm here for that purpose and BOAC is here for that purpose and you will never be estranged, lost, undefined while *we* are here. Oh, come BOAC, Miss Quigley said, all ye who are heavy laden . . .

'Jakarta,' Eve said, 'you might pencil in,' and Miss Quigley was so grateful to her. Then, moving her head, she saw gold-slippered feet on a level with her eyes and wondered how long Stevie had been eavesdropping on the stairs and so she grew curt and cool to Miss Quigley and hung up.

Stevie was leaning on the stair rail and regarding her with a look of displeasure, the look of a jilted hostess. Stevie was boss now, their roles reversed, incredible, impossible to believe this had once been her child. 'Just inquiring about going back the other way,' Eve said, feeling she was standing on the mat in the headmistress' office. The silence was pointed.

'But what do you have to go back to?' Stevie asked.

Eve stood in first position ballet, toes turned out. Her feet and legs as she stared down looked astonishingly young to her; her dark-blue linen skirt cut a good clean line across her knees and she was standing, as had just been pointed out to her, on the very last cliff of life, beyond which is endless void. She sighed and, after waiting a bit, hearing a clock bong somewhere, she said:

'Just the grave, I suppose.'

'Oh, well, we can get you back in plenty of time for that,' Stevie said and laughed that strange laugh of hers that began of silent heaving and developed into bubbles of sound breaking finally into long-drawn-out hootings that were empty of mirth, a terrible laugh, Eve thought, the laugh following her all the way upstairs. Down on her like a heavy object off a shelf fell the thought that Stevie had no imagination. That she had no real perception of people at all and therein lay her cruelty. Could that be right?

There on the bed that evening when she came upstairs from the long afternoon of sitting and looking was an embossed box tied in velvet ribbon and in it a bed jacket designed for the Empress Eugénie perhaps, Brussels lace and too beautiful for anything but to be buried in. 'Mother from Steve,' said the scrawl. She sat on the bed feeling suddenly quite weary, as though she didn't have the strength to go through the routine of thanking Stevie. The gift made her feel more estranged than ever. It was true then that Stevie had no perception whatever of people. If you would only tell me why I'm here, Steve; not bed jackets but a point is what I need. But Stevie only saw the haziest outline of where somebody existed and she was very little interested even in that. She played the piano fortissimo with technical clarity but really like a stevedore. Her musical technique was like her handling of people, easy. People were there when she saw them or they were not there at all, non-existent.

So she could dismiss Miranda. 'She wants to stay with Bill,' Stevie told everyone with an air of such munificence you'd have thought it was *she* getting the divorce, not Bill. 'She's so mad for her father it's practically incestuous and I wouldn't *dare* budge her.' So that dismissed Miranda for all time, that was the end of her.

So there was no point in looking for a point. There was no

point to her being here except that Stevie needed a prop. Some people need pets or guests to gain a sense of –

Was that the telephone?

She put down the pot of cucumber cream and listened intently to the coffin silence of the house.

She'd wanted to interrupt her thought but forced herself to go back to it. A sense of . . .? Self-value. It doesn't matter really whether the pets and guests are grateful and happy or not, provided they don't try to escape their function of furnishing that self-esteem. So we bank the fires to warm ourselves.

'Amazing,' she said aloud and slapped her own face hard with cold cream, astonished not at being fifty-seven but at being this age before facing this fact of herself. *He* had said to her in one of his very rare expositions, 'Get rid of Cissie for your own sake,' and no, she protested. Get rid of her old friend? Not even for *you*, Heath, she'd said. One of the few times she had ever fought him about anything. She'd felt alarmed and, not knowing why, walked from him along the dark veranda. But now, being a prop herself, she knew why. Bea had known. When Cissie had walked off with the last laugh, Bea had said with pity, 'Never mind.' That had been the last straw, pity at a moment like that, and so she'd said with mock innocence, 'About what?'

Breeze lifted a long veil of curtain into the room. It touched her hair and she brushed it away with a gesture of shooing away a bird, a hand touching her, like avoiding an unwanted caress, like hearing Cissie say again, 'Oh, but it's all forgiven and forgotten years ago, my love.' Meaning the dog episode.

She had wanted to make peace with Cissie but Cissie had seized the opportunity to testify to her own morality (she had grown old) and to assure Eve that during the time that Heath had come to her for advice and comfort, 'I swear to you, love, sex never happened *once*.' Eve had tried to ward off this cheap placating. Had they spent every minute of the five days together in bed, it couldn't have mattered a damn to her compared to the real hurt: that he had turned to someone else at this moment and kept it dark from her. 'It couldn't matter to me less,' she had told Cissie, who continued to placate and to forgive *her*. Oh, there there, pet, Cissie's voice went on and on, you're not as bad as you like to think you are. All forgiven and forgotten.

There, there, the curtain waved at her soothingly, and she got up and closed the window. Heath and Cissie were dead and this brooding over the unchangeable past was due to too much sitting around in her room alone.

She cleaned off her face thoroughly and then put on her makeup carefully and spent time choosing what she would wear that evening, taking out first one dress and then another and finally putting on the white wool. She buckled on the black patent leather belt firmly with calm hands so that any eyes looking on from metaphysical peepholes could see that she was a free and independent agent. Walking around the room, putting on her bracelet, she let them see that she was not going to be used for anyone's ulterior purpose.

So whatever the outcome of this thing between Stevie and Gabriel, she would go home soon. No matter what was ahead of her, even if it *was* going to be nothing, dry rot, erosion, her skeleton found sitting bolt upright in a wicker chair reading Jane Austen, or slow senility, wandering around wailing and talking to herself, it would still be better in her own space. She saw the mountains, she saw the vines climbing around the burned-out ruin of the old hotel.

But (her hand on the glass doorknob) it came over her with a spooky certainty that there was something she might have to do before she would be free. No doubt of it. No getting out of it. Something would have to be said or done that might draw blood.

Anyone seeing Eve St James come out of her bedroom at this moment of her life could have remarked, what a very contained woman she is, look how admirably she is put together from top to toe. See how she holds herself with assurance; her walk is the walk of a woman with direction, a mixture of grace and disdain which is charming and which she knows is charming, knows without being vain about it that she is watched as all beauties know they are watched. But then she has been loved thoroughly in a way that is unique and gives to beauty an added prescience, a touch of the impertinent, she has been so loved that it has given her a conviction nothing can shake, Olympian, and therefore it is apparent in the flick of her feet descending stairs in her excellent crocodile shoes (worlds can be told of a woman by her shoes) that, however, she is a woman it would be wise not to cross. She is whole, admirable, unusual in this day and age.

(Anyone seeing Eve St James coming downstairs at this moment of her life might have been surprised to see her stop suddenly half-way down and remain very still, transfixed. Anyone knowing her would certainly have been surprised to see that what has stopped her is the sight of herself in a mirror. She is not a mirror gazer, she is apt to treat mirrors impatiently because, having complete self-assurance, she doesn't need their advice or congratulations. She is inclined to sneer at the sight of herself in mirrors as though what she sees is amusing or even ridiculous and here she is, poised in flight, one hand touching her breast and transfixed at the sight of herself, fascinated as a kitten seeing its reflection for the first time.)

A conjunction of yellow light and tarnish must have created this trick of the eye because as she had turned a bend in the stairs she had caught sight of this young girl wearing her dress coming down a staircase to meet her. So she stopped and the young girl stopped and they looked at each other. The last ray of the sun coming through a skylight and falling momentarily on her had given back her girlhood to her. She was twenty. The direction of light on cloudy glass had youthened her, softened lines and sent her white hair ash blonde again. She was Eve Partridge again. She moved her hand and Eve Partridge did likewise. Nothing might ever have happened to them since they had seen each other last. There was not a trace of years. The young girl staring at her was so calm, untouched yet by event's and questing, asking, what have you been doing all these years, Eve, bring me up to date.

Then the light faded.

But the impression remained photographed on her mind so that the girl stayed with her, went downstairs with her step by step, and this troubled her. She could cope with the truly dead, Heath and Cissie and the Pretty Brown-haired Girl whose name she chose to forget and who also stayed eternally young. She could close the vault on all of them. But not on Eve Partridge. As she crossed the hall she heard a car in the driveway and she went to the front door hoping to see Gabriel's friendly face, hoping, it being Friday, that he'd come down at least for the weekend, hoping that he'd resolved it at last, had come down with something silly and extravagant for Stevie. And if he could be there with his bland assurance in his own driveway again putting an end to the silence and indecision, she felt she would be able, almost able to run towards him open-armed in spite of Eve Partridge looking on, the hell with her. Not that she hadn't tried to say the hell with her for years. But it was a taxi in the driveway and being extracted carefully from it as though the owner treasured it was an enormous rump followed by a familiar tartan canvas weekend bag. So it was the understudy, their protector in the absence of the host, their self appointed Cerberus. From the attitude of his back she could tell he was giving the driver an argument rather than a tip and sure enough the taxi drove off angrily and purposely across a strip of lawn.

She watched from the door as Angus counted his change. He hadn't yet noticed her in the shadow of the hall. He picked up his bag and came towards the house looking around at Gabriel's giant rhododendrons and, finding a dead twig, tore it off and tossed it behind the bushes just as the owner might do and came crunching down the gravel very much as though to his own house and because she was disappointed at him not being Gabriel and also because in the last few weekends she'd noticed this increased proprietary sense of him, astonishing gall really, she said sarcastically, coming out to meet him, 'Oh, did you have to take a taxi? Why didn't you phone us from the station?'

'The pay phone there is busted,' Angus said and led the way into the house, into apparently his hall and into his den, throwing down his suitcase and taking off his crumpled seersucker jacket. 'That earlier train stops everywhere,' he said and then to Mabel, who'd also come to see who it might be, 'Hello, Mabel, could you bring ice?'

'Evening, Mr Weekes.'

'And bring some limes, would you?'

'Sure.'

'How's your arm, Mabel?'

'It's better on the whole, thanks.'

Had her arm been bothering her then all week with nobody saying anything – But of course Angus would know. Ask him anything. Where in God's name are those cork coasters which don't stick to the glasses and he'd know they were under the wicker place mats, in the top drawer in the pantry.

How he had widened. Why, he seemed to have widened a bit more only this week since they'd seen him last Sunday. But he only widened, never grew fat. He extended laterally. She couldn't think of anyone else who could have managed this feat.

'Any news?'

'No,' Eve said. 'It's been rather sepulchral here.'

'Getting on each other's nerves?'

'No.'

'You look a bit fagged out, Eve.'

'From sitting, I suppose.'

'Been out anywhere?'

'No.'

'Any visitors?'

'No.'

'*She* all right?'

'Hard to tell. Depressed, I think.'

'Think what?'

'Depressed.'

'Depressed? Really? Or just doing the spoiled pouty bit?'

'No, really down in the dumps.'

'You think so?'

He didn't agree, of course. He knew Stevie better than she, which was true. The moustache flowered glossily and lent him with his balding head the look of a sea lion. He had a somewhat patronizing way of sitting (now listen to *me* a minute) with one ankle resting on a knee, elbow on the other knee, which drew attention to his socks, rayon with ugly white clocks, anklet socks which didn't live up to his will to inspire. He didn't get up when Stevie came in.

'Oh, it's you,' Stevie said but she looked brighter.

'Howdy do,' Angus said.

He looked Stevie up and down.

'Don't you ever change?'

'Was that a question,' Stevie asked, 'or was it an endearing statement in the sense of, don't you ever *change,* as in Don't change a hair for me, not if you care for me?'

'You were wearing those exact clothes when I left last Sunday.'

All week Eve had thought, must she abide Stevie another day in this outfit she'd taken to: knee-sprung oatmeal-coloured pants and an old Army jacket of Gabriel's, morning, noon and night. She didn't bother to change for dinner and every morning she drifted down to breakfast, same pants, same jacket. Some deliberation went into this, a form of mourning, Eve thought. But she could at least attend to her hair, which needed a shampoo and which she tied back in a dull brown ribbon which only emphasised her already sharp face. Stevie sharpening, Angus widening.

'You look like something out of an old World War Two movie,' Angus said, 'the nurses on Bataan. "This bed can be freed." "This leg must come off," and you're out of morphine.'

'As a matter of fact,' Stevie said, 'we *are* out of morphine.'

She huddled in an armchair, her feet tucked under her, and lit a cigarette from the butt of another.

'*You're* getting to look like Teddy Roosevelt,' she said.

'Wrong. I look like Earl Derr Biggers.'

Stevie went into one of her soundless hootings.

'Oh, you made him up. Earl Derr *Bu*ggers?'

'Biggers. He wrote the Charlie Chan stories.'

'Why did he do that?'

'Because he couldn't stand his wife wearing the same clothes day in and day out.'

'*I* can tell you from Earl Derr Biggers,' Stevie said. 'I can even tell you in certain lights from E. Power Biggs. I can tell you at a distance from Ivy Baker Priest and Oveta Culp Hobby. I can tell you from – Oh, thank you, Mabel.'

Thank God, Eve thought, that Mabel had brought the drink fixings, because this sort of thing could go on for hours between them.

'Thank you, Mabel,' Angus said. He got up and went to the bar. 'What can I fix you?'

'Make us all a daiquiri,' Stevie said, 'the way you used to make them for William Randolph Hearst and Miriam Hopkins.'

'Marion Davies.'

'Her too.'

'At San Simeon.'

'The name of the house,' Stevie said, 'was Olga San Juan.'

'You're probably wondering,' Angus said, 'why I asked you all to come here tonight . . . '

'No, we've *done* that one,' Stevie said.

'What one shall we do then?'

'Oh, let's do "Eugene, Eugene, I've never seen the barometer so low." '

The telephone rang.

'I wonder who *that* could be,' Stevie said and they said together, 'at *this* hour of the night?'

But Eve noticed the stretching of Stevie into a single long tendril, uncurling from the chair, and the tensity in her as she walked lazily to the bar and stood watching Angus stirring deep-opal-coloured rum.

'Remember,' she said, 'they laughed at Pasteur too.'

'She looked so little,' Angus said, 'lying there . . .'

'Try to get some sleep.'

'No, there's something bigger than both of us, Leona; it's what we're fighting for, a chance for kids to grow up in a world where there isn't war and hunger and misery and disease . . .'

Mabel said, 'It's for you, Mrs Imre.'

'Who is it, Mabel?'

'It's *Mr* Imre from New York,' Mabel said and tried to look casual and the triangle of thought pointed to Stevie although they looked at hands, feet, ceiling, furniture and Stevie pulled at her army jacket.

'O.K.,' she said and Mabel left.

Stevie turned and leaned on the bar.

'Let me taste,' she said and waited while Angus went on stirring and eventually poured the cloudy opal into a glass, which she sipped from several times.

'Mmmm. Bit too sour.'

'Too sour?'

'S'all right. Anyway, I think it's better if you make it in the blender.' Her face was fearfully sharp and white, predicting what she would be like in later life; she would be thin-lipped and prismatic. She would be of a complaining nature.

'Just a touch of sugar,' she said and waited while Angus did it and poured her another glass. 'That's nearer,' she said. 'We ought to have that Black Velvet thing Gabriel likes, that stout and champagne.'

'It's too hot for that,' Angus said. 'That's a winter drink.'

'I *mean* when it gets colder.'

She took her glass and went with paralysing slowness out of the room and they heard her say, 'I'll take it upstairs, Mabel.'

'Would you rather have Scotch, Eve?'

'No, a daiquiri's all right.'

'Here you are; taste.'

'Mmmm. I like it a bit tart. '

'I know. Here, let me get you a napkin.'

He had got quite drunk on Daddy's Médoc that first night in the mountains and had insisted on getting up and making a ridiculous speech about her saving him and it was the altitude, everybody said. She could see them all under the red glass light on the glassed-in veranda and Angus making this speech to her and Liesl had had to help him upstairs where he had been sick and . . .

'Ahhhh,' Angus said and sat down opposite her, appropriating the wing chair, ankle on knee in his proprietary fashion. 'Have you been in the pool this week, Eve? '

'No,' she said. 'It's too chlorinated for me.'

What was it Gabriel had said about Angus? Gabriel had put an arm around her and winked and said, 'This guy Angus is quite a sticker.'

Quite a sticker was putting it mildly.

'I believe he's *addicted* to Stevie,' she told Gabriel.

When they were seeing Stevie off on the boat for San Francisco in the last embarrassing moments with Miranda, Angus had greatly helped out and then hung on after the last going so as to be the last to say good-bye and Stevie had said in a flip way, 'Now come over and pay us a visit – why not? I dare you.' Angus' visit had now lasted nearly seven years.

And seeing him patronize her now in the wing chair in his rather shabby summer suit, his woeful socks and bluff and getting on to be thirty-four, Eve couldn't believe he was honestly happy, merely addicted and stuck half-way through life without having intended it, now unable to go back, fearful of going forward. His job at the New South Wales Tourist Bureau paid him only enough to live although he spoke of it in orotund tones in terms of 'my' documentary films, 'my' press releases.

He had a furnished walk-up apartment and lived on extra-man invitations. He went to any admission-free lecture or travel-film showing and, judging by his conversation, New York had hundreds of them. He went to the free concerts at the Frick Collection and was given people's unwanted tickets to Broadway flops. He had, as he frequently mentioned, good friends in Hackensack. But in the summer on weekends he became involved in luxury. Widening into the role of permanent guest he would say, 'How about having Dora do us her *jambon en croûte champagne* with the puff paste?' On weekends he was Stevie's well-fed barman, prop, jester, gamesman, distraction

'They have something good going for each other,' Gabriel said.

Whatever they had going for each other (a case of two heads being no better than one, Bea had remarked) had sprung up during the time Stevie was waiting for her divorce. They had met at an intersection both of the street and of their lives. Stevie was champing at the law's delay and the frustration of waiting to get to America, to Gabriel. Angus was faced with the unenviable possibility of not even having a frustration.

The following week Eve had been reading to Heath on the bungalow veranda when the quiet of the mountains had been interrupted by Stevie driving in wildly and unexpectedly from town and to their surprise the solid-looking man in the front seat with her had turned out to be Angus Weekes.

'Hello,' he said to Eve. 'I've come for my shoes.'

He'd had a rotten go of it, a stinking run of bad luck after what he and Stevie laughingly referred to as the Tin Pot Dome Disaster. He'd bought a partnership in a tin mine somewhere in the far north. But it had resulted in a double fiasco: he lacked experience and the mine lacked tin. Lesley Ann, who was, as they all knew, he said, very easily enthused, had come up to live with him; they thought of it in an old-fashioned way as 'living in sin'; no ties, enormous fun. But the loneliness, the total isolation during the long wet season had driven them to bickerings that in turn became bitter quarrels and in the end Lesley Ann had fled. In the end all it had taken was a large frilled lizard gazing into her face from an inch away on the kitchen shelf to finish the idyll in screams forever. Next day Angus had driven her a hundred and eighty miles to Birdum to catch a plane. Even their parting had been unfortunate. All the way driving to Birdum, she had enraged him by insisting that the failure had been hers alone, she was an all-round mug when it came to men, it had been *her* fault, until at last he yelled at her to shut up for God's sake and leave him *some* of the blame for the sake of his manhood for God's sake !

He'd stuck it out for another five months, living on tinned salmon and powdered eggs, and settled down to painting seriously, trying to win something out of this cruel bitter place by getting it onto canvas, and he felt after thirty or more tries that he had got ten landscapes that were more than just fair, they had something of the horror and awesomeness of the Never Never in them. He was modestly satisfied, he came back to Sydney with them. He even managed to get a showing at a small private gallery with printed invitations to a dry-sherry opening. Unfortunately one of the top art critics dropped in.

Eve had begun to feel a weight, an invisible weight, attached to each of her wrists, weighing her. He was shrugging off his comic disappointments with a kind of sceptical humour that sounded a lot like herself, something picked up from observing her warding off some similar embarrassment at the pity one is evoking. She smiled back coolly at him about his trials. They spoke nothing of the past that day and she had no way of knowing what he felt about her. Even now she had no direct clue. He simply treated her as a guest in Stevie's house and handed her things and held doors open for her. When they were alone he did the talking. He decided for her what they would talk about. Most often his talk bored her because it was polemic with which she agreed, it was safe to the point of being ecumenical and thus he purposely cut her off from any possible argument, any point of apposite view that she might seize and so spark a healthy spat, something human between them that might lead them back onto dangerous paths. So she sat suffocating with agreement like someone sitting through a film for the fifth time and having it, at the same time, explained and occasionally she supplied him with a word, 'yes' or 'absolutely'.

Now, leaning sideways in his wing chair, he was giving her their agreed-on-time-and-time-again opinion on something. He leaked the already known facts to her; he enunciated very clearly as though she were hard of hearing.

'Absolutely,' she said.

Did he know, she wondered, that in moments of abstraction he sucked his thumb?

The trouble with him was he was dazzlingly commonplace and she was swept with real pity for him, for the uselessness of his trying so hard, lost in his secondhand opinions and his pre-cooked wit. At times, in certain lights, he showed up as he had once been and just as she had been so startled to see her youth in the mirror on the stairs, so was she startled and often anguished when, not sure where to go next, he paused and became momentarily coltish; she saw the bewilderment of his whole life concentrated in his stare, thumb in mouth.

Suddenly he became again the boy in the gardens of the crematorium sixteen years ago and again she said, 'Come to *us* if you like.' When she crossed back over that barrier she saw herself in the red dress at the funeral handing him her card and him standing blinking in the sun in the earnest navy-blue suit; his shoes seemed too big for him and he was altogether so painfully trusting that what she was doing had seemed like daylight kidnapping. She had got back into her waiting taxi and she was all fleshed out with success (she had been thin and starving for some time) because she knew for certain he would come; the event seemed extraordinary to her and fatalistic: only a sudden whim on her part to pay respects to the sister of her long-ago dead friend. She had recognized him by a certain likeness in

247

the nape of the neck (he had turned around and looked wonder-ingly at her) that had the look of Victoria as you stood behind her. She sat and thought about Victoria. About the time Victoria went on strike, refused to eat or bathe or attend classes until some wrong was righted, and had almost succeeded; she was so enormously strong and Eve was not, couldn't even keep any-thing secret from Victoria, and the only time she had ever tried, Victoria had quickly got it out of her by the simple procedure of pretending she already knew. Oh, Partridge, Partridge, Victoria sang, in a pear tree, Even Partridge, you don't fool me. What Victoria had never known to the day she died when a sports pav-ilion collapsed was that Eve had been afraid of her. But Victoria was not sensitive. Angus was. She could tell from the back of him, from his pretence of detachment and not giving a damn, he was suggestible and also he was as thin and starving as she was and it was possible (here the idea was born) that they required each other. So she gave him her card. Come to *us* if you like, she said as casually as she could and he cast her a quick look of hope and then hid his wonderment at her. She spun away in the taxi. She was suddenly all fleshed out with hope and the cab went miles, was almost to the railway before she had been ready to admit anything, admit her motives were selfish; she had lost her children, she might as well never have had any; if she called to them they wouldn't have heard, they no longer recognized any signal from her, and for some time now, although she kept it scoffingly hidden, she had been in desperate need of some little admiration.

'To a T,' Angus said, telling her of some new frustration in his job, 'they are made in the image and likeness of that cartoon character John Q. Publin, and I'm surrounded, swamped, by displaced parochialism.'

The area between her and the man in the wing chair was vast in the waning light. The air seemed still and stifling. One of Gabriel's clocks coughed, whirred and donged. There were

248

people who should not be disrupted and tantalized by perspectives beyond them and perhaps Angus was one of them. Left alone he probably would have done nothing but wouldn't have been aware of it. Had she led him on by suggesting heights to him? Had she set him off on a treasure hunt for which she couldn't assure any prize? What she may have done (she stared at him truthfully in horror) was to have given him an imagined potential. 'So they rejected my design in favour of the tried and true koala bear in a wattle tree,' he said. He really had become pompous; left alone he might not have cared.

'I'm sorry,' Eve said, but he was talking over her as he refilled her daiquiri glass.

Mabel came sidling in, turned on some lamps. Time seemed imponderable. Hours might have gone by. The cook was wondering, as it was a roast . . .

'We won't wait for Mrs Imre,' Angus said. He told Eve, 'The girls are supposed to get off by nine on Fridays and I don't see why we should hold them, do you?'

She would not take the whole blame; it was spiral. If she had misguided him, she had been misguided, and in turn he would misguide someone else. She thought, watching his hands pour the wine, we are all interdependent, indivisible, touching, the blame is passed around, passed on endlessly, hand over hand, overlapping, overlapping.

They were past the roast into the endive salad, before they heard Stevie coming downstairs. She appeared in the doorway. She was holding the little white china horse that always stood beside her bedroom telephone; always stroked and fiddled with it while she was talking. She was quite unaware that she'd brought it. 'Angus,' she said, 'can I speak to you, please?'

Angus got up and followed her out to the hall. Neither of them glanced at Eve. She heard the door to the side patio slam. She went on eating her endive salad. She finished her wine

249

slowly. After a while she tinkled the little glass bell. Mabel came and took away the salad, took away the three different cheeses, dusted the tablecloth and left. Eve put the salt and pepper neatly together. She sat. Sat and looked. I wonder, she thought, if there is ever a moment like this even in great lives, great *fulfilled* lives, when you know you've run out of everything, run out of everything that ever made you, there is just no more fuel.

Mabel set before her an egg cup of *mousse au chocolat*.

Both heard the hooting sound. An owl?

'I don't think I want it,' Eve said.

There it was again, a hooting, cawing sound, some sea bird shot through the wing but not dead. But was Stevie laughing or weeping or raging? Mabel was a pearl, she was faceless, she calmly took away the *mousse au chocolat*. 'Well, would you care for some strawberries, Mrs St James?'

'I don't think I want *anything*, thanks, Mabel.'

Both heard Angus shout to *shut up*. Then absolute silence fell.

'Ice-cream?' Mabel's eyes were dilated in her golden face. 'We got peach, we got butter pecan, chocolate chip ...' She wanted to be of help, she wanted to preserve the illusion, she was put on earth to assure Eve there was nothing odd about being left at the table while news was breaking like thunder.

'Just coffee,' Eve said.

Mabel brought coffee and thin cookies. She closed the window against any possible sea-bird cries. 'Gettin' breezy out,' Mabel said and hung soothingly about with spoons. 'You try a cookie?' she asked.

'Delicious,' Eve said.

Mabel polished unused shining spoons, kept company until Eve could use her no longer and so laid down her napkin. She and Mabel seemed to agree that the silence was worse than the wounded-bird cries.

'You can clear,' Eve said.

'No hurry,' Mabel said. 'You set as long as you want.'

Anything, said huge, kind Mabel, who knew she'd been slighted, knew she was not happy in this house because, well nobody was. 'You want some more coffee?'

Eve shook her head. She was not good at gratitude.

'*Thank* you, Mabel.'

She took her coffee with her more as a prop than anything. She held the demitasse carefully, opening the door to the patio and stepping into the situation, hard to gauge by the silence and the frozen figures, Augus seated in the big bamboo shell and Stevie sitting on the stone-coping wall directly under the appalling yellow insect-repelling light that dyed her the colour of old newspaper – hair, face, Army jacket.

'Did –' Eve began but Angus held up a finger without looking at her. Stevie was drawing a line along the back of the white china horse, over and over, all the time taking deep drags on a cigarette and making a whistling sound through her teeth as she did so, the sound of being hurt touching flame. She turned the horse over in her hands and examined its delicate legs and then lifted her face towards moving vines above her. There were pouches under the eyes, her face was wet. Then she raised her knee and embraced it and, nuzzling her face into it, spoke into her thigh until Angus said, 'What?'

'The dog, the *dog*. I said, "Even the dog misses you," and he said, "I'm glad *some*body does." I said, "Gabriel, that's just stupid" and he said, "Oh, is it?" and so I said, well, as I couldn't very well get the dog to come to the phone would he believe *me*? And then there was another of the long silences – like I said, there were these long pauses with just him breathing – and I said, "Don't you believe me?" and he said, "I don't know." Then he said the most peculiar thing; he said, "The dog's name is Bimbo, you know," and I said, "I'm *talk*ing about Bimbo," and he said, "But you always call him the *dog*," just as if it was very im*port*ant to him, you'd think it was suddenly the most im*port*ant thing in the world to him what I call the *dog* for God's sake and so I said – because I suppose I was mad for a minute, I really was mad with him because here we were ... and I felt so sort of stranded and here he is criticising me about what I call the *dog,* can you believe it – so I said, "I can't believe you'd make an issue out of that, Gabriel," I said, "I can't believe we're going to argue about a thing like what I call the *dog,* not a little thing like that when here we are two grown-up people," and do you know what he said? He said, "Well, *Bimbo* is a person to *me*." I mean, the whole thing, it's so ...'

Stevie turned the white horse over and over and examined its cold shining underbelly for a time, breathing hard and deeply. 'You see, not being able to get any sort of a real answer, any real reason out of him. I said over and over again, I said, "For God's sake you've got to give me a reason I can *understand*." You see, if there was another woman I could under*stand*, but there isn't and he swears there's *not*. In fact, I wish there *was* another woman. I wouldn't care if that was all it was, if he was shacking up with some other woman, I mean I could *cope* with that, but it's this – this nothing, this nothing, no reason, just breathing on the phone and I was crying by this time and I said, "Oh, please don't do this, darling, don't do this to me ..." '

Stevie nuzzled her leg for a while.

'Oh, do you know what he brought up? I don't remember how it came up exactly but do you remember when I was going to Rome two years ago and he gave me the new black mink?'

'Yes,' Angus said.

'Well, I was showing it to you and you said to me, "What are you going to do with the old one?" and I said something flip like I was going to have it cut up into winter jockstraps for *him.*'

'Did you?'

'He said that hurt him. He said it wasn't the joke that hurt him but me not *knowing* he was hurt. So I said, "Well, why didn't you *tell* me you were hurt?" Apparently he's been storing up . . .'

She shook her head. 'Can't believe . . .'

She threw away her cigarette and watched the spark die. 'I can't believe this is happening to me,' she said.

'Well, is he coming down?' Angus asked.

'What?'

'Is he coming down?'

'I said, "Tell me what you want me to do," and again there was just this silence and once I thought he was crying and I said, "Daddy, tell me what you *want*," and he said in this tired sort of way, "I don't want to be Daddy any more." He said, "I can't think of anything more to give you, nothing I give you seems to make you happy." I said, what a lot of balls and that he knew how happy I was with everything he gave me, how happy I was with the sauna bath for instance and he said he wasn't talking about that *kind* of happy and I said, "What then?" and he said, "Well, I'll try to explain to you when I come down," and I said, "No, tell me now, tell me *now*," because I was in Trauma City by this time, I must have smoked – I bet I smoked half a pack of cigarettes just while we were on the phone. I said, "I insist you tell me now." So he did, in a sort of way.'

'What?'

'I don't understand. It doesn't make any sense. He says I take away his reasons for doing anything.'

'How?'

'I don't know. He said even if he came back it wouldn't be any good because all he'd really wanted was to make me happy and as that had failed there wasn't any reason to it any more. He said you reach a point where there's nothing to do, no reason for it. I said, "Do you think I got a divorce and gave up Miranda and all that without a *reason*? Isn't *that reason* enough?" I said, "Gabriel, what can I do to prove it to you?" I said, "Do you want me to move into town?" and he said no and I said, what then, tell me *anything*. "Do you want me to go fishing with you?" and he laughed and said, oh, Christ or something and then he said, "Is anybody winding the clocks?" and I knew that was it, I knew it wasn't any use me trying to pursue it on the phone if all he was caring about was the clocks. Soooooo . . I said, "Well, when will you be down, will you be down tomorrow so we can talk?" and he said, "I don't know. I've told you how I feel." He said, "You see, you've even taken away my reason for coming down."'

'You shouldn't have let him brood so long,' Angus said, 'You should have called him a week ago before he got to thinking about all this. He's a slow man. You weren't bright. You should have called him *two* weeks ago. Now it's going to take you much longer to get him back.'

Stevie said, 'I may not have anybody to get back.'

She was looking down at the china horse and her face was in the dark, it was not possible to tell what expression might be on it, or by the fact that her shoulders shook a little whether or not this could be amusement at the whole thing. She turned the horse gently over and over and again made the wheezy indrawn breath as if she had scorched herself. Then she said, 'Oh,' in a startled way and sprang up suddenly and, as they looked to see what or who had alarmed her, she flung the horse. It shattered on the tile beside Eve.

'Well,' Angus said, 'that was intelligent, that was a display of your well-known self-control.'

She shrugged.

'Pick it up.'

'What?'

'Pick – it – up,' Angus said, plucking the words out of a steel guitar, and Eve put up her hands to her face dreading the noise of the ton of bricks that would fall on his head as Stevie stood looking down at him, all washed out in the dreadful yellow light, washed out, washed up, looking ten years older than her age. Then, strangely, Stevie did meekly what she was told, bent and picked up the broken pieces and placed them on the glass

able, and she began laughing in her soundless way and, leaning down, she pushed at Angus as the laugh emerged and enclosed him in her private joke.

'All right, all right,' Angus said. 'Now you've had your little
scene.'

'Oh ho ho ho ho ho,' Stevie hooted, the wounded snipe.

'What's funny?'

'Oh, that's so funny. It's always the *wrong* people who know
what to do with me.'

She hooted.

'Cut it out,' Angus said. 'There's nothing funny in your behaviour or in the situation and you'd better know it.'

'I'd explain it only you wouldn't get the joke. Nobody gets
my jokes, they never get the point. Nobody ever gets the point
of *me*.' She had begun to look aghast. 'In my whole life only
one person has ever really gotten the point of me. Marcus. Marcus did.'

'*Marcus?*'

'Yes. Funny? Surprised?'

'Yes.'

'Yes, well, Marcus did.'

'Yes, well, homosexuals always have greater intuition about
women.'

'Really? That's interesting. You know the time I made you
go on the perpendicular with me?'

'The perpen – oh, the coal-mine railway thingummy?'

'Over the cliff? Poor you and your acrophobia.'

'You know, I think you ought to have some dinner now.'

'You and your acrophobia,' Stevie sang, 'do *some*thing to
me, *some*thing that makes me ido*lize* you.'

'O.K., O.K.'

'You thought I was going to jump out? I wasn't trying to
scare the life out of *you*, I was trying to scare the life out of *myself*. I thought I was preggo. Fun*ny*? No. See? You don't get
the point. Nobody ever gets the point.'

255

She went into the house and they heard her call, 'Bimbo? Where are you, Bimbo? Bimbo?'

Angus said, 'A bust.'

The yellow light made a complete circle around them and in the surrounding dark the house shrank and could have been any house; they could have been sitting together on any porch in the world.

'Well, there you are, you see,' Angus said and the 'you see' passed the blame to her.

Circular light, circular time, tides crossing oceans and recrossing, returning to the same beach, lapped the same pebbles, brought them back to where they had been before. He turned his head to her. He was passing the question to her. Well? What did she have to say? What excuses to offer? He was standing a bit slack-mouthed and dull, embracing the veranda post and asking her why she had had the dog killed. She again felt the moment threaten her as it had that day when she had answered, pleaded her case like a fool because she had no case, had only then recognized in his look, in Cissie's look, what she had done. She had done it in her sleep and they didn't understand that any more than Angus could understand what Stevie had done. Stevie had been cruel too. Stevie had said to Gabriel, 'Not *you*.' Eve got up and walked to the edge of light and stared out towards the dark beach. She felt the question before he asked it.

'What are you going to do?' Angus asked. 'Take a walk? Go and shout it to the mountains?'

Just there beyond the rim of light was the rock path that might have led from the bungalow past the burned-out ruins to the cliff. But now she couldn't take the easy path away.

'No,' she said, turning around. He was sitting back in the wicker throne, supposing. He was supposing this was all news to her and pointing a look at her, of deep resignation and pity for her ('Tch tch,' he said and then looked up at the sky. 'Wow,' he said) in this moment of shock, at this moment when at last the albatross was tied around her neck, the blame for all this laid at her feet, the sitting-looking-do-nothing mother of this confusion and woe. And she was going to run, was she? Well then (he spread his hands in a gesture of exculpation), run.

She wondered if it were possible to explain without pleading, to explain what she was in cold blood, explain that she had seen Eve Partridge in the mirror on the stairs only that afternoon. She sat on the stone coping and looked at him squarely and said in ice-water tones, 'Don't intimate something to me I already know.'

'What do you know?'

'I perfectly understood your remark.'

'Well then, what are you going to do? Take a long walk? Take a pill? Knowing you, you will extricate yourself from all this with your customary aplomb.'

'Don't arbitrate,' she said.

'Can I mediate? Can I mediate on behalf of my poor crazy mixed-up friend in there who unhappily was left an orphan at an early age?'

'Oh, I didn't think you could be so obtuse, Angus,' Eve said. 'Are you purposely obtuse or are you just being bitchy?'

'Are we getting angry, one *might* suppose?' he said in a merciless imitation of how she used to address servants at the Ritz Hotel. She felt the blood sizzling at the back of her neck and it took all her experience not to snap open her temper and bite his head off, the way he was smiling at her, head on one side. She looked at the moving vines; she was quiet for a minute and then she said calmly, 'If you're going to intercede, intercede with *her,* not me.'

'How I wonder what you are, Eve.'

'And you *can* intercede with her, did you know that? You do know how to handle her and Gabriel doesn't, so I leave you with that thought, Angus. I think you are the only one now who can straighten her out.'

'Parting words?'

'Yes.'

'Leaving us?'

'Yes, possibly; yes, I think so.'

'Oh, suddenly, like that?'

'Not suddenly, no. Just that I must go home, I want to go home.'

'Yes, I see.'

They sat quietly for a time. Someone passing would have thought them two contented people listening to the night sea, listening to the little night insects.

'Yes,' Angus said pleasantly. 'Well, I think that's right. I think that is probably a wise decision on your part. You don't want to stick around now things are in a shambles. You never know, you might accidentally say something ... drop a piece of advice or something. Even someone as meticulously careful as you might be tempted to rock the boat.'

'I am not in the boat,' she said.

'You really are the coldest, aren't you?'

'So it must seem.'

She almost laughed. She was beginning to feel a ninety-degree heat.

'Aren't you ever affected, ever touched by *anything*?'

'I would have to think about that,' she told him to stop him.

'In all the years I've known you, I've only seen you really thrown once.'

'Yes, well, that was unforgivable.'

'Do you mean,' Angus asked leisurely, 'killing the dog was? Or do you mean your giving way to hysterical behaviour was unforgivable?'

She counted one, two, three.

'I'm inclined to think what you couldn't forgive was the breakdown of your classic cool. In your declension of demeanour –'

She saw that she was on her feet in a red mist and that she

was squawking to him in an ugly shrew voice to leave off, leave off using those damn silly words, please; if he was going to attack her, well and good, but attack her please in simple language.

He looked pleased. *'Anger,'* he said. *'Anger*...Fancy.'

'Fancy,' she said. 'And not just your God-awful prose but your assumption that I don't know anything about myself; I know exactly what I am. I was told very plainly by my son. Only he put it more amiably than you and without a lot of messing around and hinting, and furthermore *he* had a right.' She felt her anger was an emetic and that she could even brag about what Tip had said and when Angus started to rise, making a signal for truce, apology, she said, 'Hold on, it is my turn.' She wasn't going to let him out of the chair until he'd heard all the details right down to the menu Liesl had served during that endless meal, the rich Austrian food on a sweltering day, begining with thick kidney-bean soup and going through to Sacher torte. 'What did Tip say?' Angus asked. 'Never mind about the food.' The food was part of it, she told him. She had been outmanoeuvred by the food, as if Tip and Liesl had known she had come to lunch with something to say and so had made certain her mouth would never be free to say it; by first debilitating her in that humidity with warm sweet Madeira, which they gave her only moments to swallow down before they hustled her to the table, where a punishing gorge began, course after course, overlapping without pause, herring and stuffed cabbage and roast duck with potato pancakes ('He was only ninety-eight pounds when they released him,' Liesl said, 'and now look, please'), sausage, dumplings, fried onion rings, carrots in cream sauce (she ate on and on), which they forced on her; there was no other outward existence for them but food, no conversation passed between them apart from asides to please pass this, try the sauce on that, and there was no foothole in this wall of food for her to speak her thought. All she could do was raise her glass and say with her mouth full, 'To you both,' but

Liesl used the moment to spoon a huge new helping of red cabbage onto her plate and Tip responded to the toast by saying, 'Leave room for Liesl's *apfelstrudel*.' The contest was theirs and, stuffed like a Strasbourg goose, she could only groan and protest the mountainous salad, the melting aspic, steaming sweet rolls. She observed her son and he appeared to observe her (he was totally obsessed with food; he was still picking on a duck bone) and while Liesl was in the kitchen making the terrifying sounds of oven doors being opened, more dishes being taken down, and knowing the moment to be inappropriate and that her thought was inadequate but it being the only moment, she said, 'I want to tell you something.' Then in the sharp six seconds he gave her attention, she faltered because how can you explain your life in a sentence (though it had been put to her in two words once)? 'I'm sorry for a lot of things,' she said. He had put down the duck bone and wiped his mouth severely and said, 'Don't, Mother, it's worse when you try.' Well, he was right, he was justified. What is later than a twenty-year-late apology?

And Liesl, coming in with the *strudel* and mistaking this as a moment of war between them, flew to his rescue, spreading her feathers and clucking, 'Now, now, we don't want long faces here only fun now.' She waved a fork in Eve's face. 'Since where he's been was no fun, do you know that? Where he's been we don't talk about this, this is hell, do you know? Now we say only good things to him.' Mrs St James junior chided Mrs St James senior for her manner. 'I didn't imagine, Liesl,' Eve said quietly, 'that it had been a tropical-island paradise.' Then Tip had laughed and patted her approvingly and said, '*That's* more like my old mum.'

'I think I'll have a cigarette,' Eve said. 'I very rarely smoke but I think I'll have a cigarette.'

She motioned towards a gold box and Angus rose obediently and passed it to her and lit her cigarette.

'He was jealous of me, did you know? Did you know Tip

was jealous of me?' Angus asked. He was trying to appropriate some of her exposition and he seemed young again for an instant, still trying eagerly to get into her room, into her heart, into any place she would let him.

She felt her anger cooling and in its place a rising sense of wonder at herself; no anger, pity, justification, merely a huge wonder. She was capsuled, she saw a continuity of herself as though she were under Sodium Pentothal. She could have drawn a straight line from the beginning up to this hour; not from the beginning of her life but from when her life had begun, which was an entirely different thing, 'because nothing had happened to me up until then, I was nothing, I was an empty dish. I was a beautiful empty dish.'

Then she was born, aged nineteen or thereabouts, quite painlessly, and came to life wearing a pale-green sprigged muslin dress on a piney veranda in the Blue Mountains, standing with a bunch of girls and seeing a horse and buggy drive up with a whole gaggle of boys in bathing suits and him among them, standing out because he was the shortest, the smallest in this tall lot, and he seemed to command attention not from being small but by his sense of large dignity while they had none, were pretty forward and rickytick, you might say, even for 1918, and she immediately saw him, getting out of the buggy, and he was exactly like a young woodsman, she thought (she saw him stripped down to his golden waist, the axe flying in sunlight), and, walking towards the girls on the veranda, who were now strenuously pretending not to see them and preening like ridiculous swans, he alone, she saw, was truly aware of everything around him, of sky and trees and veranda and girls, she knew and that the other, big ones the tall handsome longlimbed passionate heroes, were all dull and sensationless. 'All in an instant,' she said, describing the moment to Angus, but of course he was unable to recreate it as she could; now the Victorian boarding-house built itself in a second, piling gable on gable, crenellated towers rose majestically, flagpoles and dormer windows and stained glass and the instant smell of oil lamps and cedar and the pretty girls all preening like swans while the boys swarmed up onto the veranda. Then they were being introduced. She did not remember a single name but when he shook hands with her he said, 'How do you do, Miss Partridge.' The other girls, as he was introduced to them by Mrs Louise Lillianfels, the proprietress, he greeted by their first names, saying, 'How do you do, Irene,' 'How do you do, Ruth,' but then 'How do you do, Miss *Partridge*,' and the difference struck her as being contrived and therefore the first message she had ever received and so afterwards she looked back on it as the moment of her birth.

At meals he sat alone with a very pretty girl whose name she could not remember, never remember, had obliterated forever for obvious reasons. From time to time she turned her head to watch him with the Pretty Girl, who laughed a great deal and shook her head about because she had exceptionally pretty hair, and he was always full of deep attention to her but as Eve turned, turned to the view, turned to find the bread being handed to her, turned always to catch a sight of his astonishing blondness, once in a while he looked just beyond the Pretty Girl and saw her and once he winked and for some reason she carried the moment around with her the rest of the day.

In the evenings the girls dressed for dinner and the boys wore stiff serge suits, shirts with celluloid collars attached with a brass stud, which caused them discomfort and forced on them a hauteur. Now in lamplight he looked like a young King George V in his high collar coming in to dinner, always last (for the Pretty Girl took a great time dressing), and most of them were past the soup when this stunning, Olympian couple came gracefully into the room, and every night he paused, passing her table, and bowed ceremoniously to her and said, 'Good evening, Miss Partridge,' and then going on to his table with the Pretty Girl, apparently forgot her forever. 'Do you think,' Cissie asked, 'that Heath St James is ribbing you, Eve?' The situation was unusual for them because although Eve was far the more beautiful, it was Cissie who got the attention; it was always Cissie who attracted the boys and Eve, stately, beautiful, empty, stood by being beautiful, stately and empty until time to go home party after party. 'Thank God you have looks,' her mother used to say, meaning you have nothing else, 'so put on cold cucumber cream every night and take every advantage of them.'

Then it happened she and Cissie were sitting having afternoon tea on a little sheltered bluff and half watching the tennis going on below them and Cissie pointed under the table and said, 'Oh, look, Eve, somebody's lost their bag in the grass.' But the next minute Cissie was on her feet screaming and screaming. They had both seen the bag move and present a tiny forked tongue. Eve stood behind her chair absolutely still and motionless, unable to utter, and Cissie screamed and screamed until all tennis stopped, all chat stopped and two of the boys came running. 'A snake, a snake,' Cissie screamed and hung onto Eve, and they both looked away while the killing was done and the snake hung over a fence. 'Because even if you break their back a dozen times they don't die until sundown,' Cissie told the crowd, Cissie having successfully drawn a crowd and being calmed and consoled by several muscular boys. 'Did you guess?' she kept asking them. 'Did you know why I was screaming?' When Heath came up, casually swinging his racket, Cissie pursued him in her ecstasy of attention. 'Did you guess, Heath? Did you imagine I'd lost my senses or something, the way I was screaming?' Then he looked at Eve and said, 'I was more interested in why Miss Partridge was *not* screaming,' and it was as though she had received a strange and wonderful compliment.

That evening she was the first girl he asked to dance and they went out onto the floor, she a little conscious of being half a head taller than he and thinking quickly she mustn't offend him by crouching. But then he was unaware that he was short; he was very powerful, she was surprised to find when he took hold

263

of her, and he held her in a way that was more possessive than the tall long-limbed boys; it was meaningful, sexual and quite frightening, the power of this small and beautiful man, and she felt other people must see this, must see that they were transmitting this thing across the room in lights, and it made her feel faint with some evanescent desire she'd never had before and she felt that he knew it although he said nothing, never glanced at her, which made the message seem even more mysterious, like a note being pushed under a door, this saying nothing, just turning her endlessly around in his careful, clever hands, managing her; the feeling threatened to eclipse her, made her want to die on the spot. 'Thank you, Miss Partridge,' he said and left her. For the rest of the evening he danced with the Pretty Girl, who tossed her hair about wildly and said things he seemed to find amusing; he was frequently laughing into her neck and Eve felt as though she had swallowed sharp prune stones. That night, later, as she leaned out of her attic window before closing out the chilly mountain air, she saw across the copper roof someone else close a window against the night air, saw the Pretty Girl draw down the blind, but not before Eve had seen Heath's blond head beyond the lamp. She sat on her bed for a long time before turning out her own lamp.

'No, stay,' Heath said quietly. She had started to get up from the table where six or seven of them were sitting one night in the card room and Cissie was telling fortunes and the girls were giggling and showing off to the boys but the mention of a dark stranger sent them into fits, especially the Pretty Girl, whose secret was safe and who, every time Cissie saw a heart card in her life, whooped and shook her hair and laughed herself into paroxysms and protested innocently and fell on, leaned on Heath from time to time, grew prettier by the second, and he laughed too, admiringly, Eve thought, and so picked up her gold bead bag and started to rise and, 'No, stay' he said, without even glancing at her and she obediently sat and stared at the cards and later Cissie told Eve her fortune which was mostly melancholy, hearing of a death, bad news in a letter and warnings to beware of a false friend. '*Tant pis*,' Eve said, not being quite sure what it meant, and, looking up from her wretched cards, saw he was looking at her and the power of him looking at her was frightening. All the time he looked at her the noise went on like surf around them and then he said, 'You are not overdemonstrative, which I greatly admire.'

The next instant he had withdrawn, he might never have said it, he turned his concentration and mesmerizing blue eyes on the other girl. 'It's Heath's turn,' said the Pretty Girl and tickled his chin in her marvellous sureness and safety. 'It's your turn, chickie.' And Eve got up and left the table and walked out of the room and onto the veranda, where she meandered along and smiled at the other couples who were sitting on deck chairs under rugs admiring the night and, passing along the length of the veranda, she went idling down steps into the garden and as soon as the dark had closed around her did a strange thing: ran, ran through scrub and bushes, ran up against a tree and embraced the hard trunk and beat her head against the sharp knotty bark and cried, cried with despair into the bark. 'Oh, God,' she said aloud. 'Oh, God, if I could have that man I would be anything he wanted.'

Long after all the lights had gone out in the house and the wind was biting into her she stayed under the dark tree and said it over and over to herself until it became more like a vow than a lament; she never noticed the cold, her mind was opening to such an infinitude of possibilities.

She became neutral by degrees, she became all greys, she watched herself become a periphery around his edges; she sat as cool as stone and let the others exhort around him and she felt from time to time that he was at least puzzled by her, he cast her a look or a smile sometimes just in time because there were dangerous moments of fire in her that sometimes made her want to touch him; there was something about him that made people want to touch him; men and women touched him, arms and hands fell lightly on his shoulders and knees and a tiny dislike flicked in him when they did. The Pretty Girl, leaning across him for the fruit knife, let her breasts touch him but the unseen shiver went through the girl, not him.

Eve sat very still. 'Are you hatching an egg, love?' asked Cissie. The last days went. Heartlessly, they all exchanged addresses, knowing they were summer friends and would never see each other again. 'Do you like museums?' was the only fragment of hope he gave her at the railway station.

She existed deep in a cave under water and after three weeks she had the impression her hair was turning grey but when his voice on the phone (even the primitive phones of those days could not make *that* voice ridiculous) said, 'Miss Partridge, this is Heath St James,' she had willed it so often in that exact phrasing that she was able to be calm at the prospect of seeing with him next Sunday the skeletons and stuffed carcasses of giant extinct animals. In the dark, dreary museum among the glass cases of stuffed wombats he was so alive that in order not to touch the blond hair on his neck, she bent down to read about the queer habits of the lyre bird. I am completely yours, she told him silently, reading aloud about the ambivalent platypus. 'Interesting that you'd like this,' he said sceptically but she would not fall into the trap of being caught lying enthusiastically and he seemed a bit curt, he walked ahead of her, he walked briskly with small steps and over a dismal, watery tea with stale pink cakes in a green glass kiosk lashed by rain he said, 'Has it been a dreary afternoon?' She said, 'I am completely happy.'

'Don't you go to anything besides museums,' her mother asked. 'Are you studying for something?' 'Yes,' she said.

Ores, metals, elements, oxides, the external mingling of natural resources in their correct chemical balances since the planet began interested him (they were sitting in the cold Technological Museum). 'That is truth because it can't be contradicted,' he said. 'And that's my religion in a way, anything that is incontrovertible. Do you agree? The fact that has always been

o. I mean, for instance, empires going *phhht* but this and that will always produce a nitrate. I love the idea of changeless things.'

He was sizing up the possibility of their correct balance perhaps.

'I won't be the same person in seven years,' she said, 'all my chromosomes will have changed.' 'But so will mine,' he said.

More and more he let her know what kind of man he was and she applied the information to herself. There began to be a subtle interlocking between them. Her confidence gave her a sense of immutable calm.

And then one day she had walked into his lodgings and there curled up in a chair by the fire was the Pretty Girl.

Who knew where the cups were, where to rinse out the teapot in the bathroom along the hall, where he kept the folding table hidden, and presented these facts victoriously while he went back and forth between them with sweet biscuits and the mirror cracked from side to side. He sat between them nursing his cup and glancing from one to the other. 'Have you been to see *Chu Chin Chow*?' the girl asked. 'It was truly spectacular, wasn't it, Heath?' The wedge drove further in. And here was a little bedside clock in the shape of a turtle she had given him for his birthday. The girl curled into the shape she had long ago made in the chair, her shoes off. Heath said nothing. Eve stirred her tea. The curse has come upon me, cried the Lady of Shalott. So it was all over, it never had begun, it was nothing; all the learning and studying and arranging of herself in a shape that was desirable to him had been a fake, a false alarm. This is what had been going on and this is what he really wanted. This crackling energy and enthusiasm, girlish ecstasy; there was such cosiness between them.

Or was there entirely? Was the Pretty Girl pulling frayed threads from the chair out of boredom or was there something a little desperate about it? Could it possibly be that she was just as thrown by the appearance of Eve? Heath spoke with exactly

267

the same courtesy to both of them. He paid them equal attention as though he had measured the amount beforehand. 'A meringue for each of you,' he said and there was. He was totally impartial, a judge, and he was secretly weighing the evidence. It came over Eve with absolute certainty that if she made the wrong move now she would do herself in forever. She must draw on her reservoirs of calm, she must now be everything she hoped he liked in her. She must quietly take charge.

'I think I will have a cigarette,' she said. 'I very rarely smoke but I think I will have a cigarette.'

She relaxed in the chair, she made herself concentrate on the best ways to cook rhubarb. She let her arm lie at ease on the green baize table and looked into the fire and listened while the Pretty Girl became chattery and amusing, pulling at threads, throwing her hair about while Heath stood by the fireplace and watched her with a pride of ownership. She flashed, she made jokes and teased him (he was scrupulous, it was her turn), and when he chuckled at her, it gave her renewed zest. She had the trick of saying something daring with a look of wide-eyed innocence and then being amazed at the laugh it got, at having hit the target, and when he guffawed, she slapped at his leg and threw her hair around enchantingly and said, 'Oh, you are awful, darling. I didn't mean *that*, you dreadful man.' She was a bit intoxicated with attention, she was showing off for the grownups, so Eve joined Heath in being quietly delighted with her, Eve sat and paid her rapt attention, paid out rope, sat gracefully relaxed until she achieved what she wanted, the serene contrast, never moving her arms from the side of her chair, her head resting on the cushion so that the outsider peering through the window might have taken her for the hostess, patiently and graciously putting up with a guest who was — wasn't she? — going on a bit too long. And this idea she conveyed to the girl, the implication that Heath and she were the hosts. Heath and she, entertaining; Heath and she in their quietness were one and the girl caught the thought and it made her furious and also uneasy and gradually her wit soured and her laugh grew clackety-clack and she raced on. When she sometimes jittered to a halt, Eve would wait a beat and then say something entirely bland, which in the blessed pause often managed to sound wise. Heath had begun a solemn dance from one foot to the other and no longer looked at the girl although she looked at him often for a laugh or a sign; the girl rattled on, she became a clockwork thing and wound up, she flailed around, tugging threads from the chair and making them into little bows which she threw in the fire, she was machinery, she was a typewriter. She was eager to explain, to make little of her hatred for cats but she was no longer amusing, she was catty about cats, about other girls too; certain girls who posed as virgins but could give any tart a tip or two. The only laughs she was getting now were her own, which had begun to sound like hiccups, and she knew she was beaten, she lay back in the chair looking damaged, a long piece of hair lying across her face looked like a crack; she lay back against the cushions like an exhausted child and gazed out at the fading day. 'Oh, what a *mis*erable day,' she said. 'I hate winter coming on, don't you?' she asked anyone there, looked up at Heath for help but he merely arched his eyebrows and whistled something and so after a pause the Pretty Girl said, 'Well, I must go.' 'Must you?' he said but he went and fetched her fur coat and her bag and gloves and she stabbed a pin through her little hat, which was a bird of pink feathers. 'I simply hate this hat,' she said and stabbed it. 'Good-bye,' she said to Eve and she went out. She was very pretty and had bad posture, hunched in a way that would soon give her round shoulders. Eve stood by the fire and after a time she heard the outside door shut and he came back into the room, closing the door, and came and stood beside her by the fire. 'I must go too,' she said eventually and he said, 'That's the first and only insincere thing I have ever heard you say.' He looked at her severely. She could not imagine what he was thinking or feeling; she was a little dizzy with what had gone on and a little faint at the thought of being alone with him and the fact that, bronzed like this and bleached in the red and yellow of the fire, he was excruciatingly beautiful; the animal magnetism of him was like a too strong scent, lilies, lilac; he put out his hand to her. 'Don't wear drop earrings,' he said, 'they spoil the contour of your neck,' and he took them off one at a time and . . .

'And?' Angus said eventually; she must have been silent for a long time. 'And?' Angus asked. He was extremely docile, gentle with her. Stevie was crouched in the doorway fondling the dog.

'Nothing,' Eve said.

No one knew, nobody could conceive what it was like. Nobody had had their experience, she and Daddy for all those years, and it must not be taken out and looked at because, like certain hothouse plants, it could not survive being looked at and the only way it could be described accurately would be in words that are to be avoided and phrases such as 'an unspoken passion.' Nothing was so charged with energy as that unspoken thing because it translated itself into lifelike terms. Just when she thought he was drifting away, had become casual about her, used to her now, he would put a hand on her. 'No, stay'; 'no, stay, don't go to the children'; 'no stay, no, stay with *me*.' Never to say 'I love you' was the hardest rule she had to obey but her repaid her triply for her obedience, her divine coolness. For her absolute dedication to him; her protection at all costs to herself, to the children, to anyone, of their secret thing. So one day she made the discovery that when someone needed her to show tenderness or even wrath, or any emotion for that matter in lieu of love, she had lost the ability. She had long ago become what Daddy wanted.

'I often was very lonely,' she said.

'Perhaps yours is the right way,' Angus said. 'Hard but perhaps right. Look at the mess we all make by trying to be something to everybody. Maybe yours *is* the only real way. I mean, if

u are going to have the one thing you want. So you did it
d you had it.'

Poor Angus. Obvious to the end.

The end.

'I must tell you about the end,' Eve said. 'I have never told
yone about the end. He hadn't been able to speak for some
ne. He couldn't say anything without the utmost difficulty.
ne day we were sitting opposite each other on the veranda ...'

He had looked about ninety. 'And suddenly I saw that he was
ying to say something to me.' She had bent over the chair,
cking the plaid rug around him. What, darling? What,
eath? 'He looked up at me and he was completely conscious,
mpletely lucid, and his eyes were very wide open and he
ade ... a little motion with his hands of – of warding me off
d then he said just two words. I heard him say with absolute
arity' – heard his summing-up of her – 'I heard him say with
solute clarity, "Not you."'

Not *You*.

She saw the whole thing once more. Then it faded out.

Now she was able to see, instead of Daddy, their looks of
mplete dumbfounded innocence (Stevie moving, Angus suck-
g a thumb) and, knowing they might say something to her
a deadly pity or even apology, she got up from the wall and
ent quickly off the patio into the dark without a plan, without
ny idea of where this path led, without any sound except her
wn footsteps going down steps, down steps without a pause,
uite quickly, briskly, which being the only sound in the
hole world, began in a little while to seem as though they
ere taking her somewhere.

More about Penguins
and Pelicans